# DEAD MAN'S SINS

CAIMH MCDONNELL

Caimh McDonnell

Visit my website at www.WhiteHairedIrishman.com

ISBN: 978-1-912897-25-4 (Paperback)

ISBN: 978-1-912897-28-5 (Hardback)

# AUTHOR'S NOTE

Dear Reader,

Normally, I use the author's notes in the front of my books to prepare North Americans for an onslaught of things being spelled 'correctly'. You know, the Irish way which as far as my Ma (who is the arbiter of such things) is concerned, is the only way. However, this time around I would like to dedicate this note to the subject of chronology.

*Dead Man's Sins* is set in March 2000 in Dublin. It takes place a few months after the events of *Angels in the Moonlight* – meaning it is effectively the sequel to a prequel. I realise that this is incredibly confusing and I humbly apologise for it.

In my defence, the book was written between 2020-2021 when, frankly, reality sucked big time. I wanted to retreat to a simpler time when bats were only mildly unpopular and people wore masks to scare people, as opposed to the other way around. In this golden era the pubs in Ireland were all open unless actually on fire, and even then, it was acceptable to take your pint outside and wait for the fire brigade to finish up.

The point I'm trying to make is, there's a sixteen-year gap in

Bunny McGarry's story between when *Angels in the Moonlight* ends and *A Man with One of Those Faces* begins. This book is the start of that timeline/story being filled in.

I hope you like it!

Caimh

# YOU CAN'T TRUST WRITERS

**Dublin, 2000**

Bunny pulled his coat around him tightly and stared down at the water, the resolutely blue water.

"Howerya, boss."

He didn't turn around. He didn't need to.

"Deccie, how would you describe the colour of that water?"

The youngster moved to stand beside Bunny and looked down. "D'ye mean the sea, boss?"

"Of course I mean the sea. What other body of water is there knocking about the place?"

Deccie pointed. "There's a puddle over there."

Bunny sighed. Talking to Deccie was never an advisable activity this early in the day. Bunny had woken up hungover at 11am after a night that was longer than it should have been, and he'd not eaten yet. In order to grapple with the peculiar mind of Deccie Fadden, you needed a good meal inside you to achieve the requisite level of inner peace beforehand. If he was like this at twelve years old, heaven knows what he'd grow into.

Bunny waved a hand at the expanse of water before them. "Let's assume I mean the majestic Irish Sea and not that, or any other, puddle."

"Right," said Deccie. "Well, it's not my area of expertise, but I'd go with periwinkle blue."

This earned him a sideways look.

"Me granny likes them DIY programmes, and we've only the one TV."

"Right, but definitely not snot green?"

"What? No, course not. What kind of a dipshit would say that?"

"James Joyce."

"I don't know him. Does he go to O'Connell's?"

"Does he ... No, Deccie, he's considered one of this country's true literary geniuses. His school days are behind him – as are all of his days, for that matter. I'm currently taking yet another run at reading a book he wrote called *Ulysses*, in which he describes the sea here at the Forty Foot as snot green."

"He's clearly full of it, boss. You can't trust writers. They make up nonsense for a living."

"That's an interesting take, Deccie."

"He's not related to Fiona Joyce, is he?"

"Who's that?"

"Girl a couple of years above me in school. She used to be able to belch the whole alphabet, but she won't do it any more. Says it isn't ladylike."

"I don't believe so, no."

Deccie nodded. "I just thought of it because she's always making stuff up, too. Told everyone Darren Simonds shat himself on the waltzers at Funderland, and he never did."

Bunny looked back down at the resolutely blue water as the low winter sun sparkled off it. "You just can't trust them Joyces." He glanced over his shoulder at the spot along the pier where a chip van had just pulled up. "C'mon, Deccie, I'll buy you lunch."

. . .

Bunny pursed his lips and studied the burger van's limited menu. "I will have ..."

The facial expression of the woman serving made it clear that him turning up and trying to buy something was already a massive inconvenience to her, and the very least he could do was be quick about it.

"... sausage, chips and a can of Fanta, please, love." He looked down at the assistant manager of St Jude's Under-12s hurling team. "Deccie?"

"Skinny decaf latte."

Bunny rolled his eyes. "He'll have the same as me."

"D'ye want salt and vinegar?" asked the woman.

"Actually," said Bunny, "any chance of a spot of mayonnaise?"

The woman pulled a face more suited to the question of whether or not one's granny is at home to receive gentlemen callers. "Of course. Will sir be having that with the redcurrant jus and pomegranate infusion?"

The woman followed Bunny's gaze as it fell pointedly on the sign behind her head that read THE CUSTOMER IS ALWAYS RIGHT. She gave him a smile with no smile in it.

"It's covering up a rust spot."

Five minutes and a monumentally optimistic nod at the tip jar later, Bunny and Deccie sat down on a nearby bench to eat their food.

"What exactly is the Forty Foot?" asked Deccie around a mouthful of chips.

"'Tis a popular swimming spot. People dive in there every Christmas morning."

Deccie nearly choked, which necessitated a firm slap on the back from Bunny.

"People jump in there? In, like, just a pair of trunks? What the hell is that? Some kind of mass suicide attempt?"

Bunny shrugged. "They love it."

"We've not got the weather for that kind of carry on."

"'Tis Ireland, Deccie. If we waited for the weather to be nice before we went to the seaside, we'd have to send someone out every few months to check the sea was still there. If memory serves, we used to get a few nudists out this way as well."

Deccie lit up in the way only a boy careering towards puberty can, his face aglow with terrified, horny excitement.

"Cool your jets," said Bunny. "A person going skinny dipping in France is embracing the beauty of nature, or whatever. Doing it in Dublin in winter? 'Tis a mental illness. Trust me, anyone who wants to show themselves off around here invariably has the kind of body no one wants to see."

Deccie tutted. "Fair enough."

They finished their food in amicable silence. It didn't taste bad, considering, but then you couldn't really go that far wrong combining batter, grease and a sausage on a cold winter's day.

"So, are you no longer a rozzer, then, boss?"

"Incorrect," said Bunny. "I am, in fact, still a card-carrying member of the Garda Síochána, Deccie. I'm just on sabbatical."

"Oh right. I didn't even know you were Jewish."

"What are you on about? Sabbatical just means I'm taking a bit of a break."

"Got ye. Is that because your best mate got shot to death and then your girlfriend did a runner?"

Bunny raised his eyebrows and gave Deccie a look.

"Ah, this is one of those situations we talked about, isn't it? Where I shouldn't say what I'm thinking?"

Bunny gave him a slow nod.

"Sorry about that, boss. I'm still working on it."

"Work harder."

"Right. Noted."

Bunny reached across and tossed his Styrofoam packaging into the bin. "So, how are things at home?"

"Fine. Grandad gave me a lift out."

Deccie jerked his head in the direction of the car park. Bunny had already clocked the Opel Corsa parked up there with Deccie's grandfather sat in the front, his heavy overcoat on, a newspaper in his hands.

"School?"

"Same old, same old."

"How come you're not there?"

"Training day. You'd think they'd have already trained the teachers before they let them loose on us, but apparently not."

"Right." Bunny watched as a couple of mothers with prams power-walked by. "I guess what I'm getting at, Deccie, is why exactly did you want to meet somewhere so far away from your typical stomping ground?"

"I don't want to get fitted for no snitch jacket."

"What have I told you about watching those American cop shows?"

"Life on the streets ain't easy, boss. I'm keeping it real."

"If memory serves, you live on a rather nice cul-de-sac."

"That's a type of street."

Bunny's stomach made a noise that was loud enough for them both to hear. "While I hate to disrupt your natural oratorical flow, Deccie, can we move this along? I'm getting the feeling that sausage is only a short-term rental."

"Who could have guessed sausage meat bought from a dodgy-looking van wouldn't be the highest quality?"

"Deccie!" said Bunny, starting to lose his patience.

The boy nodded. "Do you remember how Larry Dodds broke his arm last year jumping off that roof?"

"I do. Made us all sign his cast."

"Yeah," said Deccie with a smile. "There ended up being that many cock and balls on it, he had to put a bag over it before that woman would let him on the bus."

Deccie's grin fell away when Bunny's facial expression made it clear that he hadn't known that particular fact and wasn't impressed by it.

"Anyway," Deccie continued. "My point is he was mad proud of it."

"I know. They had to force him to get it removed in the end. Bloody thing stank."

"Exactly. Lads that age are obsessed with that kind of thing."

Bunny frowned. "You do realise that you are also that age?"

Deccie entirely ignored the question. He found half a chip sitting in the folds of his anorak and popped it in his mouth.

"So, what's up with Larry?"

"Nothing. Larry is grand. It's Alan."

"With one or two Ls?"

"One. I still reckon two was a spelling mistake."

"For the last time, it's French or Scottish or something. Foreign anyway. Now what about Alan?"

"He's got a bruise on his arm. Like, a proper belter. Several different colours. The lot."

"OK."

"And he doesn't want anyone to see it."

Bunny nodded. "Didn't Alan and his ma recently move in with Gary Kearney?"

"Yeah. The great white dope of Irish boxing. I lost twenty quid on his last fight."

"You shouldn't be gambling."

"Not on that waster's matches. You're dead right, boss."

"And we think ..."

Bunny watched Deccie, who turned his eyes away and bowed his head, his normal bravado deserting him. "We do."

"Have you mentioned this to anyone else?"

The youngster looked up at him, incomprehension writ large across his face. "Course not, boss. Who else would I talk to?"

"Fair enough. Leave it with me."

"Will do. So, what's this information worth?"

"Excuse me?"

"I'm a busy man."

"You are, in fact, neither of those things."

Deccie ploughed on. "Fifty quid?"

"Absolutely not."

"Can I pick the team for the next game?"

"No."

"I'd like a bigger input on tactics."

"Definitely not. You shot your bolt with your 'sharpen the edge of your hurley' speech. I had to check equipment for weeks."

Deccie raised his eyes to heaven. "D'you know what your problem is, boss? You've no appreciation for the fundamentals of the game."

"I'll take your criticism on board," said Bunny, getting to his feet. He buttoned up his coat as Deccie sat there, his arms folded, scowling. "I'll tell you what, you can pick man of the match in the next game."

"But it'll be Paulie. It's always Paulie."

"I know," said Bunny. "And you get to pick him."

Deccie thought about this, then nodded. "Alright. Good deal." He held out his clenched hand for a fist bump.

Bunny placed his palm over the top of it. "Paper covers rock. One–nil. Tell your grandad I said hello."

"Will do."

Bunny's phone started to ring. He fished it out of his pocket, looked at the screen and groaned.

"Who is it?" asked Deccie.

"Nobody you know."

"Ah, ignore it, then. I know everybody important."

Bunny almost put the phone away but at the last second, his guilt got the better of him. He sighed and answered it. "Hello, Mrs Spain …"

The flurry of panicked words that burst forth from the earpiece almost caused Bunny to yank the phone from his ear.

"Alright, calm down. I'll be right there."

Bunny hung up. "Do you reckon your grandad will be up for giving me a lift to Clontarf?"

"I'm sure he …"

Deccie didn't get a chance to finish as Bunny was already halfway to the car park.

# HOMOPHOBIA IN SUBURBIA

The drive from the Forty Foot over to Clontarf was nothing if not educational. Bunny was not in a very chatty mood, which was just as well as, with Deccie and his grandad in close proximity, there was absolutely no room in the conversation for anyone else. Not that it was actually a conversation. Bunny soon realised it was more like an endless spouting of opinions from both ends of the family tree as the pair spoke with absolute certainty on absolutely everything, seemingly paying almost no attention to their interlocutor.

"I'll tell you what's wrong with Japan ..." began Grandad Fadden.

"Raw fish," continued Deccie. "Ye can't be eating raw fish."

"The cars are good, but they don't look like they're good."

"How busy are they that they can't cook the fish?"

"Yeah, they're fuel-efficient and probably very safe, but they don't look very safe."

"I mean, you're not eating any other animals raw, are ye?"

"It's like the reason lads get tattoos. You stay out of a fight by looking like you'll win a fight."

"What makes people think fish can't kill ye? Just look at *Jaws*."

"Now, the Swedes, they make a car that looks like it's good."

"I don't get the fuss about meatballs, though."

"You could hit an elk in one of them and still walk away."

"It's just meat shaped like a ball. Get over it."

"And if you hit an elk, it's yours. Could be a nice little earner, that. Worth a few bob, your elk."

"Come to think of it, the name itself is suspicious. 'Meat'. Go up to someone on the street and ask them if they want some 'meat'. They'll run a mile. It's dangerously unspecific."

"An elk is basically nature's version of a deer with tattoos."

"I'd not eat elk meat. Or alpaca or kangaroo, or anything like that."

"Big horny buggers, though. I'd not want to hit one in a Japanese car."

"If kangaroo was nicer than cow, then we'd have fields full of kangaroos already."

"Japan's problem is their wildlife is too timid. Couple of elks knocking about and the cars would improve soon enough."

"It's like they're trying to rerun an election we already had. Cow won, get over it."

"The problem with French cars is they're made by the French."

"Snails. There's another one."

"They're too into pleasure."

"Snails don't taste of anything; I ate one as a bet that time at that summer camp. They're just a bit wriggly."

"If Pierre or François think it's a nice day, they'll be off to sit under a tree and eat chocolate bread. That's how you end up with not enough bolts in your car."

"They're just pretending to like stuff to be awkward."

"That's the French for you."

"Yep," agreed Deccie. "That's the French for you."

The pair continued in this vein for the entire journey. Two parallel streams of consciousness spewing forth opinions and intertwining only occasionally. It would have been oddly hypnotic only Bunny wasn't able to relax. Diana Spain had sounded distressed. Her irate calls had become a regular part of his life, but this one had been different.

As they got closer to Clontarf, Bunny gave directions to Grandad Fadden, who managed to follow them without breaking his seemingly endless monologue.

They pulled up to the house on Williams Street and Bunny was out the door before the car had come to a stop.

Two men were standing at the front door of the property. One was big and broad-shouldered in the way that looked like that's what got him the job. The other man was by no means small – about the same size as Bunny, in fact – but his companion made him look dinky by comparison. The not-small small fella was holding a clipboard – the brains of the outfit, evidently. They were both wearing suits, the kind that looked as if they were fulfilling a minimum requirement, and were quite obviously the cheapest you could get without trawling charity shops, hoping someone had died in your size.

Neither of the men noticed Bunny as he made his way through the garden gate. The big lad was trying to wring some water out of his suit while Clipboard was shouting abuse through the letterbox. "That's assault, ye mad old cow. You'll be up on charges for that."

"What in the feck is going on here?" asked Bunny.

Both men turned around to look at him.

"None of your bleeding business," said Clipboard.

"Wrong answer. Have another go."

"Who are you?" asked the big wet lad.

"He's Bunny McGarry," came a shout from behind.

Bunny turned to see two generations of the Fadden family now perched on the bonnet of the car, watching on.

"I'll handle this," said Bunny.

"*I'm* handling this," said Clipboard. "Nobody asked you to get involved."

"Two grown men hassling a couple of defenceless little old ladies? I decided to get involved all by myself."

"Defenceless?" said the big guy. "The mad old one just turned the hose on us."

"Well, you do look like you could do with a wash."

"Excuse me," came Deccie's voice. "Can I just check – neither of you knows who Bunny is?"

Clipboard pointed. "Who's the little fat kid?"

"Hey," said Grandad Fadden. "That's my grandson and the assistant manager of St Jude's Under-12 hurling team. He's not fat. He's big boned."

"Lads," said Bunny to his cheerleading squad, "could you let me handle this, please?"

"Fair enough," said Grandad, before Deccie added, "We're here if you need us, boss."

"Boss?" asked Clipboard.

"Bunny's the manager of the St Jude's Under-12s," chipped in Grandad, which earned him a glare from Bunny. "Right. Sorry. Shutting up now."

"Whoever the fuck you are," said Clipboard, "you and your hurling team can piss off."

"Hurling is a stupid game an' all," said the big fella.

"Oh Jesus," said Deccie with barely suppressed excitement in his voice. "You should not have said that."

"There's only one way this is going to end," concluded Grandad.

Bunny tried to block out the closest you'll get to the two old lads from the Muppets in real life and turned to Clipboard. "This house belongs to a good friend of mine."

The big fella, seemingly not keeping up with the conversation, turned to the gallery. "Hurling is only a bunch of faggots with sticks, chasing a ball about."

"Right, that's it," said Deccie.

"Leave it, son. Bunny will deal with it."

"No, Grandad. I'm not standing for that kind of homophobic language."

"Deccie!" snapped Bunny. "Will you shut up?"

"Right, boss. Sorry, boss."

"Now," said Bunny, "like I said, this house belongs to a good friend of mine."

"Well, he's not paid his debts so now we own it."

"That's not possible."

"It's a fact," said Clipboard.

"Wait a sec," said the big fella. "'Faggot' isn't whatchamacallit?"

"Homophobic," supplied Grandad. "And it is."

"This is the first I've heard about this debt," said Bunny.

"So?" said Clipboard. "Ask your friend about it."

"I can't. He's dead. He was a guard, shot in the line of duty."

"My heart bleeds for him," said Clipboard with a sneer.

Such disrespect was met with a sucking-in of air from the gallery.

"Forget the hurling thing," said Deccie. "You're in for a whole other world of hurt now."

"Some things you just don't say," agreed Grandad.

Bunny took a step towards Clipboard and lowered his voice. "I'm going to say this only once. Leave the paperwork, and if this is legit, I will sort it out."

"No. I have instructions. We own this house."

"Over my dead body."

"Suits me."

"Hang on," said the big fella. "I can't be homophobic. I'm gay."

"Oh right," said Grandad. "That puts a different spin on it, alright."

"Does it, though?" said Deccie.

"Rory," snapped Clipboard, "you dozy poof. Shut up!"

"Now that," said Deccie, "we can all agree, was homophobic."

"Agreed," said Grandad.

"I'm a guard," said Bunny.

"Show me your ID, then, officer?" said Clipboard.

"I don't have it with me," said Bunny. "I'm on sabbatical."

"You don't look Jewish," said the big fella.

"It means he's on a break, ye dozy eejit," said Deccie.

"So, you're not currently a guard, then, are ye?" said Clipboard. He pointed at the front door. "That woman is getting out of there today. This house belongs to us."

"Let me see that." Bunny snatched at the clipboard but its holder wouldn't release it and the pair began to wrestle over it.

Bunny had been in more than enough fights and sensed the big fella's haymaker heading in his direction. As he ducked, it glanced off the top of his head and mostly made contact with Clipboard instead.

Right before all hell broke loose, Bunny heard Grandad Fadden behind him, shouting cheerfully, "And they're off!"

## A BETTER CLASS OF TEA

Bunny was peering into the bottom of his Styrofoam cup of tea when the door opened. He glanced up. "Detective Inspector O'Rourke, as I live and breathe. This is an unexpected honour."

Fintan O'Rourke took off his overcoat and walked across the room. "Bunny, always a pleasure."

"I had no idea you were working out of Clontarf Garda Station now. That's a bit of a fall from your lofty role in charge of task forces and what not."

"Oh no," said O'Rourke, pulling out the chair opposite Bunny and sitting down. "I still have the lofty role, alright. About to be bumped up, in fact."

"Congratulations. I'm glad to see the work we did on the Tommy Carter task force has paid off for you. So, what in the fecking hell are you doing here?"

"I could ask you the same thing, Detective."

"It's just Bunny. I'm on sabbatical."

"Indeed you are. Which does rather bring us to the question of what you're doing getting into fights in Clontarf of all places."

"Sure, I can't get into scraps around where people know me. All the gobshites there have wised up to what a bad idea that is."

"Well, from the provisional report I've just read, it sounds like it won't be long before your reputation spreads. It certainly will if Messrs Rory McDaid and Martin Dean have anything to do with it. Those are the names of the two men you kicked the crap out of – in case you didn't know."

"They started it."

O'Rourke nodded. "I've no doubt they did. I've also read the witness statements provided by Declan Fadden Junior and Declan Fadden Senior."

"I didn't know Deccie's grandad was a Deccie too. Family tradition, I expect."

"Yes. I'd imagine if this were to go to court, they'd be quite the double act." O'Rourke pulled a piece of paper from the inside pocket of his jacket and unfolded it. "The younger's statement, while hitting the same key points as his grandfather's regarding your total innocence, is still quite the piece of work. Here's my favourite bit: 'The big gay fella swung for Bunny and missed but hit the homophobic fella, who took a swipe at Bunny. Only then did Bunny defend himself by smacking the homophobic fella right in the face and then kicked the big gay fella right in his big gay meat and two veg. He didn't mean that in a homophobic way, it was just to stop the big gay fella from walloping him.'" He looked up. "It goes on like this for quite some time ..."

"Deccie has quite a way with words."

"That he has. By the way, your opponents – whose sex lives the Fadden family seems to know a remarkable amount about – have no serious injuries. Bruising, a sprained wrist, some cuts, and, one assumes, a tender big gay meat and two veg."

"For the record, I'd have much preferred to boot the homophobe in the knackers, but ye have to go with the flow in these situations."

"I'll take your word for it."

Bunny picked up the now-empty Styrofoam cup. "Have you tried the tea here, Fintan? 'Tis incredible. I don't know if it's because they're nearer the sea, or if they just have nicer teabags owing to this being fancy-pants Clontarf, but, honest to God, with a cuppa this good, why would you not get yourself arrested?"

"I'll keep it in mind, but while we're on the subject, when the locals turned up at the site of your little contretemps, why didn't you just tell them who you were?"

"What's that got to do with anything?"

O'Rourke rolled his eyes. "Christ, you're an awkward bastard, McGarry."

"You're not the first to say it."

"Oh, I know," said O'Rourke. "Believe me, I know."

"Which brings us back to: what the hell are you doing here, Fintan?"

"One of mine got arrested. When they realised who he was, eventually, they gave me a call."

"I'm not one of yours, though. That task force was a temporary assignment."

O'Rourke rested his elbows on the table. "But seeing as it was the last thing you did before taking your extended leave of absence, it counts. Now, would you stop being so bloody difficult and tell me what's going on. Why are you slugging it out with two of Coop Hannity's boys on Gringo Spain's lawn?"

"Those two lads work for Coop?"

"You didn't know that?"

Bunny shrugged. "We were never properly introduced. Things escalated quickly."

"Yes, I've noticed they have a tendency to do so when you're around. So, what was going on?"

"They seemed to be of the opinion they were owed some money and I was endeavouring to find out what was going on. Gringo's ma is living there now with her friend. She rang me."

O'Rourke raised an eyebrow. "I met his mother at the funeral. She gave me quite the bollocking."

"Yeah. She does that."

"You and her are close, then?"

"I wouldn't say that."

the name Tim Spain coming up again in any capacity other than its appearance on a bronze plaque.

Bunny leaned back in his chair. "I said I was going to handle it, and I am."

O'Rourke shrugged. "Alright, fine. You know where I am."

"I do."

"Speaking of which, when are you coming back to work, Bunny?"

Bunny smiled. "Why, Detective Inspector, are you missing my company, or would you rather I was somewhere you can keep an eye on me?"

O'Rourke got to his feet. "Can't it be both?"

Bunny ignored the question. "Am I free to go?"

"Of course. For Christ's sake, if you'd have just explained yourself to the locals, you wouldn't have been here in the first place."

Bunny looked around. "Ah, it was nice to see how the other half lives, though. I got a chocolate digestive with my tea. What a level of service!"

O'Rourke headed towards the door. "Do fill out a comment card on the way out."

"Any chance of a lift?"

"You don't need one," said O'Rourke. "Messrs Fadden Junior and Senior are sitting out in reception, chatting to the desk sergeant. They refused to leave."

"Oh."

"Yes. Just a thought, but judging by the look on the poor man's face as I came in, you might want to get them out of here in case he has access to the gun locker."

Bunny nodded. "Good tip."

## RED LETTER DAY

Bunny rang the doorbell and took a step back.

"Who is it?" asked a tremulous female voice from inside.

"It's Bunny, Mrs Spain."

"I don't know anyone by that name."

Bunny nodded, as if a part of his mind were confirming to himself why he dreaded coming here. The woman could try his patience at the best of times, and now was certainly not that.

"It's Detective Bernard McGarry, Mrs Spain. You rang me earlier."

*But then, you knew that*, he thought to himself. Even at the gates of heaven the woman could complain to St Peter about the wait.

"I see. Just a moment."

Bunny turned and looked back at the car. The Deccie Fadden Collective was sitting in the front, watching him. He gave them a wave. They'd offered to drive him to where he needed to go and, seeing as he currently had no means of transportation, he'd taken them up on their kind offer. He really needed to sort himself out with at least something temporary. His car had been in the shop for months now. It turned out that driving a vehicle off a cliff and into the sea caused all kinds of damage – James Bond's underwater car must've been a nightmare to maintain.

It had necessitated more time than it should have to convey to them both that their assistance was very definitely not required in talking to Mrs Spain. Without a doubt, the two Deccies and Diana Spain conversing would be a spectacularly watchable car crash, but Bunny had come here looking for answers, not entertainment.

The door opened a couple of inches, held in place by the chain.

"Good afternoon, Mr McGarry."

"Howerya, Mrs Spain. Could I come in, please? We need to talk."

The one eye visible through the crack stared at him intently. "Will you be behaving in a dignified manner?"

"Excuse me?"

"The last time you were here, you were brawling on the front lawn. I was mortified. I mean, what would the neighbours say?"

Bunny bit his lip. Clearly, Diana was having one of her good days. Couldn't fault her memory when it came to other people's faults. Many possible responses to her question offered themselves up, but none of them would go down well in the current circumstances. Seeing as Bunny knew for a fact that she had, on various occasions, reported the neighbours to the local police for an overly loud radio, a cat shitting on her lawn, excessive horseplay from children, playing ball on the road, and, Bunny's favourite, suspicious gardening, he had a fairly good idea what the neighbours would say.

"We just need to have a chat."

She huffed for a moment before conceding. "Very well, then."

The door closed and reopened fully. Mrs Spain waved him in quickly, as if she were keen to get him inside before anyone saw. As he stepped into the hallway, he noticed Fionnuala standing at the top of the stairs, peering down at him while hugging her cardigan around herself. Bunny didn't know much about the woman, other than she had never married and was the very definition of mousy. He had tried to be friendly to her every time he'd visited, but she still acted as if she were terrified of him. He had no idea if she was like this with everybody or just him.

Bunny made his way into the front room. Mrs Spain had made pointed noises about wanting to redecorate it as soon as they'd moved her in, but Bunny had determinedly ignored them. He and Gringo had spent a weekend decorating the entire downstairs when Gringo had first bought the place and the flock wallpaper was a reminder of happier times.

She directed him to the sofa and took a seat in the armchair opposite. She was wearing a summer dress, unsuited to the current season, but then Bunny knew that she point-blank refused all entreaties to go out for a walk as the area was "far too dangerous". So, in a house where the heating was always up full whack, it was indeed summer every day.

Every time Bunny looked at Diana Spain, he was reminded of Gringo's ex-wife's description of her mother-in-law: "She has a face on her like the whole world is one great big, blocked toilet and it's not her job to fix it." It did sum her up perfectly.

Seeing as the divorce hadn't gone through when Gringo died, Mary wasn't technically his ex-wife, but Bunny noticed that she referred to herself that way and so, out of respect, he did the same. Perhaps she preferred it to thinking of herself as a widow. Still, he remembered her collapsing in floods of tears at the funeral. Bunny knew more than anyone that Gringo hadn't been a perfect man, but, despite the couple's problems, there'd been love there – any fool could see that.

Bunny and Mary had never been close, but she'd been very decent in helping out with the mess that her soon-to-be-ex had left behind – not least, what to do about the woman now sitting opposite Bunny. In contrast to Mary, Diana had spent the funeral stony-faced, even glancing with disapproval at her former daughter-in-law's display of emotion.

Diana herself had been widowed at an early age, after her husband, the accountant-cum-investment-guru to Ireland's rich and famous, had committed suicide after it was discovered he'd been embezzling money from his friends and clients. Gringo had found him in the garage. The topic only ever came up when Gringo had been really in his cups, and Bunny was certain he'd never discussed it with Mary.

Diana regarded Bunny with the air of a school principal about to deliver a strong reprimand, "I hope you have an explanation for that debacle this morning?"

"Actually," replied Bunny, "I was rather hoping you did. Those two fellas seemed to think there were some outstanding debts. Do you know what they're talking about?"

She dismissed the question with a wave of her hand. "I don't concern myself with such things. Timothy always dealt with the finances, and before that, his sainted father – God rest his soul – handled all the family's affairs."

Bunny nodded. Mrs Spain was very sensitive about her late husband, particularly when it came to any suggestion that he had been involved in any impropriety or had taken his own life. In her version of the world, he'd been hounded over some bookkeeping errors he'd been in the middle of correcting then died tragically while cleaning a shotgun. Bunny still remembered well the moment Gringo hadn't been able to take it any more and had laid out for his mother the cold truth of how and why his father was no longer with them. The pair hadn't spoken for almost a year and their stalemate was broken only when, out of the blue, Diana had rung Gringo to inform him that the washing machine wasn't working. That was as close as you got to an apology from Diana Spain.

"The thing is, Mrs Spain, apparently those two gobshites—"

"There is no need for that kind of language."

"What should I call them?"

"Gentlemen."

Bunny paused. "OK. Those two gentlemen from this morning – the ones you were kind enough to turn the hose on ..."

Her eyes flashed with anger.

"They had some paperwork. Have you been receiving any letters?"

"All manner of things. So much comes through the letterbox these days. Honestly, why the Gardaí aren't doing anything about it I don't know."

"Right. Any letters with red writing on the front of them?"

She tutted. "I don't know. I leave all of that in the drawer in the kitchen."

"Grand," said Bunny. "Am I alright to go and look in the drawer?"

Mrs Spain thought about this. "Very well, but please refrain from touching anything else."

"Do you think I'm going to rob the place, Diana?"

For a moment Bunny fancied that even she thought her last remark might have been a step too far.

"No, I ... I'm just very particular about how everything is."

Despite the china-doll vibe she liked to give off, Diana Spain must have been stronger than she looked. There was so much post rammed into the drawer that it took Bunny three attempts to open it.

"Careful!" she admonished.

He ignored her and focused his attention on the treasure trove of unopened correspondence before him. Letters from the Garda Representative Association; bills – most of which Bunny knew, thankfully, were handled via direct debits; the normal charity mailers; flyers for double-glazing companies; pizza menus; a letter from Áras an Uachtaráin, the office of the President of Ireland herself no less; and there, buried at the bottom, were the letters Bunny had felt with leaden certainty in his stomach he would find.

As he opened them, he noted that, for a woman who seemingly paid no attention to her post, the envelopes with the big scary words in red lettering on them were shoved right at the bottom, as if they could be crushed out of existence by the weight of banality on top of them.

Bunny read the first one, cursed under his breath, loud enough to earn a tut from behind him, and then ripped open another one. It was the same, only worse.

Bunny sighed. "This is bad. Very bad."

He turned to see Diana Spain standing half in and half out of the kitchen, as if preparing to run.

"What is it?"

"Well, I need to talk to a lawyer, but according to these letters, the company those men work for aren't saying that Tim owes them money."

"That's good, isn't it?"

"Unfortunately not. What they're saying is that they own this house."

Mrs Spain went pale. "That is utter nonsense. This was – is – Timothy's house. Why would he sell it?"

"I don't think he sold it as such. Like I said, I need to look into it further."

"I'll hire a lawyer to deal with this."

Bunny nodded. "Alright, Mrs Spain, but unless you have some money to pay them, I can't see how that'll work exactly."

"But ... but ... I am a respectable woman."

For a moment, behind the acid tongue and haughty disapproval of the world, Bunny saw a glimpse of the real Diana Spain: a scared woman in her seventies whose carefully built-up world was being rudely ripped down from around her – and not for the first time. Oddly, when she showed just a hint of vulnerability was when she looked most like Gringo. It was something in the eyes.

Then, the flash of the ghost of his old friend vanished just as quickly as it had appeared, only to be replaced by anger. Diana jabbed a finger at Bunny. "How could you let this happen?"

"Me?"

"Yes, you. Timothy left you in charge of his estate."

"Timothy didn't leave me in charge of anything. What he left was a mess, which I've been endeavouring to sort out."

"I think you're stealing his money!"

Something in Bunny snapped. "Am I? Really? Not that you'd know, Diana, but I've been paying your electricity bill out of my own pocket for the last couple of months. Believe me, there is no money to steal. Tim left behind a lot of debts ..." He picked up the letter and waved it at her. "... More than we realised, because you haven't been opening the post. So don't go taking a pop at me about how everything's gone tits up. I can't sort out what I don't know about."

Mrs Spain turned on her heel, stormed down the hallway and back into the front room.

Bunny stood there, seething, and annoyed with himself for having lost his temper.

He decided to give it five minutes, and used the time to check through all of the post again and make sure there were no other nasty surprises. The only one seemed to be from Better Tomorrow Lending Limited. Bunny had a strong suspicion who that really was: Coop Hannity, whose muscle he had met earlier in the day.

After he had judged enough time had passed, Bunny knocked softly on the door to the front room. There was a pregnant pause before Mrs Spain said, "Come in" in a quiet voice.

She was sitting in the same chair she had occupied earlier. She was trying to hide it, but Bunny guessed she had been crying. He felt truly awful.

"I apologise for losing my temper, Mrs Spain."

She gave a curt nod and rearranged a doily that did not need adjustment on the nest of tables beside her. She cleared her throat. "How bad is it?"

"I honestly don't know. Like I said, I'll have to look into it. I'll talk to the lawyer from the Garda Representative Association and see if they can help with it."

"Very well."

"If those men from earlier – or anyone else you don't know – turn up and start asking questions, or whatever, ring me. Day or night." Bunny took a tentative step forward and held out a piece of paper. "If you can't get me, call any of the three numbers on this piece of paper."

She took it and looked at it.

"They're other guards," said Bunny. "I'll let them know you might be in touch."

"I don't want other people knowing our family's business."

"I understand. These are all friends of Tim's. They'll be discreet. It's only in case of emergency."

She folded the paper and placed it on the doily. "Very well."

"And if any other post turns up, just let me know."

"I will."

Bunny shuffled his feet. "Alright, then. And try not to worry."

When Diana Spain didn't say anything, Bunny turned and made his way towards the front door. "I'll see myself out."

He'd just placed his hand on the handle when she called his name. He turned to see her standing in the doorway to the front room.

"My Timothy was a good man. Wasn't he?"

"The very best."

She pursed her lips. "He gambled, didn't he?"

Bunny was taken aback. Until now, Diana had seemed determined to stay wilfully ignorant of that fact. "He did, yes."

She looked down at the carpet. "I suppose we all have our flaws."

"We do," agreed Bunny. "Lord knows, we do."

She looked up at him and gave him that same piercing look Bunny had seen Gringo use a thousand times when trying to break a suspect. "But he was a good man?"

Bunny nodded and turned back to the door, but paused. "Oh God, sorry. With all of the fuss, I forgot." He took the other letter out of the back pocket of his jeans, flattened it out on his chest and then handed it to Diana. "Congratulations. It looks like the President would like to give him a medal."

# CASTLES AND MONSTERS

As soon as the car turned the corner, Bunny couldn't help but bark a laugh.

"What's funny?" asked Deccie Sr.

"I just got it," replied Bunny. "When I rang my old friend to ask for Coop Hannity's address, he'd only give me the road name. Said I'd know it when I saw it."

Deccie Sr pulled up in front of the large house that dominated the end of the cul-de-sac.

"Do you want us to come in with you, Bunny?" asked Deccie Jr. "As back-up, like?"

"No need for that," said Deccie Sr. "I'm sure Bunny can handle everything just fine on his own."

The two men locked eyes and Bunny gave a nod of acknowledgement. Senior knew the Hannity name and being here made him understandably nervous.

"Your grandad is right, Deccie. I've got this from here. The two of you should head home for your dinner."

Senior did a bad job of hiding his relief. "Are you sure?"

"Absolutely. I've an old mate up the road that I might pop up and visit after."

"But," protested Deccie, "how're we supposed to find out what's happening?"

"I'm sure Bunny will tell you about anything that is your business to know, Deccie. C'mon. Your granny will be getting annoyed. It's sausage night."

"It was sausage night last night," said Deccie.

"It'll be sausage night all week." Senior looked at Bunny. "I got a very good deal from a lad down the pub. Forgot the missus doesn't actually like sausages."

"Oh right."

"How was I supposed to know?"

"You've been married for forty-eight years," said Deccie, earning him a dirty look from his granddad. "What? I'm only repeating what Granny said."

"And what have I told you about doing that?"

"Anyway," said Bunny, opening the car door. "Thanks very much for the assistance, gentlemen. Deccie, I'll see you tomorrow at training."

Deccie nodded huffily.

"We'll do fitness work and I'll let you be in charge of the whistle."

His assistant manager's face lit up at this. "Brilliant!"

Bunny said his final goodbyes and watched the car pull away, the Deccie Fadden Collective no doubt already deep in two parallel but separate conversations.

Bunny turned to look at the house behind him, illuminated by various strategically placed lights to fend off the early evening darkness. The reason an exact address was not needed was obvious as soon as you saw it. James "Coop" Hannity had grown up in the seven towers of Ballymun, the lights of which were just visible in the distance. Clearly, he'd not wanted to move too far away from his roots, so down the road in Santry was as far as he'd felt comfortable venturing. This left him with the issue of being rich enough to afford a mansion but only having the housing stock in a fairly run-of-the-mill middle-class suburb to choose from.

The solution Hannity had hit on was to buy up the neighbouring houses and expand. He now owned an almost palatial spread that sat incongruously between the other three-bed semi-detached houses on the street. Bunny guessed the neighbours weren't wild about it but had the sense to keep those thoughts to themselves. On the upside, he'd wager very good money that no houses on this street ever got burgled. Even the dimmest of local independent operatives in the field of unlicensed acquisitions would have more sense than to do anything that would bring them to the attention of Coop Hannity.

Now that Bunny had a better look, he realised that the word "castle" might be a more appropriate descriptor. The thing looked somewhere between Disney and Dracula Gothic, complete with actual towers at both ends of the property. It had a mock-stone facade but Bunny was disappointed to note the lack of a drawbridge.

Hannity operated in that grey area of legality that coppers hated. He could at best be described as a loan shark, although that was a bit like describing da Vinci as a decorator, or Bill Gates as an IT guy. Being a loan shark wasn't illegal, although Bunny had read in the paper that there was talk of finally doing something about that. Hannity had made his name by lending to people nobody else would, and then charging them through the nose for the privilege. Most of his clients – usually ordinary people who'd fallen on hard times – ended up paying back the loan several times over, or just drowning in the compound interest.

Hannity and his sort were leeches, who clamped on to the skin of communities and sucked the life out of them a little at a time. The loans might not be illegal, but the collection methods often were, extending far beyond strongly worded letters. Muscle, such as the type Bunny had clashed with earlier, were on the payroll, making threats and, when required, carrying them out. It was nearly impossible to get any of the victims to testify in court, and even if they did, people like Hannity were insulated. "Sorry, Your Honour, I'm as horrified as you are. I had no idea my employees engaged in such activities off their own bat." And the activities often involved the brutal application of said bat. Hannity's various operations produced the only two things that mattered in the modern world: money and plausible deniability.

To give the man his questionable due, there was nobody quite like him. Most money lenders reach a certain position within their own community and stop, but Hannity had managed the rare feat of growing his empire far beyond his geographical roots. A combination of factors had gone into it; first and foremost, he had a brilliant understanding of risk. Maybe if he'd been born in Blackrock or somewhere like that, he'd be running a bank or an insurance company now. Instead, he'd been born in Ballymun, the youngest of six, and he'd clawed his way up from the streets. He was blessed with the kind of shrewd business sense you couldn't teach, a prerequisite comfort with brutality, and a preparedness to be truly hated if necessary. It had been a long time since anyone had dared to express such feelings to Hannity's face, not unless it was as their last words.

Of course, he didn't wield any bats or dig any holes himself these days. For a man in his position, delegation was key. Back in the day, though, rumour had it that he had personally broken his own brother's legs when he'd been unable to make his loan repayment. Bunny wasn't sure if this was true or not, but it didn't matter – only the legend had any significance. Anyone thinking of pleading their case would remember how Paul Hannity walked with a cane now, and would then go back to trying by any means necessary to find the money they owed.

For all his "talents", the secret to Hannity's longevity was that he never expanded into other areas of crime. Most criminals like him did. Drugs were easy money, and God knows they gave him enough business indirectly, but he didn't want anything to do with the supply line. It also meant he didn't clash with other figures from the criminal underworld. They stayed off his patch, and he off theirs. That's not to say he didn't have involvements, but always at a remove. Say someone couldn't make their payments and was desperate to find a way – he could pass their details on. Somebody somewhere always had a use for the truly desperate, and were willing to pay for it. If, later on, that person was stopped at Dublin Port with a car full of something illegal, or was involved in administering a beating, or even in a gangland shooting, nothing splashed back on Coop Hannity.

No, instead, he focused his attention on his area of expertise: credit. He even had a more legit arm of the business now, providing no-questions-asked credit on that new sofa you could probably almost certainly afford. Much of suburbia would have been scandalised to learn that behind the various innocuous company names on those bits of paperwork from the car dealership or the furniture showroom lay Coop Hannity. Keep up with your payments and you need never find out. Don't keep up and, well, there are lawyers and then there are other people who don't cost as much or dress as nicely.

And so Coop Hannity existed in the in-between and got rich by adding up the numbers in the margin.

Bunny took a step towards the house and stopped. Some instincts you can't explain. He'd felt that prickle on the back of his neck, as if something wasn't right. He looked back up the cul-de-sac, examining each of the parked cars in turn. Nothing was obvious, but still ... He stepped back and, as soon as he did so, the engine of the blue BMW, a few cars up on the far side of the road, roared into life. Before Bunny could move another muscle, it drove off. Only as it reached the end of the road did its lights come on, which prevented him from getting the number plate.

Maybe it was nothing. Somebody making a phone call before setting off, or something equally innocuous. Maybe.

Concrete lions sat at the end of Hannity's driveway, which led to a garden that had been landscaped to within an inch of its life. The hedges on the far side had been pruned into the form of cherubs, with roses growing where the arrows would be. The lawn looked like the kind of greens they play the Masters on and the flowerbeds were explosions of colour. In the middle sat a pond, where a solitary garden gnome fished for eternity, a rather perplexed look on his face.

Bunny walked up the gravel drive and rang the doorbell. It sounded a chime of sequential tolls, more suited to the ordaining of a new pope than something you'd hear every time you got a pizza delivered. Warm light spilled through the stained glass on either side of the large oak door, before it was all but eclipsed. The door opened and Bunny realised what had obstructed the light. An immense amount of humanity stood before him in the doorway, beaming a friendly smile down at him. The voice that came with it was incongruously cheerful.

"Alright, buddy, how can I help you?"

"Jesus," said Bunny, "who in the name of holy giant haystacks are you?"

The man smiled. "The name is Samoan Joe."

"The size of you. You should play rugby or something."

"Oh, I did that exact thing, mate, but I blew out the old knee." He tapped his right leg and gave a rueful smile. "Got brought over by one of the clubs. Would you believe I did it in my first training session? Straight off the plane."

"Christ, that's fierce unlucky."

"Ah, worse things happen at sea, though, eh? Club paid for the surgery, which was decent of them, and there's always work for a big fella."

"Don't you miss Samoa?"

"I've never been. I'm from New Zealand, but my mum is from Fiji."

"So how come ..."

Joe laughed. "Guys preferred 'Samoan Joe' to 'Kiwi Joe', I guess. No skin off my nose." He favoured Bunny with another warm smile. "Anyway, what can I do for you, sir?"

"I was hoping to have a word with the master of the house."

Joe shook his immense head, despite seemingly lacking a neck. "No can do, fella. I'm under strict instructions that he's not to be disturbed."

"I'm sure he'll want to see me."

"Everybody is. Nobody is right. Mr Hannity likes to keep his evenings separate from work. He is most emphatic on that particular point. Let me take your number and I promise I'll pass it on."

"My name is Bunny McGarry. Just ask him."

Samoan Joe sighed. "Look, fella, you gotta take no for an answer here. The boss'll rip me a new one if I disturb him, and I'm just not gonna do it. Alright?"

Bunny had got around many noes he'd received in his life, but this one was being delivered so politely it was making things tricky. Joe seemed like a cordial fella. When you're big enough that life has to go around you, as opposed to the other way round, Bunny reckoned you could afford to be.

"Look, Joe, I promise I'm not trying to be a pain in your arse, but I came here to speak to the man and I'm not leaving unless I do."

Samoan Joe managed to pull off the combo of cracking his knuckles while giving Bunny a sympathetic look. "I'm afraid that's not an option. Now, I'm sure you got good reasons, but believe me when I say that whatever you need to talk to him about, he'll be a lot more receptive in the morning."

Bunny rolled his head around his neck. "I really didn't want this to go down this way, Joe. You seem like a nice fella."

"Likewise. Mind if I take my jacket off?"

"Not at all. Be my guest."

"Appreciate it." Joe slipped off his suit jacket. "Got to have them made special and they keep ripping."

Bunny nodded. "Price of the job, I guess."

"That and the blood stains."

"Bleed a lot, do you?"

"Me? No."

Generally, Bunny preferred his opponents to be so riled up that they'd make a mistake, or so over-confident that they'd do the same. Joe seemed unrilable and possessed of an utterly justifiable confidence. Bunny hadn't come here looking for trouble, but if he was going to resolve the situation before it got any worse, he couldn't afford to be fobbed off.

Joe gave a rueful smile as he bunched his fists. "Last chance. There's really no need for this to get unpleasant, Mr McGarry."

"McGarry?" asked a female voice from behind Joe.

Joe turned his head. "This is nothing to concern yourself with, Mrs Hannity."

"Get out of the way, ye big lug."

Joe sheepishly took a step to one side to reveal a brunette woman in a blue flowing dress. She held a martini glass in one hand and wore a black glove on the other. Her eyes widened. "Bunny?"

Bunny stood there for the longest time, flat-footed. In his defence, he'd been preparing himself for a kicking but now found himself in a game of Guess Who.

"Shitting Nora. Angelina Quirke, is that you?"

"That it is," the woman said with a smile, striking a jaunty pose. "Come on in."

"Ehm," said Samoan Joe, shifting awkwardly, "the boss said ..."

"He's not here to see him," snapped Angelina. "Now he's here to see me."

Joe nodded and ushered Bunny inside. "No hard feelings, I hope?"

Bunny shook his head as he stepped past. "Not at all. I'm just glad I didn't have to hurt you."

# SHOULD OLD ACQUAINTANCE BE FORGOT?

Bunny felt awkward sitting in the drawing room of the Hannity house. He only knew the room went by that name as that's what Samoan Joe had called it as he'd directed him through the doorway. Everything around Bunny appeared to be made from leather, mahogany or velvet. He was wearing the same coat he'd been rolling around in on Diana Spain's lawn earlier in the day, and suddenly worried that he'd picked up one of her neighbour's cat's shits and might now be depositing it on the indecently expensive soft furnishings. While Bunny was no fan of Hannity or his ilk, he was here to try to resolve a tricky situation, and although smearing cat shit all over the man's sofa was a strong opening move in any negotiation, he felt as if it might set the wrong tone.

One wall was filled entirely from floor to ceiling with books, and even they looked expensive. In the hearth that dominated the room, a log fire was burning. Bunny sat watching the sparks dance around each other and then disappear up the chimney. Once you looked past the opulence, however, the place was missing something. There were no pictures of family or friends anywhere. No sense of a life lived. It lent a peculiarly oppressive feel to the space. As if it were a museum exhibit.

The door swung open and in strode Angelina Quirke with Samoan Joe trailing awkwardly in her wake. Bunny was still trying to get his head around her. In his mind, she was still the little girl he remembered from back in the day when he'd helped out with the North Paw Boxing Club and it had been used as a venue for ballet classes for the local kids a couple of evenings each week.

Angelina had been a shy little thing, and the teacher, Mrs Glynn, had made the other girls watch her as an example. Bunny imagined quite a few had done so and then given up on dancing entirely. Seeing true talent can have that effect on the less gifted.

He could still recall the day he'd been sent to collect Angelina from class. Her mother had been found dead and her father had not taken the news well. As Bunny was known in the community, he'd accompanied the social worker to pick up the young girl. When faced with the tiny ballerina's big blue eyes the woman had bottled it, and it had been Bunny who broke the news to Angelina that her mother had died. John Quirke ended up being sectioned for his own safety and from that day on, Bunny had kept an eye on Angelina until she went off to see the world. On some level he knew he had no reason to feel guilty – after all, all he'd done was pass on the news – but then he'd long ago realised that guilt didn't need a reason. It was just something you collected more and more of as you went through life.

"Sorry about that," said Angelina, "just sorting something. Bunny McGarry, as I live and breathe. Now, here is a sight for sore eyes. C'mere and give me a hug."

Bunny got to his feet and awkwardly did as she asked. Angelina was still slight of build and smelled of jasmine with just a hint of gin. As they embraced, Bunny caught Joe's eye from where the bodyguard was standing beside the door. He looked decidedly ill at ease.

Angelina drew back, placed her hands on Bunny's arms and looked up at him. "My God, it's been what? Nine, ten years, and you've not changed a bit."

"Neither have you."

She gave a hearty laugh. "Thank you for lying."

"Last I heard, you'd deferred your university place and gone off to do modelling in London, or LA, or Milan – something like that?"

"Yes," she said ruefully. "All of the above. I took my turn on that particular wheel. Not as much fun as they tell you. Don't do it if you get the chance."

Bunny rolled his eyes theatrically. "Ara shite, now you tell me? I've only gone and signed a contract with Calvin Klein."

Angelina laughed again, harder than the line warranted. "Well, international fashion's gain will be law enforcement's loss. You're still with the guards, aren't you?"

"More or less."

"Glad to hear it. Sit, sit, sit."

Bunny nervously took his seat again.

Angelina turned to Samoan Joe. "This here is Bunny McGarry, the last honest man in Dublin. Hero to the working man, and especially the women."

"Ah, here now," said Bunny, "you're laying it on a bit thick."

"No, I'm not. If something went wrong back in those days, you didn't ring 999. You sent one of the kids down to the cop shop and asked for the big fella from Cork. Back when we were barely teenagers, a monumental arsehole from the estate was trying to push my old friend Mags to do, well, things she didn't want to. Bunny stepped in, sorted it right out." She gave him a sideways smile. "An honest-to-God hero in a world that doesn't allow them to exist. In olden times, they'd have written songs about you."

"Come on now, Angelina. You're embarrassing me in front of the man mountain over there."

She waved dismissively at Joe. "Don't mind him. He's harmless. It's me you have to worry about."

"How is Mags these days? Are you still in touch?"

"Oh yes. She's got a nice apartment over in Rathfarnham. Her and her boyfriend, Bobby. I visit her when I go see my dad – he's in a care facility out there."

"Great. The two of you were always thick as thieves. The 'terrible twins' we called you."

"I remember." She laughed. "And us with the terrible matching outfits."

"Tell her I was asking for her."

Angelina slapped her forehead playfully. "Sorry. I'm so thrown by seeing a ghost from my past, I've totally lost my manners. Joe, a drink for our guest. Still a whiskey man?"

Bunny nodded.

"See? As unchanging as the North Star." She turned to Joe. "Go get him a double, please. From the really good stuff my husband keeps locked in his little cupboard in his study."

Joe opened his mouth to speak but Angelina silenced him with a wave. "Don't embarrass me in front of our guest."

"Honestly," said Bunny, "there's no need to—"

"It's no trouble," Angelina said, the brightness returning to her voice. "And I'll have my usual."

Bunny felt for Joe as he shifted on his feet, trying to decide between the best of two bad choices before bowing his head and slipping through the doorway.

Angelina glided across the room and perched on the oversized couch. She'd always been a sweet kid but had blossomed into a real beauty and ended up coming second in Miss Ireland, or some similar competition. Despite everything going on around her at home, and there had been plenty, Angelina had been a top student too. On the estate, her success had inspired that peculiar mix of jealousy and pride. She'd got out. Gone off to live the life less ordinary.

She might only have been in her late twenties now, but there was something very different about the woman who sat opposite Bunny. Still beautiful but possessed of a bruised quality. As if she'd seen the Promised Land and found out it was all papier mâché and plasterboard scenery.

"How's your dad?" Bunny asked.

"Not great. I go and see him when I can. Sometimes he's talking up a storm, sometimes ..." She left the sentence unfinished.

"Sorry to hear that. He was always a lovely fella."

"Not everyone would agree with you on that front."

"Ah, people rarely know the full story."

Angelina brushed her long hair over her shoulders and leaned back, moving the conversation on. "So, did I hear you made detective?"

"I did. I get to dress myself now. Not that it's a particular strong suit – no pun intended."

"If there's one thing you learn in the fashion business, it's that clothes don't make the man. Believe you me."

"That's a relief." Bunny noticed that what he'd taken to be a glove was in fact a bandage. He pointed at it. "What did you do to yourself?"

She held up her wrist. "Oh, this? I'm an idiot. I've set up a gym upstairs and I should've checked how to use all of the machines properly before jumping in. Trying to get this old pile of flab and bones in shape."

"Go on outta that," said Bunny. "You look great."

She laughed again. "You old smoothie, you. My husband could learn a thing or two from you."

"How long have you been married?"

"A few years now."

"Congratulations."

She looked down at her shoes. "Oh please, don't. Needs must when the devil drives."

"Have you been back home long?"

She shrugged. "A while. The modelling world, well, it can mess you up if you're not careful, and I wasn't careful. When I got back here, I was broke and broken."

"Sorry to hear that. You should've ..."

Angelina raised her eyebrows. "What? You can't save us all, Bunny." She traced a finger through the air. "Besides, it's all ancient history. Look at me now. Living the good life." There was an undercurrent of bitterness in her voice.

Bunny looked around. "Worse spots to end up."

"All that glitters."

Bunny jerked his head in the direction of the bookshelves. "If memory serves, you were always a big reader."

"Those aren't even real books. He bought them by the yard."

"Really?" Bunny stared at the rows of what he had thought were leather-bound books.

"My husband is far more concerned with how things look than what they actually are." She lowered her voice, looking suddenly lost. "Rather superficial, truth be told, and for an ex-model to say that ..." She tried out a laugh that she couldn't make fit. "It's all hollow ..." She met Bunny's gaze and then looked away.

Bunny tried to gather his thoughts, but before he could, the other Angelina was back, bright and beautiful.

"So, what brings you here?" she asked. "Am I under arrest?"

"You're alright for the minute. I'm on sabbatical."

"Oh really?"

It was Bunny's turn to look away. "Yeah. Needed a bit of time away. Figure out what I want to do with myself."

"You're sounding like a man looking for a change, Bunny."

He shrugged. "Maybe I am."

"The Gardaí without Bunny McGarry. I'm not sure how well either side would cope with that."

"Ah, I'd imagine there'd be a fair few in senior management that would be popping the champagne."

"I might be way off," said Angelina, "but I'm not sure you ever did it for them, did you?"

"'Tis just a job."

"Not the way you did it."

Bunny laughed. "Are you working in recruitment for the Guards now?"

"No. No. I promise," she said, leaning forward. "I guess a small part of me is still that little girl who remembered seeing you walking round the estate, like the last of the real cowboys."

"That horse cost me a fortune in oats, though."

She shook her head. "You didn't need it. You had the swagger."

"D'ye know what caused that? Piles."

Angelina threw back her head and roared with laughter at the ceiling. "You're an awful man, Officer McGarry. And for the record, even if it was haemorrhoids, you made it work."

"I think you've got some of those rose-tinted glasses."

She gave a slight shrug. "Maybe. Every little girl needs her hero." She slipped off her high heels and drew her feet under her. "So, can I ask what brings you to the infamous Coop Hannity's door?"

"A personal matter."

Angelina raised an eyebrow a fraction.

"Trying to help a friend out."

She nodded. "Now that is the Bunny McGarry I remember. Can't stop yourself." She looked towards the door. "Although, sorry, it looks like you might die of thirst trying. I—" As she spoke, the door opened. "Speak of the Kiwi."

Samoan Joe ambled through. "Mr Hannity will see you now."

Angelina sat upright. "What the hell happened to our drinks?"

Joe looked like a man with no good answers to give and lots of other places he'd rather be.

"Honestly, don't worry about it," said Bunny, standing up. "My doctor keeps telling me I need to be cutting back."

"Yes," said Angelina, not taking her eyes off Samoan Joe. "The world is full of people who don't know what their job is."

Bunny leaned down to give her a hug as he passed. "Take care of yourself. 'Twas great to see you."

She squeezed him tightly for a little too long. "You too."

They broke apart and she gave him a brief, embarrassed smile before Bunny turned towards the door.

"Bunny."

He looked back at her.

"Word to the wise. Be careful. Deals with the devil are for life. I should know."

# FOR THE BIRDS

Bunny stood and waited.

He got it. The message being sent very clearly was that he would have to stand and wait for as long as necessary while James "Coop" Hannity went about his business.

The three men – Bunny, Hannity and Samoan Joe – were gathered in Hannity's back garden. It was an unusual-looking space – at least, it was if you weren't aware that it was actually the merged gardens of the five houses upon which Hannity's castle now stood. That was why it was wider than it was long. The trio were standing on the left-hand side, which was dominated entirely by the very things that had earned Hannity his nickname. Outside of business he had one interest, and one interest alone, and that was the breeding, rearing and racing of homing pigeons.

Bunny watched as Hannity examined and fed his prized possessions. The coops stood on a platform three feet above ground, surrounded by fencing. Arc lights on high poles threw bright light down upon them. Given that the garden was bordered on all sides by mature coniferous trees for privacy, from the perspective of the surrounding properties, it was probably like living near a UFO landing site with an infuriatingly blocked view. Albeit one that came with its own soundtrack. Classical music blared out of speakers dotted around them. Bunny guessed the neighbours loved that. He also guessed they didn't ever mention it.

He reckoned there were maybe a hundred pigeons in the cages, although the word "cages" didn't do the enclosures justice. There were heaters, lights – the whole set-up had a no-expense-spared look to it, which was much in keeping with everything else in the Hannity residence.

Beside Bunny, the big non-Samoan shifted from foot to foot.

"You alright?" whispered Bunny.

Samoan Joe nodded. "Bum knee. Gets sore in the cold."

It certainly was cold. Early March, with a biting wind whistling through the trees. It'd be below freezing soon – if it wasn't already. While there were plenty of heaters close to where they were standing, they all appeared to be directed towards the birds, as if to make clear the pecking order.

Even though Bunny was well aware of Coop Hannity by reputation, he had never met the man, who looked disconcertingly normal. If you were to pass him in the street, you wouldn't give him a second look. Average height, slim build, thinning sandy hair – he was neatly if unflashily dressed in trousers, a jumper, a warm-looking overcoat and a pair of leather gloves. He looked like most every other bloke in his late forties, save for the complete lack of even a hint of middle-age spread. To look at him, you wouldn't guess Hannity was sitting on top of a large semi-criminal financial empire. He looked more like the manager of a mid-sized supermarket.

Hannity pressed a button on the controller beside him and the music faded away. Without looking around, he spoke for the first time. "Do you know much about pigeons, Detective McGarry?"

"I can't say that I do, no. Just the usual ..."

"And tell me," said Hannity, "what is the usual?"

"Y'know, very good homing instinct. Fond of a bit of bread. Used to carry messages in the war. There was that cartoon. The one with Dick Dastardly, trying to catch the pigeon. Can't remember what it was called."

Hannity stood upright and only now looked directly at Bunny. "Actually, they've carried messages since around 3000 BC. The Egyptians used them."

"Is that right? Fair play to them."

"They are also self-regulating. They breed until the point at which their numbers match the available food supply and then they stop. We humans could learn a thing or two from them."

"Sounds like it."

Hannity addressed Joe. "The vet will come tomorrow. I want him to take a look at Iris, and Apollo's wing still doesn't look right."

Samoan Joe grunted and took a little notebook out of his pocket to take down his boss's instructions.

"I assumed, Mr McGarry, that you must be a very keen pigeon enthusiast. Why else would you come here and disturb me at home, where everyone knows I do not like to be bothered?"

"I'm very sorry about that," said Bunny.

"No, you're not. If you were, you wouldn't be here."

"It couldn't wait. I need to talk to you about—"

"I know," interrupted Hannity, "exactly why you are here. It is my business to know such things. Did you think I would be unaware that a Garda detective beat up two of my men earlier today?"

"I'm on sabbatical. And, to be fair, I didn't know they worked for you. They didn't make that clear."

"Did you give them much of a chance to do so?"

"It was them who started swinging."

Hannity gave a dispassionate nod. "As I believe the Garda report makes clear. I'm sure they wouldn't show any favouritism to one of their own in such circumstances."

Bunny, trying to play nice, let that dig slide by. "I apologise—"

"Don't," said Hannity. "Those men were hired on the understanding they had certain capabilities. It turns out they don't. Information, however it is obtained, is always useful. They no longer work for me." He took a seat in a deck chair on the raised platform in front of his birds and looked down at Bunny. "Do you know how much a pigeon costs?"

Bunny opened and closed his mouth, slightly thrown by the non sequitur.

"A good one, I mean?"

"I suppose it'd mainly be the cost of the feed and the cages and all that."

"No. A true champion bird is a good deal more than the cage it is in. One of the birds behind me is worth eighty thousand pounds."

"For a pigeon?" said Bunny, forgetting himself. "Jesus, Mary and Josephine. Not bad for a rat with wings." He couldn't fail to notice Hannity's scowl. "I mean, they're not rats. They're much nicer than rats. Rats never deliver anyone a message other than 'you probably need to clean up the place a bit'. I mean ..."

"Shall we get to why you are here?"

"Right. Yes. I wanted to talk to you about Tim Spain. I believe he owed you some money."

'No. He did not."

Bunny's brow furrowed in confusion.

"A man in my position, I don't deal with much of the day to day. I oversee and I deal with what we refer to as the 'special cases'. Your friend, Detective Spain, was such a case."

"Detective Sergeant." Bunny didn't know what made him say it. Maybe it was the effort of kowtowing to a man who represented something he couldn't stand, or maybe it was just the tone of Hannity's voice when he referred to Gringo.

Hannity looked at Bunny for a moment and then bowed his head in acknowledgement. "Of course. Detective Sergeant Spain. A guard in serious debt due to a chronic gambling problem. That is a 'special case' in anyone's book."

Bunny went to speak but stopped himself.

"I sense you are inclined to object, Detective. Put yourself in my shoes. My job is to assess risk and decide whether or not to lend someone money based on that assessment. It is not my job to live anyone else's life for them."

"And you still lent him money?" Bunny could sense Joe tensing beside him.

"No. As I said. I didn't. He was a bad risk."

"But ..."

"I knew when he showed up that he was in debt to me for a certain amount, and to two of my competitors for similar sums." The way he said the word "competitors" made it clear that he didn't see them as a true threat. "When I pointed this out, he assured me that he had a way out of his predicament. He was about to come into a large sum of money, he just needed a little time. The thing with degenerate gamblers, though, their one unifying trait, is that they all believe they are about to come into a large sum of money. They've just been unlucky."

Hannity withdrew a packet of cigars from his coat pocket and selected one. He cut the end off and lit it as Bunny stood there quietly. He then puffed it into life before he spoke again. "Your colleague, however, assured me that this was not the case. He swore his gambling days were over. He had a big pay day coming. This was on 18 November last year, by the way."

Hannity smiled down at him. Bunny tried to keep his face as a mask while he slotted together some dates in his head. That was three days before the Carter gang robbed a plane on the runway at Dublin Airport containing millions in uncut diamonds, and then Gringo, Dara O'Shea and Jessica Cunningham had attempted to ambush the gang as they swapped vehicles, which had resulted in O'Shea's death. Gringo never would have told Hannity about any plan, but it wouldn't have taken the loan shark much to piece it together after the fact.

"So, I made him a deal. I bought his house for sixty thousand pounds. I have the deeds, if you'd like to see them?"

"Sixty?" exclaimed Bunny. "It's worth at least five times that."

"True," said Hannity, puffing out a ring of smoke, "but beggars can't be choosers. He also had the option to buy it back for eighty thousand within ninety days."

"Alright. Give me some time and I'll see what I can do."

"The ninety days ran out a few weeks ago. There is nothing for you to do."

Bunny went to take a step forward but Joe placed a hand on his arm. "Be reasonable."

"I am being reasonable," said Hannity with a smile. "I've sent Mrs Spain three eviction notices."

"You fecking parasite," snarled Bunny.

Hannity laughed. "How refreshing. It's been a very long time since anyone has dared to stand in front of me and hurl insults. Most people have far too much sense."

"You'd throw an elderly woman out on the street?"

Hannity gave the merest shrug. "Business is business."

"The mother of a decorated Garda officer who died in the line of duty? D'ye not reckon that might bring your business a lot of unwanted attention?"

Hannity raised an eyebrow. "It's been even longer since someone came here to threaten me."

"You're a good-for-nothing bottom-feeding leech, Hannity. You do this and, believe me, I'll get you one way or another, if it's the last thing I do."

"Oh, I have no doubt you'll try. Your reputation for both violence and belligerence precedes you, Detective McGarry. Tell me, does it give you pause for thought that I am so entirely unfazed by your threats?"

Bunny glanced at Samoan Joe, who stared at him, poised to move if Bunny tried anything.

"Bullies are always full of piss and vinegar when the odds are on their side."

Hannity nodded and then turned at Joe. "Joseph, be a good boy and go and look at the rhododendrons for a while."

The big man gawped at his boss in confusion. "But ..."

"Don't worry. Detective McGarry will be on his best behaviour. I'm sure of it."

Bunny said nothing. He was trying to control his temper, and was very aware he was being messed with.

Joe hesitated.

Hannity's voice dropped to a lower register. "You know how I feel about having to repeat myself."

The big man withdrew. Bunny and Hannity watched as he walked to the bottom of the path and then they locked eyes.

Hannity leaned back. "Feel free to move closer, Detective."

"I'm fine where I am."

"As you wish. Now, where were we?"

"You were throwing the widowed mother of my best friend out on the street."

Hannity flicked some ash off the end of his cigar. "That's right. And you were warning me of the dire consequences if I were to do so. Rest assured, Detective, I very much wish to stay on the right side of the law. In fact, did I read in the newspaper that there's going to be an inquiry into the Carter affair? Lessons to be learned. Three officers losing their lives et cetera."

Bunny said nothing. His palms were starting to sweat and he was calculating how many pigeons he could feed to Hannity before Joe could pull him away.

"Tell me," continued Hannity, "as a law-abiding citizen, do you think it is my duty to turn over the tape I have which shows a supposed hero police officer discussing how he is about to come into a massive financial windfall three days before he and two other officers ambush some criminals in possession of highly valuable diamonds? It might rather change the context in which their actions have been viewed, don't you think?"

Bunny tried to keep his expression blank but clearly failed.

"That's right, I have a tape."

"Bullshit," spat Bunny.

"Do I strike you as a man who doesn't take every necessary precaution? I'm recording this meeting, in fact."

Bunny glanced around.

"It's amazing how far microphone technology has come, isn't it?" Hannity continued. "Well, as a police officer, I'm sure I don't need to tell you that."

"I don't believe you."

Hannity laughed. "Don't bluff, Detective. You don't have the face for it, and you certainly don't have the cards."

"Gringo was just doing his job."

"And I'm sure that the inquiry will, of course, draw that conclusion. I'm sure there is another explanation for the large amount of cash he was confident he was about to come into. I wonder, were you about to benefit from a similar windfall?"

"What is it that you want, Hannity? Or do you just like watching people squirm?"

Hannity leaned forward. "I must confess, I had no idea you knew my wife."

Bunny shoved his hands into the pockets of his coat. "And?"

"Just interested," said Hannity. "When we met she was ..." he gave a humourless laugh, "... at something of a low point. I did all I could to help her and her poor father. Even now, I'm paying a frankly extortionate amount to keep him in a very fine care facility."

Bunny said nothing, confused as to where Hannity was heading.

'My point is, I understand Detective Spain's— Forgive me, Detective *Sergeant* Spain's determination to take care of his mother. And I appreciate those bills can really mount up, even if my ungrateful wife is blind to that fact."

"If you're looking for marriage guidance, I'm really not qualified."

Hannity laughed heartily and took another deep drag on his cigar. "Ha, very funny. But no, I don't require your services for that. You would be very useful to me in other areas, though."

"I've already got a job."

"And I wouldn't dream of interfering with it. If you came to work for me, it would be in a discreet, off-the-books, supplemental role. A man with your connections, with your access – you could be very useful. And no doubt we could find certain scenarios in which we could let that violent temper of yours off the leash." Hannity tilted his head and gave Bunny an appraising glance. "If I'm any judge of these things, you must be so damn tired of always having to keep that beast at bay. Think how good it would feel to have permission to let it loose. As well as making our current issue disappear, you would, of course, be handsomely compensated. What do you say, Detective? Would you like to be my friend?"

"I'm not interested."

Hannity shrugged. "That's a shame. Still, though ..." He stood up and looked down at Bunny. "It's Monday today. I'll give you three days – until this time on Thursday evening – to think about it. We can be friends or ... Well, on Friday morning, I give that tape of my conversation with DS Spain, which I may or may not have, to interested parties and I complete the steps necessary to take possession of the house that I definitely own."

Bunny clenched his fists.

"Uh-uh, Detective," said Hannity, wagging a cautionary finger. "I strongly advise you not to say anything you might come to regret. I appreciate your dander is up. How about you turn around, walk away, and have a long hard think about your options."

Bunny and Hannity locked eyes for the longest time and then, without a word, Bunny turned and headed back up the path.

As he walked, a relieved-looking Joe fell into step behind him.

Hannity's voice carried across the cold night air. "Show the man directly out, Joe. And, Detective, I look forward to speaking to you very soon."

# QUESTIONS WITHOUT ANSWERS

Bunny stared into the abyss.

Metaphorically speaking.

In real terms, he stared into a half-drunk pint of Guinness, with an empty whiskey chaser keeping it company. He was a few in and, despite his best efforts, was still feeling remarkably sober. What he wanted more than anything was to get blind drunk. The logic being that you can't remember your problems if you can't even remember your own name. Yes, it was only a short-term solution, but seeing as he had no long-term one, it'd do.

He'd left Coop Hannity's a couple of hours ago, and had engaged in one small act of defiance on the way out. Since then, he'd been propping up the bar in O'Hagan's and had accounted for most of the drink sales from the dozen or so patrons scattered around the place. It was the quiet time between the post-work rush and closing, when only the hardcore manned the battlements.

He took another sup of his pint and looked down the bar to where the young assistant manager, Tara Flynn, was watching him with concern while trying, unsuccessfully, not to be seen doing so. She'd been working there only a few months but, seeing as Bunny had been a fixture for most of that time, they'd become friends. Right now, he was wishing she'd ignore him.

He nodded at his pint. "Same again, please, Tara. And another for my friend here."

Tara walked over and stood across from Bunny. "Don't you think he's had enough?"

Bunny looked down at the gnome that was sitting on the bar beside him, having been relieved of his gig at Coop Hannity's pond. "He seems fine to me. Still standing."

"Even so," said Tara, "maybe he should pace himself. He's been trying to catch a fish off the side of this bar for hours."

Bunny gave her a look.

She held up her hands. "Alright. Fine. I'm not your mother." After taking a pint glass from the shelf, Tara held it under the Guinness tap at exactly the correct angle and looked at Bunny. "Do you want to talk about it?"

"Nothing to talk about."

"Really?" she said, incredulity in her voice. "In that case, would you consider professional mourner as a future career? You'd do an excellent job at setting the right tone."

"This is a pub, isn't it? Aren't people supposed to come in here to drink without being nagged?"

Tara slammed the untopped pint down on the counter. "Excuse me for caring."

Bunny realised he was being an arse. "I'm just ..."

"None of my business." Tara returned to the other end of the bar.

"What are my chances of a packet of cheese and onion Tayto?"

She didn't turn around. "You've two. Fuck and all."

Bunny glanced at the gnome as he raised the remnants of his pint. "And you didn't even get your whiskey."

The glassy eyes looked back up at him but didn't respond.

The problem was that Bunny's options were as limited as they were unappealing. He laid them out for himself again as he ran his finger through the small puddle of stout that he'd spilled on the counter earlier.

Option one – tell Coop Hannity to shove his offer up his arse. While it'd feel momentarily wonderful, so too does flying until you realise you're actually falling. For a start, he'd need to find somewhere else for Diana Spain to live. Sure, there were state-run homes, but the prospect brought to his mind the image of Gringo's face as he lay dying on a beach, in Bunny's arms. His final words had been, "Take care of Mum." The woman might well be a massive pain in Bunny's arse but, like it or not, she was his responsibility.

And that wasn't even the worst part. Maybe it was all an elaborate bluff and Coop Hannity didn't really have a tape of Gringo discussing how he was about to come into a large sum of money, but if it was a bluff, it was a damn good one. If he really did have a recording, it would be enough to change the whole context of the inquiry. As things stood, three officers had died in the line of duty. All anyone was expecting were tributes to the fallen, recommendations for bulletproof vests to be more readily available, and, inevitably, an extra bit of paperwork to be filled out.

However, throw Hannity's tape into the mix and the actions of those involved would be shown in a whole different light. What had at first appeared to be dedicated officers not paying due care and attention to the chain of command in their rush to achieve a result, suddenly looked very different. DI O'Rourke already smelled a rat, and Bunny was guessing so too did those above him in the chain of command, but they appeared to be taking a pragmatic "don't look a gift horse in the mouth" approach to the Carter gang's dramatic fall from grace. That would soon change, though. O'Rourke was, above everything else, a political animal. If he sensed the wind had shifted, he'd be moving at the speed of light, because where you stand for reflected glory is also in the splatter zone if the shit hits the fan.

Even if no firm conclusions could be reached, Gringo's name would be dragged through the mud. He'd go from hero to disgrace – an embarrassment to the force. Suspicion would also fall on Bunny. What he did and didn't know. Not that he cared much about that. He hadn't had anything to do with their dirty little get-rich scheme, bar figuring out that something was up and trying to stop the train that had already left the station.

Gringo had been a flawed man who made a terrible series of mistakes. Bunny should have seen it sooner, or maybe just not wilfully ignored all the signs that his partner was going off the rails. Even if all of that didn't make Gringo's failings his problem, there was the other thing. In order to rescue the woman he loved, Bunny had completely stepped outside the boundaries of the law himself. His actions had resulted in the deaths of two men – two appalling men. Bunny didn't feel a shred of guilt about that. Justice and the law weren't always compatible. And yet, without Gringo's help, Bunny and Simone would both be dead now. Burying two bodies in the Wicklow Mountains was almost the last thing they'd done together.

He had a responsibility.

Then, there was the other option.

Become Coop Hannity's man. The mere thought of it made Bunny sick to his stomach. He might not always play by the rules, but whatever he'd done he'd always done for what he saw as the common good. That would change now. Once they had you, they had you. Some lines you can't uncross.

So yes, Bunny wanted to get very, very drunk in peace. He took a long drag on his un-topped pint.

"Howerya, Bunny."

He turned to see Detective Pamela "Butch" Cassidy standing behind him, dressed in sports gear, kit bag in hand.

He wiped the back of his hand across his mouth. "Butch! What're you doing here?"

She looked exasperated. "What am I ... You asked me to come and meet you, you drunken dipshit!"

Bunny slapped his hand to his forehead. "Oh shite, course I did. Sorry, Butch. Pull up a pew. Drink?"

"Lime and soda," she said, hopping on to the stool beside him.

Tara nodded, having caught the order.

Butch's nickname was as inevitable as it was ironic. Coppers were never the cleverest, and her surname of Cassidy had sealed her fate.

Butch tapped the garden gnome on its head. "And who is your little friend here?"

"No idea. Annoying little gobshite hasn't shut up, though. To be honest, I thought it was you in fancy dress at first."

She rolled her eyes. "Those height jokes never get old."

Bunny sucked his teeth. "You and your short fuse."

"I'd tell you to go fuck yourself, Bunny, but nobody deserves that kind of disappointment."

He nodded approvingly. "Good one."

"Thanks. I've been practising."

"Speaking of which, were you off doing judo in your jimmy-jammies this evening?"

"Krav Maga, actually."

"Crack your ma? I thought you did judo?"

"I did." In fact, she had been a national champion. "I'm doing this for a bit of a change. It's a hybrid thing developed by the Israeli Special Forces. I'm thinking of getting a collection of black belts. They go with everything, and they really bring out my eyes."

Bunny turned and looked at Butch, who wasn't much more than eight stone and five foot two. You could physically pick her up, although it'd be a mistake that'd probably leave you walking funny for quite some time.

"Be honest with me, Butch – pound for pound, are you the most lethal person in Ireland?"

She brushed back her red hair and gave a wolfish grin. "What's this pound for pound nonsense? I took down a bloke who looked like a sumo wrestler last week on a raid. He actually cried. Was a thing of beauty."

"I bet it was. Would've liked to see it."

Butch slapped him on the arm. "Well, come back to work, then, and you'll see the next one."

Tara placed Butch's drink on the bar and withdrew.

"Thank you," said Bunny.

"Yeah, thanks," chimed Butch. "And you, stop avoiding the question. When are you coming back?"

"Ah, we'll see."

She folded her arms. "We'll see? That's the kind of nonsense answer you give to a child."

"Well, you are only little."

Butch scoffed. "How would you like to see this little girl send your fat arse over that bar?"

Bunny grinned. "Stop flirting with me, Butch. I'm not your type."

She chuckled. "To be clear, if I was into men ..."

"I'd still not be your type."

They both laughed this time.

"Ah, come on," she said. "Come back. Since Dinny transferred to Galway for a quieter life, I've had to work with this new lad, Carlson. He wets himself if he's left alone too long. It's no fun any more, without you and ..." Butch stopped herself and the smile fell from her lips. "Oh God, sorry."

"It's alright," said Bunny, turning to pick up his pint. "You can say his name, y'know?"

"I know, I just ..." Butch reached across and picked up her lime and soda.

They both took a drink.

"So," said Butch. "Your text mentioned you needed a favour?"

"Right. One of the lads on the team. Got bruising on his arm. Bad, so I'm told."

"Where did he get it?" asked Butch, now deadly serious.

"His ma's boyfriend moved in with them recently. Gary Kearney."

"The boxer?"

Bunny nodded. "It would appear the useless prick finally found a bout he can win."

Butch put down her drink with more force than was necessary. "Shall we go and visit him?"

Bunny turned to look at her. "Easy, tiger. I thought I was supposed to be the loose cannon?"

"Well ..." Whatever else Butch said was lost in a mumble. Bunny knew she took a particular interest in this area. He'd never asked why. On some matters you just don't pry.

"I happen to know some nuns who owe me a favour," Bunny continued. "They can help get her and him away from Kearney."

"Nuns?" asked Butch, sounding taken aback.

"Never mind that. First things first. We need to get her and the lad out of there."

"And after first things?"

"Let's play it by ear."

"OK."

"His mother will pick up Alan – that's the kid – after training tomorrow night. I figured it'd be better if you made the approach."

"I'll have to move several hot dates around, but I'm in."

"You're a good woman."

"And you're an awful man. Do you need a lift home?"

"I'm grand, thanks," said Bunny.

"You sure? No offence, but you look like an early night wouldn't be the worst thing that could happen to you."

Bunny patted the gnome on the head. "I'd love to, but himself has just got out of a long-term relationship and it wouldn't be right to leave a man drinking on his own."

Butch blew a raspberry in response.

"Classy bird. Give O'Rourke and your new partner my regards."

She gave him another lupine grin. "Prick. I'm away home for my dinner. I'll see you tomorrow night."

"It's a date."

"And now I've lost my appetite."

As Butch left, she passed Terry Hodges on his way in, who held the door open for her.

Bunny turned back to the bar and gave his now almost-empty pint glass a mournful look. Before he could order another, an arm was thrown around his shoulders and Terry beamed a gap-toothed smile at him through the fog of his cologne. It was a move of familiarity that their relationship did not warrant.

Terry currently held second position in the "most irritating regulars of O'Hagan's" rankings that Bunny kept in his head. Behaviour such as throwing his arm around you while you were trying to enjoy a quiet pint was why Terry had always been top three, and why he was in danger of reaching both the number-one spot and the floor if he wasn't careful.

"Tara," Terry roared unnecessarily loudly near Bunny's ear, "have you asked this man yet?"

Tara looked up from her book. "No. I was waiting for the right moment."

"Sure, isn't now a great moment?" shouted Terry.

Having just popped in, Terry was stone-cold sober. It shouldn't matter but Bunny gave some allowances to people who were annoying when drunk. Terry was annoying when born. He probably came out of the womb trying to stick his grubby hands in somebody else's crisps. He also often told stories about people that nobody in the room knew and therefore made no sense. Any time anyone pointed this out, he'd just laugh and say, "You had to be there." As if that excused it. He was like watching a TV series you'd only joined in with halfway through episode six.

The man's only redeeming feature was that at least he wasn't ...

Mark Kind's insidious little head popped up from the other side of the bar. "What did he say?"

Mark was known for two things. One – his freakishly small head. It was tiny. Weirdly tiny. Small enough that people actually wondered how an adult brain could fit into it. That is, until they talked to Mark. In fact, it was so small that every time he entered a room, anyone present was left with the unnerving impression that his body had got there first and his head was running late. In a more sensible world, people would hire him to stand in show homes to create the illusion of space.

The head thing was weird but it wasn't what made him annoying. That was what came out of the head – Mark was also known as the classic topper. Nobody could tell a story without him having done whatever it was better or worse, depending on the story's narrative direction, and he would always have done it first. Bunny wouldn't mind so much if his lies were entertaining. He himself was malleable on the importance of truth in relation to a good story. However,

Mark's tales were dry retellings of most of what the other person had said, delivered in a dull monotone. The man was the living embodiment of those "previously on ..." recaps at the start of TV shows.

"He hasn't said anything yet," Terry answered.

"Are we discussing it?" asked Mark.

"Discussing what?" said Bunny.

"No," replied Tara. "Like I said, I was waiting for the right time."

"When do you think that'll be?" said Terry.

"It's fecking now," said Bunny. "This is winding me up."

"I'll tell you who got very wound up, Jimmy from work when—"

"Nobody cares, Mark" said Bunny, feeling considerably less polite than usual.

"Why've you got a garden gnome there, Bunny?" asked Terry.

"I liberated it."

"Funny you should mention that," continued Mark, in what was, even by his small-headed standards, a poor reading of the room. "One time I stole two garden gnomes—"

"The lads and I were wondering," interrupted Tara, correctly guessing that Bunny was about to involve the gnome in a case of actual bodily harm, "would you be up for emceeing the pub quiz?"

"Oh right," said Bunny. "You should have said. No, absolutely not."

Terry gave Bunny a playful rub on the belly. "Ah, come on, amigo."

Bunny whipped round in a blur and grabbed Terry by the collar with both hands. "Don't you dare call me that."

"Bunny," shouted Tara, loud enough to attract the attention of the rest of the patrons.

Bunny looked at his hands as if they were working of their own accord and released Terry. "Sorry, I ... Sorry."

Terry took a step back. "No problem," he said in a quiet voice.

"It just means 'friend' in Mexican," added Mark.

"Thank you, Mark," said Tara. "We are aware. Could you give us a moment, please, lads?"

Mark and Terry nodded.

"By which I meant, could you bugger off to the other side of the bar or something?"

Tara stood in front of Bunny and watched as the two men did as they were told. Only once they'd gone, and she'd looked round the bar to confirm that everyone else was once again minding their own business, did she speak in a low voice. "What the hell are you playing at, Bunny?"

"I'm sorry."

"I mean, you don't have to tell me how annoying the two of them are, but you get to leave when they become too much. If I want a break, I have to pretend one of the ladies' loos is blocked."

"I'll apologise."

"No. We'll forget the whole thing. Besides, Terry could do with a reminder about other people's personal space. You're emceeing the quiz, though."

"Ara ..." started Bunny. "Hang on, doesn't Cian do that?"

"He used to. To be honest, I think the pressure got to him after 'the incident'. He's taken up pottery."

Bunny turned his pint glass slowly. "Oh feck. We're all getting ash trays, aren't we?"

"I'd imagine so, yes. He offered one as a prize in the quiz you're hosting."

"I don't want to."

"I know," said Tara with a smile. "But I've already hired a guy to provide the questions and answers. The quiz was my big idea to drum up business and it is going to work. We just need someone with your considerable presence to stop them arguing about every bloody question. And besides, you owe me a favour because of that thing last month."

"What thing?" started Bunny before his brain caught up with his mouth. "Oh yeah, that thing. Sorry again."

"Prove it. I'll throw in free drink for the evening while you're doing it."

Bunny sighed. "Fine."

"Great," said Tara. "No spirits." She raised her voice. "He says he'll do it."

Her announcement was greeted with a cheer.

"But," said Bunny, raising his voice to meet hers, "no questions about cricket. I refuse to acknowledge its existence. It's a waste of a perfectly good field."

"Ah, come on," said Terry, "cricket is a brilliant sport."

Bunny turned back to the bar where Tara was already pouring him another pint. "Congrats, Terry, you just made number one on the list."

"What list?"

"Speaking of lists ..."

# THIS IS MY RIFLE ...

There was a moment ... a very particular moment. Call it what you will – the point of no return, the tipping point. It was the instant when the kindling caught and the fires of rage were not going to be put out until they'd had their say, taken their pound of charred flesh.

Riots were mercifully rare in Ireland. During his policing career Bunny had stood the line in riot gear only a couple of times. On the last occasion he'd been linked arm-in-arm with colleagues protecting Dáil Éireann from a massive demonstration by taxi drivers.

Politicians versus taxi drivers – it was impossible to pick a side. As far as Bunny was concerned, the problem with politics was the type of people who wanted to get involved in it. Jobs leading the government should be given out like jury service. Anything was better than allowing the sort of lunatic who dedicated their life to the dream of being in charge to actually get their wish. On the other hand, Bunny had spent many a rainy night standing with his thumb out while taxis that hadn't bothered to turn their light off cruised by in the torrential downpour. It was like picking a favourite out of diarrhoea and vomiting – you should really just go and eat somewhere else.

In the eyes looking back at him now, he could see the same level of simmering resentment that he had seen at the taxi-driver demo. If something wasn't done soon, all hell would break loose. It wasn't exactly the same, though. For a start, the eyes staring up at him belonged to an exhausted and exasperated squad of twelve-year-old hurlers, who'd given up their Tuesday evening's for hurling training and got a lot more than they'd bargained for.

Bunny looked out into the sea of pre-pubescent rage and made a decision. He would hold the line. The St Jude's Under-12s hurling team had right on their side, but he wasn't going to allow them to exact vengeance on his assistant manager. It would set a dangerous precedent.

He clapped his hands together. "Right then, lads. Good tough session this evening. Hard work but it'll stand you in good stead." The glares coming back at him made it very clear that nobody was buying the speech. Bunny checked his watch. There were fifteen minutes left and the first parents were trickling in to pick up their offspring. Time to pull out the big guns.

"OK, tell you what we'll do, lads. Let's put the bucket up on the crossbar there, and you can all take shots at knocking it off from the twenty-metre line. If anyone gets it I'll treat everyone to McDonald's after the match on Sunday."

This at least put an end to the staring contest. In many ways, pre-teen boys were like dogs – not least because they always appeared to be hungry. That, and because they seemed to think peeing on stuff was a great idea.

The boys all looked expectantly at Paul Mulchrone.

"Doesn't have to be Paulie," said Bunny. "Any of you could hit it."

A hand shot up for a question. Bunny pre-empted it. "No, you cannot give your go to Paulie."

His proclamation was met with widespread groans.

"Can we not—"

"Any more objections and I'll make Paulie wear a blindfold for his go."

"He'd still be our best shot."

"Right," roared Deccie, moving out from behind Bunny, "you heard the man …"

Bunny put a hand out to stop the whistle from reaching Deccie lips, thus saving everything from going full-blown *Lord of the Flies*. "Off you go, lads, off you go!"

The team reluctantly trotted back out on to the field.

"Declan, a word, please." Bunny led Deccie by the whistle around his neck towards the prefabs that served as their dressing rooms. It would also take them out of the range of any wayward "attempts" at the bucket. Retaliation was always a possibility.

"Ouch, you're hurting me there, boss."

"Not as much as they will if you blow that whistle again."

Bunny glanced around to check no parents were standing within earshot, then he pulled the whistle from around Deccie's neck. "How do you even have a whistle? I took yours away."

"Got to carry a spare, boss. Always be prepared and all that. The Scouts taught me that."

"I'm glad you learned something before they booted you out."

Deccie raised his chin defiantly. "We had a difference of opinion."

"Hard to believe."

Bunny glanced at the field to see his team nowhere near knocking the large bucket off the crossbar. Quite a few of them didn't even manage to make contact with the ball. Still, at least they were distracted.

"Right," said Bunny. "So, how do you think this evening went, Deccie?"

"Pretty good, I reckon, boss."

Bunny's eyebrows shot up so fast that he very nearly pulled a muscle. "Really?"

"I mean, OK," conceded Deccie. "Some of the lads didn't respond well to my training methods."

"Some? I told you that you could do forty-five minutes of fitness work. I meant a few sprints, a couple of laps. Maybe a bit of that circuit-training-type thing."

"Yeah. I went a different direction with it."

"That you did," said Bunny, pulling an envelope out of his back pocket. "I took some notes. Let's see here – ten minutes in, you told Larry that you were going to break your foot off in his arse."

"I did."

"Normally, we'd be having a chat about that, but twenty-two minutes in, you told George you'd ..." Bunny pointed at the envelope for emphasis. "... rip his eyeballs out and skull-feck him to death. Where the hell did you get that from?"

"*An Officer and a Gentleman.*"

"The film?" asked Bunny. "The romantic drama?"

"Yeah. Granny loves it. She's got it on video. That bit where he carries her off at the end – I cry every time." Deccie looked around, suddenly nervous. "Don't go telling anyone I said that, boss."

"Right. You're fine with telling George you were going to ..." He pointed his chin at the envelope. "... do that to him, but God forbid anyone should find out you got a bit weepy at a movie."

"Exactly."

"That one sentence might have summed up entirely what is wrong with our gender, Deccie."

"I'm glad I could help, boss. Now, if there isn't anything else ..."

Deccie turned to head back to training but Bunny spun him around.

"We're just getting started, Declan. Please explain the logic behind the hose?"

Deccie tutted. "We live in Ireland. We often have to play in wet weather."

"So you thought you'd blast the lads in the face using a hose?"

"I will not have my methods questioned."

"You most definitely will."

"Do you know what your problem is, boss? You ..."

Deccie kept going even as Bunny joined in with him, "... have no appreciation of the fundamentals of the game."

"I had a feeling," said Bunny. "Still, I feel obliged to point out when your training methods contravene the European Convention on Human Rights."

"Bleedin' EU bureaucrats, coming over here, telling me how to run training."

Bunny took a deep breath as Deccie looked up at him defiantly. "I know what you're doing, Deccie. Stop trying to drag me off course."

"Alright. But ye could at least shit-sandwich it, boss."

"What?"

"Shit-sandwich. Start and end with good bits, put the criticism in the middle."

"Oh, thank God. I thought you meant ... Doesn't matter. And seeing as I'm taking *your* criticism on board, your two slices of bread are, well done for learning the drill sergeant's speech from *Full Metal Jacket*."

"Thank you."

"And for updating it to remove the homophobic language."

"You're welcome. I'm very hot on that as we got taught about homophobia in Civics."

"Right." Bunny was suddenly aware he was on tricky ground. "I think that's a great thing, and if you or any of the boys ..." A thought popped into Bunny's head. "Wait a sec, who teaches you Civics?"

"Ms Rogers. She doesn't like being called Miss or Missus. Did you know that they are sexist terms too, boss?"

"Fancy that. If memory serves, is she the attractive young lady with the ... Who has the ... Y'know what, never mind. She's clearly doing a great job. Anyway, Deccie, here is the bacon, lettuce and tomato for your shitty sandwich. One: don't tell Paidi he's a weapon and a – what was it?"

"Minister of death, waiting for war."

"Yeah. He's had a hard enough time getting his head around the fact that he's a goalie. Let's just stick with that. Secondly, don't tell the lads to give their hurl a girl's name. That they're married to their hurleys and they've to sleep with them. They're pre-pubescent boys ..." Bunny looked down at the entirely innocent expression on Deccie's face. "Just don't. Trust me on that one."

"But boss, you give your hurl a girl's name."

"That's entirely different." Bunny raised his hand to forestall the inevitable objection. "It just is. Moving on. The song ..."

Deccie raised his voice to sing before Bunny could stop him. "We are the Saint Jude's Under-12s, all other teams can go fu—"

Bunny slammed his hand over Deccie's mouth, conscious of the increasing number of parents that were gathering.

"That's the one. It doesn't set the tone we're looking for."

Deccie gave Bunny a pointed look and Bunny quickly liberated his assistant's face. "It has some inventive rhymes, though. You've got to give me that, boss."

"Be that as it may, if I hear it again, everyone is doing push-ups. Including you."

"Philistine."

"Also, I noticed that as the lads became increasingly angry with your methods, you enlisted Dono and Jar as your assistants."

"I did."

"The two biggest members of the team."

"Are they? I'd not noticed."

"My giddy aunt you hadn't. Are you aware of the Stanford Prison Experiment, Deccie?"

"No."

"It's the one where half the students were guards and half were ... Do you know what, never mind about that either. The point is, we're trying to put together a half-decent hurling team with one purpose in mind ..."

"Giving the ball to Paulie."

"No," said Bunny. "To build a bit of camaraderie."

"While giving the ball to Paulie."

Bunny nodded. "Well, yeah."

"Exactly," said Deccie. "Mission accomplished."

"What are you talking about? They all hate you."

Deccie threw up his hands triumphantly. "See. They all hate *me*. I bonded the team. Look at them now."

Bunny did. They were all standing round, egging each other on as they made dreadful attempts to knock the bucket off the crossbar.

Despite some of the attempts being unlikely to hit the side of a barn, never mind the bucket, each one was greeted as a near miss.

"Well, alright," said Bunny, "I'll give you that. But, well ..."

Bunny trailed off as Paul Mulchrone walked up to the spot. In one fluid motion he hopped the ball up onto his hurl, bounced it and struck it.

Bunny watched as the bucket tumbled and the rest of the team mobbed Paul. "Y'know, that has cost me a small fortune in Big Macs but damn it if it isn't a thing of beauty."

"And look how bonded all the lads are."

"Hmmm. Is your grandad picking you up?"

"Oh yeah. Can't walk home after this. I'd be wearing my undies as a scarf before I even reached the gate."

Bunny glanced over at the group of parents and saw Janice Craven, mother of Alan with one L, standing to one side. "Right, get out of here now, Deccie. Probably best you get a head start."

"Good idea, boss."

# A QUIET WORD

Bunny surveyed the sea of happy faces before him that had been on the verge of violent insurrection not ten minutes previously. It was amazing what the promise of junk food could achieve.

"Did ye see, Bunny? Did ye see?" asked Phil Nellis.

"I did," he said, not hiding his smile. "Paulie's cost me a fortune in chips."

"They're not chips, Bunny. They're fries!"

"What's the difference?"

"They're better."

"Is that right? Well, you can all consider it compensation for that fitness work I had my assistant manager put you through." The trick to good policing was spotting the trouble before it actually became trouble. "What was that, Sean Nolan?"

"I didn't say nothing, Bunny."

"Sean. Look at me, Sean." Reluctantly, Sean did so. "I'm sure you did. I'm sure you said that Deccie was only doing what I told him and that nobody will be saying anything about it to him."

Sean studied the ground sullenly and spoke around the six moustache hairs that he'd already managed to grow. "Yeah, I was saying nobody was going to bother Deccie."

"Good boy." Bunny raised his voice again. "And boys, don't think I've forgotten what happened the last time I promised you lot a feed after the match. When we suddenly found ourselves with all manner of hangers-on, well-wishers and, in young Diarmuid's case, what he referred to as his 'groupies'."

Bunny's words resulted in Diarmuid looking a mixture of embarrassed and delighted.

"To be crystal clear," Bunny continued, "I'm buying grub for the team, not half of north Dublin." A thought struck him. "Although, Eoin, if your little sister and brother would like to come, we could use some enthusiastic cheerleaders." Bunny made a mental note to drop over to their house soon with another hamper of food someone had inexplicably given him. He clapped his hands. "Right, boys. Straight home, no messing. Here at 10am on Sunday for the bus."

The team began to disperse.

"Alan with one L, hang back a second."

The rest of the boys walked off, engaged in the random jibber-jabber and sporadic violence that was the mainstay of pre-pubescent boys' lives.

Bunny looked down into the nervous face of the kid, all blond hair and a smattering of freckles. Anger and sadness swirled in his gut. Alan was small for his age, too. Never mind that, though – any twelve-year-old was far too small to face up to a full-grown man, and a professional boxer to boot. The kid had that nervy edge to him, as if life had already taught him that all he could expect from it was bad.

Bunny gave him a big smile. "Don't look so worried, fella – you've not done anything wrong." He put his arm around Alan's shoulder and started walking him towards the gate. "Quite the opposite, in fact. I just wanted to say that I've noticed how hard you work in training, week after week. If we had fourteen more of you, we'd be national champions."

Ahead of them, the parents who'd already been waiting had collected their chattering offspring, while the group of lads making their own ways home had drifted towards the exit. Alan's mother stood there alone, her arms folded, looking nervous. She had that same twitchy look to her.

"Howerya, Janice."

She gave a tight smile. "Hi, Bunny. Is everything alright?"

"Oh yeah, great, thanks. I was just commending Alan here on how good he's getting. He's a dynamo on our wing."

Janice's smile transformed into a proud beam and Bunny swore he could feel the warmth of the blush off her son.

Bunny caught himself and turned around. "Ara, feck it. I forgot I've to pick up all these cones. D'ye mind if Alan gives me a quick hand?"

"Sure," said Janice. "No problem."

"Fantastic." Bunny wafted a hand to his left. "By the way, this is my friend Pamela."

Janice turned to see the short redhead who'd been standing around. She'd wondered who she was, knowing all the other parents already. They smiled hellos.

Bunny ruffled Alan's hair. "C'mon so, dynamo, I'll race ye. Most cones collected wins."

Butch cleared her throat. "That's a great young fella you've got there."

Janice's eyes crinkled. "Yeah, he's a good boy."

"Twelve is a brilliant age, isn't it? Still a kid, full of beans, none of that teenage angst yet."

Janice turned her body to face Butch. "Have you kids yourself?"

"No," Butch admitted. "Lots of nieces and nephews, though, and I used work with children a lot."

"Oh right," said Janice with a nod. "So, you and Bunny are friends, then?"

"Yeah, we're ..." Butch stopped herself and blushed as she realised what Janice meant. "Not like that."

"You could do a lot worse."

"True."

The two women watched in silence for a few seconds as Bunny

chased Alan round, trying to grab the cones he'd picked up. "You'd never know from looking at him that he was a guard, would you?"

"He does hide it well."

"That's how I know him. We work together. Well, he's having a bit of time off."

"That's right," said Janice. "I know he was involved in that bad business last year, wasn't he?"

"Yeah. Lost his partner."

Janice tutted. "Awful thing."

Bunny had now grabbed Alan by the legs and was holding him upside down, the kid snorting with laughter as he did so.

"If you don't mind me saying," said Janice, "you don't look much like a guard yourself."

Butch smiled. "Between you and me, that's kind of the point. You'd be amazed how handy it is not to have the 'my older brother got the farm so here I am' look that most guards have. Nobody is picking me out as a copper."

"Ah right, yeah. That makes sense. For undercover stuff and the like?"

Butch nodded. "And before that I worked a lot with domestic-abuse stuff. Child protection – that kind of thing."

She felt the other woman tense – a sure sign.

"It's a tough area," continued Butch, keeping her tone steady. "Things have improved a lot, though. There's a lot of ways these days to ask for help if you need it."

Janice said nothing, but turned her attention to Alan.

"A lot of it's being taught how to spot the signs in a victim. Becoming withdrawn, moody. Unexplained bruising, of course."

Janice checked her watch. "We should probably get a move on."

"All the time I spent working in that area, d'ye know what I learned? Nobody hits a kid by accident. They hit a kid because they're the kind of arsehole who hits a kid. And they never ever do it just once."

Janice's head lowered and she sniffled. "It's not like that."

Butch softened her voice. "If I'd a pound for every time I heard that. It's not just the kid he hits, is it?"

"He promised that he'd—"

"Janice, they always promise."

Anger flared in Janice's eyes as she turned to Butch. "It's nothing to do with you."

Butch took a step back, wanting to give the other woman room. "All I'm saying is, I understand. I really do. Just say the word and we can help."

"Yeah, because the law does such a brilliant job of protecting women and kids, doesn't it?"

Butch shrugged. "No, it doesn't. Nobody knows that more than I do, but I'm telling you, we can get you some place safe tonight and—"

"He'd find us."

"He wouldn't."

"How many women have you told that bullshit to?"

Butch held up her hands. "OK. Look, I get it. You don't know me and you don't trust the law." She pointed to where Bunny was now giving the laughing Alan a piggyback. "But you do know him, and you know he'd go to hell and back to protect one of his boys."

Janice bit her lip as tears trickled down her face.

"I understand," said Butch in her calmest voice. "You're scared to leave, but deep down you know it'll happen again." She took a card out of her pocket and held it out to Janice. "Here's my number."

The other woman looked at it but didn't move to take it.

Butch pointed at the printed wording on the card. "Look, it says Atlas Cosmetics. If he sees it, just say you got asked to do some make-up parties for extra cash. Even if he rings the number, that's all he'll get, I swear." She looked over at Bunny and Alan. "I think they're finishing up."

Janice turned her face away and wiped the tears from her eyes. As she looked back again, she took the card and slipped it into her pocket.

"Any time," said Butch. "Day or night."

"C'mon," shouted Janice, waving at Alan. "We'd better get a move on or your dinner will be burned. Say goodbye to Bunny."

Alan and Bunny shared a high-five then the lad ran off after his mother, who was already hurrying towards the exit.

Bunny put down the pile of cones he was carrying. He walked over to stand beside Butch and they watched the pair leave.

"Well?"

"I don't know, but at least she took the card."

Bunny shook his head. "I don't get it. Any of it."

Butch glanced up at him and then looked away. "I know you don't."

"You could probably use a drink after that?"

Butch gave him a stern look. "No. I'd rather vent my frustrations by going for a jog, and you promised me if I helped out with this, you'd go home and get an early night."

"I worry about you running around on your own at night."

"Really?"

"Yeah. Always training. Nocturnal. Be honest with me – are you Batman?"

Butch laughed and then pursed her lips. "I'll tell you what, I do look good in leather." She punched Bunny on the arm.

# UNDER A BLOOD-RED MOON

Coop Hannity looked down at his pride and joy. She was a beauty. The last time she'd been sent across to a race in Europe, Guillaume, the annoying Frenchman, had tried to make him an offer for her. He hadn't even let him get as far as proposing a figure. Athena was his first truly great bird. A three-time winner.

The music swelled pleasingly in the background. He ran the back of his index finger over her breast feathers then unfurled his palm so that she could peck the seeds out of it. All of the birds needed exercising but he allowed Deirdre, the college kid who came around on weekdays to check on the animals, to handle most of it. She wasn't as good as Peter, but he'd noticed the guy smiling at Angelina and he couldn't have that. People needed to know where the lines were.

This was why he preferred his birds. Pigeons were blessed with a singular focus: the desire to return home as efficiently as possible. There was a cleanness to it. In contrast, people were messy. He knew it shouldn't bother him, but it did. After all, if people could make simple logical decisions, he wouldn't have a business.

In fact, his understanding of the human capacity to screw up had been the driving force behind everything he'd done. To take advantage of it, he himself had to be able to anticipate people's behaviour and think several moves ahead. To see the turn in the road where the reckless driver would inevitably fail to slow down and the black ice would do the rest. Coop prided himself on being a strategic thinker in a world full of over-emotional fools, blundering from crisis to crisis.

The wind changed and a chill passed through him. March was such an annoying month. It could be bright sunshine one day and snow the next. He spoke without looking around. "Joe, move that lamp over beside this coop." He couldn't have his prize girl feeling the chill.

Coop heard a clunking noise behind him.

"Be. Careful."

Joe did not respond. The man was undeniably useful. Just the look of him was enough to stop all but the foolhardiest from trying anything. In essence, the big man was just a visual reminder of Coop's power. People might make stupid decisions all the time, but the sight of the big, dumb, musclebound clod stopped them from making a terminal one. That's not to say that having him around didn't come at a cost. Apart from his salary, he had to be fed, and that was a sizeable amount. However, Coop objected to the spectacle more than the cost. He'd seen to it that big Joe now ate his meals in the kitchen where he didn't have to watch him masticating his way through enough food to feed a family of six.

Coop himself was, of course, capable of acts of violence. You had to be, to be in this game, but it had been a long time since he'd had to do anything personally. He had taken life, because it had been necessary to send a message, but also because he wanted to know that he could do it, if required. The whole thing had been a tremendous anti-climax. These days, he preferred not to touch people at all. He'd noticed that his opinion of people had sunk further and further over the years, perhaps a result of constantly seeing them at their worst.

Earlier today, he'd let Dean and McDaid go. Hired muscle who got themselves embarrassed by one man, even if that man was a police officer, were of limited use. Dean, the fool, had decided to start issuing threats on his way out the door. Saying he knew where the bodies were buried. One glance in Joe's direction had been enough to remind him of his situation, but it hadn't stopped him from talking about the "severance package" to which he felt he was entitled. The man simply talked too much, so Coop had set the wheels in motion. Before the end of the week, Mr Dean would be reminded of the other meaning of the word "severance".

Coop also appreciated that Joe was good at the art of silence. A grossly under-rated skill. Previous occupants of his current role had been stupidly keen to butt in. They'd felt the need to make threats on Coop's behalf, to literally throw their weight around. In contrast, the man mountain just stood there. He had a blissful disinterest in small talk of any kind.

Coop felt the presence behind him.

"Just put it over—"

He noticed it was wrong. All wrong. But too late.

He felt the blade in his back. The word "frenzy" popped into his head randomly as the weapon pistoned in and out of him repeatedly. He slumped forward against the cages, looking into Athena's eyes as he tasted his own blood in his mouth. The knife continued to beat out the rhythm of his death.

His coat caught on the side of the cage and spun him around as he fell. As the last breath escaped his body, he looked into the face of death.

He hadn't seen this coming.

# MOURNING HAS BROKEN

DI Fintan O'Rourke got out of his car and looked up at the eyesore that was Coop Hannity's castle – a gaping abscess on an otherwise perfectly ordinary suburban street. If you ever wanted an example of how having all the money in the world couldn't buy an ounce of class – well, look no further. If anything, the police tape improved the aesthetic. Turrets – how in the hell did Coop Hannity get planning permission to build fucking turrets? O'Rourke was a DI in the Garda Síochána and last year the county council had turned him down flat when he asked to build a shed.

He signed in to the scene. He wouldn't admit it, but a part of him still enjoyed the thrill of the uniforms standing upright and doing their best to look alert upon his arrival. There was something gratifying about being a man people wanted to impress. It was 7am and they'd be at the end of their shift, looking forward to their beds.

O'Rourke himself had been due to take the day off but Coop Hannity being dead was interesting. Him having been murdered was downright fascinating, and it wasn't the first time somebody had attempted to make that happen. The man enjoyed the kind of popularity normally only experienced by dictators.

Strictly speaking, Hannity and his operations did not fall under the remit of the organised crime task force O'Rourke now headed up. It was a temporary one, assembled to deal with the Carter gang, but had now proved itself useful enough to get a twelve-month audition to become a permanent fixture. However, O'Rourke had said they wanted the Hannity case as soon as he got the call. Hannity lived in the margins, but the tentacles of his empire spread far and wide.

Organised crime hadn't changed since the days of Capone. Following the money was still the easiest way to find out what was really going on. There had long been suspicions that Hannity was laundering money for some of the gangs but, as always with Coop, all lines of enquiry led to dead ends. To give the dead his due, with the notable exception of taste in architecture, the man had been highly intelligent and perceptive. He'd made himself untouchable – at least, until now.

Whoever was responsible for his murder was the most fascinating of all the pieces of the puzzle. If the task force was to survive and O'Rourke's meteoric rise to continue, then he was under no illusion – they needed to take down some big game. Coop Hannity might just be the blood in the water needed to attract some really big prey.

Detective Pamela Cassidy was standing on the doorstep waiting for him, blowing into her hands and stamping her feet to keep warm. He made a point of not using her nickname. If asked, he'd say this was a propriety of management thing, but in reality, he hated his own nickname that he'd been saddled with for fifteen years – Rigger – and honestly, he was hoping the whole practice would die off. For Christ's sake, they were law enforcement, not a university rugby team.

"Pamela."

"Boss. Sorry about messing up your day off."

"So you should be. I'm missing out on three hours traipsing around after the wife as she tries on silly hats for a wedding I don't want to go to. The sacrifices this job forces us to make are brutal."

"Sounds it."

"How are you the initial on this?"

"DS Quinn has got that dental thing and Burke is in Belfast for the—"

"Right," said O'Rourke. "Makes sense."

"I'm holding the fort until Quinn gets here."

He stopped for a second, then nodded. "No offence to anyone, but I'm going to call Paschal back from Belfast. This thing is too high profile."

"Understood. The main event is out in the back garden."

She led him through the house. O'Rourke was surprised by the lack of suits of armour and stuffed buffalo.

The garden was a hive of activity as the tech bureau worked the scene. O'Rourke pulled on the requisite overalls and stood beside Cassidy. "Alright, take me through it."

"Yes, boss," said Cassidy, referring to her notepad filled with precise details written in a tight hand. "The wife, Angelina Hannity, came home last night at 11:30pm after her regular Tuesday-night visit to her father at Cedarwood Hospital and then dropping in to see a friend afterwards. She first noticed something was wrong when she got up to her bedroom and realised the lights in the back garden were still on, as was the music."

"Was the absence of her husband from the bed not a clue?"

"Apparently not. She and the hubby have separate bedrooms."

"How long are they married?"

"Three years."

Cassidy turned back towards the house and pointed to the right-hand tower. "Her bedroom is up there."

"Let me guess," said O'Rourke. "He sleeps in—"

"Yep, the other tower."

"Jeez. If the murder weapon's a glass slipper, I'm going to lose it."

Cassidy continued to flip through her notes. "No murder weapon as yet. Coming to that." She started to walk across the neatly trimmed lawn beside the paved path. "Mrs Hannity comes out, first thing she sees is the bodyguard – a Joe Stowers – who is sprawled on the ground, alive, having been walloped on the back of the head with a large blunt object while sitting there." She indicated an overturned chair. "There was a fire extinguisher near by with blood on it.

Forensics have taken it away to confirm it was the weapon used on him."

"He's lucky to be alive."

"Bodyguard, guv. Not seen him yet but I hear he's a big boy. First officers on the scene said the ambulance crew had a bugger of a time getting him in the wagon."

"Right."

"Initial reports are while he's had a vicious wallop to the head, it's not life threatening, and apparently he's conscious and talking."

"Good. He'll be doing that talking to you and me at the first available opportunity."

"Yes, boss. He told the guards on the scene that he didn't see anything before he passed out, but hopefully he'll be a little bit more forthcoming once he's no longer bleeding."

Cassidy moved further up the lawn and stopped beside the raised wooden platform.

"Jesus," said O'Rourke. "I'd heard about the pigeon thing, but I didn't realise there were this many."

"Yep. I asked Mrs Hannity if she knew how to take care of them. If there was anything we needed to do." Cassidy noticed her superior officer's facial expression. "Yeah, I know, guv, but remember that case over in Dalkey when the ISPCA went mental about the six cats not being—"

"Alright," said O'Rourke, holding up a hand. "I get it. I think I may even have signed the memo."

"The guard in charge of that thing still gets death threats."

"Don't worry, Cassidy. We will ensure your bird-loving reputation remains intact."

O'Rourke saw the nervous smirk flash across her face as she tried to decipher whether he meant that as a joke or not. He kept his face deadpan. "And the body?"

Cassidy nodded, all business. "Over there, beside the cages. Multiple stab wounds to the back with what the examiner unofficially says was a long serrated blade."

"Hmmm, not exactly the professional assassin's weapon of choice."

"No, guv. Like I said on the phone, I've put in a request for manpower to search the area as we've not located it."

"I made the call. You'll get them." He turned and pointed at the overturned chair. "Can we go back here? Am I missing something? The big lad gets smashed in the back of the head with a fire extinguisher and Coop still gets stabbed in the back?"

"Yes, sir." Cassidy pointed at the poles located around the pigeon coops. "Speakers, sir. Apparently, Mr Hannity regularly played classical music while he was out here. According to the maid, he said it relaxed the birds. Probably meant he didn't hear them coming."

"You're kidding? He sat out here, blasting out Bach or some shit like that?"

Cassidy nodded.

"He must've been wildly popular with the neighbours."

"Given who he was, I doubt there were many complaints."

"Sure," agreed O'Rourke. "Nobody did it twice, at least."

"Which brings me on to the weird bit, sir. The first weird bit ..." Cassidy pointed at the speakers again. "... is that we don't reckon they're just speakers. They're also mics."

O'Rourke raised an eyebrow. "I assume he wasn't spying on his own pigeons?"

"No, guv." She turned and pointed up into the trees. "Also, up there, there and there are cameras concealed amidst the branches."

"Cassidy, are you about to tell me we have Coop Hannity's last breath caught on film?"

"I'm afraid not, boss. It's very much one of those good news, bad news scenarios."

She indicated the far side of the garden before leading the way. Hidden behind bushes was the kind of door you'd associate with a bunker, or perhaps an air-raid shelter. Neither of which he'd ever seen in person. "How did we find this?"

"It was open when we got here. One of the uniforms noticed it but had the presence of mind to leave it as is, except for a glance to make sure it was unoccupied." She pointed at the door. "It's thick, and there's a serious-looking lock on it."

As Cassidy led O'Rourke down the six steps into the subterranean room, the first thing he noticed was the bank of monitors on a desk to the right, their monochromatic light barely reaching the bottom of the stairs. All three screens were showing a live feed of the forensic team outside, from different angles. A couple of VCRs were located beneath them, and a ratty-looking swivel chair sat in front of the desk, upon which lay a clipboard and a jar of pens.

Cassidy stood to one side. "No tapes in any of the machines. Tecchies have already dusted it for prints."

"Is there something else I'm missing here?" asked O'Rourke.

"Well, guv, there is this." She flipped a switch on the wall and O'Rourke turned to watch the fluorescent lights click and flicker into life, illuminating the rest of the room.

"Holy ..."

The space must have stretched nearly all the way back to the house, and the only thing it contained were shelves and shelves of video tapes.

"Is this—"

"Yep," said Cassidy, failing to keep the glee out of her voice. "I mean, we've not checked, but judging by the labels on the tapes and what we've seen in that ledger, Mr Hannity has been keeping video recordings of his meetings going back at least ten years."

O'Rourke licked his lips. "Fuck me, Cassidy. This is an intelligence motherlode. I mean ..." His mind was racing. He twirled around and clapped his hands together. "Right, nobody touches anything that isn't immediately pertinent to the investigation. I need to talk to the Director of Public Prosecutions as lawyers will have a field day with this, but, as of now, this is all evidence. Everything in this room speaks to motive in the sainted Mr Hannity's murder. I want a uniform – no, two uniforms. Actually, screw it – I'll ask for two armed officers outside this door twenty-four-seven and I will personally sign off the overtime in my own blood if I have to."

He pointed back at the monitors. "We suspect the tapes from last night were taken by the individual or individuals responsible for a first-degree murder. This is officially all part of our crime scene. Clear?"

"Yes, boss."

O'Rourke scanned the room again. "Do we know if anything else has been removed?"

Cassidy indicated the clipboard on the desk. "From what I can see on the log, a tape from Monday night is possibly missing, but I've no idea what else might have been taken."

"OK, OK." O'Rourke rubbed his hands together. "Christ, Pamela, this place is Aladdin's fucking cave."

"Yes, boss."

"Butch?" The shout came from outside. "Where the fuck are you?"

Cassidy grimaced. "Down here, Detective Carlson."

Carlson was sweating despite the morning chill. He was a man who could be on the brink of starvation and still have something about him that said fat lad. O'Rourke didn't know for sure, but he'd put money on him being lumbered with something terribly clever like Tubs as his nickname.

The detective spotted O'Rourke and looked as if he might lose his breakfast.

"Calm down, John. I like my squads to project an air of control."

Carlson looked embarrassed. "Sorry, boss. I've just been looking through the camera footage."

O'Rourke gave Cassidy a confused look.

"Sorry, sir, I was getting to that. There are other cameras that aren't linked to these – ones that cover the perimeter. I asked Carlson to scan through the tapes from last night."

O'Rourke nodded. "I don't suppose the murderer was kind enough to ring the doorbell?"

"No, boss."

O'Rourke stopped smiling. The look on Carlson's face was not a happy one. "Jesus, John, you look like you've shat your nappy. Just come out with it, whatever it is."

Carlson drew an intake of breath. "The tape – it shows no visitors last night, just the wife leaving and returning. But ..." He glanced at Cassidy.

O'Rourke could feel his good mood dispelling. "Last I checked, Carlson, Detective Cassidy doesn't outrank me. You don't need to check with her. Come on, you'd better show me whatever the hell has got you so worked up."

In contrast to the bunker outside, the control room for the more mundane security system was pretty basic. To O'Rourke, it didn't look like much more than a converted cloakroom. He, Carlson and Cassidy had managed to squeeze inside, but nobody would be able to bend down and pick up a pen without at least one other person leaving first. The system itself seemed to be run on a computer, which marked it out as considerably more modern than the videotape one used out back.

Carlson took a seat at the controls and, on the bottom left of four screens, he rewound the recording to the night before. When the time stamp showed 9:14pm, a figure clad all in black, including a balaclava, appeared on screen.

"Freeze it," said O'Rourke. "Now, what am I looking at?"

"That camera," explained Carlson, "covers the wall on the right as you look down the garden, sir. It's actually mostly on the far side of the wall. Hannity's neighbour's garden."

"And are we sure the time stamps are correct?"

"We have to double check them, sir," said Carlson, pointing at the top-right screen, "but the one on the front door, covering the drive, does show Mrs Hannity leaving and returning at the exact times she told us."

"OK. Roll it."

As the tape played on, the trio watched in silence as the balaclava-clad figure disappeared from view behind the tall hedge, and then, about a minute later, a head and shoulders could be made

# WE NEED A BASTARD

DI Fintan O'Rourke strode out of the gates of Garda HQ and looked around. He really wasn't in the mood for this. He had hot-tailed it here from the Coop Hannity crime scene, as he'd needed to speak to the Commissioner immediately. Upon arriving for his meeting, he was informed by his boss's PA that Commissioner Ferguson had "gone for a walk with Kevin." Where? "Out."

O'Rourke didn't know a Kevin – at least, not one who was a senior guard. More importantly, given the revelations of the day, he didn't have time for a game of hide-and-seek. With that in mind, he'd asked if the Commissioner had left any more detailed information about his location other than "out".

The Commissioner's PA – a matronly woman with a hairdo that looked as if it had been welded in place in the 1970s – had laughed at the question. "Yes, the Commissioner said you might ask that."

"And?"

"And," she'd said, reading from a Post-it note attached to her monitor, "he told me to remind you that you are one of the most highly decorated detectives in the country, and if you can't find him, then God help us all." She had smiled up at O'Rourke. "He does so enjoy his little jokes, doesn't he?"

So here he was, wondering where the hell he was supposed to be.

O'Rourke examined the evidence. He wouldn't say Commissioner Gareth Ferguson was a fat man – mainly because nobody in their right mind would make that statement out loud for fear of it getting back to him. The Commissioner could be a sensitive soul and, more importantly, he had a legendary ability when it came to holding a grudge. Besides, the man wasn't fat – the word didn't even begin to do him justice. It was like describing the Grand Canyon as a hole. Ferguson was six foot four and immense. It was as if someone had taken an avalanche, stuffed it in a finely tailored suit and then made it the most high-ranking police officer in Ireland. You wanted Ferguson on your side, because the only other choice was to be crushed by him one way or the other.

For all of that, he was indeed fat, and had a well-established aversion to physical exercise. In practical terms, this meant that wherever he was at this moment in time could not be that far away.

Second, the Commissioner, while a dedicated servant of the public, was not their biggest fan. O'Rourke hypothesised that wherever his boss had gone for a walk, he wouldn't wish to be in their company. That ruled out turning left from HQ, which led to the park gates and a particularly busy stretch of the North Circular. It also ruled out straight ahead, as that led down to Dublin Zoo where, even from this distance, O'Rourke could hear the roar of dozens of school trips collectively losing their damn minds.

O'Rourke turned right and started walking up North Road. After just two minutes he found Ferguson and his entourage. The Commissioner was leaning against an oak tree, panting heavily. The duo of Garda protection officers strategically stationed around him were ever present but there was also a new addition, which took O'Rourke by surprise.

"Commissioner, I didn't know you were a dog lover."

Ferguson shot him a dirty look. "That very much depends on what you consider a dog to be. When someone mentions a dog, I, for example, think of a German Shepherd, possibly a Labrador or, at the risk at coming over all pant-wettingly patriotic, an Irish wolfhound.

My beloved wife, however, thinks of something very different. This is Kevin."

O'Rourke looked down at the hound beaming up at him cheerfully. He had closely cropped, brown curly hair and a lolling tongue.

"The missus," Ferguson continued, "devious wench that she is, was, in hindsight, far too keen to compromise. I expressed the firm opinion that I wanted a Labrador, for her part she wanted a poodle, and what we ended up with was Kevin. He is a Labradoodle, which I belatedly realised was what my wife wanted all along."

"Well," said O'Rourke, "he seems nice."

"Nice. Yes, well, nice – that is exactly the problem. What I wanted was a manly hound, man's best friend. What I got was something that looks as if it should be playing keyboard in an 80s pop band. I feel frankly ridiculous walking him about. And he doesn't play fetch! What kind of a dog doesn't play fetch, I ask you? I throw the ball and he looks up at me, like, 'Oh, did you not want that?' I can't decide if he's incredibly stupid or incredibly smart. Either way, I don't like him. You might be wondering why I've brought him to work with me, then?"

In fact, O'Rourke had not been wondering that, but he had more than enough experience of Commissioner Gareth Ferguson to know that the path of least resistance was to let him get whatever he wanted to off his chest.

"Kevin is spending the week with me as he has developed behavioural issues, which my wife – in conjunction with the animal behaviourist, who we are paying more than you would believe for his services – has decided are the result of Kevin getting the impression that I do not like him. He can pick up that, but a ball, apparently, is beyond him."

Ferguson started to walk, and tugged on the lead in his hand to drag the excitable Kevin along with him. The dog veered left and right, as if everything he could see was the most exciting thing ever. O'Rourke followed in their wake.

"To be fair," Ferguson continued, "my problem is not with Kevin per se." The dog yapped repeatedly at some leaves, earning him a disparaging look from his owner. "Well, not just with Kevin. It is rather what he represents. Did you know Dr Jacobs?"

"No."

"Nice old duffer. Used to do the annual check-ups for myself and the other senior gardaí. You'd drop in, he'd run a few tests, whack your knee with a hammer, give you a light scolding about cutting out this, that or the other, and then you'd both enjoy a nice cigar. It was all very civilised."

"Certainly sounds it."

"Then Jacobs went and ruined a good thing by going off and dying. Inconsiderate arse. Had the wrong kind of stroke in a swimming pool, apparently. Now we have a new sawbones." Ferguson's eyes narrowed and his tone dropped to a low growl. "Dr Mansfield."

Kevin began to whine, sensing the dip in the conversational temperature.

"Fresh-faced, charming girl, doesn't drink or smoke. Also, takes what I consider to be an unhealthy interest in the health of her patients. Last month she gave me my annual medical and failed me. I thought the only way you could fail a medical was by being dead. Worse than that, she sent the results home, where my beloved opens all of the post."

"I'm sorry to hear you're not well," said O'Rourke.

"Oh, for God's sake, don't you start. When, as a species, did we become so obsessed with living for ever? Jesus only lived to thirty-three, and back in those days, that was a pretty good innings. Nowadays, we're all obsessed with coffin-dodging until the end of time. Personally, I'm a big believer that when your time is up, you should shuffle neatly out of the way and not cause a fuss. I made the mistake of expressing this opinion in the presence of both my wife and doctor, and I've now had to give up having opinions as well.

"My beloved, despite all the evidence to the contrary, has expressed how much she wants me to live a long and happy life. Well, at least a long one. I can only imagine the woman does not wish to experience dating in the twenty-first century. That's why she has made it her mission to render me immortal, whether I like it or not. I've been forced to give up everything. I can no longer smoke a cigar, I can't drink – never mind whiskey or port, I can't even have a glass of wine. I mean, wine, for God's sake – the French give wine to children! I have also been betrayed."

Ferguson glared in the direction of each of his close protection officers in turn. O'Rourke immediately recognised the facial expressions of two men caught between the rockiest of rocks and the hardest of hard places.

"My detail – who, as far as I am aware, are still members of the Garda Síochána, the organisation which I allegedly run – has agreed with my wife to no longer assist me in the acquisition of what I consider to be necessary provisions. Let's call it what it is – treason! My personal assistant, who I have long suspected of being engaged in espionage at my wife's behest, is now similarly in open revolt. In the last fortnight there has not been a single biscuit at any meeting I have attended. The biccies were the only reason I was willing to go to most of those godforsaken bore-fests in the first place. My existence has become an unbearable trudge towards immortality, a path I must apparently travel in the company of Kevin the Labra-fucking-doodle, as it was felt a dog would motivate me to take more exercise."

As if on cue, Kevin jumped up on O'Rourke and grabbed his leg firmly between his paws.

Ferguson tugged the pup away. "For Christ's sake, Kevin! What have we said about humping in public? If I wanted an animal that did that, I'd have offered to adopt the Minister for Foreign Affairs' son, the randy little bugger." O'Rourke disengaged himself and moved slightly further away. The dog had a surprisingly strong grip.

"Anyway," said Ferguson, "I hear Coop Hannity is dead, the lucky bastard."

And there, thought O'Rourke, endeth what could be referred to as the "small talk" section of the meeting.

"Yes. It happened last night. We've been working the scene all morning. Canvassing the neighbourhood and conducting a search for the murder weapon, as none is present at the scene."

"Thank you for the explanation of how an investigation works. I particularly appreciate you putting it in simple terms as I've seemingly won a competition to meet a police officer. I do hope you'll let me have a go on the siren later."

O'Rourke tried to smile. Ferguson could be a challenge to deal with at the best of times, and it was alarmingly clear that these were not those times. He decided to keep moving forward as the odds on his boss's mood improving were not great, given that O'Rourke didn't have a packet of Hobnobs about his person.

"The good news is, it appears we have stumbled upon quite the treasure trove. There's a bunker beneath the back garden of Hannity's gaudy castle, which contains hundreds of video tapes. It seems he's been surreptitiously recording many of his meetings, stretching back to at least 1989, if the labels are to be believed."

A smile attempted to dawn across Ferguson's face, but it couldn't quite break through the perma-scowl.

"Really? Well, well, well. I would imagine there will be many hours of interesting viewing in that little collection."

"Yes, I'm sure there will be. I'll be having a chat with our friends at the office of the DPP later on, as I'd imagine there will be some legal issues accessing it."

"Speaking of which, I feel obliged to ask – although he is no great loss to mankind – do we know who introduced Mr Hannity to the choir eternal?"

"Not as yet. We do have CCTV of a man wearing a balaclava, entering the property and exiting it seven minutes later – a short time after 9pm. Coop's bodyguard was knocked unconscious with a fire extinguisher, and the man himself was stabbed from behind, numerous times, with a large blade, while feeding his pigeons."

"Ah, the bloody pigeons. So, you have to figure out who killed one of the most unpopular men on the planet? I have every confidence in your abilities, Fintan. Haven't there been attempts on his life previously?"

"Yes, sir. A Mrs Rita Marsh was done for attempted murder in 1992—"

"Christ. Yes. I remember that. What a fucking mess. And the other time?"

"The brothers Fairchild – two low-end car dealers from Skerries – got involved in a messy deal with Coop. There were reports of a gunshot outside his office, but Hannity didn't cooperate with the investigation. Oisín, the younger Fairchild, was found burned to a crisp in an oil drum a week later."

"And the other one?"

"Cian. Location unknown. Best guess is he's dead too, or running for his life."

Ferguson arched his back to stretch it and farted unapologetically. "What a bloody mess. Let's hope his video collection is going to be incredibly useful to your investigation."

"Yes, I believe it will be. Although, unfortunately, it appears our murderer was aware of it – they had the presence of mind to remove the tape from last night. It would have made things considerably easier. It's possible a couple of other tapes have gone along with it."

"Do we know exactly which ones?"

"We're looking into that. Hannity had a secretary whose job apparently included maintaining his little library. We're trying to interview her, although she's lawyered up and is being less than helpful."

Ferguson nodded. "I'd imagine she will continue to be so, until you can get our friends from the DPP to give her immunity."

"Yes. That will form a large part of the chat that I'll be having after I leave here."

"Lovely. Who discovered the body?"

"The wife."

The Commissioner raised an eyebrow and O'Rourke shook his head, aware of where his boss was going – the people who discover bodies being well-known suppliers of them in the first place.

"She went to visit her father at his care facility last night, before having a drink with a friend. We're checking, but Cedarwood have already confirmed that she visited her old man between 8:15pm and 9:26pm last night."

"Shame," said Ferguson. "I wish more wives would kill their husbands. Mariticide is so neat and tidy, and everyone is happy to assume the bastard had it coming. Does wonders for the crime stats." He glanced at his protection detail before lowering his voice slightly. "And now that you've danced me around the floor a couple of times like the perfect gentleman you aren't, can we please get to the part where you try to grab my boob?"

"Excuse me, sir?"

"You are in the early stages of a significant and challenging investigation, Detective Inspector. Everything you have so far updated me on you could have covered in a five-minute phone call that would not have been anything more than a courtesy. The reason you requested a meeting is that you felt moved to come and ruin my already-ruined day in person. So, please do get to the point, because if it is as bad as I think it might be, judging by your facial expression, I'd rather keel over from the heart attack here than have to walk all the way back to the office and do it there."

Annoyingly, the man was, yet again, absolutely right.

"There's also a CCTV camera on the front of the Hannity property. We recovered footage from the night before last of Detective Bernard 'Bunny' McGarry paying the house a visit." O'Rourke elected to neglect to mention the theft of the gnome – the Commissioner's face was already an alarming shade of red.

Ferguson turned around and started walking in the opposite direction, back towards Garda HQ. "Am I to take it that this is the same Bunny McGarry whom we have recently discussed promoting to the rank of detective sergeant and having the President herself pin a medal on his chest?"

"Yes."

"Good. If I were to find out this force has two individuals with the nickname of Bunny, I'd start to feel as if I were running a petting zoo." Ferguson came to a stop and gave O'Rourke a penetrating stare. "And the rest?"

"Sir?"

"You have the look, Fintan, of a man who is waiting for his other bollock to drop. Stop waiting for a better time – I assure you there will not be one. You have a theory as to what McGarry was doing there. Given that you have yet to share it with me, I can only assume that it will not be good news either."

O'Rourke hesitated.

"Just spit it out, there's a good boy."

"Two days ago I got a call from Clontarf Garda Station. McGarry had been involved in an altercation with two men – muscle in the employment of Coop Hannity. The incident took place at an address that belonged to DS Tim Spain and is now occupied by his mother."

"And there we have it. I seem to recall you assuring me that DS Spain's financial difficulties had all been resolved?"

"I was under the impression they had been, sir."

"Well, it appears – not unlike that talentless hack somebody hired for last year's Christmas party – your impression was wrong. What exactly did McGarry tell you?"

"Nothing. He's even more concerned about protecting DS Spain's reputation than we are, sir."

"So, just to make sure I have this completely clear in my head, what you are telling me is that one officer, whom we are about to hold up as a hero, may have been involved in the murder of Coop Hannity, in an effort to protect the reputation of another officer, now deceased, whom we have already been lauding in the press as a paragon of virtue the whole country can be proud of?"

O'Rourke paused before nodding. "I should point out that we're still in the very early stages of the investigation."

"But am I correct in my assumption that you believe the video tape of McGarry's meeting with Hannity to be one of those taken by the murderer?"

"We haven't yet located it, but that doesn't ..." O'Rourke decided to stop digging the hole. "I agree it sounds bad."

Ferguson laughed humourlessly. "It sounds bad? Good God, Fintan. If this is the end of your policing career, you really must consider moving into the real-estate business. It's like referring to Pompeii as a bit of a fixer-upper. This is an unmitigated fucking disaster."

"Again, sir, we shouldn't jump to any conclusions. Hannity was rumoured to be money laundering. For all we know, this could be the start of a gang war."

"And you have to wonder how fucked up things are that we're hoping something is a gang war now." Ferguson moved off at such a surprising pace that O'Rourke needed to hurry to catch up with him. His boss was mumbling beneath his breath, dragging the witless Kevin in his wake. All of a sudden he stopped and turned sharply. So sharply that O'Rourke very nearly ran into him.

The Commissioner jabbed a chubby finger in O'Rourke's face. "Let's be honest with ourselves here, Detective Inspector. Both you and I know that there was something deeply fishy about the deaths of DSs Spain, Cunningham and O'Shea. The planets aligned in such a way that they could die heroes and the force could take a massive victory from a sticky situation. A large part of that was because McGarry's version of events tallied so well with that narrative. However, any suggestion that McGarry or Spain is not the clean-living paragon of virtue that we have been extolling, and people might start asking questions that do not have good answers. More importantly, you are currently leading a murder investigation and one of your main suspects is on sabbatical from your team."

"I'm aware it looks bad," O'Rourke repeated.

"No, Fintan. It *is* bad. At the risk of getting an answer I don't want ... As someone who knows McGarry, do you think he could have done this?"

O'Rourke licked his lips. He'd been running that question backwards and forwards in his mind all morning. "That is not a simple question."

"And that is not a good answer."

"Is Bunny McGarry capable of murder? Probably. Most of us are, given the right circumstances."

"And is trying to protect his former partner's reputation the right circumstances?"

O'Rourke shrugged. "Here's the thing, Commissioner: I think Bunny might be capable of just about anything. But still ... I don't think he did this."

"And why is that?"

"Hannity was stabbed in the back. McGarry is many things – chief among them is painfully direct. He's not the sneaking-up-behind-you sort."

Ferguson rolled his eyes. "Well, let's hope that if this comes to trial, he has better character witnesses lined up than you. So, you think he was in the wrong place at the wrong time?"

O'Rourke nodded.

"Here's the problem. There are certain lines you do not cross. When it comes to Spain, Cunningham and O'Shea, we've all decided that it's for the greater good not to ask certain questions. Justice was done, even if some of the surrounding circumstances stink like French cheese." Ferguson closed his eyes momentarily and spoke to the sky as if offering up a desperate prayer. "Cheese. God, how I miss cheese."

He opened his eyes and continued as if nothing had happened. "But now, this is something different. This is what sets us apart from the criminals. We need to make sure this thing is investigated to within an inch of its life. No stone will be left unturned. Nobody, especially a defence lawyer at a later trial, could dare to suggest that the Garda Síochána failed to do everything in its power to bring the guilty to justice. You, Fintan, will step down from being in charge of this investigation immediately."

"Who'll take over?"

"An excellent question. And one with a simple answer. You see, in these circumstances, what we need is a bastard. An utter bastard. The kind of bastard who would turn in his granny for nicking sweeties. One who would happily walk over the flaming corpses of his brothers and sisters in uniform to get a result."

"You don't mean ..."

Ferguson grimaced and patted himself down instinctively, in search of a cigar he did not have. "I do. Our friend from Limerick. A man who would lose a popularity contest against syphilis but who nobody – *nobody* – is going to suggest is a team player."

"I feel obliged to point out, sir, that I'm fairly sure McGarry and that individual have a bit of history."

"How so?"

"I'd rather not say, sir."

"And I'd rather not have a lunch featuring tofu sitting on my desk and waiting for my return. To quote the bard, life is shit. Now, what history?"

"I believe McGarry pantsed him, sir."

Ferguson looked genuinely flummoxed. "I'm sorry, he what?"

"He pulled down his pants."

"When?"

"On the day they both graduated from Templemore. At least, that's the story I heard."

Ferguson shook his head and looked at the ground. "I can't believe I give some of these people access to firearms. It's like being the class prefect in *Porky's* fucking *Revenge*."

"Gladstone, over in Galway, is an excellent—"

"No," said Ferguson. "It will be our friend from Limerick. He and McGarry not getting on is perfect. Let's give the man his chance at sweet vengeance, because make no mistake about it, McGarry's own pants are down and his bollocks, my friend, are blowing in the wind."

# ALCOPOPS

Bunny awoke to a pounding noise. No, that wasn't right – two pounding noises. One appeared to be in his head, but the other was coming from an external source. They were infuriatingly out of sync with each other, as if the outside world and his hangover were conspiring against him, possibly in an attempt to produce prog rock.

He looked around. It appeared that at some point in the night he had tried to get himself to bed, but not managed to make it all the way. He had fallen asleep on his own staircase. Various parts of his body were making known their objections to this state of affairs, but at that point in time the excruciating pounding in his head was filibustering for all of his attention. It was as if someone was trying to drill through his skull in the hope of striking oil.

The second noise resumed, and increased in tempo. He could see the front door visibly shaking under the assault.

"Alright, alright, alright, I'm coming. Keep your bollocks on."

He made the mistake of running his tongue around his mouth and had to pause for a second, fearful he was about to throw up. The disgusting taste was unlike anything he had ever experienced, akin to losing a bet and having to eat a urinal cake. As he reached the bottom step, he tripped over his own discarded trousers and stumbled to the door, before opening it to reveal Detective Pamela Cassidy. His colleague and friend was standing on the doorstep, looking highly agitated.

"Jesus, Butch, I know you martial-arts types love smashing bits of wood with your bare hands, but could you not practise on my front door? Use the doorbell like a civilised human being."

Despite his weakened state, Bunny caught the look in Butch's eyes and took half a step backwards. She had the air of a woman who would delight in punching out his lights and her exquisite self-control was the only thing stopping that from happening.

"Funny you should mention that, Bunny. I've been standing here for fifteen minutes. I gave up ringing the doorbell after the first ten."

Bunny rubbed a hand over his face. "Oh. Right. Sorry about that." A thought struck him. "This isn't about Janice and Alan, is it?"

"No. She hasn't rung me yet."

"In which case, what's so fecking urgent? I was enjoying a nice lie-in."

Butch rolled her eyes. "Would you listen to yourself? Enjoying a nice lie-in? Pull the other one – I could see you through the letterbox. The only reason I haven't called an ambulance yet is that I clocked you scratching your nuts every now and then."

"This feels like a shocking invasion of privacy, Butch."

"I will invade your privacy with my boot in a minute." She looked around surreptitiously. "Now, stop being an idiot and invite me in."

Bunny opened the door fully and stepped to one side. Butch walked past him.

"And, if at any point you feel like rearranging your underwear so that it covers at least some of your genitalia, I, for one, would be delighted."

Bunny obliged as Butch walked down the short hallway and into the front room.

"Holy shit, if you were keeping a panda in these conditions, you'd have the World Wildlife Fund camped out on your doorstep by dinner time."

She had a point. The room was not looking its best. "I'm between cleaners at the minute."

"Was the last one killed by the Black Death?" Butch kicked a couple of the empty bottles sitting beside Bunny's chair in front of the TV. "Well, the good news is, if any shops are still paying for the return of empty bottles, this room will be worth a fortune."

Bunny sagged against the doorframe. "To be completely honest with you, Butch, I'm not feeling great. Is there any chance you could drop by again in the afternoon and give me this bollocking then?"

"First off, I'm afraid I have to inform you that it is already the afternoon. And secondly, no this cannot wait."

Bunny sighed. "Well, can't blame a guy for trying."

Butch narrowed her eyes and turned her head to one side quizzically. "What on earth is going on with your mouth?"

Bunny raised his hand to his face self-consciously. "What are you talking about?"

"What am I talking about? It's blue! How is your mouth blue? Have you been drinking Drano or something?"

"No, I ..." He ran his tongue around his mouth again. "I don't think so. Not unless bleach is a lot sweeter than you'd expect. My gob feels like the Honey Monster and Bertie Bassett have been shagging in it."

Butch wrinkled her nose in revulsion. "Evocative imagery as always, Detective."

"I didn't get that gig as poet laureate for nothing."

Butch leaned forward across the armchair and picked up a bottle from the floor. It was about the size of a beer bottle but its label depicted what appeared to be a Smurf riding the sun. From somewhere in Bunny's subconscious a little alarm bell of guilt tolled.

"Were you drinking alcopops last night?" Butch made no attempt to keep the disgust from her voice.

"No," said Bunny, ignoring the evidence before his eyes. "Of course I wasn't."

Butch reached down and picked up several similar-looking

bottles from the floor and held them up accusingly. "You were! You were drinking alcopops."

"For Christ's sake, woman, would you keep your voice down? I have a reputation to preserve."

"As what exactly?"

"If memory serves, I may have run out of all other options."

"How did you even have these in the house?"

Bunny ran his hand through his hair. Even his hair felt painful. How could your hair hurt? "I caught some young lads with them a couple of weeks ago. I confiscated them."

"That makes sense. I'm pretty sure nobody over the age of eighteen has ever drunk one intentionally. Well, until now, that is."

"I've been meaning to get rid of them."

Butch dropped the empty bottles on to the chair. "Mission accomplished." She waved her hands over the detritus. "Can we agree that this must be rock bottom? I mean, I know you've been playing out this Hunter S. Thompson thing for a while now, but even you must see that it's gotten way out of hand?"

With a groan, Bunny pulled himself upright and walked towards the double doors that led into the kitchen. "I'm going to get myself a drink of water, so, if you'd like to follow me, you can continue to dance on my grave in there. Sorry, where are my manners? Can I get you anything?"

Butch followed him. "Yes, please – I'll take a tetanus shot if you've got one."

"Very good. You know, some people in your position might feel inclined to go easy on a fella." Bunny considered the pile of washing-up in the sink then turned the tap to one side so he could get his mouth to the stream of water.

"I am going easy on you. By now, a lesser woman would have made a comment about the state of the back of your underpants."

Bunny leaned against the counter and belched. His mouth filled with the taste of unhappy memories. "Thanks. You're like Mother Teresa meets Chuck Norris. I've always said so."

"What did you do after training last night?"

"Seriously, I'm a little too long in the tooth to be getting my botty spanked by my mammy."

Bunny saw the genuine anger writ across Butch's face. "Just answer the bloody question."

"If you must know, I came straight home – just like I promised you I would. I was here all night like a good boy."

Butch folded her arms. "Shit. I was afraid of that."

Bunny scratched at his three-day-old stubble with both hands. "I'm not exactly at my sharpest, Butch. Would you mind filling me in on what I'm missing here?"

"Coop Hannity was murdered last night."

"Really?"

"Yes. And O'Rourke asked me to come around and officially ask you if you have an alibi."

"I'm afraid I don't. Although, Coop is not exactly a big loss. Is he?"

Butch gave an exasperated sigh. "Try not to look quite so happy about it."

Bunny shrugged. "What do you expect? Mankind hasn't had news this good since they announced they had a vaccine for polio." His eyes widened suddenly. "Is his wife OK?"

"Other than a bit shook-up. She found the bodies when she came back from visiting her da."

"Bodies?"

"Sorry. Body. The bodyguard got knocked out but he'll live. Hang on – you know Coop's wife?"

"Since she was a kid. Saw her for the first time in years when I dropped over on Monday evening."

"Speaking of which. Why were you there?"

"Private matter."

Butch put her hands on her hips and furrowed her brow. "Bunny – don't be an idiot. The man is dead. You know that won't fly."

"I was there on somebody else's behalf. I'm not at liberty to discuss it."

"Fuck's sake. Seeing as you just admitted that you have no alibi, and the authorities have some rather embarrassing footage of you leaving the corpse's abode on Monday night and acquiring without permission the man's garden gnome on your way off the premises, I'd perhaps try to come up with something better than that."

"Thank you, counsellor. I'll take that under advisement." Bunny opened the back door. "Excuse me a moment, please."

"Oh, don't mind me. I'm just here briefing a murder suspect about the investigation. I've got all the time in the world."

Bunny stepped out into his back yard. He was surprised to discover that he had some washing on the line. It consisted mainly of a couple of vests that had seen better days, and a few pairs of underpants that had seen too much. The paving stones were wet beneath his bare feet and he was not dressed for the cold March air, but the breeze did at least have the effect of clearing his head somewhat.

"Howerya, Bunny," came a female voice that he recognised instantly. Margaret Byrne, his neighbour on the left, was leaning over the fence, a cigarette dangling from her lips. "You need to get yourself a dressing gown. You'll catch your death."

Another head popped up over the right-hand fence. It belonged to Mrs Cynthia Doyle, his other neighbour, wearing her hair in curlers under a pink headscarf.

"Good afternoon, Bunny." The warm smile dropped from her face. "Margaret."

The air around Bunny grew colder still. The two women had a long-running feud – so long-running, in fact, that Bunny doubted anybody could remember how it started. It was ever-present, a constant level of passive-aggressiveness interspersed with occasional peaks of actual aggressiveness for a bit of variety.

He tried to give each woman a winning smile but his face wasn't up for it. "Apologies for my state of undress, ladies. I was just nipping out to bring in the washing."

"You'll catch your death," said Cynthia.

"That's what I said," Margaret chipped in. "He needs to get himself a good dressing gown."

Cynthia nodded her head reluctantly, conceding the point. "Actually, I have a lovely one that belonged to my Albert. He's not using it any more, God rest his soul, so you're welcome to it. He was a smaller man than yourself, but it was always very big on him."

"Thank you very much for the kind offer, but I have one already. It's just in the wash."

Bunny was fairly sure he did indeed have a dressing gown, although the chances of it being in the wash were remote. Odds on it could do with it, though. Still, wherever it was, it seemed a better option than a dead man's hand-me-downs.

"You would want to be taking better care of yourself, though, Bunny," advised Margaret. "I'm going to drop round a casserole."

"I'll do you another one of those lasagnes you like," offered Cynthia.

"Lasagne," said Margaret, derision dripping from her voice. "Would you hark at her ladyship and her fancy foreign food."

"Oh, here we go. Don't go getting all offended just because Bunny has a more sophisticated palate on him than you do."

"Sophisticated palate, my arse. You're only getting pretentious 'cause you can't do a basic decent coddle."

Coddle was what Dubliners – "proper Dubliners" – called stew. It was like a shibboleth for those whose blood ran truly navy blue. Back in his early days in the capital, Bunny had made the mistake of saying it was just stew. For his trouble he had got a clip around the ear from an eighty-year-old. It was different to stew, although nobody could explain how.

"Shows what you know, Margaret Byrne. My coddle is the talk of the town. The parish priest loves it."

"Yes," said Margaret. "Did you hear he was in hospital again? They don't know what it is yet."

"It has nothing to do with my coddle. I'll tell you that for nothing."

Bunny held up a hand. "Sorry to interrupt, ladies, I just need a moment to ..." He turned around and did what he had come out to do because he simply couldn't hold it in any longer. That's to say, he threw up down the drain.

"Jesus!" exclaim the ladies in unison.

"Are you OK?" asked Margaret. "You've not been eating badly prepared Italian food, have you?"

"You keep talking, Margaret Byrne, and I'll come over there and give you something to be sick about."

"You're all mouth. By the time you get halfway here you'll be retreating, just like the Italian army."

Bunny wiped a hand across his mouth. "Apologies, ladies, I'm not feeling the best. Now, there's no need to fall out and, please, let's leave the Italian army out of this. They've had a bad run of it over the years."

With a wave, Bunny turned and headed back inside. The last thing he heard was Cynthia Doyle speaking in a stage whisper. "God, how was it blue?"

Inside the kitchen, Butch was leaning against the counter. "Did you just—"

"Yes," said Bunny, "I did, and it has done me a power of good. Before I forget ..." He reached into a jug on the windowsill and took out a set of keys, which he handed to her. "Save you booting the door in next time."

Butch went to say something but stopped. She noticed that "B's place" was written on the tag in Gringo's distinctive handwriting.

Bunny picked up the remains of a sliced bread from the counter and sniffed it warily. "It'll do." He turned to her. "I'm having myself a cheese toastie. Do you want one?"

"You threw up, like, thirty seconds ago."

"I know. Cleared a bit of room. Now I'm gonna put down a solid foundation to see me through the rest of the day. So, do you want one or not?"

"I'm alright, thanks."

"Suit yourself."

"Look," said Butch. "We need to talk about —"

Bunny opened the fridge and removed a block of cheese that was about the size of a small suitcase.

"What on earth is that?"

Bunny dropped the slab onto the counter heavily and looked over his shoulder at his colleague. "What? Have you not seen cheese before?"

"Yes, I am familiar with cheese. I just didn't know that you apparently own all of it. What in the hell are you doing with that much cheese?"

"As it happens, I won it off a fella in the pub."

"How exactly?"

"It was a bet about how much cheese one man could eat," said Bunny with a grin. "Not for the first time in my life, I exceeded expectations."

"Congratulations. You're now the proud owner of the EU cheese mountain."

"You should have seen how big it was when I got it. Took me ages to get it down to a size that could fit in the fridge. My diet has been rather cheese-based recently."

Butch made a retching face. "Wow. If you listen carefully, you can hear the sound of your arteries screaming."

Bunny held up a finger and cocked his ear. "No. All I can hear is two women who should know better, arguing about Italian food." He looked along the counter. "Where the hell is my big cheese knife?"

"Maybe it went all *Fantasia*, grew legs and danced out. I can't say I'd blame it."

Bunny stuck out his blue tongue at Butch and started to open drawers. "I must have another one somewhere."

"Seriously. Forget about the bloody cheese. This is serious."

"No, it isn't. I didn't kill anybody. I know I didn't kill anybody. You know I didn't kill anybody. Even DI O'Rourke must have a fairly good idea that I didn't kill anybody."

Bunny pulled a clean butter knife out of a drawer and held it up in triumph before turning back to his massive block of cheese.

"And, while, not unlike this implement, I'm not the sharpest knife in the drawer, even I wouldn't nick a guy's gnome then go back the next night and kill him. I mean, I don't want to brag, but I've been around enough investigations to avoid making such an obvious mistake."

Butch leaned forward and punched him on the arm.

"Ouch! What the feck was that for?"

"Do you think I'd be here if this wasn't serious? Laugh it off all you want but they're taking it seriously enough. They've brought in somebody to take over the investigation. O'Rourke is stepping aside. If you've been dismissed out of hand as a suspect then they wouldn't be doing that, would they? Oh, and you didn't hear this from me, but apparently, Hannity's been recording all of his meetings for years, so your chat with him is about to become evidence."

Bunny turned from hacking ineffectively at his cheese monolith. For the first time, he looked at Butch with actual concern in his eyes. "Really?"

"Yes, really, you big, cloth-eared idiot. Assuming it isn't on one of the tapes that we think the murderer swiped. And if it *is* on one of those, well, that's bad for other reasons."

Bunny scratched his head. "Right. Yeah, that's not great."

That's what I've been trying to tell you."

"Who've they brought in to take over the investigation?"

"I don't know him," said Butch. "Well, other than by reputation. O'Rourke's asked me to pick him up from the train. I'm heading straight there. It's the guy from Limerick who turned in those three guards for fixing speeding tickets."

Bunny dropped the knife on the counter loudly. "Marshall?"

"I take it you know him?"

Bunny sighed heavily. "You could say that."

Butch arched an eyebrow. "Is there anything I should know?"

"Yes. If there's a man in existence who wants to put me in jail, it's Tommy bloody Marshall."

# MEET THE NEW BOSS

Butch was trying to keep an open mind about DI Thomas "not Tom" Marshall. She had tried not to form an opinion when she'd picked him up from the train station and, after a grunt of acknowledgement, he'd handed her his suitcase to carry back to the car. She had tried not to form an opinion when he'd got into the back seat and had her drive him to the Hannity residence as if she were a taxi driver and not a detective in the Garda Síochána. She had even tried not to form an opinion on the man when she realised why he looked so familiar: it was as if somebody had made an extra Baldwin brother out of bits of the Baldwin brothers that nobody wanted. The effect it yielded was peculiar – even though each of the man's features was fine when taken in isolation, they somehow combined to make a highly punchable face. His hair was gelled efficiently into place and, although he looked as if he was in decent shape, there was something overly jowly about him. Despite all of this, Butch was not allowing herself to form an opinion.

He was capable of human speech. She'd heard him give one of the guards on duty outside the house a dressing-down when the officer had failed to ask to see his ID. He really seemed to enjoy showing people his ID. Technically, he was in the right, but the guard had probably assumed that Detective Pamela Cassidy wasn't bringing in a tourist for a gawp around. Mind you, perhaps DI Marshall was confused by the fact that his taxi driver was being given free rein at a crime scene.

Marshall listened in silence as Butch and Detective Carlson took him around the property and essentially gave him the same briefing as she'd given O'Rourke earlier in the day. His eyes lit up when he watched the CCTV footage of Bunny waving the gnome around like an idiot. Butch really liked Bunny, and considered him a close friend, but right there and then, she felt as if she could slap him around the head until the cows came home.

"And, as per DI O'Rourke's instructions," she concluded, "we've arranged for two uniformed gardaí to be stationed outside the late Mr Hannity's little video library for now, subject to other measures being put in place at a later date, and until the DPP has determined what we can and can't do with the tapes."

Marshall nodded. It seemed to be his go to move. He studied the pad in his hand, on which he'd been taking copious notes. Both Butch and Carlson stood there awkwardly as he flipped back a few pages and started to reread his scribblings while chewing on the end of his pencil. After about two minutes he looked up. "Who was in charge of the fruitless search conducted outside the property for the murder weapon?"

"Ehm," said Carlson. "That would be me, sir."

Marshall nodded again. "I see. Could you both come with me."

It was not a question. He turned around, walked back up the path and led them through the house. He exited through the front gate, turned right and started to walk back up the cul-de-sac. When they reached the main road he turned left and strode forward with purpose. He stopped outside a house where extensive building work was being carried out, although at that moment the only sign of activity was four builders sitting around the radio and drinking tea while listening to a horse race. They had driven past it on the way in.

On the road in front of the house was a skip. Marshall stopped beside it. "Can you tell me what you see, please, Detective Carlson?"

Carlson looked like a dog that knew he was about to be hit but didn't know quite what for. "It's a skip, sir."

"That is correct. Have you observed anything else about it?"

"It's empty, sir."

Butch noticed that they had attracted the attention of the builders.

"Again," said Marshall, "I cannot fault your basic observation skills. However, your data interpretation does leave something to be desired."

Butch was painfully aware of what Marshall was getting at, but she reckoned he was the type that would deliberately make it worse for Carlson if somebody else tried to help him. Despite this, she found herself mentally repeating the answer, over and over again, in the hope that Carlson might somehow pick it up telepathically.

He didn't. He stood there with his mouth open, gradually becoming sweatier and sweatier, to the point where he looked as if, given enough time, he might melt away entirely. Marshall continued to look at Carlson for an uncomfortably long period, like a meal he was about to send back, before he eventually turned his eyes to Butch.

She felt bad for Carlson, but all she could do now was move this on as quickly as possible. When you're having a nightmare, the best thing that can happen is for it to end. She turned to the builders. "Sorry, lads, was your skip emptied recently?"

"Yeah," said the one in a Manchester United jersey. "It got taken away first thing this morning. Why?"

A groaning noise John Carlson had never intended to be audible escaped from his person as the realisation hit him. Butch glanced in his direction and tried to look supportive.

"Sorry, Detective Inspector. I'll get on this right away."

Without another word, DI Marshall started walking back towards the Hannity residence.

For the second time that day, Butch found herself in the presence of a man who appeared to be about to throw up. "Don't worry about it, John," she whispered. "He's just ..."

Marshall, without turning around, raised his voice. "Carlson, with me, now."

"Quick, fella," shouted one of the builders. "Your mammy's calling you in for tea."

Amidst the uproarious laughter from the other three, Butch moved forward and gave them a smile. "Very funny. Now, who here would like to be the first to get his road tax checked?"

The laughter died off quickly.

Butch turned and watched John Carlson catch up to Marshall as the DI power-walked away from him. In that moment, she finally allowed herself to form an opinion on the man. He was a massive arsehole.

# TROUBLE'S DAWNING

Bunny's hangover was starting to clear, but his mood was only getting darker. He was sitting in his front room, staring at the TV that wasn't on. It had been a couple of hours since Butch had come to visit him. Enough time for his brain to have belatedly started to process things.

Coop Hannity's death, while no great tragedy, was bad news for him. In fact, the more he thought about it the worse he realised it was.

He and DI Tom Marshall had a history. Marshall was a good copper, but he was also not above bearing a grudge. It wasn't as if he was going to set up Bunny, but he certainly wasn't going to do him any favours. The problem was, given some of the wrinkles in this particular situation, Bunny was going to need a favour.

If what Butch said was true, and Hannity had indeed been recording all of his conversations, including the one he had with Bunny, then there was no way he'd be able to keep Gringo's situation a secret. Questions would be asked. The very thing Bunny was keen to avoid.

There was something else. He had that sickly feeling, like something was scratching away at the back of his brain, trying to get his attention, but it was somehow out of reach. And whatever it was, he was willing to bet it was bad news. That was just the kind of day he was having.

Mixed in with his concern about the situation was a healthy dollop of self-loathing. He had laughed off Butch's jibes at the time, but as he looked around the room now he saw it through her eyes. He needed to pull himself together, and fast. Gringo's memory, his own reputation, and who knows what else was hanging in the balance, and here he was, dragging himself upright after another knockdown night of messy, self-indulgent drinking. He wasn't just hurting himself now. There was a real danger that damage would be done to others too. Gringo's memory deserved better. Even Diana Spain deserved better.

He got to his feet. He needed to move. He needed to try to get his brain into gear and finally start thinking. First things first, though – a bit more food. He walked through to the kitchen where he discovered he'd forgotten to put the big block of cheese back in the fridge. Lacking any other supplies, he had the core ingredients for another cheese toastie and nothing else. Along with whatever else he had to do today, he made a note that he needed to do some shopping and buy some actual food. He might also want to find a better home for the rest of the cheese.

Butch's diatribe about the dangers of excessive dairy consumption had also hit home. She was a good friend; maybe he should start listening to her more. Quite aside from anything else, he didn't have that many good friends left. He should stop driving away the ones he had.

He looked down at the cheese. The best course of action would be to give it away to the neighbours. Half to Mrs Byrne, half to Mrs Doyle. The last thing he wanted was to look as if he was showing favouritism to one side or the other – that would only lead to six months of reprisals, recriminations and inedible lasagne.

He slapped his hands together. "Right so, while I've enjoyed our time together, I'm afraid it's time I split you in two and we start to see other people."

Bunny scanned the counter. All he could lay his eyes on was the butter knife he'd used earlier. It would be entirely ineffective at carving the slab of cheese in half. What he needed was the big knife. He looked in the sink, peeked under some errant crockery from around the kitchen and filled half a bin bag with rubbish. The knife was nowhere to be seen.

"Where the hell are you? You can't have just ..."

And there it was. The itch.

A horrible feeling that was nothing to do with the after-effects of alcopops hit Bunny in the pit of his stomach. He immediately fished his phone out of his pocket and dialled.

Butch was fiddling with the radio, trying to find something upbeat. She wasn't great at being a passenger. She was also aware that if she was the one driving and somebody else was messing with the radio, it would be getting on her last nerve. Still, John Carlson had the air of a man who was on his way to his own funeral and, try as she might, she was really struggling to cheer him up. She had never been great at the cheerleading rah-rah positivity stuff. It just wasn't in her nature.

Carlson was on his way to the head offices of Wallace Recycling, the company they had determined, after an infuriatingly long time, was responsible for the skip that had been removed from outside of the house near Coop Hannity's earlier that morning. He was dropping Butch back at the station en route, as Marshall wanted her to be second chair on the interview with Coop's wife. Butch didn't take it as any kind of compliment, but rather a reflection of the long-held belief amongst coppers that a woman was more likely to open up to another woman. Personally, Butch thought the idea was spectacularly overrated and outdated thinking. However, because it got her to where the action was, she was prepared to live with this particular piece of prehistoric thinking. Plus, it meant she wouldn't be spending her day dumpster-diving.

"I am so dead," said Carlson for about the fourth time.

"Oh, for God's sake, John," replied Butch. "You made a mistake.

Everybody does it from time to time. Loads of people probably wouldn't have picked up on the skip either."

"You did."

"I'm a woman," said Butch, trying for levity. "We are genetically programmed to notice other people's mistakes. Have bad sitcoms taught you nothing?" She fired a grin at him, but she might as well have been trying to put out a forest fire with a water pistol. Nothing seemed to permeate the dark cloud enveloping Detective Carlson.

"I'm still on probation on the team. You saw how angry Marshall was. I'm going to get booted for this. I mean, who loses a murder weapon?"

"Alright, let's just get a grip here, shall we? You didn't lose a murder weapon. You didn't check a possible dumping site. Let's not get carried away. I mean, look at it this way—"

Butch was interrupted by her phone ringing in her pocket. She was glad for the disturbance as she had no idea where she was heading with her last-ditch attempt to cheer Carlson. Once she'd looked at the screen, however, her temporary moment of happiness dissipated. Bunny McGarry.

She considered letting it go to voicemail, but then she thought about having to play the message for DI Thomas Marshall. She answered the call.

"OK, Bunny. Before you say anything, I need to inform you that I, and the rest of the investigation team, have been instructed not to communicate further with you regarding our current case, or anything else for that matter."

Carlson turned to look at her, causing the car to veer slightly. Butch glared at him and jabbed a finger at the windscreen to give the strong suggestion that that was where he should direct his attention.

"Fair enough," said Bunny. "I just need to know one thing."

"Look, Bunny, I've already explained – I can't say anything. I need to hang up the phone now. I'm sorry, but you understand why."

"Alright. No problem at all. You don't need to say anything – just listen. I need to know how Coop Hannity died. I'm going to list some methods, and when I say the right one, just hang up the phone. OK?"

Butch said nothing.

"What's he saying?" asked Carlson.

Butch covered the phone's mouthpiece with her hand. "He's asking if you know where he can rent a skip?" She felt bad for saying it, but Carlson was really getting on her nerves.

"OK," said Bunny. "I'll take it you're on board. Was he shot?"

Butch did nothing.

"Was he drowned?"

"Beaten to death?"

"Died of boredom?"

"Stabbed?"

Butch hung up.

Bunny sat there and looked at the phone in his hand, then at the back door he never bothered to lock, then back at the phone.

"Oh shite."

# THE WIDOW'S WORDS

Butch hated this. The silence. She had never been good with silence. Somebody – anybody – needed to say something. It was beginning to remind her of the last date she'd been on. An utter disaster. The woman had turned up late – a pet peeve of Butch's – and then, over her starter, had proceeded to explain how the police were the jackbooted thugs of the establishment, whose only purpose was to keep the population in their place. After that, the conversation had rather dried up. It was also the reason Butch now had a firm and fast rule about never being set up on a blind date ever again.

This might not be a date, although she was sitting opposite an attractive woman. Angelina Hannity was not what she'd been expecting. A younger woman married to an older, richer man – well, the mind has a tendency to fill in quite a few gaps there. Angelina didn't seem to fit between those well-defined lines and Butch silently admonished herself for falling into such lazy thinking. As somebody forced to carry the weight of more than their fair share of grating stereotypes, she should be better than most at keeping an open mind.

Angelina Hannity appeared to be possessed of a sharp mind and, despite the best efforts of the man sitting beside Butch, she had shown herself not to be someone who was easily intimidated. Butch caught her eye for the fourth time, and for the fourth time they both looked away awkwardly. Seeing as they were sitting in an interview room, their problem was that the choices of places to look was really very limited.

Jonathan Robinson, who had been Coop Hannity's lawyer and was now representing his wife, cleared his throat purposefully. The look on his face made it clear that he had had his fill of silence too. "Will this be much longer, Detective Inspector Marshall? My client has had a traumatic and exhausting day, as I'm sure you appreciate. So, if we have covered everything ..."

Butch glanced at Marshall, who didn't look up from his A4 pad of notes as he raised a finger. Robinson looked at Butch, who resisted the urge to shrug.

After what felt like a very long minute, Marshall dropped his pad. "Apologies for that. As I'm sure you appreciate, it's vital to ensure that we've covered everything."

Robinson bent down and picked up his briefcase. "Of course. Do let me know if you require anything further."

"Oh, I'm sorry," said Marshall. "You've misunderstood. We are not finished."

Robinson glared at Marshall over his briefcase before slowly lowering it to the floor again. Seeing as they had already gone through Angelina Hannity's movements on the night before in great detail – three times – Butch was fairly confident that if the DI started another sentence with the words "Please take me back to ..." he would be finishing it with the hands of one of Ireland's most highly paid lawyers wrapped tightly around his neck.

Marshall favoured Angelina with a smile. "Mrs Hannity, as far as you are aware, did your late husband have any enemies?"

Angelina gave a bitter little laugh.

"My client," interrupted Robinson, "as I believe I mentioned previously, had absolutely nothing to do with the running of her late husband's business. She has no knowledge of who he was dealing with."

Marshall tapped his pen on the table. "May I ask about your reaction to the last question, Mrs Hannity?"

"My reaction?" said Angelina.

"Yes. You laughed."

"Actually," said Robinson, "for the benefit of the tape, I would characterise it more as a sigh of exasperation."

Marshall shrugged. "Very well. Can I then ask—"

"I reacted that way, Inspector, because, respectfully, it seems like a rather silly question. The man was stabbed to death. Describing him as universally loved would be really pushing it, don't you think?"

Butch tightened her lips to avoid a smile slipping by.

"Yes. Point taken. Still, may I ask if he had any enemies in particular that you were aware of?"

"As Mr Robinson has already pointed out, I had nothing to do with my husband's business. However, I know what he did and I'm sure that didn't make him a popular man. In fact, weren't there a couple of attempts on his life previously? He always kept the details from me."

"He probably didn't want to worry you." Marshall took a note, continuing to write as he spoke. "I believe your husband carried out most of his meetings at home?"

"Yes. Mostly."

The DI looked up. "Mostly?"

"He did leave the house from time to time."

"And where did he go?"

Angelina folded her arms. "I have no idea. My husband did not discuss his business with me."

"But presumably, if he had most of his meetings at home, you would have seen people coming and going?"

She shrugged. "The doorbell would ring but I was told to ignore it, and I did. People came and went but I took no notice of it."

"I see. And yet, when Bernard McGarry rang the doorbell, you met him?"

"Excuse me?" said Angelina, looking momentarily confused. "Do you mean Bunny?"

questions you have, we can deal with them tomorrow, when she's had a chance to get some sleep."

Marshall kept his eyes on Robinson but spoke to Angelina. "Are you returning home, Mrs Hannity?"

She nodded.

"Well, in that case, I should inform you that the bunker in the back garden will be under police guard, and —"

Angelina's brow furrowed. "The what where?"

She continued to look utterly mystified as Marshall briefly explained about the tapes.

Despite the DI's instructions beforehand, Butch decided to speak up. "Did you go out to the back garden much, Angelina?"

Angelina looked at Butch for a second then shook her head. "To be honest with you, I couldn't stand those bloody pigeons. Can I ask, is there an update on Joe?"

"If you mean Joseph Stowers," Marshall said, shooting Butch a look, "Mr Hannity's bodyguard, I can tell you that, following an interview with my colleague, he has been discharged from hospital of his own volition."

"That's good, then."

Robinson placed a hand on his client's shoulder, and she stood up to leave. She made it as far as the doorway then turned around to the room. "Sorry, I'm very tired, but ... Am I right in thinking that all of the money owed to my husband – all those debts – are now owed to me?"

"Yes," said Robinson. "That's my understanding."

"In that case," she said, looking at Butch, "when you see Bunny, tell him I said that whatever debts he was worried about are written off. I owe him that much at least."

As the lawyer and his client left, Marshall looked at Butch with an excited glint in his eye. Angelina Hannity might have meant well, but Butch was pretty sure she had done Bunny no favours.

# THE IRRITATED BOWELS OF JUSTICE

The offices of O'Leary, Mensah and Goldberg Associates were on the third floor of a converted Victorian house just off the North Circular. The first two floors of the building were taken up with the administrative headquarters of a plumbing supply company. Bunny walked up the creaking stairs and was alarmed to find himself out of breath by the time he had reached the top landing. He was a man in his thirties – the prime of his life – and, not for the first time that day, the thought that some serious lifestyle changes might be called for loomed large in his mind. Of course, he had more pressing immediate concerns, which was why he was here.

This was the first place he'd come to since renting the car he'd decided he needed. He'd discovered that car hire on the day was a lot like trying to insure your house when it was already on fire – very much a seller's market. If he'd spent a bit more, he could just have bought a car.

The important thing to know about O'Leary, Mensah and Goldberg Associates at Law was that, despite the impression the name gave, it was a one-man operation – and always had been. Kofi Mensah had come to Ireland from Ghana as a three-year-old. His mother had cleaned offices at night while his father had cleaned the streets, all while raising five children. At the last count, their family tree had sprung an architect, an accountant, a psychiatrist, a chartered surveyor and a lawyer, not to mention fourteen grandchildren. A classic immigrant story.

Bunny was here to see the lawyer. The logic behind the name of the firm was that Kofi had decided he needed an O'Leary because people were wary of leaving their fates in the hands of a "foreigner", albeit one fluent in Gaelige and an expert in Irish history. The reason for the Goldberg was that prior to striking out on his own, Kofi had worked for the legendary Maurice Goldberg. Back in those days, that name meant a lot in Dublin legal circles. Maurice had gifted him the use of it upon his retirement, much like a key to the inner circle, handed down from one outsider to another.

These days, fifteen years down the line, a lot of Kofi's clients couldn't even tell you the name of the firm. Everyone just knew it as "Kofi can" – the slogan he'd had emblazoned on the snow globes he gave out to all potential clients. Bunny knew for a fact that Kofi could have moved on a long time ago and made a great deal more money, but he liked serving the community in which he'd grown up.

On top of that, when you offer the best legal defence available to the everyday Joe, nobody cares if you're a little bit on the eccentric side. Kofi was also well known for being a soft touch when it came to "negotiated payment", which was why Bunny was unsurprised to see an eight-foot-tall teddy bear in one corner of the waiting room, and what appeared to be thirty-six cans of purple paint sitting in another.

"Howerya, Louise," said Bunny.

The woman sitting behind the reception desk gave him a steely stare.

"Hello, Bunny. Is he expecting you?"

"No. I'm just dropping in on the off chance."

Louise scurried her blood-red nails on the desk. "I'm afraid he's booked solid. He's just finishing up with a client now, and then Mr Gallagher here is his last appointment of the day."

Bunny turned to the young man sitting behind him, who smiled at him nervously. Bunny shot him a broad grin in return. "Picky Gallagher, as I live and breathe. I've not seen you for a while."

Picky Gallagher was rake thin and suffered from a nervous disposition, which meant that at any given time his body was never entirely stationary – some part of it was always moving. That, coupled with the fact that there was something about him reminiscent of a cat recently dragged out of a canal, gave him the air of a man who was never destined to be one of life's big winners. He wasn't possessed of a temperament suited to stressful work either – just another of the many reasons he was such an awful thief. It was a mystery that he had managed to reach his late twenties and it still hadn't dawned on him that a change of career was called for.

Picky nodded, then shook, and then nodded his head again. "Yeah, no, yeah, Bunny. How have you been? I'm fine. How have you been?"

"I'm grand, thanks," said Bunny, taking the furthest of the two empty seats from Picky. "What have you been up to?"

"Nothing!" he said, sounding alarmed. "Nothing. Whatever you heard, I didn't do nothing."

"Glad to hear it."

Louise cleared her throat pointedly. "As I was saying, Mr McGarry, Kofi doesn't have any space today. Would you like to make an appointment for later in the week?"

Bunny held up his hands. "I know, I know, I know. He's a very busy man, but like I said, I'll just take my chances and hope for the best."

He met her glare with a smile. He could see that she was considering saying something else. Instead, she sighed and went back to typing.

Bunny smiled at Picky.

Picky smiled back nervously.

Bunny kept smiling.

Picky stood up. "Ehm, could I use your toilet, please, Mrs Mensah?"

Louise didn't look up. "I'm no longer Mrs Mensah, Picky. Remember? I explained that to you last time."

"Yeah, sorry, yeah, sorry, you did, yeah, sorry." He stood there awkwardly for thirty seconds. "Ehm, sorry, Mrs no-longer-Mensah. I still need the loo."

She rolled her eyes and pointed to the door in the far corner. "If it's a number one, you can go in there. If it's a two, you'll have to go down to the ground floor."

Picky's head bobbed up and down. "It's alright, I'm only looking for a piss." He hurried through the door and locked it behind him.

Louise looked over at Bunny again. "You'd think that given that the building is owned by a plumbing supply company, they'd be able to actually fix the plumbing."

Bunny went to say something, but Louise had already gone back to her screen.

He'd been sat there for ten minutes, leafing through a copy of *Woman's Weekly*, when the phone rang and Louise picked it up.

"O'Leary, Mensah and Goldberg ... Oh, hi, Cheryl ... What?" Louise looked at the bathroom door, then back at Picky's empty chair, and then back at the bathroom door again. "Oh, for God's sake. I thought he'd been in there a while." She moved across the room, opened the window and leaned outside. "Mr Gallagher, exactly what are you doing climbing down the drainpipe?"

"I, ehm, I, sorry. I was ... I just ... I ... fancied some air."

"Did you?" asked Louise, looking over her shoulder at Bunny.

"Don't look at me," Bunny objected. "I just sat down. Hardly said two words to the lad."

Louise leaned back out of the window. "Only, I can't help but notice, Mr Gallagher, that you're looking a bit stuck."

"Yeah, yeah. You're right," said Picky. "To be honest with you, I sort of got out here and remembered I was afraid of heights."

Before Louise could respond, there was the sound of another window being opened below.

"What the hell are you doing hanging off my drainpipe?"

"Hello, Mr Reardon," shouted Louise.

"Oh, hello, Louise. Is this fella one of yours?" He didn't sound happy.

"He's a potential client, yes. But he asked to use our toilet and may have found himself embarrassed due to its pathetically unfit-for-purpose flush capabilities."

"Here we go. For the last time, I'm going to fix it at the weekend."

"Is that right?" shouted Louise. "I'd be delighted to hear that, if you hadn't told me the same thing every week for the last six."

"I think we're getting off the point. There's a man dangling off my drainpipe. That's an AFT 20. It's a fine bit of piping, but it's not meant to handle that kind of a load. What are we going to do if he falls?"

"Well," said Louise, "I'd imagine Mr Gallagher here will sue the owners of the building, after finding himself in such a precarious situation owing to plumbing failures."

"Ah, here now – you can't go blaming this on me."

"I can. And I am."

Just then, the door to the main office opened and out walked Kofi Mensah, with a young couple trailing in his wake. The man from the couple was holding a snow globe he almost certainly didn't want.

"Rest assured, Mr and Mrs Blake, everything will be taken care of. You have my word. I will just ask Louise to ..."

Kofi noticed Louise hanging out of the window. "Is everything OK?"

"No," she snapped. "Our toilet doesn't flush properly."

Kofi laughed awkwardly and looked at the Blakes. "Well, I'm sure we can get that sorted out."

"It might be too late," Louise called over her shoulder. "It may prove fatal."

Bunny didn't need a demonstration of Kofi Mensah's prodigious negotiating talents, but the next five minutes gave him one anyway. With a warm smile and a calm voice, Kofi managed to usher the Blakes on their way, coax Louise back to her desk, persuade Mr Reardon to close his window and get on with his day, and, with the help of an eight-foot teddy bear thrown down to act as an improvised crash mat, talk Picky Gallaher through a controlled descent that

NASA would have been proud of. Having achieved all of that, he ushered Bunny into his office and closed the door.

"Detective McGarry, to what do I owe this pleasure?"

"Before we get to that – did I hear Louise say that you and her are no longer married?"

Kofi took a seat behind his desk and indicated that Bunny should take the one opposite. "That is correct, yes."

"I'm very sorry to hear that."

"Oh, do not be. Divorce has saved our marriage."

"Excuse me?"

Kofi leaned back in his chair. "We were not able to find a buyer for the house, so we still live together. In fact, because Louise's mother has had to move in with us – owing to her hip – we are sharing the same bed."

"Oh right," said Bunny. "Hang on, I've seen your house. You've got more than two bedrooms."

"That is correct. But one of the bedrooms is taken up with Louise's crocheting and sewing equipment, and the box room has my train set in it."

"Excuse me?"

"I collect model trains."

Bunny shrugged. "It takes all sorts."

"Indeed. So you see, after some rigorous negotiation, Louise and I have come to suitable arrangements on many things. It has been far easier than if we were still married. And ..." added Kofi, favouring Bunny with an exaggerated wiggle of his eyebrows, "... between us men of the world, Louise has taken to jumping me in a sexual manner at the most unusual of times. It is like living with a horny Cato from the *Pink Panther* movies."

"Right," said Bunny, entirely at a loss as to how to respond to that particular piece of information.

Kofi sat forward. "But you are not here to discuss my sex life, robust and healthy though it is. So, which of my clients is in trouble now?"

"Ehm, that would be me."

Bunny's revelation was met with raised eyebrows. "I wasn't aware you were my client."

"I find myself in need of legal representation and, as members of the legal profession go, I've always found you to be the least offensive."

"Well, obviously I am flattered. But doesn't the Garda Representative Association normally assist with such matters?"

"I'm currently on sabbatical," said Bunny. "This would be a private matter."

Kofi ran a hand over his neatly trimmed goatee. "I see. And may I ask, this matter wouldn't involve any of my existing clients, would it?"

"No."

He opened his desk drawer, took out a snow globe and placed it in front of Bunny. "In which case, I am delighted to have your business. There is just some paperwork we need to fill out."

Bunny raised his hand. "Before we get to that, I think it's only fair that I tell you what you'll be getting into."

Kofi shook his head. "That will not be necessary. It is my job to provide the highest standard of legal representation to anyone who requires it. And may I say that as members of law enforcement go, I've always found you to be the least offensive too." He beamed a wide smile at Bunny, clearly pleased with himself.

Bunny laughed. "Touché."

"Although, you did throw Darren Raker down the stairs."

Bunny rolled his eyes theatrically. "As I'm pretty sure I mentioned in court, Darren swung for me and I merely deflected the blow. What happened after that was a combination of Darren's poor balance, physics and a fair dollop of karma."

Kofi shrugged. "You may well be right. Certainly Mr Raker's defence was not helped by the fact that he is a massive arsehole."

"Are you not breaking solicitor–client privilege there, counsellor?"

"I do not believe so. Mr Raker being an arsehole is a widely known fact. If memory serves, his own mother shouted the same thing at him from the gallery as he was being taken away to serve a couple of years in Mountjoy."

"You can't win them all. Still, your admirable policy of being willing to provide a legal defence to arseholes notwithstanding, I'd still like to explain the situation before we go any further."

Kofi placed his elbows on the table and steepled his fingers.

"Right." Now that it came to it, Bunny wasn't entirely sure how to begin. He studied the wall for a few seconds and ran through his scant options. "Here's the thing: I would guess that sometime tomorrow, or possibly the day after, the Garda Síochána will be inviting me in for a voluntary interview about the murder of James 'Coop' Hannity."

Kofi did an admirable job of keeping any surprise from his face.

"I don't need to tell you," Bunny continued, "that, technically, I can decline to help them with their enquiries. I say technically because, although I'm on sabbatical, I'm still a guard. So, me not wishing to cooperate – well, it would look dreadful. My legal rights aside, I can't not go – not if I still want to have a future in the Garda Síochána afterwards." He shifted in his seat nervously. "The thing is, there are questions I'm not willing to answer, so I can't attend an interview."

"I see," said Kofi, furrowing his brow. "That is a problem."

"Yes. I—"

"You don't have to explain your reasons to me."

"Actually, I do. You see, I met with Hannity the night before he died. We discussed an issue in relation to a friend of mine that, if it became public knowledge, would be disastrous for this friend."

"Would this information not come out in the end, anyway?"

Bunny bit his lip. "Maybe it will, but I'm hoping it won't. I'm hoping to buy a little time. The thing is, I'm ninety-nine percent certain somebody is trying to frame me for Hannity's murder."

This time Kofi did not attempt to hide his shock.

Bunny looked him directly in the eyes. "I know you can't ask this question and you don't want to know the answer, but ..." He leaned forward. "... I didn't kill Coop Hannity."

Kofi's voice was quieter now. "OK. For what it's worth, I believe you. Still, as someone who is about to become your legal representative, I strongly urge you to explain that to the police as soon as possible. I know you want to protect your friend but—"

Bunny shook his head. "I can't. My only course of action is to figure out who really did kill him. And fast."

Kofi drummed his fingers on the tabletop. "You do seem to be in quite the pickle. If you don't want to talk to the police, I'm not entirely sure how you're asking me to assist you. I do want to help. While you are nice enough not to mention it, I owe you a debt."

"No, you fecking don't."

"Yes, I do. We both know that if you hadn't intervened, I might not be here."

"Don't quote me on this – it alone might get me kicked out of the Gardaí – but those willing to defend the accused are an important part of the legal system. The problem with being willing to defend those individuals accused of crimes is that, occasionally, you'll come into contact with a genuine criminal. That prick who tried to slash your throat with a shiv when you couldn't get him off? It wasn't your fault. Him managing to get that into the courtroom was somebody else's monumental screw-up. You're entitled to the same protection as anyone – probably more so, in fact."

"All true, Detective," said Kofi with a smile. "Still, thank you again for slamming my client's head through that wall."

"Don't mention it."

"Still, I'm not seeing a course of action here."

Bunny shifted nervously. "It occurs to me that if I am called in for a voluntary interview, I am entitled to legal representation."

"Of course."

"However, if my legal representative happened to be unavailable at the proposed time of said interview, it would be reasonable to reschedule for a time when he was."

Kofi tilted his head. "Ah, I see. The thing is, legally, I am not allowed to lie about such things."

Bunny puffed out his cheeks. "Oh. Right."

Kofi spun around in his chair and faced the wall.

"It was just—" started Bunny, but he shut up as Kofi raised a finger.

After about thirty seconds, Bunny's soon-to-be lawyer turned back around and smiled. "Have we ever discussed my bowels?"

Bunny scratched his head. "No, funnily enough, they have never come up."

"I'm surprised. They have been quite the issue. My bowels are highly irritable."

While he was well aware that Kofi Mensah could be more than a little eccentric, Bunny was at a loss as to where this conversation had suddenly taken a turn.

"Yes," continued Kofi. "In fact, I am on a new and very restrictive diet. However, seeing as my ex-wife and I have entirely given up telling each other what to do, there is nobody to stop me from going off the rails tonight." He stood up dramatically. "This evening, I dine at the Tandoori Palace, and I do not take any of the sensible options on the menu."

"While I appreciate the effort, is this a good idea?"

"No. It is a terrible idea, but a useful one. I hope you will not be requiring my services tomorrow – I've a sneaking suspicion I may be unavailable. The next day may be touch and go as well, but if anyone enquires, I will, of course, express my heartfelt belief that I will be fine."

"Well, if you're sure?"

Kofi rubbed his hands together gleefully. "I am one hundred percent certain. God, I have missed dishes twenty-three, forty-six, and especially eighty-seven. Me and some old friends are going out on the town tonight."

Bunny stood up. "Thanks, Kofi. I appreciate it."

"Don't mention it." He lowered his voice to a conspiratorial whisper. "And rest assured that if matters become of a more urgent nature – say, for example, you are arrested – I will be there. In a nappy, if necessary."

Bunny laughed. "Now, that'd be a sight worth seeing."

Kofi extended his hand and Bunny shook it. "Welcome to O'Leary, Mensah and Goldberg." He indicated the ornament sitting on the desk. "Please enjoy this complimentary snow globe."

# BOXERS IN BRIEFS

Butch nodded her hellos to the mostly familiar faces that were gathered in the upstairs briefing room of Sheriff Street Station. As always, the heating was a feast or famine, and on this occasion it was leaning towards famine. She took a seat beside the stone-cold radiator and silently wished that she'd kept her coat on. Some of the older and smarter heads around her had done just that.

Detective Carlson was still trying desperately to locate the skip that contained the possibility of a murder weapon, and the probability of career disaster if he didn't find it. His absence meant Butch was the most junior detective in the room. It had been a long day already and there was no end in sight. She noted the clock on the wall showed 6pm, which meant she'd been on the go for over twelve hours.

In line with the procedure that DI Marshall had already outlined to her, Butch had informed him about the phone call from Bunny. Despite having followed his instructions to the letter, more or less, she was still made to feel as if she'd done something wrong. Marshall was nobody's idea of a people person.

As the last couple of seats in the room were taken, Marshall came striding into the room with DS Paschal Burke trailing in his wake.

O'Rourke entered next, and closed the door behind him. The buzz of conversation ceased as Marshall took his position at the top of the room.

"OK. For those of you who don't know, I'm DI Thomas Marshall. I have assumed command of this investigation from DI O'Rourke. Given that we are in a live-fire situation, I'll dispense with the niceties and introductions. Put simply, you do everything by the book and we'll get on fine. There will be an update on where we are, led by DS Burke and I, but before we get to that, this investigation has some unusual circumstances, as you are no doubt aware. I have already spoken to some of you directly ..." Butch endeavoured to remain stony-faced as Marshall's eyes fell upon her. "... But let me reiterate for the entire group: Every last detail about this investigation must and will remain confidential from anyone who is not in this room. That includes any and all other members of the Garda Síochána. Anyone breaks this rule and rest assured, I will do everything in my power to make sure you're not only off this case, but off this force ASAP. Any questions?"

There weren't any.

"Right, then," continued Marshall. "Forensics is ongoing, but I've just received a provisional report and it contains little we don't already know. Hannity was stabbed in the back multiple times after his bodyguard, Joseph Stowers, was incapacitated by a heavy blow to the back of the head with what has been confirmed as a fire extinguisher. We still do not have a murder weapon, possibly due to our own incompetence, but Detective Carlson is currently working to remedy that."

Butch picked up on the slightest of twitches from O'Rourke. The different leadership styles of the two men was already evident. O'Rourke was unafraid to deliver a bollocking, but he was not a big fan of public humiliation for the sake of it.

"They weren't able to pull any prints off the wall the suspect crossed twice, which is a disappointment. We're still waiting on the full autopsy." Marshall turned to Burke. "DS Burke, if you'd like to update us on your conversation with the tech bureau regarding CCTV."

Burke stood as Marshall sat. "They verified that the time stamps on the recordings are correct, which means our suspect in the balaclava did indeed enter the property from the neighbour's garden at 9:14pm and exited via the same route at 9:21pm. They can't give us definitive numbers, but they've pegged him as somewhere between six foot and six foot three. Detective Martin is now working his way back through the recordings from the past week to establish a definitive list of visitors to the property."

Burke took a step back.

"Where are we on the wife?"

Burke looked at Detective Keogh. "Vinnie?"

Keogh cleared his throat before speaking. "I went out to Cedarwood. They've got her visiting her father between 8.15pm and 9.26pm last night. Not only is there footage of her coming and going, backed up by the receptionist who was on at the time, but we also have her on tape sitting beside her father for the duration. They record everything that goes on in all the communal areas. I've also contacted the friend she said she went to visit on the way home and, so far, everything checks out."

Marshall nodded. "Moving on, where are we with the Fairchild brothers angle?"

Burke pointed at a man sitting at the front whom Butch didn't recognise. He had the look of a boxer about him – the dog breed rather than the pugilist. "DS Anglesey, who worked the original investigation, is here to bring us up to speed."

Anglesey turned awkwardly in his chair and addressed the room. "June fifteenth of last year, 999 got a call that two shots had been fired at a vehicle on Collins Avenue – from the back of a passing motorcycle. We identified the target as a vehicle containing Coop Hannity. Nobody was injured but a bullet shattered the back window. Mr Hannity was uncooperative with our investigation. We heard rumours through unconfirmed sources that Cian and Oisín Fairchild may have been behind it."

"Where did these sources come by this information?" asked Marshall.

"We heard that Hannity's people were very keen to find the Fairchilds, so despite him telling us he had no idea who was behind it, clearly he thought it was them. Apparently, they were into him for a bundle. An ill-judged expansion of their second-hand car business had resulted in Hannity owning the lot. Ten days later, we found Oisín's body in an oil drum on wasteland in Finglas. He'd been sealed in and burned alive. A particularly nasty way to go.

"And the brother?" asked DS Burke.

Anglesey shrugged. "Dead too, or, if he's got any sense, he's gotten as far away as he can."

"Did you get anything linking Hannity to the murder of Oisín?" asked Marshall.

"No. Forensics were a dead end, and despite shaking as many trees as we could, not a sniff of a witness. For what it's worth, it's been nine months now and there's been no word on the whereabouts of Cian Fairchild. The only reason we don't think he's dead is that they didn't exactly try to hide the body of the brother. Hannity was sending a message. No reason not to make it as loud as possible."

"In which case," said Marshall, "we'll be starting from scratch and trying to locate Cian Fairchild. Maybe Hannity's demise will mean he'll feel comfortable coming up for air. Either that, or he decided to come back for another go."

Anglesey nodded but his body language made it clear he didn't think either possibility was likely.

"Finally, Mrs Rita Marsh."

Burke stepped forward again. "Some of the older heads in the room might remember this one. I worked it. Truth be told, there wasn't much of an investigation to be made. Rita Marsh, an honest-to-god housewife, attacked Hannity on his way out of a dental appointment of all things. She came at him with a carving knife. He suffered some relatively minor defensive wounds. She ended up being charged with attempted murder because she made it very clear in her subsequent statements that was what she was trying to do.

"Her son, Mark, the second youngest of seven, had got himself into an awful lot of debt to Hannity. The Marsh family blamed Hannity for the lad's suicide. She was a nightmare for her legal team. Wouldn't go for a diminished responsibility defence. Wouldn't apologise. She even said, if given the opportunity, next time she'd make sure she finished the job. The case was kept away from the media by an injunction from Hannity himself. I guess he thought a mother's tears in the papers would be bad for his image."

O'Rourke chipped in. "Weren't all the sons—"

"Yes," said Burke. "All seven of them were firemen. As was the father. The word at the time was that Hannity had better pray his house never caught alight. The Dublin Fire Brigade would turn up en masse with marshmallows and sing campfire songs as they watched it burn. Probably why Hannity kept a fire extinguisher out in his back garden. Much to the chagrin of his bodyguard."

This raised a laugh from the room but Marshall glared at Burke.

The detective sergeant gave a contrite nod and continued, "Rita Marsh was sentenced to seven years. Served four. I've made the call, and myself and Detective Cassidy are popping over to see her after this."

"Anything else?" asked Marshall, looking around the room. Nothing came back. "Alright, then. We're hoping to get access to Hannity's files and tapes soon, which will no doubt throw up more suspects, but for the moment, let's work the leads we do have. And again, not to labour the point, but this investigation must remain hermetically sealed."

With that, DI Marshall got to his feet and strode straight out of the room.

The assembled officers watched him go. Not one of them had asked the question they all wanted answered, and Marshall had pointedly not addressed it directly. As soon as the DI was out of earshot, almost as one, the room looked at O'Rourke.

"Boss," said Burke. "We're not seriously looking at Bunny, are we?"

"Not my investigation, lads and lasses," he responded. "Just do your jobs. If Bunny hasn't done anything, then he has nothing to fear."

"And if he has?"

O'Rourke turned to leave too.

"I'm going to pretend you didn't ask me that, Sergeant."

# RAWK

For the second time that day, Bunny found himself trudging up several flights of stairs. Given that it seemed pretty likely he was already being framed for murder, it felt like an unnecessary karmic boot in the arse. He could really do with somebody somewhere being on his side. The closest thing he had so far was a lawyer who was willing to seriously irritate his own bowels on Bunny's behalf. It was turning into quite the day.

Having to take the stairs this time was pure bad luck. The building was nice, but the lifts were out of order owing to an electrical short. There'd been an extremely apologetic sign up that promised an engineer was on his way. Such problems were an uncommon enough occurrence that three residents were standing in the lobby complaining excitedly to each other about it. Bunny had been in enough shitty buildings in his time to know that when the lifts were out there, nobody stood around complaining. With so many stairs to climb, they simply didn't have the oxygen to spare.

It had only taken a couple of phone calls to find the person he was here to visit. He knew she lived in Rathfarnham because Angelina Hannity had told him so, and one of his old contacts had been able to give him the exact address. Mags Walsh hadn't had the easiest start in life, so Bunny was pleased to see she was now living in a nice place.

He reached the fourth floor and stood there, panting heavily. A woman in Lycra running gear pushed through the fire door. He took out his phone and pretended he was about to make a call and was not some sweaty interloper who shouldn't have been there. He'd managed to get in by tailgating a delivery driver through the main door. It wasn't that he thought Mags Walsh wouldn't want to speak to him, but experience had always shown him that it's much harder for people to avoid somebody who is standing on their welcome mat than a disembodied voice at the other end of an intercom.

Once he'd regained control of his breath and his heartbeat no longer sounded like a samba band falling down a steep hill, Bunny pushed through the fire door into the hallway. He heard the music straight away. It took a few seconds longer for him to pick up the distinct smell of weed. The music was rock – spelled R A W K. Not that Bunny considered himself a connoisseur of the genre, but it sounded like that god-awful metal from the eighties, when the bands had dropped Satan and discovered hairspray. The music he could hear now was reminiscent of Whitesnake or Poison knocking out a B-side as quickly as they could because somebody had to get to an STD clinic.

He came to a stop outside apartment 408 and, sure enough, it appeared to be the source of both the odour and the noise. A door down the corridor opened and a man in his forties emerged carrying a couple of full bin bags. Bunny stepped to one side to let him pass. His genial nod was not returned. The man shot a dirty look first at the door and then at Bunny. Clearly he was being judged guilty by association.

Bunny knocked on the door. He waited and then knocked again. Finally, when it seemed like no other approach would yield any kind of success, he started to pound on it with his fist. After a particularly egregious guitar solo, the door flew open so fast that Bunny nearly stumbled through. He took a step back as most of the doorway was now occupied by a walking showroom for what he believed was known as body art. The man standing before him had long blonde hair that could do with a wash and was, in no particular order: topless, heavily tattooed and extremely angry. None of these three things particularly bothered Bunny, although he couldn't help but be distracted by one of them.

"What the fuck do you want?"

Bunny stared the man's torso. "Do you seriously have a tattoo of an arrow pointing down to your lad with the words 'Where the magic happens'?"

"What's it to you?"

"Well, it's your body and your choice and all that, and well done on all the muscles, but if you don't want people commenting then you should maybe get yourself a T-shirt."

"Why don't you piss off before I make you piss off?"

Bunny shook his head. "I'll be honest with you, fella, I'm not sure this meet-and-greet job is playing to your strengths. Is Mags in?"

The man took this as an opportunity to flex his muscles. "Who wants to know?"

"I have to ask: did you make your boob thingies jiggle there or do they do that on their own?"

"Are you looking for a smack in the face?"

"No," said Bunny. "I'm looking for Mags Walsh. I already said that. Maybe if you turn down the music a little bit, you'll have an easier time hearing what people are saying to you. Now, could you be a good lad and go and get her, please?"

"She doesn't want to see you."

"How do you know that? You don't even know who I am."

"She doesn't do that any more."

"Right. I think we're having a bit of a misunderstanding here. I'm an old friend."

"The hell you are." The man jabbed a finger in Bunny's face. "I can spot a fucker like you a mile off."

"Have you seriously got the word 'rock' tattooed on your knuckles? I mean, that is some serious dedication. Do you not worry it will affect your chances of gainful employment?"

"You are pissing me off now."

"Well, to be honest with you, you have not made the greatest first impression either. I imagine that if we met under different circumstances, we'd be getting on like a house on fire. Like, for example, if you were wearing clothes and ..." Bunny waggled a finger at the man's chest, "... if you weren't jiggling your musclebound boobs at me in such an aggressive manner. Now, for the last time, could I speak to Mags, please?"

In lieu of an answer, Jiggly Tits drew back his right hand, clenched it into a fist and then made a pained gurgling noise. The noise was the result of Bunny ramming the side of his left hand into the man's Adam's apple. Given the fella's aggressive demeanour, Bunny had expected that reasoning with him was probably not going to work, and his attempt to throw a right hook had been as predictable and tedious as a David Coverdale lyric. God, the more Bunny thought about it, the more he realised how much he hated hair metal.

Bunny also liked to think that he didn't enjoy violence. However, if violence was on the cards, he enjoyed it an awful lot less when he found himself on the wrong end of it. That was why he dispensed a firm right hook to the man's nether regions. He didn't do it as hard as he could, but it was still hard enough to close down the magic show for a few days.

The big fella crumpled to his knees. Bunny was about to deliver a knee to the lad's face – one of his other fundamental beliefs about violence being that the best route to minimising it is to win the fight as quickly as possible – but he held off when a woman appeared in the hallway behind the now-kneeling jiggly-titted twat. While she looked very different to what he had been expecting, there was no mistaking who she was.

Bunny put down his foot and stepped back. "Mags, how are ye?"

# UP ON THE ROOF

Bunny shook his head in disbelief as he watched a young man with his whole life ahead of him go tumbling headfirst towards concrete at high speed.

"I just don't get it."

Mags laughed. "You must've seen skateboarders before, Bunny? It's not like it's a new thing. We had them when I was a kid."

"Yeah, I know." He waved a hand at the quartet of men in their early twenties who were taking turns at trying to hop a skateboard onto a metal handrail that bisected half a dozen stone steps five storeys below them. They were passing round a camcorder, which they were using to record their failures for posterity. "That's precisely my point. You have skateboards when you're a kid. Those lads are old enough to go to war, although given the survival instincts on display over there, I'm not sure any of them would make it past minute two in *Saving Private Ryan*. I mean, none of them are even wearing a helmet. It's like watching the qualifying rounds for the Darwin Awards."

Mags slapped him playfully on the shoulder. "I'm surprised you're not down there trying to sign them up for a boxing club."

"Oh no," said Bunny. "Been a while since I've been involved with the boxing. Besides, I'm not sure it would be ethical to recruit those lads. They seem way too keen on incurring head injuries. No, would you believe I've got my own hurling team these days?"

"Is that right? Fair play to ye."

"Yeah. The St Jude's Under-12s. We are creating quite a stir."

"Under-12s? Same old Bunny McGarry. Always keen to make sure the kids are OK. God," she said with a smile, "you have not changed a bit."

"Well, may I say, Mags – you have!"

She had too. Blonde hair streaked with pink and red flopped over sparkling eyes that heavy eyeliner accentuated, but not enough to take away from her dimpled girlish smile.

"Thanks very much," she said with a giggle. "Way to make me feel old."

"You know what I mean. Last time I saw you, you were a slip of a girl. You and Angelina, the terrible twins. Inseparable and almost indistinguishable."

She gave a rueful smile. "Jesus, yeah. I do remember us wearing the same outfits a lot. To be fair, it was me copying her. I was so shy as a kid – far too nervous to decide on a look of my own. I got there eventually."

"Indeed you did," said Bunny. "You're looking very stylish."

She blushed a little. "Same old McGarry. Always a charmer." Then her smile dropped. "Sorry again about the misunderstanding earlier."

Bunny waved away her apology. "Not at all. Don't worry about it. I was as much at fault as he was."

They both knew that wasn't the case. The shirtless tattoo exhibit – apparently called Bobby – had received exactly what he'd been asking for. Mags had intervened before things got too out of hand, although the lad had learned a valuable lesson in etiquette. She'd explained that Bunny really was an old friend as they'd both picked him up and assisted him to a sofa, where he could be alone with his tattoos and traumatised testicles.

The apartment was nice, although it could certainly have done with a clean – not that Bunny was in any position to judge. While the ashtray was overflowing with roaches, he'd been relieved to see there was no evidence of anything heavier – apart from the weights in the corner. Bobby didn't get those jiggling boobies without putting in some serious work. The front room had been particularly messy, but Bunny had caught sight of one of the bedrooms on his way out, which, surprisingly, looked five-star-hotel immaculate.

"Look," Mags said. "I know Bobby made a fool of himself, but honestly, he's a good guy. Bit overprotective, but to be honest with you, there's a lot worse things a boyfriend can be."

"Fair enough."

"You just got him on a bad day. His band were in the running for this big showcase in London, but they didn't get it."

"Oh, he's a musician?"

"Lead singer. They're good. A lot of people reckon all the grunge stuff has had its day. There's going to be a return to good time showmanship rock 'n' roll, though – like Kiss and all that."

"I'll have to look out for them. What's their name?"

"Spandex Bullet," she said, sounding rueful. "I know. Believe me, there have been an awful lot of discussions about that."

"Right."

Bunny pulled his coat tightly around him as a chill gust of wind whipped past them. Mags had sensibly decided that leaving Bobby to recover in peace from his run-in with Bunny was the best option. With the lift out of order, she'd led him up to the roof, where someone had left some worn plastic garden furniture. It was probably great up there in the summer, but in early March the wind cut through any enjoyment of watching the sunset in the distance.

Mags lit another cigarette off the butt of the last one and gave Bunny an appraising look. "So, lovely though it is to see you, I'm going to guess this isn't a social visit."

Bunny shook his head. "I'm afraid not."

"I'm glad it's you who came over, though. I got a call from a Detective McGrath earlier. I guess because I saw Angelina last night when," she paused momentarily, "y'know, it happened – they just need to confirm her alibi." Her face blanched. "Jesus, when you say it like that."

"I wouldn't worry about it. It's just routine." He shifted in his chair. "Although, to be completely honest with you, Mags, I'm not here as a guard. I'm actually on sabbatical at the minute."

"Oh. Right."

"This is a personal thing. I saw Angelina a couple of nights ago, while I was dropping in to see her husband." He tried to find the best way of putting it. "I'd no idea she was back in Dublin."

"Yeah, she sort of snuck back in, to be honest with you. Didn't want a lot of people knowing. Things ended up going badly over in Milan. And her dad was taking a turn for the worse by then."

"Sorry to hear that. She did mention he wasn't great."

Mags sighed and looked at the ground. "Yeah, it's pretty brutal. I mean, you know he always had issues, but he's got a lot worse. It's shocking to see. Poor man's mind is almost gone. Sometimes he doesn't know who he is or where he is."

"Have you seen much of him?"

She looked up, as if surprised by the question, and then turned her head away. "Oh no. No. Just what Angelina tells me. She goes to see him once or twice a week, and she normally drops over here on the way back and we go for a drink. She doesn't get to see many people."

"It's good that you're both still so close."

"Yeah," agreed Mags. "She's been a very good friend to me. Helped me out with this place and with college." She raised her chin with a look of brittle pride. "Would you believe I'm studying make-up now? Doing it at night. I've got a gig on a movie over the summer. Getting my foot in the door."

"That's fantastic. You were always a very smart girl."

"I don't know about that. Fuck knows I made enough stupid decisions over the years, but thanks to Angelina, I'm getting myself back on track now."

Bunny had his suspicions about what Bobby had presumed he

had turned up at the apartment for, but it wasn't his place to ask. Thankfully, it seemed to be in the past now.

"Even as kids, the two of you were always good for each other."

She laughed. "Oh, I don't know. We had some bad ideas too. I could show you a few haircuts."

Bunny smiled. "I guess I'm just lucky. I hit on the perfect hairdo early and I know a bloke who does it for a fiver."

"A fiver?" she said with a mock gasp. "And they wonder why men have all the money."

They both looked down as a particularly large *ohhhh* attracted their attention to the steps five storeys below, where a grown man had bestraddled a railing.

"Jesus!" said Bunny.

As the guy managed to walk off gingerly, other members of the skateboard crew applauded.

"They should send the tape of that one into one of those TV programmes," said Mags. "*You've Been Framed*, or something like that. It'd be worth a fair few quid."

"Take it from me, nothing is worth that."

The rotation of dodos jumping off the cliff resumed below.

Bunny couldn't think of a segue, so he decided to be direct. "Have you spoken to Angelina since it happened?"

Mags nodded. "Yeah. Briefly." She turned to look directly at him. "She's very upset, obviously."

"I'm sure she is. I believe she found the body."

"Yeah." Mags stood up and took a drag on her cigarette. "Are we allowed to talk about this?"

He looked up at her. "Absolutely. Why wouldn't we be?"

"It's just ... If you don't mind me asking, Bunny – what's your interest here?"

"'Tis a fair question. I'll be honest – I'm worried about Angelina, and I'm worried about myself."

"Yourself?" she sounded shocked. "Why would you be worried about yourself?"

Bunny watched the red sun setting over the flats in the distance for a moment before he spoke again. "I went to see Coop the night before last and now he's dead. Doesn't look great."

"Oh, for fuck's sake, Bunny. Coop Hannity had more enemies than anybody else on the planet. The man was a pure bastard." There was a real venom in her voice now.

"I know they say you're not supposed to speak ill of the dead," said Bunny, "but it's hard to disagree with that. How was he with Angelina?"

Mags shifted her gaze away. "Oh, you know – marriages. None of them are ideal."

Bunny said nothing, giving the last statement some air.

"Yeah, OK," she conceded eventually. "It wasn't great."

"How exactly?"

Mags flicked away her cigarette and folded her arms. "Who am I talking to here?"

Bunny got her meaning. "Just me, Mags. Just me. I'm not sharing anything with anybody else – I'm just trying to figure out what's going on. You know I'd never do anything to make life awkward for either of you. You have my word."

Mags bit her lower lip nervously and, for a moment, it was like the fourteen-year-old girl was standing in front of him again. She closed her eyes and sighed. "I know. I'm sorry. You've never been anything but good to me."

He was alarmed to see tears forming in the corners of her eyes. "Here now," he said in a soft voice, "there's no need for that."

"Sorry," she mumbled as she turned away and took a tissue from the pocket of her coat. "It's just been such a weird day with all this horribleness."

She dabbed at her eyes for a moment before surprising Bunny by turning around and moving her chair to face him directly. She sat down with a look of determination in her eyes.

"OK," she began. "I don't know what's going on, but just in case Angelina is in trouble, I wouldn't trust anybody else to help. Here's the truth: when Angelina came back to Dublin she was in all kinds of shite. She owed some bad people a lot of money. She'd been living a lifestyle she couldn't afford, some things had gone badly, she was coming out of a disastrous relationship and, like I said, her dad, God love him, really is in a bad way. In answer to the question everybody asked when they saw her and Hannity: how does a man like him end up with a woman like her? Well, she was desperate, and the one thing Coop Hannity knew how to do is take advantage of that."

She pulled a packet of cigarettes out of her pocket and instinctively offered Bunny one. He waved it away. It was just as well, as the packet only contained the one, which she lit in a fluid motion. After taking a drag she continued. "Hannity decided he wanted a son. Not a kid, mind you, but a son to take over his empire." She stretched out her hands to emphasise the grandiosity of the statement. "I don't know. Maybe it dawned on him that one day he might die too. Although I'm guessing he was an atheist – as, if he wasn't, he should have been a lot more concerned about where he was headed after his death."

"You don't seem to be the man's biggest fan?"

She gave a caustic huff. "He was awful. Not just in the ways you already know he was awful, but the way he treated her. Like she was a horse he'd purchased just to breed. She had to have a fertility check before they got married. Very romantic." Mags took another drag on her cigarette. "Although that turned out to be bitterly ironic."

Bunny tilted his head. "You mean ..."

"Yeah. Turned out the prick had chronically lazy swimmers."

"Oh."

"And then he treated Angelina like it was somehow her fault. Much to her relief, they stopped trying. On the downside, though, he became insanely jealous instead. Had her followed. His own wife. It's not like she was able to go out much, anyway. He didn't like her having friends."

"At least she had you."

"Yeah," said Mags with a firm nod. "It didn't matter how appallingly rude he was to me, he wasn't going to drive me away. Although eventually, Angelina just came to see me here. Couldn't stand the hassle of him being a prick if I dropped over. And now she's not even able to go to the gym, poor girl." She sat back in her chair. "Well, I guess she is now – although maybe not, after what happened."

"What do you mean?"

Mags gave an almost imperceptible shake of her head. "Horrible thing. Somehow Coop got it into his thick head that Angelina was having an affair with her personal trainer. I remember her sitting on my sofa in tears telling me about it. It didn't even make any sense – she only ever saw Marcus while she was at the gym. In a gym full of people, mind you. What the hell did he think was going on?" She looked into the distance. "I think he just wanted to send her a message. Show her how much control he had. They roughed the poor guy up something horrible, for no reason at all."

"Christ," said Bunny.

"I know. Pure nasty."

"What gym was this?"

"Paragon Fitness. Up on the Quays. Fancy place, of course. Angelina wanted me to join with her, but I can't be doing with that kind of thing."

Bunny was about to ask another question, but they were both distracted by a scream from below. They looked down to see one of the skateboarders rolling around in agony, clutching at his shoulder.

"Jesus," said Bunny. "Looks like the gobshite has broken his collarbone."

Mags sucked at her teeth. "Oh God, that's horrible."

They watched as his friends helped him delicately to his feet then Mags checked her watch. "Look at the time. I'm sorry, Bunny, but I've got college tonight. I need to get a move on. You know what the traffic's like." She stood up and Bunny mirrored her actions.

"No worries. I don't want to keep you. Can I ask you a favour, though?"

"Of course."

He reached into his pocket, pulled out a pen and a piece of paper and wrote his mobile number on it. "Could you pass this on to Angelina? I could really do with talking to her."

Mags looked at it and then tucked it into her pocket. "Sure. No problem."

Bunny clapped his hands together to warm them. "It was great to see you, though."

"Likewise."

He held out his arms and she walked into the hug. Bunny noted she wore the same perfume as Angelina.

They released one another and started walking back towards the stairs.

"Seeing as we're being nosy," said Mags. "I can't help but notice there still isn't a wedding ring on that finger, Mr McGarry. What on earth is going on there?"

"Ara stop."

"Have you not met the right woman?"

Bunny sighed. "I'm afraid that's far too long a story to start now."

"Oops. Sorry."

"Don't worry about it. Let's just say that a good woman is hard to find. Bobby should get that tattooed somewhere."

Mags laughed. "I'm not sure he's got space. But I'll let him know you suggested it."

"I hope he appreciates it. The lesson, I mean. I'd imagine he wouldn't appreciate the suggestion."

"Honestly, Bunny," she said as she pushed open the door to the stairwell. "Like I said, I know he can look a bit ridiculous, but he's a good guy. I love him."

"In which case, I apologise to both of you for putting him out of action, in a manner of speaking."

This raised a cheeky smile as Mags stopped at the door that led back to her apartment. "I'm sure I can get everything working again with a little TLC." She waggled her eyebrows.

Bunny clapped his hands over his ears. "Please, please, please!" he squealed, laughter in his voice. "To me you're still a young girl. Some things I do not need to know."

# A BAKER'S HALF-DOZEN

It wasn't as if there were a set template for what a murderer was supposed to look like, but if there were, Rita Marsh would not be it. Attempted murderer, Butch corrected herself. If Mrs Marsh had been successful in her attempt eight years ago, she and DS Burke wouldn't be here. Still, when the door of the large four-bedroom house in Blanchardstown opened to reveal sixty-two-year-old Rita standing there, grey tinting her perm, wearing a "World's Greatest Granny" apron, the first word that sprang to mind was not "murderer".

DS Burke cleared his throat. "Hello, Mrs Marsh. I'm Detective Sergeant Burke."

"Detective Sergeant now, is it?" said Mrs Marsh warmly. "Congratulations, Paschal. Although the promotion seems to have made you very formal."

Burke laughed. "Sorry. I wasn't sure you'd remember me."

"Of course I do. You never forget the man who arrested you for attempted murder. Come on in."

She ushered them inside and made her way down the hallway. After closing the front door behind them, Burke and Butch followed suit. The smell coming from the kitchen was both overwhelming and spectacular. They walked in to find every available surface covered with baking trays filled with a cornucopia of treats. Almond slices, Rice Krispie cakes, brownies and, above all others, hot cross buns.

"You'll have to forgive me," said Rita, "but I'm going to have to work as we talk. One of the grandkids has a bake sale at school, and his mother is working double shifts as a nurse. Granny here offered to help out, but the problem is, once you offer your services to one grandchild, well ... I've been at this since 5am."

"It looks like it," said Burke.

"It smells amazing," offered Butch.

Rita Marsh favoured her with a warm smile. "Thank you." She wiped her hand on her apron and extended it. "Oh my God, I've completely lost my manners. Forgive me. I'm Rita."

Butch shook the woman's hand. "Detective Pamela Cassidy."

"It's good to see they finally have a few women in the detective ranks. When I first met Paschal here, was there one?" She slapped the counter. "No, I tell a lie. There was. They sent her in with you to talk to me the first time. Who was she again?"

"At the time she was Sergeant Campbell. Detective Inspector now."

Rita's eyes widened and she gave a big smile. "Is she? Fair play, Ms Campbell!" She looked at Butch. "So, let me guess, they bring you along to talk to any of the suspects who happen to be women?"

Butch nodded and smiled before she could stop herself. "They do."

Rita laughed. "They really think that just because we see somebody on the far side of the desk who also has ovaries that we're immediately going to start confessing? It is so ridiculous."

"Don't look at me," said Burke. "I only bring Butch here with me for personal protection."

"Butch? Such an awful name for a wee girl."

Butch shrugged. "My second name is Cassidy ..."

Rita rolled her eyes. "God. They're not going to die from an overdose of imagination, are they? Excuse me."

She bent down to open the oven and remove yet another tray of hot cross buns. She looked around before deciding to place it carefully on top of the fridge, the only flat surface currently unoccupied.

"I'm going to have to start sticking some of these in tins."

"We're sorry to have to intrude when you're so busy," said Burke.

"Don't worry about it. Let's say your phone call didn't come as a complete surprise."

For the first time since the arrival of the detectives, Rita Marsh stopped moving and leaned back against the counter to look at them.

"Is your husband around, by any chance?"

She shook her head. "I'm afraid Mikey had a heart attack and passed a while ago. Three months before I got parole."

"Oh God," said Burke sincerely. "I'm so sorry. I didn't know."

Rita waved away his apology. "Don't worry about it."

"So you know why we're here?" asked Butch.

"I do. Hannity is dead."

"Just to go through the formalities," began Burke, "could you tell me where you were between nine and ten o'clock last night?"

"I don't remember."

Burke sighed. "Come on now, Rita."

Instead of answering the detective sergeant, Rita turned to look directly at Butch. "I have – well, *had* – seven sons. Did they tell you that? Seven."

Butch nodded.

"People always asked me if I was disappointed not to get a girl? Like we were just keeping going until we finally got one or gave up from exhaustion. I'll be honest with you, Pamela – it is Pamela, isn't it?"

"Yes."

"I thought so, but my memory isn't what it was. I used to be great with the names, if I say so myself. You have to be. Seven kids – that's seven sets of friends, seven sets of teachers, and so on and so on." She leaned across to turn down her oven before continuing. "Where was I? Oh yeah, did we not want a girl? I'll be honest with you, I think it's the most spectacularly rude question I've ever been asked, and I used to be asked it a lot. I'd laugh it off, and I regret doing that now. I wish

I'd told just one person where to stick that stupid question when I'd had the chance. Do you have kids, Pamela?"

"No."

"Well, if and when you do, know this. Each one of them is special. Each one is a miracle in their own way. Love isn't a finite thing. You don't just have X amount of it and it has to be divided seven ways if you've got seven kids. Each of those kids was loved as much as if they were an only child. More, in fact. Because each of them had six brothers too and, amidst all the fights and the squabbling and the teasing, there was love there. Mountains of it. Of course, them all being boys meant that nobody called it that, but it was there all the same. You could see it when somebody from outside tried to attack one of them. It could be scary. You had to keep on top of it."

Rita looked down at a tray of shortbread biscuits and lined them up so they were perfectly symmetrical.

"The other thing that really bothered me ..." She looked at Butch, a hint of angry tears in her eyes. "And nobody ever said it directly, but it was there. It was the idea that, well, at least I had the other six boys. Like they were interchangeable or we were carrying a spare. Something like that."

Rita took a bowl from one of the cupboards, examined it, and then put it back. When she spoke again, her voice was quieter but she still avoided eye contact with the two officers. "Thou shall not kill. It sounds very simple when you say it like that, doesn't it? But if it's such an absolute, how come it doesn't count in times of war? Or, these days, in times of peace, really. War and peace used to be an either/or thing, now it seems to be much more shades of grey. Like, we can kill people if we need to. Well, take it from me, somebody needed to kill Hannity."

She busied herself opening cupboards, as if looking for something, while Burke and Butch looked at each other, trying to figure out what to say next. Eventually, Burke took a step forward and spoke softly.

"Rita, we just—"

Rita whirled around with frightening speed and jabbed a finger at him. "I know what you're here to ask me. Let me be very clear: the mistake I made wasn't trying to kill that bastard, the mistake I made was not getting the job done. If I had my time again, I'd get myself a gun. I didn't know how to do that before I went to prison, but I do now. You can't help but learn a few things inside. Girls talk. Hannity was a cancer and nobody did anything about it. How many lives? How many poor souls –" her voice cracked "– like my little Eamon did that monster destroy? Just to make a few quid? I'm glad he is dead and you should be too."

"We just need to—" started Butch.

"I know what you need to do. You need to eliminate me from your enquiries. Well," she said, straightening up, "I'm afraid I can't help you because I don't remember where I was last night. I also don't know where any of my boys were. I'm sure you can check with the various fire stations to see who was on a shift. They might be a little slow in getting back to you, though. Firemen have never been great at the paperwork. Checking on all that might slow down your investigation, I'm afraid. It might make it harder for you to catch whoever it was who rid the world of that blight. That demon." She ran her hands down her apron, as if regaining her self-control. "That's all I'm going to say, unless you'd like to arrest me?"

Butch and Burke glanced at one another before Burke shook his head. "Of course not."

"Well, then ... And for what it's worth, I appreciate you both have a job to do. You don't have to explain to me about duty. I come from a family of men who run towards fire."

"Is that your last word on the matter?"

Rita gave a firm nod. "It is. Now, if you'll excuse me, I still have a ridiculous amount of baking to do."

Butch and Burke sat in the car and said nothing for quite some time.

"Sarge?"

"Yes, Butch?"

"Rita's sons, all of them being firemen ... Isn't there still a minimum height requirement for the fire brigade?"

"I'm not sure, to be honest with you. Not that it would matter in their cases."

"Big fellas, are they?"

Burke leaned forward and turned on the ignition. "Yes, Butch. To answer your question, I'd bet they're all between six foot and six foot three."

# DINNER FOR ONE

DI Fintan O'Rourke looked down at his plate of Michelin-starred duck à l'orange and felt queasy. Le Château de Moore was one of the jewels in the culinary crown of post-Celtic Tiger Dublin, but he had little appetite. The restaurant was regularly mentioned in the society pages, as was its owner and head chef, Owen Moore. During his frequent TV appearances, much was made of his CV, having studied at the feet of some great master or other in Paris before continuing his training at blah, blah, blah, blah, blah. O'Rourke enjoyed a decent meal as much as the next man, but he had never got into the fetishization of food.

Mrs O'Rourke, on the other hand, was quite the foodie. In fact, they had eaten at almost every high-end restaurant in Dublin, with the notable exception of this one. Regardless of how many hints his wife dropped, and there had been plenty, they were never going to enjoy an overpriced meal here. He didn't want to be here now, but he had no choice in the matter.

He had agonised about his decision all day. On one hand, maybe he could let it slide. Just allow the investigation to take its course and no action would be necessary. On the other hand, if he said nothing and that turned out to not be the case, that would be bad. That would be very bad indeed. Eventually, he'd justified it to himself by reasoning there was an intelligence-gathering angle to it. After all, this was supposed to be a two-way street. O'Rourke couldn't actually make himself believe that, though. Both parties involved were extremely aware who held the whip hand. His being here proved that. They could have handled all of this over the phone, but the reason they didn't was that the other party wanted him always to be aware who was in charge.

The protocol was the same as before. He had called the restaurant from his "other" phone and requested a booking for a Mr Dylan, citing an unspecified special occasion. In reality, nobody but nobody was getting a last-minute reservation at Le Château de Moore unless they regularly played Wembley Stadium in between visits to meet the Pope. Still, as had happened on previous occasions, he had got a call back within the hour with a time. Not only that, but he'd been given the private booth.

A curtain provided ample privacy from the rest of the diners, and a discreet, nearly-invisible-to-the-naked-eye door meant that the waiting staff could come and go without entering the restaurant proper. It also meant that other people could come and go unseen. O'Rourke would have bet his left nut that a certain cabinet minister would be making use of this arrangement in order to see his mistress. O'Rourke, though, was not having an affair. No – he was on even more morally dubious ground.

Once, out of curiosity, he had surreptitiously looked into the ownership of the restaurant and found nothing untoward. Everything made it appear that Owen Moore owned it outright, save a mortgage and a bridging loan from legitimate sources. All that made O'Rourke think was how good certain people had become at hiding both their influence and their ill-gotten gains.

The door opened and the man O'Rourke was certain really owned Le Château de Moore sat down opposite him.

"Are you not enjoying your duck à l'orange, Fintan?" asked Gerry Fallon.

O'Rourke put down his fork. "It's fine – I just don't have much of an appetite."

"You should have gone for the scallops. They'll blow your mind."

"Oh well, too late now."

"Never mind. You know for next time."

The prospect of there being a next time removed what little chance there was of Fintan O'Rourke regaining his appetite any time soon.

Fallon leaned back and stretched out his arms, enjoying the comfort of the expensive leather chair. He offered O'Rourke a wide grin, enjoying the other man's discomfort. "Right. Well, now the small talk is dispensed with, United's Champions League game kicks off in about twenty minutes, so can we move this along?"

"Coop Hannity is dead."

He laughed. "No kidding? I actually own a radio, Detective Inspector, so I was aware of that. I assume you brought me here for something more than that?"

O'Rourke ran his finger around the rim of his wineglass. "I don't suppose you have any idea who might have been responsible?"

"Are you asking if I was responsible?"

O'Rourke said nothing.

Fallon picked up the bottle of red wine and poured himself a large glass. "Well, obviously, I wouldn't know much about such things but, as an avid fan of TV crime drama, it strikes me that walloping a bodyguard over the head with a fire extinguisher and then stabbing a man several times in the back while he feeds his pigeons doesn't sound like the work of a professional assassin." He noticed the look on O'Rourke's face and laughed. "What, Inspector? Did you really think you were my only source of information?" Fallon raised his glass in mock toast and took a large gulp. "Now, can we get to the part where you prove your value to me?"

O'Rourke knew he was being baited. Fallon was engaging in typical alpha-male bullshit, asserting his dominance. The thing was, he wasn't wrong.

"It seems Mr Hannity has been secretly videotaping many of his meetings for several years now." Part of O'Rourke relished seeing Fallon's smile tighten.

"What?"

"Yes. He had quite the set-up in his back garden where, seemingly, he held many of his meetings. I guess some people thought that being outdoors meant it was less likely to be bugged, but there are hidden cameras and what I'm told are very expensive directional mics – the whole shebang."

Fallon put down the wineglass and ran his tongue across his lips. "Do you have a recording of the murder?"

"No."

"Was he recording any meetings elsewhere?"

O'Rourke shrugged. "We don't know. What we do know is that we've got a large bunker full of video tapes in his back garden. It's currently under Garda protection while the DPP sorts out the legal angle. Obviously, there's all kinds of issues, given that the people being recorded were unaware. On the other hand, it wasn't the Gardaí that did the recording ... They're still figuring it all out, but even if there is some question over the admissibility of the tapes in court, we're still viewing it as the intelligence mother lode."

"This might be a problem for us," said Fallon, tugging at his ear.

Not that O'Rourke was going to find himself in a game of poker with Fallon any time soon, but he was confident he'd just figured out his tell. The man was rattled.

"Can you tell me the exact nature of your relationship with Hannity?"

Fallon leaned forward, a little snarl in his voice now. "We were humping in the back row of the pictures. What the fuck do you think was the nature of our relationship?"

O'Rourke held up a hand. "Hey, take it easy. I can't protect you if I don't know what I'm trying to protect you from."

"Yes, you can. It's not your business to know my business. It's your job to make sure nobody else does."

O'Rourke rolled his eyes but instantly regretted it. Fallon was now staring at him.

"Do I need to remind you of the exact nature of *our* relationship, Fintan?"

He tensed as Fallon picked up a fork from the unused place setting.

"I know that in the past we've referred to it as mutually assured destruction, but you get that was a little joke, right? It's not mutually assured. I have the goods to destroy you and walk away without a scratch on me. But if I go down – if I'm even inconvenienced more than I wish to be – then I will turn you into roadkill. Which of us do you reckon has more friends in Mountjoy?" Fallon reached across and stabbed a piece of O'Rourke's duck with the fork, before shoving it into his own mouth. He chewed expansively. "Are we absolutely clear, Fintan?"

"Jesus, Gerry. Alright, I get it."

"I'm not sure you do. Maybe you need me to get Owen to join us, and he can flambé your bollocks right here at the table."

"Look," said O'Rourke. "You can make all the threats you like, but none of them are going to help us sort this out. I'm going to assume that you're nervous about what might be on the tapes, yes?"

Fallon jutted out his chin almost imperceptibly, the only affirmation he was willing to give.

"OK. I suggest you get your lawyers on it. See what they can do. File an injunction, perhaps."

"Wow. Thanks very much. Invaluable advice."

O'Rourke puffed out his cheeks. "I'm not sure what else you expect me to do?"

"The amount I have invested in you, Fintan, and the leverage I have ... Let me be crystal clear: I don't pay you for information, not *just* information. You'd be amazed how cheap I can get that. What I expect from you is creative thinking." He stood up suddenly, causing the table to shake, and then leaned down so that he loomed over O'Rourke. "I'll get my lawyers on it. Meanwhile, I suggest you put on your thinking cap."

"It would help," said O'Rourke, "if we could find out quickly who actually killed Hannity."

"Why would I care about that?"

"Because as things stand, those tapes are evidence because the assumption is they speak to motive. If we have a killer, then legally, the grounds for going through them are a lot shakier."

"Fine," said Fallon. "I'll ask around. In the meantime, do not let me down. I'd hate to see a glittering career come to a crashing halt."

With that, he pulled open the nearly invisible door and disappeared back into the darkness.

O'Rourke sat there for several minutes, staring down at the tablecloth. He was woken from his reverie by a waiter he hadn't seen enter, and who was diplomatically clearing his throat.

"Is everything OK with your food, sir?"

O'Rourke looked up at him, but said nothing before standing up and walking straight out.

# HOW TO MILK A CUCUMBER

Bunny felt extremely out of place. For a start, he appeared to be the only person in the building who wasn't wearing some form of Lycra. What's more, the seats in the reception area at Paragon Fitness were so uncomfortable that he was beginning to seriously wonder if they were supposed to form part of a workout. They hit that sweet spot of being too big for one arse cheek, but far too small for two. As a result, Bunny found himself seated with half his arse floating in the air, as if he was waiting to let rip a monumental fart. Not that anyone would have noticed as scented air was being wafted through the place in an effort to achieve a certain ambience. If only they'd shut off the painfully thumping dance music, it would do the power of good on that score.

He'd been sitting there for fifteen minutes now, and the woman behind the desk had offered him cucumber water with such frequency that he was beginning to suspect she was on a commission to get rid of the stuff. It was just past 8am and a steady stream of individuals full of energy and brimming with life was already flowing through reception. Bloody morning people.

He'd actually seen two men high-five each other. Unironically. Irish people didn't high-five – they couldn't carry it off. At least, not at eight in the bloody morning. It was an American thing. Bunny had no problem with Americans – he liked them – but wherever their capacity for unbridled enthusiasm had come from in the cosmopolitan, globe-spanning genetic stew that went into making the US, it hadn't been from the Irish diaspora.

After talking to Mags last night, he'd gone home and enjoyed one of the worst night's sleep of his life. The more he thought about it, the worse his situation appeared to be. Coop Hannity was dead and Bunny had a motive, which was bad enough, but his unwillingness to explain exactly what it was made everything much worse.

Added to that, a knife had gone missing from his kitchen. He had ripped the entire place apart last night, in the forlorn hope that maybe he'd just misplaced it, but to no avail. He had to admit that his own stupidity played a large part in all this. He was Bunny McGarry, and most of the time he didn't bother locking the back door of his house because nobody within twenty miles would be foolish enough to rob him. Sheer absurd arrogance.

He knew the sensible course of action would be to come clean and tell O'Rourke – and God forbid, Tommy bloody Marshall – the whole truth. It was the only way he could get out in front of this, but to do so would mean throwing Gringo to the lions and, for better or for worse, that wasn't something he was prepared to do.

His only course of action was to find out who really had killed Coop Hannity. Presumably, it was the same person who was now setting him up. The problem was finding somebody to rule out. It was like a twisted version of the time traveller and baby Hitler hypothesis: if you knew you could save the world a great deal of suffering, would you kill Coop Hannity? Mother Teresa might have been tempted.

Finding a suspect was like finding a needle in a needle factory. The more promising line of enquiry appeared to be trying to figure out who knew enough to set Bunny up, but the more he pulled that thread, the less promising it looked. He remembered seeing the suspicious car parked up the road when he'd gone in to see Hannity. It meant anyone could have known about his visit and, from there, fingered him as a potential patsy. In hindsight, making a great show of stealing the man's gnome might have been one of his dumbest decisions ever. That would be great on his first day in Mountjoy: "What are you in for?" "Who, me? I stole a fecking gnome and things escalated."

A short woman with a smile bright enough to be a danger to oncoming traffic approached him. "Hi," she said in an overly cheery voice, "I'm Tracey. Can I show you around the facilities?"

Bunny glanced at the reception desk but the girl had stepped away, possibly to milk yet another cucumber. "Sure," he said. "Why not?"

What followed was ten solid minutes of confusion on both sides. Tracey and Bunny both spoke English and walked upright but those seemed to be the only two things they had in common. Bunny had never considered what his fitness goals were – he didn't think he had any. Despite Tracey's perma-grin, the look of alarm in her eyes at this revelation was as if Bunny had just explained that he didn't have any internal organs. After a couple of minutes she concluded with, "Right, so, weight loss, then. Great."

Bunny was too embarrassed to correct her. She then proceeded to show him a confusing array of weights machines, where a truly warped mind had come up with fifty different ways to lift something and put it down again in the exact same spot. Next was the cardiovascular section, which Tracey was particularly proud of, and where she explained that thanks to state-of-the-art video technology, you could run up Mount Everest if you so desired. To Bunny, it just looked like somebody had built a better hamster wheel.

After she showed him the communal sauna – "To be honest, Tracey, I don't think it's fair to inflict the sight of my semi-naked body on anybody without buying them dinner first" – and the hot tub – "I've always wanted to know what the last few minutes of life as a lobster would be like" – she brought him back to the reception area.

"So," said Tracey, "have you any questions?"

"Actually," said Bunny, "I do. What's the deal with the music?"

Not for the first time during their time together, Tracey looked confused. "What about it?"

"Why do you feel the need to have up-tempo dance music blasting out like we're in a terrible nightclub?"

She forced out an awkward laugh. "Well, most people love it. It's, y'know, great music to work out to."

"Right. Only I couldn't help but notice that if you look around the entire gym, every last person is wearing headphones. As in, something to block out the music."

Tracey scanned the room and nodded reluctantly. "Hmmm, that's interesting. I've never noticed that before." She turned back to him and cranked up the brightness of her smile a couple more notches than Bunny ever would have thought possible. It was like staring directly into the sun. "So, should I grab some paperwork and talk you through our exciting membership packages?"

"Oh, Jesus on a jet ski," responded Bunny. "God, no. Not in a million years." He chuckled. "No offence, but I would never join a place like this. Could you imagine?"

The smile tumbled from Tracey's face. It was like watching a star turn into a black hole. "So what the fuck are you doing here?" she said in a voice that belonged to a very different Tracey.

"I've just dropped in to see Marcus. Thanks very much for the tour, though – it was really eye-opening."

Without another word, she stalked away from Bunny and over to the reception desk. Bunny retook his seat and watched awkwardly as Tracey and the receptionist attempted to have a whispered blazing row, hissing at each other through fixed smiles while simultaneously greeting gym members cheerfully as they walked in.

Bunny noticed a man in a suit appear at the bottom of the stairs behind reception. He was looking in Bunny's direction. Even from a distance, Bunny could see that the guy's shirt was uncomfortably tight, because heaven forbid anyone should not know that everyone who worked in the building had put in the requisite amount of effort to achieve physical perfection.

The man slapped on the grin that seemed to be part of the Paragon Fitness official uniform and walked across to Bunny with his hand already extended. Bunny got to his feet and shook it.

"Hi there, I'm the co-manager, Paul Green. How can I help you this morning?"

"I was actually hoping to speak to Marcus."

The man shook his head. "I'm afraid he's not in today."

"Oh right. Only the girl at reception rang him and told him I was here. I heard the conversation."

Credit to him, Green recovered well. "Yes, that's right. He was here, but he's just had to step out. He asked me to help you with whatever you require. What is it you require?"

Bunny slipped his hand inside his coat and pulled out his ID, displaying it at a discreet angle where it was visible only to Green. "I need to talk to Marcus, please."

Bunny had been hoping that he wouldn't have to show his ID. Even though he wasn't impersonating an officer, he could be accused of misrepresentation, given he was on sabbatical. It wasn't like in the movies – they didn't make you hand over your badge and gun. He didn't have a gun, of course – this was Ireland. Certain detectives carried one for protection, but most of the time, if you needed a firearm you had to ring up and ask for one. It resulted in quite a bit of paperwork.

Green, who'd dropped the smile and the sunny disposition, told Bunny to take a seat in their small staffroom while he went to speak to Marcus. A couple of minutes later he returned and showed Bunny into a rather cramped office where a man he guessed was Marcus was seated behind the desk.

As expected, he looked physically fit but, unexpectedly, he had a wary look to him, and bags under his eyes that suggested he could really do with a good night's sleep. Bunny could sympathise. Bunny also noted the fading bruising on the left side of the man's face, which tallied with what Mags had told him. He certainly looked like someone a couple weeks removed from getting a good going-over. He introduced himself as Marcus Phillips and indicated that Bunny should take the seat opposite him. Paul Green took a position behind his colleague, leaning against the filing cabinet.

"So, Detective, what can I help you with?"

Bunny pointed at his own face. "If you don't mind me saying, it looks like you've been in the wars?"

"Yes. I'm afraid I got mugged."

"Sorry to hear that. When did that happen?"

Marcus glanced back at Paul. "About three weeks ago now."

"Have the Gardaí had any success finding the perpetrators?"

Marcus looked down for a moment and then scratched his chin. "I … I actually didn't report it. I know I probably should have done, but I didn't see anything. It would have just been a waste of everybody's time."

"You'd be surprised," said Bunny. "CCTV, witnesses, and a lot of these guys have a tendency to work the same areas. They might have mugged other people before or since. It really is important to report such things."

"Yes, sorry. You're right, of course. I guess I was just shaken up, and a bit embarrassed, if I'm honest. Stupid, I know."

"Oh, not at all. That's a very natural reaction. After all, you've been through something traumatic. It's very common for victims of violent attacks to deny anything happened or, indeed, to fabricate an entirely different story to explain it. Like, for example, telling people you got mugged when the reality is some arsehole sent the boys around to work you over."

The room grew very tense. Marcus studied the top of the desk intently to avoid meeting Bunny's eyes, whereas Paul glowered burning daggers straight at Bunny.

"I don't know what you've heard," said Marcus, "but I don't want to press charges or anything like that. It was all a big misunderstanding."

Bunny crossed his legs. "And exactly what was the misunderstanding?"

"Sorry," interjected Paul, taking a step forward. "If Marcus doesn't want to press charges, then that's the end of it. I think you should leave."

"I'm afraid," said Bunny, "that it isn't the end of anything." He turned his gaze to Marcus. "I don't want to, but if you wish to keep lying to me, then I can charge you with obstruction of justice."

Paul was outraged. "Are you serious? You're going to charge the victim? What kind of bullshit is this?"

Marcus patted Paul on the arm and they shared a look. Paul, his face red with anger, took a step back reluctantly and stood there with his arms folded. Marcus took a deep breath and looked at Bunny. "What are you after here?"

"Look," said Bunny. "I'm not trying to cause you any hassle, I promise. I just want to find out what happened. And, for what it's worth, I don't think you need to worry about any of this coming back at you. For a start, as I'm sure you know, Mr Hannity is dead."

Either both Marcus and Paul were both a great loss to the acting profession, or Bunny would have bet that that piece of information really did come as a shock to them.

"Am I to take it that neither of you knew?"

The pair shook their heads.

"Right," said Bunny. "But you know who Coop Hannity was?"

Marcus nodded. "I know he is – was – the husband of a client of mine."

Bunny gave a tight smile. "He was indeed. I guess I meant, did you know what he was?"

Marcus paused and glanced up at Paul before answering. "Only after the fact. Apparently he's some kind of gangster. We don't know anything about that world."

"Right. And he thought you were having an affair with his wife?"

"Apparently."

"And can I ask—"

"No," said Paul firmly. "He most definitely was not."

He placed a hand on Marcus's shoulder, who reached up and patted it. Bunny tilted his head back as the realisation belatedly dawned on him.

"Ah right. Am I to take it Angelina Hannity isn't your type?"

"That's right," said Marcus. "And even if she was, for the record, I was her personal trainer. I only ever met her in this building. I tried to explain that, but ..."

"I blame that slimy little bastard," said Paul.

Bunny's eyes narrowed. "Who?"

"There was a guy hanging about the place," said Marcus. "He came in a couple of times, pretending like he was interested in joining. The staff said there was something off about him. Then, another day, somebody noticed him sitting outside in a car. To be honest, we thought he was some creepy arsehole who was stalking one of the girls. I went out and had a word with him."

"And let me guess," said Bunny. "A few days after you ran him off, some big lads representing Mr Hannity came to visit you?"

Marcus scratched a hand across his T-shirt and nodded.

"If I ever see that bastard again," snarled Paul, "I'm going to rip that ridiculous comb-over clean off his head."

"Paul!" said Marcus, before turning back to Bunny. "He doesn't mean that, obviously. If he did," he added pointedly, "I'm sure he wouldn't be stupid enough to say it in front of a Garda detective!"

"He does mean it," said Bunny. "And he should. This fella with the comb-over – by any chance did he look like he got dressed in the 70s and hasn't changed since?"

Marcus's eyes widened. "You know him?"

Bunny shrugged. "I might do. It's the year 2000 – there aren't many people still walking around with a comb-over. And of them, I'm guessing there's only one whose job it is to follow people." He got to his feet. "Alright, lads. Thanks for the help. Don't worry, I won't bring you into anything. Sorry for your troubles, Marcus. Looks like you got an awful lot of shit for no good reason at all." He was about to head for the door, but turned back around. "Oh, if you wouldn't mind – could you tell me where you were on Tuesday evening between nine and eleven?"

Marcus glared at him. "As in, did I kill Hannity?" He pulled back his chair from the table and Bunny realised why the guy had been sitting awkwardly – his left leg was enclosed in a full plaster cast.

"OK. Point taken." Bunny turned his attention to Paul. "And yourself?"

"I was downstairs, as it happens, leading forty people in a Zumba class, before we all went across the road for a drink. I can give you a list of witnesses if you'd like?"

Bunny shook his head. "No, you're grand. I just had to ask." He gave them a smile. "I'll show myself out."

"Detective?" asked Paul.

Bunny looked back over his shoulder.

"Do me a favour. If you find the man that killed Hannity, shake his hand for me."

# HUMPING HOUNDS

DI Thomas "not Tom" Marshall straightened his tie, checked his cufflinks then knocked on the office door. He could hear a voice from inside but it was indistinct and offered no clear indication that he could enter. He looked back at Commissioner Ferguson's PA for a signal, but she was busy feeding documents to a shredder in the corner.

He knocked again.

"Come the hell in, for Christ's sake," came the roar from the other side of the door, removing all ambiguity.

Marshall stepped inside and closed the door behind him. "Commissioner."

"Tom," Ferguson responded, waving a hand at the chair opposite him and on which Marshall duly took a seat.

Marshall waited to speak because the highest-ranking Garda officer in the country was not making eye contact with him, instead focusing all of his attention on the plate of food in front of him. He was tentatively prodding its contents with a fork, as if half expecting them to leap up and attack him.

"Do you know what celery is, Marshall?"

"It's a vegetable, sir."

Ferguson raised his eyes for a brief moment – just enough time to make it very clear to Marshall that was not the correct answer.

“Yes, thank you, Inspector. What it is, is quite possibly a perfect moment of evolution. It is a piece of vegetation that quickly realised that its greatest chance of survival would be to evolve itself to the point where it has absolutely no taste. Hunter-gatherers would obviously ignore it. Animals would have no use for it. It isn’t even poisonous, as in a threat that needs to be removed. It reached the point of being utterly irrelevant to the rest of existence. On some fundamental level, celery must’ve been smugly pleased with itself – neither friend nor foe to any living thing. It was just there – like that music you get in lifts, or Belgium. The thing that was in between the other, far more important things.” He picked up a piece of the vegetable and held it out before him.

“It must have been absolutely gutted when enough of mankind managed to scoff itself into a state of morbid obesity, to the point where forcing them to eat Mother Nature’s wet fart is now considered a good idea.”

Commissioner Ferguson dropped the piece of celery back on to the plate, pushed it to one side and then, after giving it a queasy look, covered it with a folder from the pile on his desk so he wouldn’t have to look at it.

“If you’re looking for diet tips, sir,” offered Marshall, “I’ve read a couple of very interesting books on the subject.”

Ferguson gave him a steely look, then lifted the file and spoke directly to the celery. “If it’s any consolation to you, it appears you still have better survival instincts than a detective inspector in the Garda Síochána.” He dropped the folder once more, having made his point.

Marshall glanced around the room, and only then noticed the dog sleeping in a bed in the corner. He pulled back instinctively.

“I see you have a dog, sir?”

“You can’t teach observation skills like that. It’s just something you’re born with.”

Marshall gave a weak laugh. “Yes, sir. Sorry, it’s just – dogs make me nervous.”

"You don't like dogs?" asked Ferguson, incredulous. "Did one rip your face off as a child? Kill a family member? Something like that?"

Marshall shifted in his seat, deeply regretting this conversational segue. "No, sir. Nothing like that. I've just never been a dog person."

"What sort of a person doesn't like dogs? I can only think of two possible groups – serial killers and that bunch of nutters in Rathmines who dress up as cats every weekend. Should I be concerned?"

"No, sir. I'm sure your dog is lovely."

Ferguson thumped his fist on the table, causing the dog to startle. "He's an utter shit, as it happens, but he's still a dog."

"I ... I had a goldfish when I was a child," managed Marshall, confusing even himself as he said it.

"Do yourself a favour, Tommy – quit while you're behind." Ferguson settled his considerable bulk back in the chair. "And how goes our valiant efforts to bring the perpetrators of Coop Hannity's murder to justice?"

Marshall was thrilled to move on to more solid ground. "We're making progress. I have two of our men trying to trace Cian Fairchild. His brother's widow said she believed he was in Spain, so we're checking that out. We're also looking into the alibis of the Marsh family."

"Excuse me?" said Ferguson. "An entire family?"

"Rita Marsh, who—"

"I remember her."

"Well, she has six sons, who all work for the fire service and who all fit the physical description of the man in the balaclava."

"Christ. That's not a family you'd like to piss off."

"Following a meeting last night," continued Marshall, "a Miss Caroline Keane, the late Mr Hannity's assistant, has agreed to assist us both in unravelling his business affairs and in verifying which tapes are missing from his collection. The DPP has agreed to grant her immunity from any prosecution in return for this assistance."

Ferguson pursed his lips and nodded.

"I also have a team of four officers, assisted by the two forensic accountants I requested yesterday, who've begun trying to unpick the Hannity organisation. We've already been able to determine that there are multiple shell companies, offshore accounts and other evasion methods. It may be months, if not years, before we get the full picture."

"Given that most of what Mr Hannity engaged in was morally bankrupt but not actually illegal, do we feel all that is necessary?"

Marshall sighed. "The problem, sir, is that it's necessary if we're to understand who owed him money and, therefore, who had motive."

"It's my understanding," said Ferguson, "that we might be better off trying to find people who *didn't* owe him money. It seems like that's a considerably smaller group. Regardless, please tell me we have something more than a couple of spreadsheets?"

"Yes, sir. With the assistance of Miss Keane and pre-existing records, we're drawing up a list of the most likely suspects: any long-running enmities, people who owed him a great deal of money and those who are having difficulty paying it back in particular, and anyone else we can identify as having an axe to grind regarding their previous dealings with Mr Hannity."

"That sounds like it's going to be a very long list. It would also appear to include individuals from two of the emergency services. I imagine that by the time the day is out, we'll discover Hannity somehow managed to piss off the coastguard too."

"We have to start somewhere, sir."

"It's the finishing bit I'm concerned with."

The dog barked.

"Shut up, Kevin," snapped Ferguson, without looking at the pup. "Anything from the crime scene?"

"We've agreed to release stills of the man in the balaclava to the media today – in the hope that it might jog some memories for the public. Disappointingly, despite the man not wearing gloves, forensics haven't been able to pull any prints from the wall he jumped over, or anywhere else for that matter. A search of the area has yet to yield the murder weapon."

"Yet?"

"Yes, sir. A detective from DI O'Rourke's squad was in charge of it, but he overlooked a skip at a nearby building site, which was removed the morning after."

"Oh, for shit's sake."

"I've already added a reprimand to the file of the officer in question, and first thing this morning, he and a couple of uniforms went out to Dunsink to go through the area of the dump where that the driver thinks he unloaded the skip."

Ferguson scratched his belly through his shirt. "Well, it's nice to know that somebody is having an even shittier morning than I am. Any good news?"

"I've just come from speaking to Dr Denise Devane. Her preliminary autopsy confirmed what we suspected – namely that Hannity was stabbed multiple times, mainly in the lower back. There was also an unexpected finding in the wounds. It appears they contain trace elements of a substance she has provisionally identified as cheese."

Marshall tried to hide his confusion as the Commissioner closed his eyes and tilted his head back.

"God," Ferguson whispered at the ceiling, "I miss cheese."

"Sir?"

Ferguson returned his gaze to Marshall. "You're telling me the man was butchered with a cheese knife?"

"Again, I must emphasise the preliminary nature of the findings."

"Yes, thank you, Detective Inspector, I do understand what the word 'preliminary' means. I'm having considerably more difficulty understanding what kind of a killer uses a dirty knife?"

"I would imagine we can rule out professional assassins, sir."

"You think?" said Ferguson, not attempting to disguise his sarcasm in any way.

"It's still far too early to draw any meaningful conclusions, sir. Also, as far as we can tell, there isn't anybody obvious lined up to take over Hannity's business. Not that there's an org chart anywhere, but what little intelligence we have indicates there are three lieutenants managing different parts of the business, plus a more conventional management structure on the more legitimate side of things. We're going to have to wait and see whether this looks like somebody making their move."

"Christ," said Ferguson. "What an utter shit show. At this point, presumably Hannity is the only person we can rule out, unless we think this might have been a particularly elaborate suicide?"

Marshall said nothing, belatedly catching on to the Commissioner's love of a rhetorical question.

"And what about the other thing?"

"The other thing, sir?"

"Don't play the innocent with me, Marshall. We are both well aware of the specific reason you were brought up to Dublin to take over the investigation. McGarry?"

Marshall shrugged. "Currently he's just one name on a list. However, from Miss Keane's provisional inspection of the video-tape store, she has confirmed that the tape from Monday night – the one that would have shown McGarry's visit to Hannity – is missing."

"And how many other tapes has she so far identified as missing?"

"Just the one from the night of the murder, sir."

"I see."

"And Detective Pamela Cassidy informed me that McGarry contacted her yesterday afternoon, enquiring about the case. As per my instructions to the entire team, she didn't tell him anything, and she has Detective John Carlson as a witness to the fact. Nevertheless, sir, I will be removing Detective Cassidy from the case."

Ferguson leaned forward. "But she followed your instructions?"

"Yes, sir, but she is a friend of McGarry's."

"As is, I would imagine, a large percentage of the Gardaí in Dublin. This is Cassidy – short girl, red hair?"

"That sounds like her."

"I thought so. I remember her from the ill-fated cross-border police sports day we had with our colleagues from the North a few years ago. The one we held only the once – following the incident."

Marshall was fully aware of the circumstances. He hadn't been there, but the event had gone badly enough to have made the papers.

The Republic had won the soccer match three–two, with a couple of sendings-off for each team. The shit had really hit the fan when the captain of the winning team had accepted their trophy and decided to give his whole victory speech in Irish.

"Cassidy was our representative in the lightweight judo, or whatever it was called. She won that, then, when our heavyweight representative did in her knee playing netball, she stepped up and won that as well. In about thirty seconds too. I'd never watched judo before, but Christ almighty, I enjoyed the hell out of that. Her opponent was that woman from the cross-border cooperation committee – the one whose entire role appears to be to ensure no actual cooperation takes place."

"I'm not entirely sure how that's relevant, sir?"

"It is relevant, Inspector, because we do not take good coppers off cases for no reason when, as you yourself said, she followed your instructions to the letter. Knowing somebody is not a crime, only assisting them inappropriately is. Do let me know if that happens. In the meantime, let's allow Detective Cassidy to do her job, shall we?"

Marshall said nothing.

"Generally, Inspector, when I ask a question, I do expect some form of answer."

"Sorry, sir," said Marshall awkwardly. "I'm afraid ... It's just ... You see ..."

"Good God, man, just spit it out. This is like watching a Hugh Grant movie."

Marshall pointed behind the Commissioner. "Your dog, sir ... "

Ferguson spun around in his chair to be greeted by the sight of Kevin the Labradoodle industriously humping a cushion. "Oh, for ..." The Commissioner rubbed his hand against his forehead and then turned slowly back around. "Continue."

Marshall looked at the dog and then back at the Commissioner. "I'm sorry, sir?"

Ferguson sighed a heavy sigh and came the closest he was ever likely to get to looking embarrassed. "I have been informed by my pet behaviourist that this behaviour is stress-related, and that the best way to deal with it is to ignore it."

"I see."

"I don't," said Ferguson, staring forlornly at his desk. "I used to be master of all I surveyed, Tom-Tom. Now look at me. Sitting here eating celery while a Labra-bloody-doodle fucks my soft furnishings. I have been utterly emasculated."

Marshall reached for something to say but nothing came. He looked at the dog again. To Marshall's untrained eye, the animal's facial expression did not say stress. He appeared to be enjoying himself immensely.

"So," said Ferguson, "I believe you and McGarry have a history?"

"I fail to see how that's relevant, sir."

"And I fail to care what you think is relevant. That's my job. Now, you and McGarry – what incident sparked this bitter feud? I assume it didn't start with McGarry pulling down your pants?"

Marshall considered refusing to answer, then remembered who he was speaking to. Commissioner Ferguson, amongst his other talents, was heralded as the most gifted interrogator the force had ever seen. He could just keep asking the same question again and again until a person broke. Marshall wanted to get out of the room, and the quickest way to make that happen was by telling the truth.

"We trained together in Templemore."

"And? I assume other Garda recruits were there as well. Even you can't have fallen out with all of them. So what was it? A woman? Money?"

"No, sir. If you must know, McGarry claimed that at a social, I had made a wager with him that Limerick would beat Cork in that year's Munster hurling final."

"So it was money?"

Marshall looked offended. "No, sir. According to McGarry, the bet had been that the loser would run from one end of the training college to the other. Completely naked."

Ferguson raised his eyebrows. "Well, well, well. And who won?"

"That is irrelevant, sir. I have no recollection of the bet and, more importantly, I don't believe such a wager could take place while both parties were inebriated."

"At a wild guess, did Cork win the match?"

Marshall pursed his lips and gave a terse nod.

Ferguson scratched his chin. "So, you made a bet, and then you backed out of it?"

"That's very much not how I would see it, sir."

Ferguson nodded. "Has he finished yet?"

"I'm sorry, sir?" asked Marshall.

"The dog. Has he finished? I'm noticing an absence of grunting noises from behind me."

Marshall peered towards the corner. "Yes."

"Thank God for that. I need to dictate a letter after this and I can't bring my PA into the room while Kevin's still at it. I think that would technically qualify as sexual harassment in the workplace. So, what's the next move with McGarry?"

"I'm asking him to come in today for an interview, so that we can eliminate him as a suspect."

Ferguson ran his tongue around his mouth. "Yes. I entirely believe that is your objective, Inspector. Let me know how it goes, and if you need any further assistance. That is all."

Marshall got to his feet. "Thank you, sir."

"Would you please ask Ms Willis to step in as you leave?"

"Certainly, sir." Marshall turned and walked to the door. As he placed his hand on it, Ferguson spoke again.

"Oh, and off the record, Tommy Boy. If you'd backed out of the bet with me, I wouldn't have pulled your pants down."

"Sir?"

"No. I'd have set them on fire, with you still wearing them."

The dog barked.

"Shut up, Kevin!"

# A LOST SOUL

Hand on heart, Bunny really couldn't say why he was here. He couldn't shake the feeling that somehow, in the middle of all this, as well as everything else, Angelina was in trouble. Perhaps he was hoping that her father could throw some light on what was going on? Or maybe it was just good old-fashioned Catholic guilt?

Until Angelina had mentioned her father, it had been years since Bunny had even thought about John Quirke. Back in the early days, when he'd first been on the beat, they'd seen one another regularly. These days, Bunny hoped some things had changed for the better, but back in the late eighties, more often than not John Quirke and people like him were just dismissed as being "mad". There was no bad in him, the man just wasn't well.

His wife had been the glue that held him together and things got a lot worse after she died. The unexpected death of anybody in the prime of their life is a terrible thing, but Fiona Quirke's passing had been cruel. She left for work one day and collapsed at a bus stop, leaving behind John and Angelina, an ill man and a confused kid trying to take care of each other.

Things hadn't always been that way for John Quirke. To hear others tell it, back in his teenage years, John had been the life and soul of the party. Blessed with good looks and charm, Fiona had been regarded with jealousy for snagging him. However, John's youthful behaviour – him being a bit of a messer, a bit wild, call it what you will – began to manifest in other ways as he grew older. It was the difference between a teenager jumping into the local pond at the height of summer to impress his friends, and a lone man doing the same thing on a cold winter's morning. There were bursts of manic energy followed by the inevitable dark depths of depression, and the whole pattern inevitably intensified after he lost his wife.

No longer able to hold down a job, he slipped in and out of care. Angelina would sometimes stay with an aunt or, as she got older, with friends. The truth was that Angelina Quirke was raised by the whole estate – neighbours quietly chipping in, dropping food over, making sure the house was kept in good order. It takes a village and all that. When the Gardaí received reports of John behaving erratically, they'd collect him and, most of the time, drop him back home.

On some occasions, when he was really bad and they couldn't calm him down, they had to hospitalise him for his own safety. Bunny remembered the time he had to convince a colleague not to file a report that John Quirke had hit him. If John had been perceived as violent, he'd have inevitably ended up in court, a prison sentence would have followed, and Angelina could have wound up in care. Besides, John Quirke wasn't swinging at anybody except the demons in his own head.

Bunny also remembered dropping round several times himself, and the look on Angelina's face when the poor kid answered the door – a mix of concern and embarrassment as he explained where her father was and checked that she had somewhere to stay. This wasn't to say that John didn't have his good days too – there was the incredible treehouse he managed to build for Angelina and her friends, which, as much as anything, was a work of art and a hint of what the man could have achieved in life if the cards had fallen a different way.

While he might not have received the care he needed back then, it looked as if things had improved for John – at least they had if you were to judge by looking at the Cedarwood Hospital from the outside. As Bunny drove into the grounds, he stopped and double checked the sign to make sure he hadn't pulled into a golf course by mistake.

Undulating manicured lawns, stretching into the distance and dotted with mature trees, surrounded the cluster of buildings. What was referred to as the mental-health clinic was only one part of the complex. There were other units with euphemistic titles, such as the well-being centre, rehabilitation spa and sports medicine clinic. He'd never been here before, but Bunny had heard of the place. If you were a sports star who'd blown out your knee, a musician who'd snorted your way into needing "some time away", or anybody who had the money and desire to select their nose from a catalogue, then Cedarwood was where you ended up.

The complex was surprisingly busy. Bunny followed the signs that directed him into an underground car park. He hated these places, not least because he was driving a rental car and, on principle, he'd refused the excess cover because it was, well, excessive. He found himself corkscrewing down a ramp designed by a sadist – or, at the very least, somebody who owned a body shop – desperately trying not to scratch the bloody thing. He breathed a sigh of relief as he eventually arrived at the designated parking area for the clinic on the -3 level.

He got out and checked the sign on the wall, then read it twice again to make sure he had got it right. He then he looked around to confirm somebody wasn't trying to pull some kind of elaborate practical joke. He had to either get his parking validated or take out a second mortgage to pay for it. He found the lift and rode up to the ground floor in the company of a woman he vaguely recognised but whose face he couldn't place. His best guess what that she either read the news or had somehow been in it. She turned right as Bunny turned left, following the signs to their very different destinations.

If you didn't know where you were as you stepped into the reception at the mental health clinic, you could be forgiven for thinking you were in an upscale hotel. An indoor water feature burbled away in one corner, and abstract and expensive-looking art graced the walls while muzak softly Kenny G-ed for all it was worth in the background. Bunny had to concede that at least it was better than the music inflicted on people at the gym. A few days of that, and Bunny would end up here himself.

As he approached the reception desk, Bunny was favoured with the kind of dazzling smile you were only blessed with if you worked for an organisation that had two of the most expensive dentists in Ireland on its books and could avail of a sizeable staff discount.

"Hello, sir. How can I help you?"

"I was hoping to have a chat with one of the patients, please. John Quirke."

"And you are?"

"Bernard McGarry. I'm an old friend of the family."

The receptionist ran a finger up and down the sheet in front of her. "I can't see you here. Do you have an appointment?"

"No, sorry, I don't."

"I'm afraid we do have a strict appointment system here."

Bunny took out his ID. "I am honestly a friend of the family, but this isn't just a social call."

She nodded. "I understand. Let me call Dr Fitzgerald."

Bunny took a step back as the woman made a brief phone call then smiled up at him. "She'll be right out."

"Thank you." Bunny glanced at the comfortable-looking sofas opposite the reception desk but stopped short. He remembered himself and reached into his inside pocket. "Oh, before I forget – is there any chance you could validate my parking?"

"Of course, sir."

Bunny handed her the card gratefully. "Thank God for that. I thought I was going to have to drop over the road when I was done here and see if I could convince somebody to buy a kidney."

She laughed as she fed the card in and out of the machine on the desk. "I know," she sympathised. "Between you and me, it's absolutely ridiculous, isn't it? The guard who called around yesterday said exactly the same thing." It was noticeable how the woman's accent had become considerably less posh now she realised he was just a copper and not a relative of one of their patients.

"Oh right," said Bunny. "I imagine they were just in confirming Mrs Hannity had been here on Tuesday night?"

The receptionist nodded. "Yeah. I just showed him the records in the book and then he had a brief chat with Dr Fitzgerald. He asked to speak to the patient as well but she talked him out of it. I guess that's why you've come back?"

"I'm afraid so. We just have to be seen to be ticking all the boxes – you know how it is. Does John Quirke get many visitors?"

"No," said the woman. "Just Princess Grace."

"Excuse me?"

The woman looked embarrassed when she realised what she'd just said. "Sorry, I ... Nothing. Don't mind me."

Bunny gave her a smile. "Why do you call her that?"

She looked around nervously.

"Don't worry, you're not in any trouble. I was just curious, that's all."

"It's just," started the woman "every time she comes in, she's very aloof. We take turns covering the later shifts, me and the other girls, and Carol came up with the nickname. Always looks so glamorous. Gucci this, Armani that. Big sunglasses. Never chats."

Bunny nodded.

"I mean, to be fair to her, it can't be easy, can it? I mean ..." She went quiet as a brown-haired woman in a neatly pressed white coat appeared through the doors and made her way across to Bunny.

"Hello," she said. "I'm Dr Amanda Fitzgerald, the lead specialist here."

"Detective Bernard McGarry."

"I believe you're enquiring about John Quirke?"

"Yes."

"As I told your colleague, there is no benefit to him being interviewed, and it wouldn't be good for him."

"I appreciate that, Doctor, but as it happens, I'm actually an old friend of the family. I've known John for years."

Dr Fitzgerald pursed her lips before nodding back in the direction of the door through which she had come. She led Bunny down a hallway and into a room where a bored-looking nurse was seated, watching a bank of a dozen or so monitors.

"Hi, Claire," said Dr Fitzgerald.

The nurse sat forward instinctively, trying to look more alert.

"Is everything OK?"

The nurse smiled. "Absolutely, Doctor."

"Where is John Quirke at the minute?"

The nurse scanned the monitors and pointed to the one at the top left. "He's in the lounge."

"Could you zoom in, please?"

She dutifully hit a couple of buttons and manoeuvred the joystick on the control panel. Bunny watched as the screen filled with the image of a man he barely recognised. John Quirke, even on his bad days, had been a good-looking man. Now, bloodshot eyes sat in a gaunt face. His hands tugged nervously at his raggedy beard as he rocked back and forth, staring at the ground, mumbling to himself.

"Jesus," said Bunny softly.

"Yes," said Dr Fitzgerald. "I'm afraid there is a degenerative element to John's condition. He has good days and bad days, but I'm showing you this to emphasise my point: nothing he could say would be of any use to law enforcement and, frankly, the experience of being interviewed would be very upsetting for him."

"I understand," said Bunny. "As I said, I honestly do know him, but we've fallen out of touch. I didn't realise it'd got this bad."

"I'm afraid so. The only person who sees him now is his daughter. And honestly? On the bad days, he doesn't even know who she is. He had an episode a couple of weeks ago, when he started screaming at her and had to be restrained. As part of his condition, his paranoia can spiral. He's accused us of trying to poison him, her of being an impostor, and one of the orderlies of trying to steal his teeth in the night. As his doctor, I strongly suggest you leave him alone."

Bunny took a last look at the man on the screen. "Right. I'm sorry for bothering you."

. . .

He walked back to the car lost in his own thoughts. Such a cruel situation. There but for the grace of God. But he couldn't imagine how hard it was for poor Angelina to visit week after week and see her father slipping further and further away from her.

It was only once he'd got back into the car and carefully negotiated his way up to the ground-floor exit that Bunny realised he'd left his parking ticket with the receptionist.

"Oh, for fuck's sake!"

# A WALK IN THE PARK

As she walked along the path, the sharp March breeze slashing through the bare branches of the trees towering above her, Angelina could feel eyes on her. A couple of new mothers pushing prams, chatting away a mile a minute. An older gentleman sitting on a bench, tossing stale bread to ravenous pigeons. A sweat-soaked jogger trundling grimly by, his gait telling the tale of ambition outweighing capability. They were all busy in their own little worlds, but their eyes still invaded hers.

Not that she wanted to, but Angelina could chart the phases of her life by how she felt about people looking at her. Ballet dancing as a child, and enjoying the feeling of being the best at something – at least in the tiny universe she'd lived in – she'd revelled in the thrill of recognition. Then, as she'd become an awkward motherless teenager, she became a typical mix of wanting to be both noticed and ignored. As she grew older still, and the modelling dream became her way out, her chance at something better, she'd needed to be noticed. Being noticed had come to be the be all and end all, her very reason for living. Near the end she'd hated it, hated it so very much. It had taken her to some dark places and moments when things could have gone very differently.

She'd eventually come home and made her deal with the devil, and, for different reasons, once again she hated the feeling of people's eyes on her. She could feel their judgement, knowing what she was. She had done what she'd had to do to protect herself and her father, and those looks were part of her punishment. The subtle *drip, drip* of accusation and judgement. Nothing was ever said, of course – the Hannity name carried far too much fear for anyone ever to actually say anything, but people couldn't keep that look out of their eyes and she had seen it. Maybe because she'd been looking for it. As confirmation of her own self-image.

None of that mattered now. Everything had changed. She had more important things to worry about than herself.

She took a deep breath and tried to relax. Logically speaking, she knew that none of these people were really looking at her – they were gawping at what was behind her. Samoan Joe, immense as he was, inevitably attracted attention, even without the conspicuous bandage wrapped around his head as evidence of the injury he'd suffered a couple of nights ago.

When she'd announced that she was going to Santry Park for her regular walk, he'd insisted on coming with her. In fact, since he'd checked himself out of the hospital the day before, Joe had rarely left her side. Perhaps she should stay home, wear black, mourn – for the look of the thing, but she was royally sick of keeping up appearances. She also found herself irrationally irritated by the fact that Joe cheerfully greeted everyone they passed as they looked at him. He was just so infuriatingly comfortable in his own skin.

She checked her watch: 12:13pm. Her walk around the park, following the route she always did, had taken precisely forty-eight minutes. Usually it took fifty-one – she assumed the increase in her speed was down to nervous energy. While she hadn't slept more than a couple of hours in days, there was enough caffeine surging through her body to leave her feeling jittery and wired.

She stopped, bent down and started to tie her shoelaces. A shadow loomed over her, blocking out what little warmth there was in the spring sun.

"For Christ's sake, Joe. You don't need to stand over me."

"Is everything alright there, Angelina?"

"Yes. I'm tying my shoelace. I've been doing this since I was a kid, and if I couldn't, I'm not sure you'd be the first person I'd call."

She noticed the old man look up from his pigeons and give her a concerned look, his attention attracted by her irritated tone, then felt the sun again as Joe took a step back.

"Alright. No need to get snippy."

Angelina straightened up and headed for the exit. She turned left on to the Swords Road and increased her pace. To her right, traffic flowed by at a steady speed. This road would be at a crawl in the morning and evening rush hours, but just after midday it flowed as God and town planners had intended. A bus whooshed by in the lane beside her, causing her to jump. She resisted the urge to look behind, denying Joe the opportunity to roll out his big goofy smile and ask her to slow down.

She noticed the woman on the far side of the road walking her dog, standing there as the pooch relieved itself against a lamppost. Their eyes met. Angelina found herself focusing on the woman's face as her eyes widened and her mouth dropped open. The next thing she heard was pounding footsteps behind her and Joe's unintelligible roar, accompanied by his massive hand on her back, shoving her forward. She wasn't able to make out what he shouted as she fell and her head smashed against the stone wall. When the popping noises reached her ears, it took her a moment to identify them as she was unfamiliar with the sound. Gunshots sounded different on the TV.

She was dazed. Her vision momentarily blurry. She was only dimly aware of the screech of tyres as a vehicle made good its escape. Instinctively, she put her hand to her forehead and took it away, wet with sticky blood.

She looked up to see Joe kneeling beside her, his eyes fixed on something in the distance. Then he turned his gaze on her.

Somewhere near by, a woman screamed.

# KNEE DEEP IN SHIT

Pamela Cassidy had joined the police force because she wanted to help people. She really did. Alright, that wasn't the only reason, but it was definitely one of the reasons. So much so that if you'd told her even a week ago that a scream of terror from one of her colleagues would only result in her rolling her eyes and tutting, she wouldn't have believed you. They say a week is a long time in politics, but it turned out a couple of hours was a long time in policing – at least it was if you were doing that so-called policing in a dump. An actual dump.

"Oh God, oh God, oh God," yelped Detective John Carlson behind her, at a pitch a schoolgirl would have found embarrassing.

If Pamela was honest, it had been funny for a while. She'd also tried to calm him down and sympathise with him, because she wasn't a monster. But she was confident that she spoke not just for herself but also for the two uniforms, the three refuse technicians they'd been provided with reluctantly by the dump's manager, and Danny from the technical bureau, when she said that Detective Carlson's ongoing panic attack was getting pretty old.

They were in hazmat suits, scouring an area of about 50 feet squared for a possible murder weapon. The driver from the skip company reckoned he dumped his load here yesterday, but they weren't one hundred percent sure as he'd dumped several loads over the course of the day and, as he put it, "It's rubbish. Who bothers their bollocks keeping track of rubbish?"

She was coming to the end of her allotted fifteen-minute break, which was why she was delighted when her phone showed a call coming through from the office. Having to take it meant she'd be unable to rejoin the search for a few more precious minutes.

"Hello. Detective Cassidy speaking."

"Butch, I'm not distracting you from going through some bins, am I?"

It was DS Paschal Burke, who was nowhere near as funny as he seemed to think he was.

"Jesus," came the screech from behind her. "I'm sure something touched my leg. Something definitely touched my leg that time!"

"What on earth is that?" asked Burke.

"That," she replied, "is the worst day of Detective Carlson's life. And at this rate, it might just be his last. If he doesn't have a heart attack, there's every chance one of us might kill him."

"Oh dear."

"Did you know he was musophobic?"

"He's afraid of musicians?"

"Ha ha," said Butch without feeling. "Very funny. No. It means he's afraid of mice and rats."

"In that case, I'd imagine Dunsink dump might not be the best place for him."

"Yes, I think we all agree on that. Well, with the exception of Detective Inspector Marshall, whose apparent response when Carlson had tried to explain this was, and I quote, 'This will be an excellent way of curing it.'"

Burke laughed.

"Seriously, Paschal – this is way beyond a joke now. The lad is gonna do himself an injury."

"If you want, I can try and bring it up with Marshall again? But fair warning, whatever happened at his meeting with the Commissioner, he came back in a really foul mood."

Butch glanced over to the search site where Carlson, shovel in hand, was gamely trying to sift through rubbish while simultaneously looking in six different directions.

"I wasn't aware DI Marshall had any other kind of mood."

"It doesn't seem like he's taken much of a shine to you either. I thought that Cassidy charm worked on everybody?"

"Well, I committed the most grievous of sins: I answered the phone to someone you and I have worked with for years, and then did exactly what the DI had instructed us to do. And as a punishment for that, I'm out here." She leaned on the car and looked off into the distance as behind her, Detective Carlson gave one of his more dignified yelps. He was averaging about three a minute.

"Rest assured, your presence was missed at the briefing."

"I'm sure it was. Anything good?"

"I don't know about good," said DS Burke, "but I've been officially directed to ring Bunny and ask him to come in for an interview to assist us with our enquiries."

"That's gonna be a total waste of time. If Bunny knew anything, he'd have told us already."

Burke paused for a second. When he spoke again his voice sounded different, quieter, like he was cupping his hand around the phone to prevent himself from being overheard. "Word to the wise, Pamela: neither of us likes it, but stay out of the way of it. I was chatting to a mate from down south earlier: Marshall is a hard-nosed bastard but he gets results, and, unfortunately, it appears himself and our friend have a bit of history."

"That should have nothing to do with anything."

"Yeah, I know. Meanwhile, over here in the real world ..."

"I know," said Butch. "It just feels wrong."

From where she was standing, she could see the road running along the side of the dump. Some guy in an Audi had found himself stuck behind a bin lorry and, for some inexplicable reason, was honking his horn, presumably to jockey the bin lorry along the narrow winding road that barely had enough room for oncoming traffic. She smiled as the lorry slowed down and the binmen waved out the windows, enjoying the arsehole's unjustified rage.

"Oh, one more thing," said Burke. "You'll love this. It's about the knife that young Carlson will definitely find for us any minute now. Apparently, according to the autopsy findings, it had traces of cheese on it. It seems murderers can't even be bothered to wash their weapons of choice these days."

Butch smiled for a fraction of a second, then her mouth dropped open. "Cheese?"

Burke laughed. "I know. It's completely ridiculous, isn't it? We might need to put out an APB for Mickey Mouse."

Butch attempted to sound casual but her throat was suddenly very dry. "Are they ... sure about the cheese thing?"

"It came from Dr D herself."

DS Burke kept on talking, but Butch had stopped listening. Her mind was racing, remembering standing in Bunny's kitchen as the man tried and failed to find the knife he'd had for that bloody ridiculous block of cheese.

It wasn't funny now.

Not funny at all.

# DIMPLES

The same sequence of words kept tumbling around and around in Garda Sean Heffernan's head. *Should have gone before I started. Why did I not go before I started? I'm never going to be able to hold this for two fucking hours. Oh God, oh God, oh God – why did I not go before I started?*

The instructions he'd been given were simple: guard the door to room 312. Nobody gets in or out of this hospital room until Detective Inspector Marshall shows up. However, on his way in to the Mater Hospital, Heffernan had run into Felicity Wallace, the girl of his dreams from his schooldays. He'd never had the balls to do anything about his crush, but had just admired her from afar. Well, there was the time he and Denny had hidden in a tree outside her house with a pair of binoculars and copped an eyeful, but Denny had got overexcited and fallen, breaking his wrist as he landed. They'd had to pretend he'd come off his bike or else there would've been no end of trouble.

Seeing her again, though, it had all come flooding back. Normally, such a woman was out of his league, but she'd married straight out of college and had gone through a messy divorce only last year. Now she was like one of those products in the supermarket with the yellow *whoops* sticker on it – back in his league. She'd been happy to see him too. She was at the hospital to visit her sick auntie who, by the sounds of it, was circling the drain. Heffernan had been sympathetic, kind, sensitive. He'd been reading a book that Denny had lent him – all about hitting on women. Getting them when they were vulnerable like this was perfect. He'd got her number and then excitedly texted Denny. If he played his cards right, this could be even better than that time Denny took Karen Murphy's panties as a trophy. Yeah, alright – technically he had a girlfriend, but this was Felicity Wallace. Nailing that would make him a legend.

While he'd moved reasonably fast, it hadn't been fast enough to save him from getting a call from the desk sergeant to give him a bollocking. He was already on a warning. The sergeant's boot up his arse had taken the shine off the day a bit, but still, Felicity Wallace – hubba hubba hubba!

He'd rushed up to the third floor and been directed to a private room by the ward sister, where he'd confirmed the patient was inside, checked in with the doctor and then radioed in to update the sergeant. Before doing that, he really should have taken the time to go for a pee. He didn't dare risk leaving his post now he was here, so all he could do was hop from foot to foot and count the seconds. He just had to hope that this DI turned up soon, as he wasn't due to be relieved for three hours, and he was going to have to relieve himself one way or another long before that.

Heffernan had been so wrapped up in his own desperate need for release that he hadn't noticed the kid walking up to him until he spoke.

"Here, guard, what's the story?"

He looked down to see a pre-pubescent fat lad looking up at him with beady eyes.

"Can I help you, son?"

"You're not my dad."

"I didn't say I was. It's a figure of speech."

"Why are you guarding this door?"

"That's none of your business."

The kid folded his arms and scrunched up his face. "Just making a bit of conversation."

"G'wan, hop it."

The kid tutted. "Do you know what your problem is, guard? You've got no appreciation for the fundamentals of conversation."

Heffernan scanned the corridor to make sure they were not being observed before hissing, "I'm not in the mood. Fuck off, or I'll slap you around the ear."

"That's a terrible thing to say. And me, a cancer kid, with only six months to live."

He looked the kid up and down. "No, you're not. Look at you. You're in a tracksuit. If you were a patient, you'd be wearing one of those gown things."

"Shows what you know. Those gowns are for people having operations. My tumours and all that are inoperable."

Part of Heffernan thought there was every chance the kid was lying, but he seemed unnervingly confident about it. "If you're a patient, what are you doing wandering around?"

The kid leaned back against the opposite wall. "If you must know, seeing as I'm on one of my rest days from, you know, all the treatment and that, they let me wander about the place. I've nobody my own age to talk to. The only people I see are the staff, my family, and all the celebrities that come to visit me because I'm a cancer boy and all that.

"To be fair, I used to get all the big names, but now there's another kid who's younger than me, and he's a bit more photogenic. Dimple-faced little prick. He got a visit from three members of the Irish soccer team there last week; I got a fecking clown. I'm not going to lie to you, it was a real low point. Not even a children's TV presenter, and normally you can't move down on the ward without bumping into one of those weirdos." The kid shook his head bitterly.

"That sounds rough," said Heffernan.

"So, did you always want to be a guard?"

Heffernan scanned the hallway again. "Are you sure nobody's looking for you? Like, there's nowhere you're supposed to be?"

"Nah. So, like, what attracted you to the guards? Was it the shiny jacket or the stupid-looking hat, or do you just like ordering people about?"

"Don't be cheeky."

The kid raised his hands. "I'm not. I'm honestly curious."

Heffernan bobbed his head. "What's your name?"

"I'm not supposed to tell that to strangers."

"I'm not a stranger. I'm a guard. You know you can always trust a guard." Heffernan gave the kid his best winning smile.

"Would you get out of that garden? Do you think I came down in the last shower? Next you'll be telling me how you can always trust a priest." The kid made a snorting noise. "I can see you've not read a paper recently."

"If you don't mind me saying, you don't talk like a normal child."

"No kidding. I can feel the Grim Reaper's breath on my neck. That changes a man. It's hard to go back to playing with Lego after that."

"Right. I suppose that makes sense."

"So, you never said what made you want to become a pig— I mean, sorry, a guard?"

Heffernan bent down, placed his hands on his knees and spoke in a soft voice. "I think you'd like to be a guard when you grow up. Am I right?"

The kid slapped his hands over his face dramatically and shook his head in disbelief. "Jesus – that's an appalling thing to say. I cannot believe you said that to a cancer kid. What part of 'six months to live' did you not understand, PC Plod? I mean, Jesus Christ, wait until the newspapers hear about this."

Heffernan straightened back up. "Ehm, no, I ... I just meant I ... I think you would look good in the uniform."

"And now he's telling me how he'd like to play dress-up. Were you a Catholic priest before you signed up or something?"

"You know what I meant."

The kid gave him a big smile. "I do. I'm only pulling your leg. I like you. I've decided you're my best friend."

Heffernan felt disconcerted by this. "Oh. OK. Thanks very much."

"You're welcome. I had a fish who held the role previously, but he died. I'm not going to lie to you, it's been a tough year. So, what kind of hardware are you packing?"

"Excuse me?"

"Weapons. I know they don't give you guns and all that, but I presume they give you something. God help us all if you're supposed to defend yourself with just your charm and that goofy-looking hat. So, what do they give you? Knife? Knuckle-duster? Baseball bat?"

"No," said Heffernan. "We get pepper spray and a collapsible baton."

"G'wan, then. Give us a look at your baton."

Heffernan shook his head. "I'm afraid I'm not allowed to do that."

"You are kidding me? Dimples O'Donoghue got Bono and the Edge playing a greatest hits medley by the side of his bed, and I can't even get a look at your baton? I don't think I have the will to go on."

Heffernan looked around again and sighed. "Fucking hell, kid. You are something else." He unclipped the pocket on his utility belt and withdrew the extendable baton, flicking it out to its full length.

"Cool!" breathed the kid. "Can I hold it?"

Heffernan handed it to him. "Now, be careful with that. You don't want to go taking your eye out."

The kid held the baton in one hand and slapped it against the other. "Nice. I bet you can do a fair bit of damage with this."

"It's not about hurting people."

"Yeah. Right. Pull the other one, it's got my cancerous knackers attached to it."

Heffernan winced. This kid was beyond weird. "Right, come on now. You should be getting back to your room. Give me that back."

"Ah, do you not want a game of chase?"

"I can't right now because— Ouch, you little fucker!"

The invective came as the kid whacked Heffernan in the shins with his own baton, causing him to crumple to the ground. He took off down the hallway with a surprising burst of speed.

"Come back here, you little prick!"

As Heffernan raced around the corner, he collided with a large man in a sheepskin coat coming the other way.

"Jesus, fella. Watch where you're going. Running around the place like a greyhound in heat."

"Sorry, sir. Did you see a fat kid?"

"I did," said the man. He pointed down one of the perpendicular corridors. "He went that way."

Heffernan ran off in hot pursuit.

Bunny watched for a few seconds, long enough for the guard to make it to the other end of the hallway and around another corner, before he lifted the sheet off the gurney he was standing next to and looked at Deccie crouching underneath it.

"Alright, you can come out now."

Deccie slipped out. "That was brilliant. I love messing with a guard."

"Remember what we agreed. That was a one-time thing."

"Yeah, yeah. I remember, boss. Don't worry. But don't you forget your end of the bargain."

Bunny nodded. "I'll go around to that shop that sold you the dodgy ice-cream and threaten to arrest the guy."

"And I get to watch?"

"Yes."

"And throw a couple of digs into him."

"Absolutely not."

Deccie shook his head in disappointment. "I did a terrible job negotiating here. I could have got a lot more."

"You live and you learn. Now, get out of here fast. Go and sit in the car with your grandad. I'll be out in a couple of minutes."

"You're the boss, boss."

"And Deccie ..." Bunny held out his hand and gave Deccie a pointed look.

His assistant manager pulled a face then handed him the extendable baton from his pocket.

"Can't blame a guy for trying."

# SO MUCH TROUBLE

Bunny slipped into the room and closed the door behind him as quietly as he could. Angelina was asleep on the bed. Looking at her lying there, it struck him how small she was. There was a bandage over her left eye and a bit of swelling in evidence around it. One of her wrists was also bandaged, but he remembered that had been there on Monday.

He moved across to stand beside the bed. He felt bad about waking her but time was of the essence; the guard on duty would eventually remember himself and return to his post, having given up on retrieving his collapsible baton and conferring upon Deccie the clip around the ear he so richly deserved.

He placed his hand on Angelina's forearm and shook it gently. "Angelina. Angelina."

Her eyes opened at half mast, groggy at first, but then they widened with surprise as she looked up and recognised him. "Bunny! What are you doing here?"

"Sure," he said, trying to give her a reassuring smile, "when I heard somebody was taking pot shots at little Angelina Quirke, of course I was going to come in and check she was OK."

She smiled up at him but winced and brought her hand to her forehead.

"Are you alright?"

"Yeah. It's nothing too serious. I just walloped my head against the wall, I think, when Joe pushed me to the ground."

Bunny puffed out his cheeks. "Jesus, it was very lucky the big lad was there."

She repositioned herself to sit upright. "How did you get in here?" She squinted towards the door. "Wasn't there a guard outside? I remember some guy ... Yeah, he stuck his head in, said that Detective Inspector Marshall arsehole was on his way."

"So you've had the pleasure of making Tommy Marshall's acquaintance, have you? What a delightful shit-sipping shandy-drinker he is."

"Didn't seem like he was your biggest fan either. What's the story there?"

"I'm afraid we don't have that kind of time. Listen, I don't know what's going on here at all, but I'm going to try and find out. OK?"

Angelina nodded.

"Have you any idea who would try and take a shot at you?"

Angelina drew a ragged breath and looked away. "I've no idea. I mean ... I guess Coop had a lot of enemies. The lawyer, Robinson, he pulled me aside after we spoke to Marshall. He made a big deal out of the fact that Coop's business interests, with all these shell companies and what not, are all very convoluted. He said there wasn't a will so, in the absence of that, everything has come to me."

"Oh. Congratulations, I guess."

"No," she said, grabbing Bunny's hand. "You don't understand. Anybody who owed Coop money now technically owes it to me. I mean, if it's all been legally signed and stuff, which, according to Robinson, the vast majority of Coop's deals were. He might not have been popular, but apparently, most of what he did was legal."

"I see. But if you're no longer in the picture ..."

"Then," said Angelina, in a hoarse voice, "I guess everybody's debts are written off. At least, that's what they think. I don't even want the bloody money." She raised her hand to her mouth as she started to cry. "Oh Jesus, Bunny. I'm in so much trouble."

"Hey, come on now, none of that. I'll make sure you're OK."

"No. You don't understand ..."

"Explain it to me, then. You know I'd always do anything I could to help you."

She looked up at Bunny and started to wipe the tears from her eyes. "You're a good man, Bunny." She laughed. "Last of the real cowboys."

"Look," he said, "I know this is gonna sound mad, but trust me, OK?"

"Always."

Bunny took a deep breath. "I have no idea why, but it looks like somebody's trying to frame me for Coop's murder."

Angelina's mouth dropped open and she gawped at him in disbelief. "That's ... That's impossible."

"It's not. A —"

The door behind him swung open and two men stood framed in the doorway. The look of shock on DS Paschal Burke's face was nothing compared to the look of outrage on DI Marshall's.

# OLD FRIENDS

Bunny hadn't seen Thomas "not Tom" Marshall in a good eight or nine years. It didn't seem like the time had been particularly kind to him, but then again, maybe he wasn't seeing him at his best. Incandescent with rage is rarely anybody's finest look.

The three guards had moved to the corridor outside Angelina Hannity's hospital room. Bunny was smiling calmly in the face of Marshall's fury, and poor old DS Paschal Burke was caught in the middle, looking like a man who would rather be anywhere else.

"Give me one good reason," barked Marshall, "why I shouldn't arrest you right now for attempting to pervert the course of justice?"

"What the feck are you on about?" asked Bunny, before turning to Burke. "Has he been drinking? Lunchtime piss-up, was it?"

"What am I talking about?" said Marshall, in a voice loud enough to attract the attention of a group of onlookers, who were gathered at the other end of the hall, wondering what was going on. "You were just in there with one of the key witnesses to a murder investigation in which you're a suspect."

"I'm being accused of murder?" Bunny threw out his hands in ostentatious shock. "This is news to me. Why have I not been told about this?" He jabbed a finger in the direction of the beleaguered

Paschal Burke. "I got a phone call from you, Paschal, earlier this afternoon, asking me to come in to answer some questions regarding the investigation into the death of Coop Hannity, but at no point was it mentioned that I was a suspect."

"Yes," said Marshall. "And I find it very interesting that you have not come in for that interview."

"I was more than happy to come in, but, given your unjust and ridiculous vendetta against me, Detective Inspector, I quite legitimately asked to exercise my right to have legal representation during this interview. And I'm glad I did, because apparently, I was being brought in under false pretences."

"Alright," said Burke, looking back and forth between the two men. "Let's everybody just calm down."

"So," continued Marshall, "seeing as you're available, would you like to answer a few questions now?"

"After this revelation, I will be doing no such thing without proper legal representation. And again, to be absolutely clear, I will be thrilled to do so, just as soon as my poor lawyer is available. The man is at death's door."

"Oh, give me a break," said Marshall. "He has IBS."

"Indeed he does," responded Bunny, "and that is a very serious complaint. As we speak, the poor fella is at home shitting blood, as you well know, seeing as you weren't willing to take his word for it and sent an officer round to check on him earlier today."

Paschal Burke was looking particularly embarrassed. Bunny guessed it had been him who Marshall had instructed to verify Kofi's condition.

"Rest assured," continued Bunny, "I'll be bringing this matter to the attention of the Garda Representative Association. And I hope that Kofi Mensah, a highly respected lawyer in this town, will be bringing your attempts to intimidate him up to the Law Society. I don't know how you do things down in Limerick, but in the big cities, like here and Cork, we show some respect for the law."

Bunny could feel Burke grow tense, as if he was preparing to intervene should Marshall try to take a swing. Wouldn't that be a dream come true? The long-awaited scrap with Marshall and witnesses to verify that Bunny hadn't swung first.

Disappointingly, the detective inspector took a deep breath and managed to get his emotions under control. "I left instructions that an officer was to be on guard outside of this room and to let nobody in except me. Where the hell is he?"

"How am I supposed to know?" said Bunny. "I only just got here, after hearing that Angelina, who I have known for a very long time, was involved in a traumatic incident. I wanted to check she was OK, so I found the room, went in to see her, and then you turned up, screaming and shouting, and accusing me of murder."

"I did not accuse you of murder."

"Yes, you fecking did!"

"Actually," said DS Burke, "he didn't."

Bunny nodded. "You're right, Paschal. I stand corrected. He informed me I was a suspect, that he was bringing me in for an interview under false pretences, and then he accused me of trying to pervert the course of justice by dropping in to check up on an old friend. Is that your recollection of events, DS Burke?"

Burke said nothing, but his eyes were pleading for a quick and painless death.

"Fine," said Marshall. "Just so we don't have any other misunderstandings ... As the lead officer in the investigation into the death of James Hannity, let me be crystal clear: you are to speak to no one involved, specifically any of the officers on my team, Mrs Hannity or anyone in the employ of the Hannity organisation or with even a tangential association with this case. And stay away from the Hannity house. Is that unambiguous enough for you?"

"Absolutely," said Bunny. "I just wish there had been some proper communication before this point. In particular, I'm concerned that Garda resources are being put into a wild goose chase, trying to pin something on me, for reasons I hope you'll be happy to explain to the Garda Representative Association, Detective Inspector Marshall. Meanwhile, a murder is going unsolved. I look forward to coming in for an officially documented interview, just as soon as poor Mr Mensah is able to do so."

"Excellent," said Marshall.

Bunny slapped Marshall convivially on the shoulder. "Indeed it is. You're looking good, Tommy. Almost didn't recognise you with your trousers on."

As Bunny reached the end of the corridor on his way to the exit, Garda Sean Heffernan came puffing around the corner and nearly ran into him again.

"Whoa. Go easy. I think somebody up there is looking for you, guard."

Heffernan's face dropped as he looked up the hallway. "Oh shite."

"Yeah, that Marshall is quite the prick." Bunny patted him on the arm and walked off. "By the way," he called back over his shoulder, "I think you dropped something."

Heffernan turned around to see his extendable baton lying on the ground behind him.

# NO BUSES FOR AGES AND THEN...

Bunny clapped his hands enthusiastically. "Alright, lads, bring it in, bring it in. That's enough of a warm-up."

The St Jude's Under-12s duly gathered around him on the sideline, their breath fogging under the floodlights in the sharp March air.

"I see we have a good turnout for training this evening. Clearly the big news that I'm treating everybody to McDonald's after Sunday's match has got around. Jimmy Dolan, nice to see you've got over that debilitating ingrown toenail that sidelined you for the last three months." This barb was met with a sarcastic cheer. "I'm only taking the piss, Jimmy. It's great to see you. Welcome back. And," Bunny continued, turning slightly to the man standing beside him, "seeing as we're welcoming back some old friends, I should introduce a new one. This gentleman here is Richard Chaplin."

Bunny's introduction elicited no response at all.

"Howerya, lads," said Richard. "Nice to be here. Bunny has told me great things. People call me Dick."

Bunny winched at the predicable sniggering. "Shut up. We'll stick with Richard."

Richard was a cheerful-looking man in his forties. Short, pudgy and bald in the peculiar way that a person has masses of hair, none of which has reached the top of their head.

Bunny favoured the team with a wide smile. "Richard is going to help out from time to time, and if, for any reason, I'm not around, he'll take over as manager."

Until that moment, he'd always thought the phrase "you could hear a pin drop" was just hyperbole. He swore he could hear birds' wings flapping a couple of hundred yards away.

Ruairi Thomas was the first to speak. "Where the fuck are you going?"

"Ruairi. What have I told you about swearing?" Bunny looked into the sea of concerned faces. "I'm not going anywhere, but, you know, just in case."

"In case of what?" asked Phil Nellis.

"Just ... Just ... I might have to go away with work."

"But you're not even working at the minute," countered Phil. "You're off because of that circumcision."

"For the last time, it's a sabbatical – it's not a Jewish thing, I don't know where you all got that idea from. It just means you're taking a break for a while."

"Are you going to be taking a break from us?" asked Paul Mulchrone, and Bunny felt a little piece of his heart break.

"No, no. Nothing like that."

"But you reckon," persisted Ruairi, "that you might be going away with the job you're not currently doing? Are the Gardaí going to start policing other countries or something?"

Bunny opened his mouth and closed it again. He hadn't given this much thought beyond ringing Richard earlier in the day and convincing him to get on board with the idea. He was belatedly realising that he hadn't prepared any kind of a cover story, and as interrogators went, the Spanish Inquisition had nothing on twenty confused twelve-year-olds.

"Richard is just a contingency plan, should anything happen to me."

"What's going to happen to you?" asked Phil.

"Nothing, just ... Look, lads, you're taking this far too seriously. This is a 'just in case' kind of thing." He gave a half-hearted laugh. "I mean, you never know, I could get run over by a bus tomorrow."

"A Dublin bus?" asked Phil. "How is that even possible? I've never seen one move fast enough to bruise you, never mind kill you." The assertion was met with a murmur of agreement from the entire group. "In fact," continued Phil, a lad not accustomed to having a lot of people agree with him, "the only way you could hurt yourself with one, is by running up the pavement and hurling yourself at the bleedin' thing."

"It's an expression, lads," said Bunny, growing exasperated. "Just an expression."

"And besides," chipped in Larry Dodds, "you told us not to talk to strange men. How is this bloke supposed to be the manager when we can't even talk to him?"

"But that's exactly what we're doing here," said Bunny, waving a hand at the increasingly bemused Richard Chaplin. "I'm introducing you to him. That way, he's not a stranger any more, is he?"

"We don't know anything about him," said Phil.

"Well, what do you want to know?"

"Where's he from?"

Bunny turned to Richard, who cleared his throat. "I was born in Bray, but I've lived up in Phibsboro for the last fifteen years."

"What do you do for a living?" asked Ruairi.

"As it happens," said Richard, "I'm a bus driver."

A horrified gasp escaped from the group of boys and Bunny slapped his hand to his forehead.

"Bunny," said Phil while jabbing a finger at Richard, "is this fella going to run you over so he can take over the team?"

"No," responded Bunny, doing his best not to shout. "Look, I asked Richard to be here. He's doing this as a favour to me. The whole getting-run-over-by-a-bus thing – that's just an expression. Admittedly, and I'll hold my hands up here, it's a truly awful choice of expression, but I promise you, I'm not getting run over by a bus, driven by Richard or anybody else."

"Besides," said Paul, "why is he coming in to be the manager if you're gone when we already have an assistant manager?" He indicated Deccie to emphasise his point.

Deccie stood beside him, looking aghast. It was also dawning on Bunny that he hadn't thought through the other part of this idea either.

"It's not like that," he said quickly. "You know – you *all* know – Deccie is invaluable to this team, but he can't be the manager."

"Why not?" asked Deccie. "What's this Johnny-come-lately got that I haven't got?"

The sea of heads before him bobbed together as one.

Bunny could not believe what he was seeing. "Need I remind you, lads, that two days ago you were all fit to lynch poor Deccie."

"Well," said Ruairi, "he is a bit of a prick."

"Language, Ruairi!"

"But," continued Ruairi obstinately, "he's our prick."

A cheer went up at Ruairi's words.

"OK, boys, I think you're misunderstanding me here."

"We should have a vote," said Deccie.

"We are not having a vote," said Bunny, before turning to Deccie. "And didn't you say to me last week that you'd no faith in democracy? That voters were a bunch of sheep too easily fooled?"

"I did," said Deccie with a firm nod, "but I've never been the shepherd before."

Inspiration struck. "The minibus," said Bunny, with enthusiasm typically only seen in shipwrecked sailors noticing a ship on the horizon. "The manager has to be able to drive the minibus!" He waved triumphantly at the increasingly alarmed Richard. "Richard, as previously discussed, is incredibly well qualified for that part of the job. It will literally be a busman's holiday."

"What's a—" started Phil Nellis, but Bunny cut him off.

"Doesn't matter. It's just another one of those expressions that I need to remember not to use. The point is, great as he is, Deccie cannot drive the minibus."

"If we need a driver," said Larry Dodds, "I'm willing to do it. And I do have relevant experience."

"Larry Dodds, stealing an ice-cream van with your cousin and taking it for a joyride is not relevant experience. Do I need to remind you of the promises you made me when I spoke to the judge on your behalf?"

Larry Dodds lowered his eyes to the ground, suddenly sheepish. "No, Bunny. Sorry, Bunny."

"So, it's settled. If anything happens to me, Deccie shall remain in his vital post as assistant manager ..."

Deccie stepped forward. "With increased responsibilities in the areas of team selection, fitness and tactical planning."

"What? Ah, feck it, fine," said Bunny.

"What?" said Richard.

Bunny turned to him. "We'll discuss it later." He focused his attention back on the main group. "But Richard here shall be the manager."

"Slash bus driver," added Deccie.

"OK," said Bunny, wiping the sweat from his brow, "so that's all sorted, then."

"Alright," said Ruairi, before stepping towards Richard and looking up at him defiantly. He pointed at Bunny. "But if he gets run over by a bus, we're all coming looking for you."

With that, the team took to the field to practise their passing while Bunny escorted the shellshocked Richard to one side and tried to reassure him. That hadn't gone well, but needs must when the devil drives. What was he supposed to say? "Lads, it looks like I'm being framed for murder, so if the next couple of days go badly, I might be missing training for the next twenty to thirty years." They would have had an awful lot of questions about that too.

Once Richard had left, Bunny found himself alone with Deccie.

"I'm sorry about that, Deccie. I should have discussed it with you first."

"What's going on, boss? I wasn't gonna say anything in front of the lads, but you're getting into fights out in Clontarf. You've got me distracting coppers so you can get into hospital rooms, and now you've got bus drivers with no appreciation for the fundamentals of the game coming in to take over. Seriously, is everything alright?"

Bunny looked down at his assistant manager. "I'll be honest, Deccie, I've had better weeks. Speaking of which, I can't help but notice that Alan with one L isn't here."

Deccie nodded. "I've been meaning to talk to you about that. He wasn't in school yesterday, or today. I was asking around, and none of the lads have seen him either."

Bunny sighed. The trouble was, given the circumstances, he couldn't ring Butch. That meant it was time to call up the big guns. "Alright, Deccie, split the boys into two teams and get them practising shooting."

"And what are you going to be doing?"

"I need to go ring a nun about a favour."

"Is that another one of those expressions?"

"I wish it was. I really wish it was."

# GET OUT

Bunny parked the car and looked around warily. This wasn't a great area to leave a vehicle unattended at night. Normally, he didn't worry about such things. Nobody wanted the kind of hassle in their life that would come with stealing Bunny McGarry's car, but this car was a rental and there was no way for interested parties to know it was his. He briefly considered leaving a note in the window, but decided against it. Sometimes, it doesn't pay to advertise, and he was here on business. Besides, it was a rental.

He looked up at the flats. At the far end of the fourth floor was the one belonging to Janice and Alan Craven, and, recently, Gary Kearney, who was the reason for Bunny's visit. Alan had been absent from school for two days and had now missed training. He had never missed a session before. He wasn't the biggest, most skilled or fastest of players, but you couldn't fault him for his reliability or determination. Something was wrong and the thought of it turned Bunny stomach.

"He's been—"

Bunny jumped and turned to see Sister Bernadette standing behind him. "Where the fecking hell did you come from?"

She rolled her eyes. "In case you've forgotten, I'm here doing covert surveillance. The covert part is not only half of the job, but they also put it before the surveillance to show how important it is."

"I know, I just ... Thanks for doing this, by the way."

She dismissed his gratitude with an upwards jerk of her head. "Unfortunately, this looks like it's exactly the kind of thing we do, and sadly, business is booming. As I was saying, Kearney's been in the pub just up the road there for ..." She checked her watch. "... ninety-four minutes."

"Are you sure?"

This earned him a stare from Sister Bernadette's extensive collection. "I'm going to pretend you didn't ask me that, Bernard, as I know you're not that stupid. This isn't my first rodeo."

Sister Bernadette was five foot nothing of bespectacled nun from Tipperary. In his life, Bunny had met ham-fisted brutal savages, cold-blooded professional killers and straight-up insane psychopaths, but none of them had the ability to be as intimidating as Sister Bernadette. He estimated that she was maybe sixty, but he wouldn't be surprised if that estimate was off by two decades in either direction. Nuns didn't age in human years, and in Bernadette's case that was doubly true. Bunny guessed she'd been forged from the melted-down remains of old nuns mixed with equal parts shoe leather, iron and venom.

Part of the reason Bernadette's age was so impossible to determine was that evidently she had managed to combine clean living with a hard, eventful life. The Sisters of the Saint was an order shrouded in mystery, but what Bunny knew from his limited exposure to them, they were diametrically different from your regular nuns. Excommunicated back in the mists of time, they were technically a rogue order, under nobody's control but their own. They were also uninterested in the thoughts-and-prayers approach to solving problems. They saw a world full of wrongs that needed righting and were prepared to get their hands dirty in order to get the job done. He had known of their existence for only a few months, but Bernadette in particular left an impression – often a permanent one, if you weren't careful.

"Are we ready to make a move?" she asked.

Bunny held up his hands. "No time like the present."

He was taken aback when she touched her ear under her wimple and said, "This is Eagle, we are go. Can I get confirmation on Kearney?" She listened for a second, then nodded before noticing Bunny's shocked expression. "What? Did you think I was just going to stand out here and watch? What kind of amateur organisation do you think we're running here?"

Bunny looked around. "How many of you are there exactly?"

"Exactly as many as we need. Come on."

Bunny glanced at the front door of the flat then back at Bernadette. "If he decides to leave the pub, how long do we have?"

"Don't worry about it."

"I am worried about it."

Bernadette looked up at him. "Technically? Eight minutes."

"But —"

"With the emphasis on the word 'technically'. If it looks like he's coming back, it will be dealt with."

"What does that mean?"

She sighed pointedly. "It means – don't worry about it. You asked for our help, now let us do what we do."

Bunny turned back to the door and gave a little shake of his head. It didn't feel as if his life was going to get any less weird any time soon.

He knocked on the door and, after about thirty seconds, he heard some movement behind it. Then came a nervous-sounding voice. "Who is it?"

"Howerya, Janice. It's Bunny."

"Oh, hello. Now isn't a great time."

Bunny glanced at Bernadette. "Just give me a couple of minutes, Janice. I promise I only want to help."

"Honestly, everything is fine."

He moved closer to the door and spoke more softly. "I think we both know that isn't true, Janice."

"Please. This will just make everything worse."

"I promise it won't. You know I only want the best for you and Alan. Just give me a couple of minutes and then I won't bother you again. I swear."

Bunny held his breath for a few seconds and then heard the latch being taken off the door.

Janice had tried to hide the bruising with make-up, but it was still easy enough to see if you knew what to look for. She attempted to explain, excuse and prevaricate, then she leaned against the wall and started to cry softly, big fat tears rolling down her face. "I'm such a fool. You tried to warn me. He swore – he swore it would never ever happen again."

Bernadette moved forward and took Janice's face between her hands. "Now, you listen to me. This is very important. This is not your fault. None of it. All abusers are masterful manipulators, that's how they get away with it. They lie, and we believe them, because we are decent people who think like decent people. It's only natural to believe it will never happen again, because decent people can't believe it happened the first time. But you know now, don't you? You have to do something or it will happen again."

Janice wiped a hand across her face awkwardly and then looked at Bunny. "Who is this?"

"She's a friend."

"Forget that," said Bernadette. "What I am is a one hundred percent guarantee of safety, and a fresh start for you and your son."

"Oh no," said Janice with a pleading look in her eyes as her gaze flitted between the two of them. "We can't go anywhere. He'll find us, and when he does ..."

"Listen to me. He will not find you – not if you come with us. We've been doing this for a long time."

"I'm sure you mean well, Sister, but he's a violent man."

"They're our speciality."

Bunny saw what happened next, but he still wouldn't have been able to describe precisely what happened. Sister Bernadette casually flicked her wrist, and then somehow, it contained a small handgun.

Janice shared Bunny's disbelieving look then turned back to Bernadette. "What kind of nuns are you?"

"Have you seen the *Sound of Music*?"

"Yes."

"Not those kind of nuns," Bernadette said with a tight smile. "Now, we need to get moving. Pack a bag with everything you'll need: clothes, medicines, family heirlooms, valuables. No domestic appliances, please. Where's your son?"

Janice nodded towards one of the doors leading off the hallway. "He's in his room. He won't come out."

Bunny knocked quietly on Alan's door, fully aware that the young lad must already be aware of their presence. It wasn't as if it was a very big flat.

"Alan?" No response. "Alan?" Bunny repeated. "Is it OK if I come in?"

In the absence of any response, Bunny slowly opened the door. Alan was sitting on the single bed in the corner, hugging his knees up under his chin. He tried not to look at Bunny as he entered.

Bunny closed the door quietly behind him. He looked around, taking in the posters on the wall. The Dublin football team. A soccer player Bunny didn't recognise.

"Howerya, fella. How's it going?"

He could see Alan's thin arms shaking, the white tightness in his lips. Bunny recognised the look – trying to cover everything in anger, because the rage was the easiest thing to hold on to. He moved across the room slowly and sat at the end of the bed, careful to give Alan space, but close enough to put himself in the boy's eyeline.

"Everything's going to be OK," said Bunny softly. "I'm here, and I brought a friend with me. We're going to help you and your ma."

Alan stared steadfastly at the wall above Bunny's head. "I don't need help."

"Right. Well, I still reckon it'd be best for everybody if you both came with us."

He gave his head the merest of shakes. "I'm not going anywhere."

"Look, I know how hard this must have been for you."

Bunny drew back in surprise as Alan's voice came out at a near shout. "You don't know anything. Mind your own business."

He put his hands out in a placating gesture. "Alright. Calm down, son. No need to go upsetting yourself." As he spoke, Bunny noticed that Alan was clutching something in his hand, but he couldn't see what it was. "What have you got there, fella?"

"Nothing. Never mind."

Bunny sighed. "Here's the thing, though, Alan. You know me, I'm a nosy bastard, always have been. I know you think I don't understand what you're going through, but believe me, I do."

"It's my job," said Alan.

"What is?"

"I'm the man of the house. It's my job to protect my ma." As he moved his arm Bunny saw the scissors. "He's gone to the pub. Sometimes, when he comes home, he falls asleep in front of the TV. I'm going to kill him."

"Right. OK," said Bunny, trying to think carefully about what to say next. "Here's the thing, though. If you were to do that, I'd have to arrest you."

Alan attempted a shrug.

"And," continued Bunny, "what do you reckon that will be like for your ma? She wants a fresh start. She's a good woman and I think she deserves that, don't you?"

"It'll be better when he's dead."

"Maybe," said Bunny. "Maybe it will. But do you know what I don't like about that option? It means he wins."

Alan didn't say anything, but he looked directly at Bunny for the first time since he'd entered the room.

"He'll have done the thing that he's trying to do. He'll have ruined your mother's life."

When Alan spoke again, it was in a voice so quiet that Bunny struggled to hear him. "It's my job."

"It isn't, though. I promise you it isn't. You might well be the bravest and toughest twelve-year-old I've ever met, but you're still only twelve. He's a full-grown man. No, I take that back – he's not a man. Not a real man. Real men don't behave like he does. You're better than him. You're worth a hundred of him, and you've got your whole life ahead of you, I swear. But not if you do this." Bunny held out his hand. "I'm asking you to please trust me. The both of you can leave here right now and you'll never have to see him again."

Alan fixed his eyes on Bunny as the tears began to swell in them.

"You have my word."

Twelve minutes later, the Craven family had all of their worldly possessions worth taking packed into a large, battered old suitcase and three bin bags. As Janice closed the door of the flat, Sister Bernadette held out her hand.

"OK. Everybody just wait here for a second."

"Is everything alright?" asked Bunny.

"Yes," said Bernadette with a curt nod. "It's just, he's on the move."

Bunny saw the panic in Janice's face, but Bernadette laid a hand firmly on the woman's arm. "Trust me. This is what we do. Just give me a minute."

In the end it was only thirty seconds – albeit a tense thirty seconds – before Bernadette nodded once more and said, "He's down. Let's go." Then, without another word she turned and headed for the stairs.

While trying not to be obvious, Bunny hurried to catch up with her. "What do you mean by 'he's down'?"

# WHAT YOU MEAN BY DOWN

Jason Potts knew his place. He was not "the man". No, Jason was, at best, the man who stood beside and slightly behind "the man". Through a cruel twist of fate, he was born short and not very likeable. He didn't know why this was – he came from a family of largely tall and largely likeable people. However, life had provided Jason with ample evidence that he was neither.

People who made sweeping statements about life usually said stuff like, there are only two types of people in this world – those who take and those who get taken from. Kill or be killed. The hunter and the hunted. All that kind of crap. Sure, those two categories were the most popular ones to fit into, but if you didn't have the chops to be in group A and you had the common sense not to want to be in group B, there was a third option: you could be the hanger-on, the hype man, the water carrier. You could ingratiate yourself with the predator to avoid becoming the prey. It wasn't a particularly fun life, but it was a life. Even hippos have those little birds that clean their teeth for them.

Gary Kearney was the hippo and Jason was his little bird – in the teeth-cleaning sense. Not that he actually cleaned Gary's teeth, but he went to the bar, got the drinks in, picked up Gary's dry cleaning, listened to his problems, had the common sense not to bring up any of his own – that kind of thing. Gary's problems fit into two distinct categories: his girlfriend and her son, who were annoying him; and his boxing career, which had taken a big hit owing to his inability to do the same. Having watched Gary's last fight, Jason was aware he had not attached himself to the apex predator, but there wasn't much he could do about that now. In this pub at least, in the street, maybe even in the postcode, Gary was still "the man", and Jason was the little bird who cleaned his teeth.

As they got ready to leave the pub, Jason was nervous. He'd actually been nervous all night because he needed to do the one thing you never did. Last week, Gary had asked for a loan of fifty quid, which Jason really didn't have but had given him anyway, on the understanding it was definitely coming back. There had been no mention of it since, except at home, where Jason's ma mentioned little else. They needed that money for the gas bill. Despite being thirty years old, Jason was also frightened of his mother. True, she wouldn't physically kick the crap out of him, but then she wouldn't need to. The woman could inflict the kind of psychological damage that would make you yearn for a good old kicking. And so it was that Jason was desperately trying to find the right moment to ask Gary for his money back.

And now they were leaving the pub. The walk back to the flats wouldn't take long and Gary was in a foul mood. He always got like that when he drank.

As they stepped outside into the cold March air, Jason could feel himself sobering up fast. The anticipation of what was about to come next was making his guts boil. He wondered if he was going to be sick.

"People think Muhammed Ali was so great," slurred Gary, continuing a monologue he'd started while taking a piss in the toilets, "but he wasn't all that. He'd get eaten alive in the modern game. Wouldn't last two rounds with me."

Jason nodded. He'd always found that was the best course of action when confronted with statements of such monumental bullshit.

Given the late hour, he was confused to see two nuns, holding collection boxes, standing on the pavement ahead. They looked quite comical, if you were in the mood for a laugh, which Jason definitely wasn't. One of them was a very large girl, and the other was small and thin. They also looked surprisingly young for nuns. He'd been educated by nuns at St David's, but he'd never seen one that looked under fifty – at least, not unless they were African. Africa seem to be the only place in the world still producing nuns. They were a dying breed, like box-to-box midfielders and affordable housing.

As Gary and Jason approached, the two women shook their tins enthusiastically.

"Donation for the orphans," said the little one in what sounded like a Northern Irish accent. "Help save the orphanage."

Gary laughed. "Would you fuck off out of that. Orphans? I'm not giving away my hard-earned money just because somebody else doesn't want to take care of their kid. I'm already taking care of one that isn't mine."

While Jason was used to Gary being an arsehole, this was a whole new level. These women were nuns. If his education had taught him anything, and God knows he had not learned much, it was that you never, ever fuck with nuns.

Gary shoved his way roughly between the two women, causing the bigger one to stumble backwards and throw out an arm to prevent herself from falling. Jason cringed behind Gary's back and made an apologetic face. He couldn't actually apologise, not without pissing off Gary, but he tried to convey his regret through the medium of mime.

Gary strode on for a couple of steps.

Then he slowed to a drunken stroll.

Then, a stumble ... An unexpected pirouette, during which he looked back at the nuns, a look of stupefaction spreading across his face, then he fell back, hard. Anyone who had attended Gary's last couple of fights would have experienced an overwhelming sense of déjà vu as he crashed to the ground like a felled redwood. This time, though, there was no uppercut, no right hook. He just went down.

Jason looked at the nuns and could have sworn he saw the little one shove something back into her pocket. She caught sight of him and favoured him with a quick smile before looking down at the unconscious form of Gary Kearney.

"Dear oh dear. Isn't drink a terrible thing? Some people just can't handle it." She nodded to the other nun. "Come on, Assumpta. We should be getting back."

As they walked away, the little one touched her ear. "He's down."

The two nuns disappeared around the corner, leaving Jason alone in the street with the supine form of Gary Kearney.

"Gary? Gary, are you alright?"

He didn't move. Jason bent down to check him. He was still breathing, there was no blood. It appeared that he'd just fallen unconscious. Jason wasn't sure what to do next. It would take four of him to pick up the man and take him home. He could go back into the pub and ask for help but Gary was not a popular man. The only reason he hadn't been barred was because nobody was brave enough to do it.

Jason looked around and considered his options. Then, a voice inside his own mind that he'd never heard before spoke to him.

He reached inside Gary's jacket and pulled out his wallet. One hundred quid. The prick had a hundred pounds just sitting there and he'd made no effort to pay Jason back. Jason snatched the notes, closed the wallet and shoved it back inside the pocket.

After a quick glance around to confirm he wasn't being watched, Jason stood up and started to walk quickly away.

He got all the way to the street corner before stopping. What the hell was he doing?

As he hurried back to Gary Kearney, he checked again that nobody had witnessed what he'd done.

"Gary? Gary, can you hear me?"

No response.

Jason glanced around one more time then gave Gary Kearney the mother of all boots in the bollocks.

# THAT SINKING FEELING

What was the phrase? It's not the despair, it's the hope that kills you. Bunny tried to calm the thumping heart in his chest as he fumbled with the keys to his own front door. It wasn't Simone. It couldn't be. Still, the hope, the terrible hope.

He opened the door and raced down the hall towards the sitting room, where a light had been visible through the closed curtains.

He burst into the room then slouched against the wall when he saw Detective Pamela Cassidy sitting in his armchair, looking back at him. "Butch," he said, failing to keep the disappointment from his voice, "it's you."

"Yeah. Did you forget you gave me a key? Were you expecting somebody else?"

Bunny ignored the question, took off his coat and slumped down onto the sofa. The text from Mrs Byrne had read, *Your lady friend is back*. He had jumped to conclusions.

"So, to what do I owe the pleasure of this visit?"

Butch extended her leg carefully, so as not to wake the cat that was sleeping on her lap, and kicked Bunny in the shin.

"Ouch! Jesus, Butch. What in the fecking hell was that for?"

"It could be for a lot of things. Like, for example, how I had to drive over here, and then go round the area for an hour, making sure you weren't under police surveillance, before I came in. Anyone finds out I'm here, forget my career being over, I could go to jail too."

Bunny looked at her. "So why are you here?"

She took a deep breath before speaking, as if she were trying to keep her temper under control. "Lots of reasons. I guess I'm here to warn you. To convince myself I haven't done something stupid. But mainly, I'd like the explanation I think I deserve as to what the hell is going on?"

"I don't know what you're talking about."

"Bullshit!" snapped Butch. "Guess what I found out today? The autopsy on Coop Hannity came back with an unusual little finding: traces of cheese in the stab wounds. You know, like he'd been stabbed with a large knife that had previously been used to cut cheese." She jabbed a finger in the direction of Bunny's fridge in the next room. "I'm guessing like the massive fuck-off slab you have in your fridge. For Christ's sake, I was here when you realised that knife was gone."

Bunny went to speak but she cut him off.

"And before you say anything, you rang me to confirm that Hannity had been stabbed to death. You must know that somebody is trying to frame you for this thing, so why the hell are you dodging coming in for an interview? I could even give a statement confirming that I was here when you realised the knife had disappeared. All of this you know, so seriously, Bunny, what's going on?"

He lowered his eyes to the worn carpet. "I'm sorry, but I can't say."

"This is Gringo, isn't it?"

Bunny said nothing but glanced up at her briefly.

"Jesus," said Butch. "Only you would get yourself into this much shit in order to protect a dead man." She petted the still-sleeping cat and then looked back up at Bunny. "I'm not an idiot. He was my friend too, but we both know whatever the hell happened in that investigation, it stank to high heaven. Gringo and the others getting into a shootout somewhere they had only the weakest of justifications for being? And you and him ending up on that beach? I don't know exactly what happened and, to be clear, I don't want to know, but I've lost one friend already and, annoying prick that you are, I'd rather not lose another."

Bunny gave his famed wonky-eyed smile. "Are you hitting on me?"

Despite herself, Butch laughed. "So help me God, McGarry, I am this close to hurling your own cat at you."

He nodded. "Would this be a bad time to bring up the fact that I do not own a cat?"

Butch considered the sleeping feline. "What? But the thing was sitting on your doorstep and walked in like it owns the place?"

"Yeah," said Bunny. "It's a cat. That's what cats do. As a lesbian, I thought you had a fundamental understanding of cats? Aren't they like the national animal of Lesbania?"

"OK, well, first things first – fuck off. Secondly, I probably shouldn't have fed it, then, should I?"

"No," agreed Bunny. "That was less than ideal."

"Why didn't you say something when you walked in?"

Bunny shrugged. "I thought you were going for a sort of Bond-villain vibe."

"Why would I ... Never mind. Forget about the cat," she said, while stroking the cat. "What are we going to do?"

"*We* aren't going to do anything. This has nothing to do with you."

"That's a shitty thing to say. I came here to help and whether you like it or not, I'm going to. You do know Marshall is this close to having you arrested? Sure, they haven't got enough to pin Hannity's murder on you, but I know for a fact that he and Rigger O'Rourke went a couple of rounds this evening – about whether or not he could bring you up on charges for obstructing the course of justice."

"That's a bit of a reach."

"Which I believe was O'Rourke's point. Still, this is Marshall's show, and from what I hear, you gained access to Mrs Hannity's hospital room through unconventional means."

"I've no idea what you're talking about."

"Yeah," said Butch. "On an entirely unrelated note, you remember I have met your assistant manager previously?"

"And heaven help anybody who brings him in for an interrogation."

"Do you reckon he'll stay quiet?"

"Oh no. I guarantee he'll talk. And talk and talk. Incidentally, have they any idea who took a shot at Angelina Hannity?"

Butch shook her head. "Investigations are ongoing, and I can confirm that all manner of resources are being thrown at it. The higher-ups are freaking out that we've got a new gang war in the offing, and we don't even know who the players are. By the way," she added, looking at her watch. "Training finished a couple of hours ago. Where have you been?"

"Janice Craven."

Butch's eyes widened. "She never rang me. Is everything ..."

Bunny nodded. "It wasn't, but it is now." He considered his words. "Well, I hope it will be eventually. They're somewhere safe, which is the main thing."

"Jesus. Even with all this going on, you find time to try and deal with that too, huh? You're some man for one man, McGarry."

"And they say men can't multitask." He leaned forward on the sofa. "There is one thing you can help me with. Let's assume I am being set up for this murder. What I can't figure out is why haven't I been *properly* set up for murder, if you see what I mean? There's the murder weapon, which I'm guessing has my fingerprints on it, and I believe there's a tape of my meeting with Hannity ... Is it just me, or does it seem odd that neither has been found?"

"Well," said Butch, "I don't know what's happened to the tape, but there is a possible explanation for why the murder weapon hasn't been found. The new lad, Carlson, messed up on the search, and a skip from up the road from Hannity's house got taken to Dunsink without being checked. If I was to dump the murder weapon – I mean, somewhere I wanted it to be found but believable enough not to look obvious – that's where I'd have put it."

"Ah, I see."

"Yeah, I was out there today. It's the shit duty Marshall gave me as a punishment for knowing you. To be honest, if it is there we should have found it by now, but there were some unexpected delays."

"Like what?"

"I'll tell you about it when this is all over. Just be thankful that, despite DI Marshall's protestations, it was too big an area to bring in lights to search at night. But we're due back out there at eight in the morning with a much bigger team. If it's there, odds on we'll find it. The clock is ticking, Bunny."

"I know. I just need a little more time."

"I hope you're right," said Butch. "Because a little more time is all you have. I should probably get going."

"Thanks for dropping in. Can I interest you in a massive block of cheese?"

Butch shook her head. "No, thanks." She looked down at the feline still sleeping on her lap. "Have you ever considered maybe getting a cat?"

# SEX DUNGEONS IN SUBURBIA

Garda Mark Finlay clapped his gloved hands together and hugged himself, trying to generate some warmth.

"Why are we here?"

Garda Alan Maguire scratched at his goatee beard and considered the question. "Do you mean in an existential sense?"

Finlay scrunched up his face. "What?"

"As in, what is our place in the universe? What is the meaning of life? Is what we consider to be our lives actually our lives or maybe a projection from another state of existence?"

"No, ye fuck-trumpet. I just meant why are we standing out here at three in the morning in a back garden in Santry?"

"Oh," said Maguire, failing to hide his disappointment, "we're here to guard this door." He pointed a thumb back over his shoulder at the door in question to emphasise his point.

"Yes, smart arse," said Finlay. "I know we're here to guard that door. My question was: why are we here to guard a stupid bloody door?"

"Actually, that wasn't your question. What you said was 'why are we here?'. That's a very different question with a lot of possible interpretations."

Finlay glared at him. "This garden has already been a murder scene once this week; are you trying to go for the double?"

Maguire turned his head and, when Finlay couldn't see, stuck out his tongue. It was fair to say that neither man would be the other's first choice for spending a night standing a post together. Still, got to get along to get along.

"I heard it's a sex dungeon."

"No way."

"That's the word on the street."

"The street?" scoffed Finlay. "How would you know? Does your book club meet on it?"

The reason Finlay disliked Maguire, at least as far as Maguire could tell, was that he'd taken the unusual step of dropping out of a philosophy degree to join the Garda Síochána. Either that or Finlay could smell the books off him. The man's determination to avoid all levels of intellectual engagement was almost impressive. Maguire guessed he hadn't read anything more involved than the instructions on the back of a microwave pizza packet in a decade.

"If it's a sex dungeon," continued Finlay, "then why is it under twenty-four-hour guard?"

"Obviously it played some part in the murder."

"No, it didn't. I was here on the first morning. Coop Hannity's body was found over there, by the bloody pigeons."

"It doesn't mean the sex dungeon wasn't involved."

"And who would even build a sex dungeon in their back garden?"

"Well," said Maguire, "sexual deviants. Obviously."

"Right, yeah. You'd definitely put your sex dungeon down here, just between the pigeon coops and the washing line. People don't do the freaky-deaky stuff in their own back yard," said Finlay knowingly. "They go somewhere else to do that."

"Like where?" Maguire deeply regretted asking the question as soon as it came out of his mouth. What followed from Finlay was tediously inevitable.

"Amsterdam."

It took every ounce of Maguire's self-control not to shove his gloved hand into his mouth and scream. Two months ago Mark Finlay had gone on a stag weekend to Amsterdam with his football team, and had been laboriously shoehorning it into conversation ever since.

As it happened, Maguire himself had done a weekend in Amsterdam a couple of years ago, but he didn't bring it up, primarily because it was very obvious that, unlike his trip, the stag do had not taken in the Van Gogh Museum, the Anne Frank House or the Royal Palace Amsterdam. It might have involved a canal, but only if somebody threw up in it.

Still, the stag weekend had made Finlay one of the world's leading experts on the cornucopia of human sexual desires. Seeing a woman dressed as a French maid shoving a feather duster up somewhere unexpected apparently had that effect.

Maguire turned around to look directly at the innocuous-looking blue metal door. "So, what do you reckon is behind the mysterious door, then?" he asked, keen to move the conversation away from the Dutch capital at any cost.

"I reckon it's a vault. Got to be."

"A vault?" said Maguire. "Do you mean as in a crypt?"

"No, idiot. Like a bank vault. Behind that door is millions of quid in gold bars, and probably priceless works of art and all that."

"Right. And they're leaving two unarmed guards and a padlock here to protect it, are they?"

Finlay gave him a huffy look and folded his arms. "I've nearly got my firearm certificate"

"Brilliant," responded Maguire. "I hope you brought the documentation with you. You can show it to the robbers when they turn up. It'll be a real conversation piece."

"Do you know what your problem is?"

Before Maguire could find out, their conversation was rudely interrupted by the tip of a silencer being placed against the nape of his neck. He knew it was a gun because out of the corner of his eye he could see a figure dressed head to toe in black camouflage gear holding one to the back of Finlay's head too.

A calm, English-accented voice spoke from somewhere near by. "If you want to live, you don't move, you don't speak. Understand?" The voice actually laughed. "You may nod your heads extremely slowly to indicate compliance."

They did.

A figure clad in identical black camouflage gear stepped out of the darkness and stood in front of them. The source of the voice.

"As long as you're both sensible, this doesn't need to get messy." He nodded at the two men still standing behind Maguire and Finlay. "You are going to get down on your knees very carefully, then lie on the ground. Try anything stupid, and all that will happen is my colleagues will add to the extensive list of people they've already killed. Don't be a hero."

The man noticed Maguire staring at him and nodded.

"Yes, they are brown – the same eye colour as between fifty-five and seventy-nine percent of the world's population, depending on who you ask. Still, you've got that for the debrief."

As the pair lowered themselves to the ground, Maguire had an excellent view as the man silently dropped his kitbag and withdrew some kind of welding kit.

Ten seconds later, he heard the bunker door creak open. By this point, his hands had been cuffed behind his back. The man put the welding kit back into the bag then withdrew a large, heavy-looking object.

He stepped through the door, flicking on a torch as he did so. Two minutes later, he returned, put the device, whatever it was, back in the bag and picked it up. While he'd been gone, Maguire and Finlay had been gagged too, which honestly relieved Maguire. Bad as this was, at least he wasn't going to have to listen to Finlay talk while they waited for the humiliation of being found.

Five minutes after their arrival, the three men disappeared back into the night.

. . .

Four hours later, Finlay and Maguire were indeed found by the next shift. As soon as Finlay's gag was removed, he blurted out the words, "Brown eyes. The guy had brown eyes."

Such an arsehole.

# UNDER SURVEILLANCE

Bunny closed the front door behind him and threw out his arms in a world-encompassing stretch. He'd heard something somewhere about people who do yoga "greeting the sun", or something like that. That wasn't what he was doing. Last night, for the first time in a while, he'd slept reasonably well. God knows, it wasn't through a lack of worries in his life – quite the opposite. There were a lot of ways today could go badly, and maybe it was a survival instinct on the part of his own body, but something somewhere must have reasoned that, today of all days, he really did need to be at his best.

He'd had eight hours of quality sleep. The world really was your oyster with a decent night's kip in the bank. He could feel his brain firing on all cylinders, which was definitely what was needed. For the show of the thing, he decided to lean against the wall and throw in a few hamstring stretches. And it was a show because, as expected, he was being watched.

You have to understand the politics of parking. In this day and age most people, even from a working-class background, have a car. Or rather, to be more exact, most households have a car. This means that on a road of terraced houses that don't have driveways, the space outside of your house is yours. Not by law – at least not by any law written down – but rather by a collective understanding of how things should work. Once you know that and you know the area, reading the street becomes easy.

In the past, Bunny may have been lax in the area of home security, but not with parking. Parking he had always paid attention to. Last year, for example, when a couple of commuters had the bright idea to park on his street and cycle the rest of the way in to avoid the extortionate parking rates in central Dublin. Bunny, being a guard, had gone to great lengths to not notice how, after a couple of weeks and a couple of polite notes had been ignored, one of those commuters had returned to find all of his car was still there, but that it had been neatly disassembled into its constituent parts. After that, the parking situation quickly returned to residents only.

As he stretched, Bunny had taken in the road in both directions. Mr McCall's, Mrs Clark's, the Killfoyles's, Nancy Jacobs's, Jerry Marks's, Mr Ranganesh's, Tony Baker's, young Vivian Clark's (who got herself a job in a bank last year and parked her car outside of the widow Reed's house, who she drove to the hospital when she had an appointment), Johnny Rogers's, Mr Danaher's, Mr Byrne's, Bunny's spot currently occupied by the rental car, Mrs Doyle's, Carl Mullins's, John McCullough's, and finally, on the end as always, Dave Tiernan's Ford Cortina. Once you knew the familiar topography, seeing what was out of place was as easy as noticing if you'd woken up with extra teeth in your mouth. There was not one, but two interlopers parked in the street. Bunny didn't look directly at them, he just hopped in the rental car, sent a quick text and pulled away.

As expected, one of the vehicles followed him and the other stayed put. Ironically, they were both watching him, but he guessed neither was aware of the other.

The thing about being followed by the Gardaí is that fleeing really does make you look guilty. Unfortunately, while Bunny wasn't guilty, he needed to go about his day without the tail DI Marshall had assigned to him cramping his style. On the upside, at least Marshall had had the common sense not to use anybody that Bunny knew.

Bunny glanced in the rearview mirror and saw the man and woman in the innocuous-looking Opel Astra behind him. They were, of course, being careful to leave plenty of room in order to avoid arousing his suspicions. He couldn't help but smile. At a guess, they were a couple of detectives from Limerick and Marshall had seconded them to Dublin for the duration of the investigation, on the grounds that he didn't know who he could trust up here. Bunny couldn't blame him. In fact, he was thankful for it.

He pulled up at the junction at the end of Carnlough Road and was waiting to turn left on to Cabra Road, towards the city centre. It was just after nine, so the traffic was starting to flow more easily after its rush-hour peak, but it was still relatively slow-moving. Bunny reached the front of the queue, indicated and waited for a clear gap in the traffic.

On the pavement to his left, a woman who looked more granny than mother-aged was cooing at the unseen bundle of joy in the pram before her. Just as Bunny turned left, she pushed the pram in front of the Opel Astra two cars back, as if to cross the road, temporarily preventing it from moving forward. There was no traffic coming in the other direction, but the woman still looked both ways conscientiously.

As she was about to move on, she dropped the baby's rattle. With an apologetic wave, she bent down to pick it up. At this point, with both of the cars in front of them having driven off, the two guards in the Opel Astra were growing understandably irritated. Then, the clumsy grandmother dropped the rattle again.

DS Richard Tiernan, who normally worked out of Limerick, leaped out of the vehicle in desperation to assist the woman. He glanced into the pram. "What the fuck?"

"Oh God," said the clumsy grandmother in a cheerful voice, "would you look at that? I forgot to bring the baby with me again. Well," she added, giving Tiernan a wide smile, "that's the menopause for you, love. Makes the old brain go screwy."

With that, Margaret Byrne, next-door neighbour of Bunny

McGarry, returned to the pavement, and pushed the empty pram back towards her home and a well-earned breakfast.

DS Tiernan returned to his car, where he and his partner spent the next fifteen minutes driving around in an increasingly futile attempt to relocate Bunny McGarry, before ringing the office for a bollocking.

# IN THE ROUGH

Commissioner Gareth Ferguson was distracted from his club selection by what was becoming his least favourite sound in the world.

"Damn it, Kevin. Could you stop with the incessant yapping for—"

The Commissioner noticed the direction in which the Labradoodle was barking and looked up to see Detective Inspectors Marshall and O'Rourke approaching.

"Ah, gentlemen, what an unexpected surprise."

Marshall glanced at O'Rourke before speaking. "I was told you demanded to see us, sir."

"Yes, Marshall. I was being facetious."

The Commissioner withdrew the driver from his golf bag, selected a ball from the bucket beside him and placed it on the tee. All around them, other golfers were similarly working on their game, smashing golf ball after golf ball into the distance. Given that it was half-nine in the morning, the place was maybe one-third full.

"I didn't know you're a golfer, Commissioner," said O'Rourke.

Ferguson didn't respond verbally. Instead, he took a hack at the ball, which sent it shooting off at a forty-five degree angle from the hoped-for trajectory. Kevin whined and placed his paws over his face.

"Ah," said O'Rourke.

"Yes," replied Ferguson. "Can't stand the bloody game. I do enjoy the clubs, though. They're one of the few acceptable cudgelling implements that a gentleman may possess without questions being asked. I do feel they should have stopped there, however, rather than adding the unnecessary difficulties involving the ball."

He slammed the driver back into the bag. "The reason I am here is that in a couple weeks I have to go on a championship-standard golf course with my opposite numbers from England, Scotland and Wales, and embarrass myself in order to build bridges. I should add that I have no need for such bridges. My bridges are perfectly fine, thank you very much. However, at a recent UN convention on policing, the Junior Minister for Justice shared a hilarious joke with an individual he thought was his opposite number from France, but who, incredibly, turned out to be from the UK. You have to ask yourself, what kind of incompetent buffoon can't tell a Frenchman from an Englishman, yet somehow feels qualified to tell a joke involving an Englishman, a Welshman and a Scotsman, not to mention the Pope's penis."

"Is that the one—" started O'Rourke.

"Yes, it is," snapped Ferguson.

O'Rourke noticed that the Commissioner's face seemed redder than normal as he selected the three wood from his bag.

Marshall cleared his throat. "Have you lost weight, sir?"

The Commissioner raised his eyebrows and looked at Marshall. "Do you mean since I saw you yesterday, DI Marshall? What an embarrassing attempt at toadying. Do fuck off, there's a good chap."

O'Rourke managed to remain stony-faced, internalising his delight at Marshall's embarrassment.

"So, we know why I am here," said Ferguson. "Would either of you like to guess why you are here?"

You could tell Marshall was new to the hand-grenade juggling act that was dealing with the moods of the Commissioner. One of the first things you learned was that his questions were really more oratorical devices. The trick was resisting the urge to answer them, unless absolutely necessary.

"Is this about the tapes?" Marshall asked.

Ferguson took the three wood by the grip and held it out in front of him. "Is this about the tapes? Is this about the tapes?" he mocked. "What tapes would these be? Oh, the Hannity tapes. The ones that were not only evidence in Mr Hannity's own murder case, but also, potentially, a spectacular intelligence windfall, the likes of which this service has never seen. Those tapes? Do we think I mean those tapes?"

Marshall looked at O'Rourke nervously. "Yes," he ventured.

"Ding, ding, ding, ding!" roared the Commissioner, earning a look from a golfer a couple of bays down. "Correct," he continued. "I do indeed mean those tapes. The ones that I thought were under armed guard, although it seems I was mistaken in that belief, seeing as they were destroyed through the application of an industrial-strength magnet by a person or persons unknown while a couple of my officers watched on."

"It was persons, sir," said Marshall. "Team of three. Highly trained, apparently."

"Yes," said Ferguson through gritted teeth. "I know that. I was being facetious."

"The security arrangements for the bunker preceded my taking over of the investigation."

"Did they indeed? Service, Marshall. DI O'Rourke, would you like to return serve?"

"As everyone here knows, the assignment of armed gardaí to such a role requires sign-off from a more senior rank than detective inspector. I highlighted this to DI Marshall as an action point requiring urgent attention."

"No, you didn't," protested Marshall in an outraged whine.

O'Rourke put his hand inside his coat and withdrew the document he had brought with him in anticipation of this becoming an issue. "I have here a copy of the handover notes I left for DI

Marshall, which back up my point." O'Rourke kept his eyes fixed firmly on the Commissioner, so didn't get to enjoy the look on Marshall's face as he realised he was Wile E. Coyote and had just ran out of cliff. "Given how the detective inspector has made no secret of his disdain for how things are done up here in Dublin, perhaps he didn't feel the need to read these notes. I'm afraid there's nothing I can do about that."

Marshall's mouth opened and closed repeatedly without producing any words. It happened enough times that you could have stuck a light in there and used him to send Morse code messages to passing ships.

Ferguson nodded at O'Rourke, perhaps the slightest hint of appreciation at a hand well played. "Well, there we have it. Shall we chalk this up to a spectacular administrative error by a senior officer and move along?"

Perhaps Marshall was getting the hang of it – he made no effort to answer the question.

O'Rourke held out the copy of the handover notes to Marshall, the originals of which he'd gone to great lengths to be witnessed leaving on the DI's assigned desk. He'd also emailed them. "Would you like this copy of them, Tom? Make sure there's nothing else you've missed?"

Marshall snatched the three sheets from his hand while Ferguson tutted at O'Rourke. "Fintan, Fintan, Fintan – have you never heard of the punch Ali didn't throw? The one when Foreman was already on his way down? It does ruin the aesthetic of the moment by piling on."

O'Rourke knew the Commissioner was right, but something about Marshall irritated him more than he could possibly understand. Or maybe he was overcompensating in some messed up-redirection of guilt. "Sorry, sir."

"However, that does bring me on to the other matter. I should inform you that Detective John Carlson, who suffers with musophobia, has decided to leave the force with immediate effect. You see, musopobia is the fear of vermin and not musicians, although a certain reprobate who, until recently, was engaged to my beloved goddaughter, would fit both interpretations.

"The reason his departure has been brought to my attention is that, despite making clear his phobia to a senior officer, Detective Carlson was sent to Dunsink. Dunsink, as we all know, is famous for two things: the observatory and the dump. Seeing as Detective Carlson – or, rather, formerly Detective Carlson – is now suing the Garda Síochána for mental distress, I think we can all guess where he ended up. Apparently, on his way home last night, he pulled over his car in the fast lane of the M50 and was found in the central reservation, semi-naked and screaming about rats. Bearing in mind I'm holding a metal three wood in my hands, would the senior officer in question like to explain himself and risk being bludgeoned to death if I do not like said explanation, or would he rather take the sensible option and just say sorry?"

It didn't speak well of Marshall's survival instincts that he clearly deliberated before giving an answer. "Sorry."

"Excellent choice," growled Ferguson before looking at O'Rourke. "Can you make this go away, Fintan?"

He nodded. "Yes, sir."

"Very well. Also, Detective Inspector Marshall, do I want to know why I've had a complaint from the carpool about one of the cars being used in your investigation being flooded?"

"Yes, I—"

"Understand," continued Ferguson, "that I don't mean the engine has been flooded. I believe the entire car has been mysteriously filled with water."

"We're trying to eliminate all of the Marsh brothers from our enquiries, but the fire service is being unhelpful. I sent a couple of uniforms to check rotas at stations where the brothers work. At the Dolphin's Barn station the officers' car was broken into and filled with water. I was going to ask you to register a complaint with the head of the Dublin Fire Brigade."

"Your wish is my command, Detective Inspector. What I definitely need right now is a turf war with the people we pay to put out fires, especially as you seem so determined to start them. I'm going to hazard a guess that they have the hump with you for treating roughly one percent of their entire workforce as murder suspects. Maybe try to pare down your fishing expedition to two or three brothers and see how you get on. They seem a little touchy on the subject of the Marsh boys. Can't think why – maybe it was the whole 'locking up their mammy' thing? And do I want to ask for an update on the Hannity murder investigation, and the attempted murder I believe has now been rolled into it? I mean, we're not just looking at firemen, I presume?"

Marshall shook his head. "No, sir. Right now a much larger team is completing the search for the possible murder weapon at Dunsink." He noticed Ferguson's expression and correctly anticipated the question on the Commissioner's tongue. "I have made sure that everyone involved is happy to be there."

"I think you might be being over-ambitious reaching for happy," commented Ferguson. "Let's just aim for 'not willing to participate in a class-action lawsuit', shall we?"

"The release of the image of the man in the balaclava has led to a lot of calls to the tip line, which we're processing," Marshall added.

O'Rourke was well aware of the Commissioner's dim view on the value of tip lines, which was why he knew that his loud passing of wind at that moment was entirely deliberate.

"And," continued Marshall, undeterred, "we're pursuing numerous other promising avenues of investigation and assembling a wealth of intelligence that I am confident will lead to a positive conclusion very soon."

Ferguson stretched out his back. "You do realise who you're speaking to? I invented half of the bullshit language you just used to try to sound optimistic about an investigation that is going nowhere."

"The tapes are a big loss," admitted Marshall, "although we do have to acknowledge that somebody destroying them may not have had anything to do with the murder itself. It might have been elements within the organised crime community covering their own backsides." He eyeballed O'Rourke. "Personally, I would question how such sensitive information as their existence could have come to be leaked?"

O'Rourke turned to face him. "What the fuck is that supposed to mean?"

Marshall stuck out his chin defiantly. "The information got out there somehow. We have to examine the possibility that there's a leak in your team."

"Based on what? We weren't the only people who knew about Coop Hannity's little bunker. We have no idea how many people in his own organisation were aware of it. It's interesting that when you're desperate to cover up your own screw-up, your go-to move is to try to throw other gardaí under the bus."

Marshall turned to face him. "I resent that remark."

"Sorry," said O'Rourke. "Maybe I should have put it in some handover notes – that way you wouldn't have seen it."

The two men were squaring up to each other now.

"Gentlemen," barked Ferguson, looking up and down the range and noticing that their little group was drawing quite a lot of attention, "need I remind you that we are in public. As the senior-ranking officer here, let me assure you that if anyone is going to resort to the use of violence, it will be me." He stepped forward, not exactly putting himself between the two detectives, so much as reminding everybody involved about his considerable presence.

"DI Marshall, you shall continue with the murder investigation and, for your sake, in twenty-four hours' time, I would make sure to have considerably more to offer up than platitudes and well wishes. DI O'Rourke, you shall find out what you can about who might have wanted the tapes to be destroyed and, assuming it may not have been related to the murder, who would stand to benefit from Mrs Hannity's death. Speaking of whom, where is Mrs Hannity now?"

"The hospital kept her in overnight for observation," said Marshall. "I've already arranged for her to be under twenty-four-hour armed Garda protection when she's discharged. Incidentally, Bernard McGarry managed to get by the garda assigned to her hospital room yesterday and spoke with her."

"What the hell?" said Ferguson, looking back and forth between the two detectives. "If the man pulls another stunt like that, do make clear to him that I will arrest him myself."

"He has also, so far, declined to come in for an interview."

"A serving member of the Garda Síochána has declined to be interviewed?" asked Ferguson, sounding incredulous.

"Actually," said O'Rourke, "that's not technically correct. It's my understanding that Mr McGarry said he was happy to be interviewed, but his brief was unwell yesterday."

"And for some inexplicable reason," offered Marshall, "he was unwilling to use another lawyer."

O'Rourke shrugged. "It's his right to use his own lawyer. We can't ping him for that."

Ferguson eyeballed the two men. "Nevertheless, I would like him interviewed today. Make it crystal clear to him that failure to comply – for whatever reason – shall be looked on very dimly indeed. Have I made myself understood?"

Both men nodded.

"Good," said Ferguson. "Now, unless there have been any other spectacular fuck-ups that you've not yet told me about, then you may consider yourselves dismissed."

"Sir."

"Sir."

The two DIs headed back towards the car park.

"Oh, and boys ..." Ferguson shouted after them, causing them both to turn round. He pointed at Kevin. "His nibs here is going to the vet tomorrow to have his nuts removed – in the hope it will improve his behaviour. Any more screw-ups and you both shall be joining him."

# FINDERS WEEPERS

Sod's law.

Sod's bloody law.

Butch had had a bad feeling all morning. To be fair, everybody present had some form of bad feeling. When you found yourself in a sweaty, hermetically-sealed hazmat suit, digging your way through rubbish, nobody with any sense had a good feeling. Butch's had been more specific than most people's. Hers had been more of a premonition.

In contrast to yesterday, there was now a team of twenty-six people working the dig, and it was considerably more organised. The potential area had been mapped and broken down into a grid, with each searcher being assigned a square. Despite hers being one of only twenty-four such squares, Butch had had a feeling.

And now, with terrible inevitability, that feeling had been realised.

Amidst the rubble, the rotten wood, the insulation material, the junk-food wrappers, the plastic bottles that really should have been recycled, and the mountain of other crap, she had dug down and found the thing she did not want to find.

There was no question about it. The large carving knife lying in front of her was definitely the murder weapon in the Hannity case. There was still dried blood on it. The only problem was that she'd bet every last penny she owned that it also had Bunny McGarry's fingerprints on it.

This would be all Marshall needed. She would be as good as handing over one of her best mates for a crime he did not commit. And yet, what other choice did she have? She was a guard. A member of law enforcement. If she took the knife and shoved it down to the bottom of the rubbish pile, what would she be then? Some lines you can't uncross. She would have wilfully tampered with evidence. Interfered with an investigation. Used her position to protect her friend.

If she were to do it, she could justify her actions in lots of ways. Bunny was a good man and she believed one hundred percent that he was being set up. Still, wasn't the whole point of this thing that if they gathered all the evidence and did their jobs right, the real guilty parties would be brought to justice? If not, what the hell were they doing here?

Either she was a copper or she wasn't. And coppers, regardless of their personal instincts, don't ignore evidence.

Butch ripped off the mask of the suit and took a series of shallow breaths. She thought she was going to be sick, and it had nothing to do with the foul stench or the rank unpleasantness of the filth that surrounded her.

She closed her eyes and gave a silent prayer. Fuck's sake, Bunny, whatever rabbit you're gonna pull out of a hat, you'd better get to the reveal pretty damn quickly.

She reopened her eyes and spoke softly and only to herself. "Sorry."

Then, she put up her hand and raised her voice. "Here. Over here. I've got something."

# WORSE THINGS HAPPEN AT SEA

For the second time in a week Bunny found himself at the seaside. In fact, technically speaking, he was no longer at the seaside, because he was now on the actual sea.

He'd paid a brief but highly informative visit to the offices of Muldoon Investigations before heading to Dun Laoghaire Marina. He was putting a lot of faith in a tip, but he was running out of other options. It had taken him a while, but eventually he'd found somebody willing to take him out. March wasn't peak tourism season, so anybody already at the marina had a good reason for being there and wasn't interested in unusual propositions from wonky-eyed strangers. Then, he'd met Margot.

A short woman in ragged overalls, she'd been sitting in her boat – a small, unremarkable fibreglass fishing boat – reading *Sense and Sensibility*.

"Are you available for hire?"

"That depends," she said, turning the page without looking up. "Have you got the urn with you?"

"What? What urn?"

She glanced up from her book. "Normally at this time of year, it's mostly people trying to scatter ashes. I've decided to stop doing those.

They're a bit depressing. Plus, a lot of people spend an inordinate amount of time trying to find the right bit of water to do the scattering over. You try to explain it to them – that it's all the same sea at the end of the day – but they don't listen. To be honest, it feels like people are expecting a lot more from the experience than it can offer. As far as I'm concerned, the best you can hope for is not to get any of it in your eye."

"No," said Bunny, "I'm not trying to scatter ashes."

She looked up at him properly now. "Well, you've not got fishing gear." She rolled her eyes. "This isn't a suicide, is it?"

"What?"

"You'd be surprised. I've had emails. A lot of people can't face jumping off stuff or swallowing stuff or, I don't know, dropping a toaster in the bath. I've had a couple of people ask if I could just drop them off at the middle of the sea and leave them there. The answer is no by the way. I mean, do what you want, but I'm not getting involved. It's the kind of thing the coastguard will get very arsey about."

"I'm not trying to do anything like that either."

"OK," she relented. "I'll bite. What's the story?"

"I'm hoping to surprise a friend."

She considered this then shook her head. "Nah. I don't believe you." She opened her book and went back to reading.

"Alright. You got me. Cards on the table. Right now, somewhere out there, is a piece-of-shit private investigator called Andy Muldoon. He's sitting in a boat with one of those telephoto zoom lens cameras, trying to get compromising pictures of a couple of people shagging who shouldn't be."

"And what?" said the woman. "Are you a friend of the shaggers?"

"No. I couldn't give a shit either way. But I think this gobshite might be able to help me stop an innocent man from getting arrested for murder."

The woman tilted her head. "Ohhhh, interesting. Who's the man?"

"That'd be me."

"Well, beats dumping Grandad's ashes. It's three hundred quid for the day."

"We shouldn't need—"

"It's three hundred quid for the day," she repeated.

"Done."

She put down her book. "Hop aboard. I'm Margot."

The problem with the sea, as Bunny had come to realise, was that the whole thing was really, unnecessarily big. There was, frankly, tons of it. The information he'd received was that Andy Muldoon had his telephoto lens trained somewhere along the Seapoint area of the coast. It was only when he got out there that he realised that was a pretty vague location.

Still, after an hour, and a couple of false alarms, he and Margot found their man. He was seated in an inflatable dinghy with an outboard motor, doing a pretty poor impression of a fisherman. The clue that he wasn't really a fisherman was that his rod wasn't actually in the water. The giveaway that he was Andy Muldoon was the sight of his comb-over wafting majestically in the breeze.

The man himself was staring into his camera while listening to the horseracing from Leopardstown on his headphones, and the first he knew about his vessel being boarded was when it rocked alarmingly. He turned around to find Bunny McGarry standing unsteadily on the bow. It was fair to say he was surprised – much more on the "unexpected snake" end of the scale than the "oh my God, you guys, I said not to make a fuss of my birthday".

He pulled off his headphones and dropped the camera, which, luckily, fell in the boat. "Jesus. What're ye ... How'd ye ... Who've ye ..."

"These are all excellent questions, Muldoon, but to be honest with you, I came here with a few of my own."

Muldoon looked back and forth rapidly between Bunny and Margot, who was still sitting in her boat. "You can't be here."

"And yet I am," said Bunny. "Isn't life full of little miracles?"

"How did you even find me?"

"Funny story that: I dropped by your offices. Your assistant was only delighted to tell me where you were."

"That bitch."

"Now," said Bunny in a warning tone, "I'm not a big fan of people using derogatory terms towards women. Although it has to be said, I don't think it would be possible to lower that particular woman's opinion of you."

"You're not wrong. She hired me because she thought her rich husband was having an affair, and she was hoping for a massive divorce settlement if he was found screwing around. Turns out what he'd been doing was playing cards – really badly. To the point where he was no longer rich. They couldn't afford to pay my bill, so she offered to work it off managing the office for me. It hasn't worked out to be the best of arrangements."

"Still," said Bunny, "worse things happen at sea. As you're about to find out."

"I've not done anything wrong."

Bunny sat down. "Nobody said you had, Andy. Although now that you mention it, you definitely have. Incidentally, seeing as you saw me at Hannity's house on Monday night, I'm a little hurt you didn't honk your horn or wave hello."

"I don't know what you're talking about."

Bunny didn't say anything, he just gave Muldoon the wonky-eyed stare that had proved to be an invaluable asset throughout his career.

"You can't just come on my boat. I have rights."

"As it happens," said Bunny, "I was made an honorary Sea Scout a couple of years ago. I believe that gives me the right to board and inspect all vessels within three miles of the Irish coast."

"No, it doesn't."

"Well, you'll have to take that up with Admiral Nelson or whoever the fuck is in charge of the Sea Scouts. In the meantime, I'm on a bit of a clock here, so let's assume I've already firmly established in your mind the strong possibility of violence if you don't play ball."

"You're a guard, and there's a witness here," Muldoon protested, pointing at Margot.

Margot shrugged and picked up her book. "I've a good book on the go. A bit of Jane Austen. And I'm notoriously focused while I'm reading."

"And I," said Bunny, "am currently on sabbatical. So, we've cleared all that up. Speaking of employment – until recently, you were in the employ of one James 'Coop' Hannity."

"I refuse to answer."

"It wasn't a question. He had you following his poor wife everywhere she went." Bunny grabbed Muldoon's camera from the deck.

"Put that down!" yelped the PI.

Bunny pulled away as Muldoon tried to snatch back his equipment before whimpering as he grabbed on to both sides of the boat.

"Are you OK there, Andy? You seem a little tense."

"It wasn't like that," said Muldoon.

"Really? So Coop didn't have you following the poor girl around every hour of the day because he was convinced she was having an affair?"

"Well ... There's nothing illegal about that."

"You're right," said Bunny, nodding his head in agreement. "But I'm going to guess that Hannity, a man who was never known for his patience, started getting a little antsy when you weren't getting results. I'm guessing that's why you gave him the name of Marcus Phillips, the personal trainer?"

"They could have been at it. You don't know."

"Another excellent point, Andy. The only problem with that train of thought is that Mr Phillips isn't a ladies man. By which I mean he has no interest in the ladies. And yet a couple of Coop's boys went around and kicked the crap out of him anyway. Broke his leg."

Margot didn't look up from her book but some audible tutting came from her direction.

"Alright. Look, I was desperate. The woman hardly ever left the house, for Christ's sake. I was on her for a couple of months and the only places she went was the gym, to see her dad, and then, on the way back, she'd call up to see her friend and they'd go for a drink."

"So," said Bunny, "she clearly wasn't having an affair, but you told a jealous husband she was, because that's what he wanted to hear." Bunny noticed a look cross Muldoon's face. "What?"

"Nothing."

Bunny spoke while keeping his eyes fixed on the investigator. "Did I ever tell you, Margot – I'm an awful clumsy man."

"I met you little over an hour ago. Surprisingly, it hasn't come up."

"Well, I am." Bunny jerked his hands holding the expensive-looking camera towards the edge of the boat.

"Don't!" pleaded Muldoon.

"Again, Andy, maybe you should reconsider the path of least resistance here? Coop Hannity is dead and soon to be in the ground, whereas I am alive, in your boat and getting increasingly pissed off. Why don't you tell me what you're not telling me?"

"Alright, alright. Hannity came to me. He was convinced his wife was having an affair. Like I said, I followed her everywhere. I had a team of three on it. We covered every angle, night and day. Hannity even told us he has a tunnel out of his place that leads to a house he owns in the next street along. We watched that too. Nothing."

"So," said Margot, still not looking up from her book, "like the man said, she was clearly not having an affair."

"Yeah," said Muldoon, "that's what I thought too. But then I paid off her doctor's receptionist. For a woman who isn't screwing anybody, she's awful pregnant."

"Bullshit!" said Bunny.

"She is," said Muldoon. "I only found out a few days ago myself. I was supposed to have a meeting with Hannity and then, well ... Given the circumstances, I'm kind of keen to forget the whole thing."

Margot cleared her throat. "Call me old-fashioned, but isn't it possible the father was her husband?"

"As it happens," answered Bunny, "no."

Margot raised an eyebrow. "Twist."

"Indeed. None of this makes sense."

"I'm not lying to you," said Muldoon. "Why would I? I've got all the proof in a file in the boot of my car."

"Where's your car?"

"Back at the marina. Let me finish up what I'm doing here—"

"No. I need it now."

"But—" started Muldoon.

"Give me your keys. I'll take the file and leave them under your front tyre."

"I'm not doing that."

"I think you're fatally underestimating how willing I am to take them off you by force."

Muldoon considered this for a few seconds before his shoulders sagged in defeat. "Alright. But you promise you'll leave them under the front tyre?"

"Would I lie to you, Andy?"

Muldoon's body language made it clear he thought that was a strong possibility, but he reached into the pocket of his anorak begrudgingly and handed Bunny the keys. "It's a blue Beemer."

"I know. I'm glad to see the sleaze business is treating you so well. Now, next question – who did you sell me out to?"

"What?"

"Who did you tell that you saw me going to see Coop on Monday night?"

Muldoon wrinkled his nose. "I didn't tell anyone. Why would I tell anybody that?"

"Because, Andy, somebody is trying to frame me for Coop's murder."

"I haven't a clue what you're talking about."

Muldoon was an untrustworthy piece of crap, but Bunny got the distinct feeling that, on this occasion, he wasn't lying.

"I was afraid you were going to say that." Bunny got to his feet and, in one fluid movement, hopped back on to Margot's boat.

"The camera, Bunny. Fair is fair – give me back my camera."

Bunny looked down at his hands. "God, of course, Andy. Sorry.

My memory is shocking." He handed the camera over carefully and Muldoon snatched it gratefully. Bunny turned to Margot. "Time to weigh anchor, O Captain, My Captain."

"Fair enough," said Margot, putting down her book and starting up the engine.

Muldoon lined up his camera at the shore, keen to check he hadn't missed what he'd been waiting for.

As the engine roared into life, Bunny shouted over the din, "Oh, and Andy ..."

Muldoon turned his way just in time to see Bunny pick up a screwdriver from the deck of Margot's boat and jab it into the side of the inflatable craft.

"There's a hole in your bucket."

Thirty minutes later, Bunny was sitting in the front seat of the rental car, going through Muldoon's file. Margot had dropped him back and then, surprisingly, waved away the money when he tried to pay her.

"Don't worry about it," she'd said. "I'm about to head back out and offer to save a man who may be in some difficulty. I'm guessing I'll be handsomely rewarded for that."

Bunny had thanked her for her time and left her to it.

As he flicked through the papers in the file, he could say this for Muldoon: he might be pond scum, but he was thorough pond scum. There was a detailed log of all of Angelina's movements stretching back a couple of months. There were time-stamped photographs of her on all the days in question – hundreds of them, in fact. And there was also a verified test from a gynaecologist confirming that she was indeed pregnant – about six weeks along, according to the dates.

Bunny checked back through the log from six weeks ago. There were three possibilities: either Muldoon had screwed up somewhere and missed something, or else Angelina and Coop were getting on considerably better than Mags had led Bunny to believe. The third possibility was that Angelina was going to experience something akin to the virgin birth and she'd have to be chasing God himself for child support.

Bunny went over the logs yet again, looking for something, anything. Assuming Angelina hadn't got pregnant by her gynaecologist, which would be the very definition of taking your work home with you, Bunny was stumped. Regular trips to the gym until she stopped. Going to visit her father at least once, often twice a week – almost always in the evenings. More often than not, calling up to Mags's apartment for a couple of minutes on the way back before heading over the road to a pub for a couple of drinks. Outside of that, rare shopping trips, which extensive surveillance showed were spent alone doing nothing but shopping, and a couple of medical appointments that were, again, covered in detail and looked utterly innocuous. Her life was mundane in the extreme.

His mind flashed back to the memory of the first night he'd seen her in years. It had only been on Monday, but it felt like a long time ago now. She'd been standing there with a drink in her hand and had the air of a woman who'd had a few already. Bunny didn't know an awful lot of mothers-to-be, but he knew they didn't drink much. At least the good ones didn't.

He tossed the folder carelessly on to the passenger seat, causing several of the pictures to spill on to the floor. As he bent down to gather them up, it hit him.

He picked up the picture that had caught his eye and stared at it for a full minute. Then he scrabbled through the other images, searching for the ones he needed.

The good news was that Bunny thought he finally might have figured something out.

The bad news was what it meant.

# THE FINGER

Butch took a deep breath and knocked on the office door. The feeling of nausea that had washed over her at the dump hadn't subsided in the hours since.

"Come in."

She entered the room to see DI Marshall sitting behind the desk, filling out some paperwork.

"You asked to see me, sir."

"Yes," he said, putting down his pen. "I appreciate we didn't get off to the best of starts, but I wanted to congratulate you on your work today. Finding the murder weapon is hopefully going to blow this case wide open."

"About that, sir. I have a theory."

He leaned back in his chair. "Go on."

"On the footage from the night of the murder, the guy in the balaclava – he appears to pause behind the hedge, out of the view of the cameras, for nearly a minute?"

"Yes."

"He isn't wearing gloves when he appears, but we didn't pick up any fingerprints from the wall he climbed over. That's because he was taking his gloves off. He wanted to be seen on camera not wearing gloves because it would give credence to whatever we found on the murder weapon."

Marshall leaned forward again. "That's a hell of a reach, Cassidy. You of all people know the ridiculous lengths we had to go to to find the weapon."

"Yes, sir. But you of all people know it should have been a lot easier. That skip should have been checked on day one and the weapon found almost immediately. Somebody dumped it there for us to find, and then we screwed up."

Marshall sighed. "I appreciate the thought you've given this, Cassidy, and we will, of course, consider all possibilities, but a common mistake we make as police officers is believing the criminals are smarter than they are. Occam's razor and all that."

"I'd imagine another common mistake is not questioning when simple solutions are dropped into our laps."

Marshall's eyes narrowed. "Is there something you'd like to say, Detective? Or, indeed, is there something you're not telling me?"

"Yes," said Butch, surprised by the word as it came out of her mouth. This thought hadn't been present in her head when she'd walked in the door, but it seemed obvious now. It was as if looking across the desk at Marshall had made stuff click into place. "I'd just like to say, for the record, how inspirational you are, sir."

"Excuse me?"

"Yes, sir. You've made me realise what policing really is. With that in mind, I wish to offer my immediate resignation from the force."

Marshall offered a strained smile. "Yes, alright. Thank you, Cassidy. Most amusing. Now, if you're done—"

"Oh, I'm done, you sanctimonious, small-minded prick. You're such a good reader of people that you don't even realise when somebody's being deadly serious. Let me make myself crystal clear: you can shove your job up your arse."

Butch turned neatly on her heels, opened the door and walked out.

"Cassidy," Marshall shouted after her, "get back here this instant."

His raised voice attracted the attention of everybody in the incident room, so they all watched as Butch raised her hand and, without looking back, gave Marshall the finger.

Marshall stood up in his office. "Cassidy! Cassidy!"

DS Paschal Burke stood in the doorway.

"Burke," said Marshall, "I want you as a witness to Cassidy's insubordination. I don't know how this team runs normally, but I am not going to put up with displays like that. Are we clear?"

Burke dealt with the question by ignoring it entirely. "The tech bureau has just been on to us. The blood on the weapon is confirmed as Hannity's, and they found fingerprints."

"And?"

Marshall noticed for the first time how pale DS Burke looked. "And ..."

# BAD IDEAS

Bunny stood outside the door and listened. He could hear definite sounds of movement coming from inside the apartment. He rapped on the door and the noises stopped instantly.

"Mags, it's Bunny."

No response.

"Mags, I know you're in there. Open up. I need to talk to you."

After about thirty seconds he heard the locks being opened and the chain being pulled across. The door opened a crack and Mags peered out at him. "Now isn't really a good time, Bunny."

"No kidding. Let me in."

She considered it for a second then stood back, opening the door wide for him to enter. He walked down the hall into the living area as she shut the door behind him. Bunny clocked the two suitcases lying open on the sofa, clothes messily piled in each.

"Are you going somewhere?"

"Yeah," said Mags, trying to sound relaxed. "Friend of Bobby's has a lovely holiday home up in Donegal. We've got a chance to use it for a few days."

"That's nice. I mean, I don't believe you for a second, but still, it's a nice idea. How about you and I sit down for a second and have a proper chat – what do you say?"

"Honestly, no offence, but this really isn't a good time."

Bunny sat down beside the two cases and looked up at her. "I know what you did."

At his words, Mags's shoulders sagged and she collapsed into the armchair opposite. "Oh God. Oh God. This is a nightmare."

He found her reaction confusing but decided to let it play out. "Why don't you tell me what happened?"

Mags held her face in her hands for a couple of seconds, and when she looked up again there were tears in her eyes. "I'm not trying to save myself, but I swear to God, I didn't know anything about it. I'd never let the damn fool do it. She rang Bobby directly, went behind my back. Offered him thirty grand. That's enough for them to record their stupid bloody album." She pulled a packet of cigarettes from her pocket and lit one with shaking hands.

"Mags, what the feck are you talking about?"

Her eyes grew wide. "Oh Jesus, I thought you ... Never mind. Ignore me. I'm, I'm just having an awful day."

Bunny replayed her words in his mind. More pieces were falling into place. "Where did Bobby get the gun?"

Mags threw back her head and pulled up her legs on to the armchair, hugging her knees to her chest like the little girl he could still remember.

"I don't know," she said, sounding weary. "He likes to pretend he's connected. He's not. Bloody idiot. But this is Dublin – Jesus, even I know a couple of pubs you could walk into and ask."

"The thing is," said Bunny, "speaking as a detective, when you buy a gun, you're really not paying for the gun. You're paying for the assurance that as soon as you walk out of the place, they'll forget you ever existed. I'm guessing Bobby Boy didn't understand that, and now people are looking for him?"

Mags gave a tearful nod. "Yeah."

"I guess that's the danger of missing the target – the target wanting to have a strong word with you about it afterwards."

Bunny looked around the room and his eyes fell on the door to the bedroom he'd noticed on his first visit. He pointed at it.

"When I was first here, I should have clocked something. The rest of the place, no offence, looks rather lived in. Yet somehow, you've got a bedroom in pristine condition, just waiting to be used. Shall we call it what it is – Angelina's room?"

Mags took a drag on her cigarette and gave an almost imperceptible nod. "How did you figure it out?"

"Far too slowly, unfortunately. If I'd got there quicker, you might not be in the shit you're in now. Sorry about that."

"It's not your fault. I guess it really is like my mam always said – I've always been too easily led."

"In answer to your question," Bunny began, as he opened Muldoon's folder that he'd brought with him and took out a photograph, "if it's any consolation, your hair and make-up work really was flawless." He held up the picture. "This is Angelina walking in to Cedarwood to see her dad on Tuesday night."

The image showed her striding across the road from the parking garage, sunglasses on, a paperback book under her arm.

"I met her the night before, and I saw her yesterday in the hospital. Both times, she had strapping on her left wrist where she'd strained it lifting weights at home." He tapped the picture with his finger. "This woman isn't wearing the strapping, because she's not Angelina. She didn't think to mention it to you, did she?"

"No."

Bunny paused for a moment. "Stop me if I'm wrong, but she obviously knew that Coop was having her followed. She figured out that they couldn't follow her down into the parking basement because it would be too obvious. It was a very clever idea, to be fair to her."

Mags dabbed at her eyes with a piece of tissue. "But then, she was never short of brains, was she?"

"Clever all the same," said Bunny. "So, you got there ahead of her, and she took your car while you went in and pretended to be her. That can't have been fun, visiting her father in her place."

"No. To be fair, it wasn't me every time. She did go and visit him properly too. On one visit a couple of weeks ago, he started rambling about how I wasn't her. I thought we were done for then." Mags looked down balefully at the carpet. "All they did was take him away and sedate him, poor bastard."

"And while you were busy pretending to be her, she was here, meeting a friend."

Mags nodded again. "And you know who?"

"Yes. I do. There are some bits I'm still a little unsure of, but I've got that piece. Did you know about —"

Bunny was interrupted by his phone ringing. He looked at the number and got to his feet.

"I need to take this. Finish packing, and I'll make sure you get out of here safely. Find somewhere to lie low for a few days. Fingers crossed this will all be over by then."

She smiled up at him. "Thanks, Bunny. I'm sorry for lying to you."

"Don't worry about it. There's a lot of it going about."

He answered the call.

"We got him," said the voice on the other end, before Bunny could say anything.

"What do you mean 'got him'?"

Mrs Byrne tutted. "What you think I mean? He's tied up in front of me now."

"Jesus! I told you just to keep an eye out. Are you safe?"

"We're fine," she said, sounding slightly defensive. "Him, on the other hand ..."

"Just ... I'll be there as soon as I can. Don't— Don't do anything ..."

"Do anything what?"

"Anything else surprising," finished Bunny.

He hung up and turned to Mags. "Right, come on, then. I'll swap cars with you – in case anybody's looking for yours. I need to get home fast. Sounds like my neighbourhood watch scheme has started taking prisoners."

# BATMAN AND OTHER BATMAN

Cynthia Doyle opened the door and ushered Bunny inside.

"Right this way, sir. Your guest is in the kitchen area."

It did not escape Bunny's attention that his next-door neighbour was holding a frying pan in her hand.

"Bloody hell, Cynthia. I mean, I appreciate the effort, but I did say just to keep an eye out for anybody acting peculiar."

She held up her head proudly. "We cannot have gurriers running around the neighbourhood, breaking into places willy-nilly. It sets a dangerous precedent."

He looked down at the frying pan. "True, but I'm a little bit worried about the precedent this approach has set. Vigilante behaviour like this, I'm pretty sure that's how Batman got started."

"I don't know who that is," said Cynthia Doyle. "I don't read the papers."

He followed her through to the kitchen. As eye-catching conversation starters went, the man sitting in the centre of the floor, gagged and bound to a kitchen chair, would take some beating.

And if anything else needed beating, Mrs Margaret Byrne was standing guard behind him, also wielding a frying pan. "Hello, Bunny," she said cheerfully.

"Margaret. So you're also part of the Justice League?"

She beamed at him. "It was me that first walloped him on the back of the head while Cynthia distracted him."

Bunny looked back and forth between the two women. "Right."

"I tell you," continued Margaret, "it's not like in the cartoons. You wallop somebody on the back of the head with a frying pan, they don't go down immediately."

"No," agreed Cynthia. "It took us both swinging a few times to put him down. We nabbed him as he was trying to force his way through your back door."

The two women shared a gleeful smile, clearly enjoying the new hobby they'd discovered.

"Yes. It was Mrs Ranganesh who spotted him, as soon as he entered the laneway out the back there."

"Mrs Ranganesh?" asked Bunny. "How many of you were involved in this? I only told the two of you to keep an eye out."

"We can't have people going around breaking into houses," said Margaret.

"That's exactly what I said," agreed Cynthia. "So yes, we told a few people. You're quite a popular man in the community, Bunny. People were very keen to help."

"Yes. Mrs Choi from over the back there came running around with her sword. Apparently, it's part of her culture. Aren't these things very interesting? We said she should bring it to the next coffee morning and tell us all about it."

"A family heirloom," said Cynthia. "Imagine that?"

Bunny took a closer look at the man sitting before him and looking up at him warily. He did a quick count of his visible limbs and features. "She didn't actually use the sword, did she?"

"No," said Margaret. "We had him restrained by then. There was no need for it. I mean, we're not savages. We only used as much violence as was absolutely necessary."

Their prisoner mumbled something half-heartedly around his gag.

"That's right," agreed the other Batman of suburbia. "I think he had some of these injuries before we got to him."

Bunny gave a wry smile. "Oh, he did indeed. Sure, didn't I give them to him myself? We had a scrap out in Clontarf on Monday morning."

"Did ye?" asked Cynthia. "God. Isn't it a small world all the same?"

The prisoner stared up at Bunny, his eyes groggy, possibly as a result of the overenthusiastic application of a frying pan. It was the guy who'd been wielding the clipboard outside Gringo's house on Monday morning.

Bunny glanced around the room. He already had a good idea of the answer, but he asked the question anyway. "By any chance, did he have something on him?"

"He did," said Cynthia. She moved a tea towel that was sitting on the counter. Beneath it lay a flick knife, a few tools that would come in handy if trying to break into a house, and a video tape.

"I expected as much. Ladies, thank you again for your invaluable and enthusiastic assistance. If you don't mind, though, I'd like a word alone with our friend here."

"Are you sure you don't need back-up?" asked Margaret, hefting her frying pan pointedly.

"No, thank you. I think you've beaten all of the fight out of him already."

"Come on, Margaret. I'll show you that new throw I've just finished knitting in the front room."

"Oh, lovely."

Bunny watched the two women leave the room, closing the door behind them.

"Well, if nothing else, your little visit has brought the two of them together. Never let it be said that violence doesn't solve anything." He turned back to the man. "I'm going to take the gag out of your mouth now. By all means scream. By the sounds of it, a couple of neighbours might drop over and see if I need any help torturing you."

The man made no movement. Bunny removed the tea towel that was serving as an improvised gag.

"So," Bunny said, "we were never properly introduced. Would you be Mr Dean or Mr McDaid?"

"Dean," he responded.

"You're having quite the bad week, aren't you? I mean, I kick the crap out of you on Monday, the frying-pan defence league kick the shit out of you today, and in between, I'm told you lost your job. Although, I'm guessing you've been rehired by the new management of Coop Hannity's organisation?"

Dean remained silent, concentrating instead on running his tongue around his mouth, as if trying to get rid of the tea-towel taste.

Bunny picked up the video tape. "I presume this was supposed to be the pièce de résistance in the frame job. My meeting with Coop Hannity from Monday night. Not only would it establish motive, but the fact that it would be in my house when the Gardaí inevitably search it would also make it a simple open and shut case. I assume it was also you that was sent around to grab a convenient murder weapon, am I right? Out of curiosity, was it on Tuesday, when I was out of the house, or earlier, when I was still there?"

Dean looked up at him and then looked away again.

"It doesn't matter," said Bunny. "After all, I made it embarrassingly easy for you. I'm pretty sure I hadn't even locked the back door. As you can see, I've upped my home security somewhat since then. Fool me once and all that." He pulled up one of the kitchen chairs and sat down opposite Dean. "There's one little bit I'm not sure about. You had to make sure I had no alibi on Tuesday night …"

Bunny left the sentence hanging, but the other man offered no response.

"Ah, sure, that's pretty simple too when you think about it. Somebody followed me back from training and then gave you a ring, right? Told you I was home alone. Then you knew it was a go. You had your patsy. You're even the same build as me. Handy for the camera that, wasn't it? A balaclava really suits you, by the way. It must have been quite the rush, seeing your picture on the news and on the front pages of all the papers. Tell me, did Coop know it was you when you stuck the knife in?"

Dean's eyes shot up suddenly to meet Bunny's. "I didn't kill anybody. Don't go trying to pin that bullshit on me."

"That's a rather ironic choice of words given the circumstances, don't you think?"

"Yeah, alright, I was there, but only after the fact. I took the tapes and the knife, but that's all."

Bunny nodded. He hadn't wanted to hear it, but it did make sense.

Before he could ask any more questions, he noticed something out of the corner of his eye. He picked up the gag, shoved it into Dean's mouth and hit the deck.

Five seconds later came the sound of the Garda armed response unit smashing in the back door of Bunny's house.

# PERSON OF INTEREST

DS Paschal Burke leaned against the wall outside Bunny McGarry's house and lit a cigarette. He was supposed to be quitting but this wasn't the week for it. He looked again at the smashed-in front door and shook his head. Detective Inspector Marshall, in his infinite wisdom, had tagged Bunny as a strong violence risk and had ordered an armed response to take him in.

Now, to be fair, Bunny McGarry was no stranger to violence, but Paschal couldn't see him trying to fight his way out of being arrested. For that matter, he couldn't see him murdering somebody either. Not that his opinion counted for anything. Marshall had gone hell for leather as soon as the fingerprints had come back, and there was no reasoning with the man. The road behind Burke was packed with police vehicles, all trying to manoeuvre around each other and find parking spaces that weren't there.

He took a long drag and blew it out slowly. This day had gone to shit.

Burke leaped up when he heard a scream coming from McGarry's house. Ten seconds later, DI Marshall stormed out, a bloody scratch running down the left side of his face.

"DS Burke, I want you to contact the ISPCA. There is a rabid cat in there and I want it caught and put down immediately."

Burke considered this. "No, sir."

Marshall stopped dabbing at his face with a handkerchief and glared at Burke. "Excuse me?"

"An armed response unit went charging into an animal's home so it panicked and tried to defend itself. I'm not having Bunny's cat put down just because it wounded your pride."

"I will not stand for this insubordination."

Burke took another drag on his cigarette. "I'll be honest with you, sir, I really couldn't give a shit. By all means put me on report, but I'd imagine even you wouldn't want to increase the rate at which serving officers with previously exemplary records are disappearing from under your command, sir."

Marshall rushed towards him and stopped less than a foot from his face. "One of your colleagues is now the prime suspect in a murder. How dare you stand there and try to interfere with my investigation."

Burke tossed his cigarette to the ground and stubbed it out under his shoe. "And for the record, Detective Inspector – how exactly is me having a cat killed going to assist with your investigation?"

For a second Burke wondered if Marshall was going to swing for him, but the spell was broken by a woman's voice.

"Excuse me, what the hell is going on here?"

They both turned to see McGarry's next-door neighbour standing on her doorstep.

Marshall stepped away from Burke and ran a hand down his tie. "This is an ongoing Garda situation, madam. Please stay inside your house."

"I will do no such thing. You can't go smashing in people's doors like that."

"Actually," said Marshall, "we can."

"He's not even in there," she said.

"Tell him something he doesn't know," said Burke, not exactly under his breath.

"Yeah," she continued. "The taxi picked him up about half an hour ago."

Marshall was about to reprimand Burke further, but then his eyes grew wide and he turned to face the neighbour. "Excuse me? There was a taxi? Did you see what company it was from?"

"I did, of course."

"Fantastic."

"I also got the licence plate, the driver's full name, and a stool sample in case you might need it."

Burke couldn't stop himself from laughing. Marshall's head whipped back towards him, his lips twisted into a snarl.

"I'm not nosy," said the neighbour. "The only reason I know there was a taxi at all is because the idiot rang my doorbell first. Taxi to the airport? Chance would be a fine thing. I've not had a holiday since my Albert, God rest him, took me to Corfu for our anniversary."

Marshall turned back around again so fast that he almost fell over. "The airport?"

"Yeah," she said. "Big building, lots of space around it." She pointed up at the sky. "Where the big metal birds come in to land."

Bunny peeked out between the curtains of Cynthia Doyle's upstairs bedroom. The smell of lavender was almost overwhelming.

On the street outside, the unnecessarily large police contingent that had descended upon his house to arrest him was trying to manoeuvre its vehicles around one another, all hurrying to chase a wild goose to Dublin Airport. Three drivers were having an argument about which one of them needed to move out of the other's way. It wasn't the Garda Síochána's finest hour.

Still, a tiny part of Bunny felt flattered. You could judge a man by how many officers they'd sent to take him down. He'd apparently warranted the full armed response SAS malarkey. The reason they hadn't nabbed him was that he was about six feet away in Mrs Doyle's kitchen, interrogating the man who'd been sent to complete the frame job on him.

He heard the door opening quietly behind him.

"So they went for it, then?"

"They did," confirmed Mrs Doyle.

"Thank you," said Bunny, turning around.

Mrs Doyle stood there looking nervous. "I do have a concern ..."

"Don't worry," said Bunny, holding up a hand, "you won't get into trouble for lying to the guards. I promise."

She waved away his assurances dismissively. "I'm not bothered about that. Nobody is locking me up. However ..." She looked around anxiously before continuing, "I'd appreciate it if you didn't let people know that you'd been in my bedroom. I am a respectable woman. I wouldn't want anyone getting the wrong idea."

Bunny almost smiled, then he saw the seriousness on her face and stopped himself. "Right! Of course not. You have my word." The things people decided to care about.

She looked relieved. "Excellent. Well, then ... By the way, there are still some officers next door."

"Yeah. They'll be searching the place."

"How rude!"

"I know," agreed Bunny.

Just then, his phone pinged. He fished it out of his pocket and read the text message. It was the one he'd been half expecting and half hoping he wouldn't get.

"Looks like I've somewhere else I need to be. Could I ask you one last favour, please, Cynthia?"

DS Burke watched as the last of DI Marshall's ludicrous armada turned on their sirens and set off to make a mess of the rush-hour traffic. Marshall hadn't got around to actually saying it before he had hauled arse out of there, but Burke was taking it as read that he had been suspended from duty. He knew he should be worried about that but somehow he wasn't.

He liked Bunny. He liked Cassidy. Hell, despite him being a tad annoying, he quite liked Carlson. If Marshall was the new boss, then

Burke was happy to get sent somewhere else. He was only a couple years off his pension, and telling a detective inspector to go blow it out his arse wasn't going to get him booted off the force. Up until this point he'd always toed the line, and it felt kind of good to finally tell somebody to shove it.

He had a quick word with the uniforms guarding the front door, and made sure they understood whose house it was and that the search should be carried out with as much respect as possible, then he sauntered off down the road. As it happened, his bus home had a stop just around the corner and he had a particularly good jigsaw on the go.

If Burke had turned around at any point during his walk to the end of the road, he might have caught sight of Bunny's next-door neighbour and two other elderly ladies leaving her house and walking in the opposite direction. One of them, rollers in her hair and a scarf over her head, was really rather tall and large.

# BOXED IN

Bunny parked the car opposite the North Paw Boxing Club and turned off the engine. It had been a few years since he'd been here, and time hadn't been kind to the place. It was a functionally built hall with rudimentary dressing rooms stuck on to the left-hand side of the building. The kind of thing you'd find up and down the country. Not much in itself, but an awful lot to an area that didn't have much else.

It was always the way with places like this – you spend ages raising funds to get them built, and then, as soon as they're finished, the thing starts slowly falling down. The club was encased in scaffolding, which at least meant they'd been able to raise enough money to hold it together for a few more years. To one side of it lay a football field, empty in the darkness, and to the other side, a playground that had seen better days. He could hear a lonesome swing creaking in the breeze.

Despite the signs making clear that the place was closed, a light was on inside. Bunny noticed the expensive-looking jeep parked up by the side. He got out, leaving Mags's car unlocked. He'd had the best of intentions when he'd given her his rental car, but in hindsight, that might have backfired now the Gardaí were looking for him. Still, on the upside, police custody was by no means the worst place Mags could be right now.

Bunny walked across the car park, crystal shards of broken glass mixed in with the gravel, and pushed his way through the double doors. Scaffolding clambered up three of the internal walls too. In the centre of the room stood the ropeless base of the boxing ring, covered in tarpaulin. On top of it sat Angelina Hannity née Quirke.

"Howerya, Angelina. I got your text."

She smiled at him. "I wasn't sure you'd come."

"Yes, you were."

"Maybe I was hoping you wouldn't."

Bunny chuckled. "I get that a lot. How's the head?"

She raised her fingers and touched the small dressing on her forehead. "It's OK, thank you. Just a scratch."

Bunny nodded as he walked in and looked around the hall. "I see they're giving the old place a facelift?"

"Needs a whole new roof, in fact. It's been leaking for years, but they had it inspected back in November. Rotten, apparently. One of the old builders did a dodgy job."

He tutted. "Damn near impossible to find an honest builder these days. Nothing is ever their fault." He looked up at the ceiling. "It's going to cost a pretty penny."

"It is," said Angelina. "I'm paying for it."

"Fair play to you."

"Might as well use the money for some good." She looked around again. "Do you know what I can't get over? How small the place is. When I was a kid, this hall seemed huge. I never saw the damp and the flaking paint. It was a palace of dreams to me." Her voice sounded wistful. "Dancing here, up and down on these boards ... D'ye know, I think that might have been the happiest I've ever been."

She pointed to the small office to the left of the main door. "And it was in there that you sat me down and gave me the worst news of my life." She tilted her head. "Thinking back on it, that must've been a horrible thing for you to have to do. Telling a little girl that her mummy had died."

"To be honest with you, the woman from social services was supposed to do it, but she bottled it. You were getting upset because you knew something was wrong. It seemed cruel to drag it out any more than necessary."

She took a deep breath. "I'm glad it was you, for what it's worth. Rather than some woman I'd never met. I think that would have felt very cold."

A silence descended between them. Bunny continued to walk around, remembering the layout of the place. Here was where they had the warm-up mats, over there was the heavy bag.

"Do you remember Anto McCarthy?" he asked, looking back over his shoulder at Angelina.

"Should I?"

"Nah, not particularly. He would've been a few years older than you. His dad sent him down here to join the boxing club – thought it would make a man of him, all that nonsense. Nice lad. He hated the boxing. Hated it. But you know how boxers skip as part of their training? Supposed to help with fitness and footwork. The lad could skip like you wouldn't believe. I mean, the speed of the thing. The rope was a blur, he was able to turn this way and that. Do all kind of tricks. It was mesmerising. No other word for it. Mesmerising."

"Sounds it. Wish I'd seen it."

"The last I heard, years ago now, Anto had moved to Australia. Became a big deal in real estate, I think. I wonder if he still skips?" He turned to look at Angelina. "Do you still dance?"

She gave a sad laugh. "No. My dancing days are over."

"Shame. That's a real shame."

"Speaking of which – shame, I mean ... I'd imagine you have a lot of questions for me?"

Bunny turned around and faced her fully. "Not as many as you'd think. I've figured out most of it now, I reckon. I got hold of Andy Muldoon – he's the bottom-feeding piece of crap who was following you for months."

She rolled her eyes and shook her head. "He's not even

particularly good at it. After a while, I could spot that stupid comb-over from half a mile away."

"I know," said Bunny. "While I'd never claim to have my fingers on the pulse of fashion, even I know that's a fight not worth fighting. Unfortunately, while he might not be great at the following, he is pretty good at the digging. Doesn't feel like congratulations is the right thing to say, given the circumstances."

Instinctively, Angelina placed a hand on her belly and rubbed it. "No, I guess it isn't."

"Can I ask – when I first saw you that night, you were drinking ..."

She shook her head. "Was I? Or was I walking around with a drink and acting drunk?"

Bunny tilted his head. "You were convincing."

"I had to be. Coop was a suspicious man."

"Still. Smart. Your little scheme with Mags to outwit Muldoon was pretty clever too."

"She told you?"

"No. Loyal to the end, your little twin. I figured out that bit myself."

"I've been trying to ring her," said Angelina.

"Yeah. I advised her and Bobby to get rid of their phones. Some nasty people are trying to locate them, but then you knew that."

Angelina looked down at the floor, a suitably ashamed expression on her face. "I panicked."

"Be that as it may," said Bunny. "Leaving aside the fact that you tried to get that dimwit Bobby to kill somebody and solve your problems for you, did you ever even consider that on a busy street innocent bystanders could have got caught up in it?"

She didn't say anything, just kept staring at the floor.

Bunny gave her a moment and then continued. "No, I didn't think so. It's fair to say you've not given much consideration to collateral damage." He turned around again and started pacing. "So, I know you were having an affair, and I'm not sure anybody would even blame you. I mean, the vows of marriage aren't sacred if you're hitched to a monster. Not your best decision that, was it?"

"Dad needed help. So did I." She shrugged and smiled a broken smile at the ceiling. "It seemed like a good idea at the time, or, at least, the least bad one. Some part of me knew what Coop was. I wouldn't be the first woman to marry a man on the mistaken assumption I could change him. Stupid as it sounds, he really was quite nice, in the beginning."

"Seeing as you mentioned your dad, and God knows it isn't the worst part, but did you not feel bad having Mags visiting him pretending to be you?"

She lowered her head and looked Bunny directly in the eyes. "I've done a lot wrong, but don't dump that on me. You don't know what it's like – sitting there, night after night, watching somebody you love slipping away, not just from you, but from themselves." She bit her lip. "Jesus, back in his day, my dad was something else. The stories he could make up. You'd be thrilled going to bed knowing it was going to be story time. Such a wonderful imagination. Such a wonderful mind." She turned away for a moment and then looked back. "So that – having to see all that taken away? Unless you've seen it up close and know what that's really like, then you don't get to judge me. I gave up a lot to help him."

Bunny raised his hands. "Fair enough. You helped yourself, though, too – didn't you?"

Angelina spoke softly. "Somebody had to."

"Was it your idea to kill Coop?"

"Does it matter?"

"I guess not. If you were going to do it, though, you needed to find yourself a patsy – right? Otherwise, suspicion would fall on you."

"I have no reason to expect you to believe me," said Angelina. "But I honestly didn't know it was you. He just told me that he'd found the perfect person."

"That's some comfort, I guess. But you didn't ask, did you? You knew an innocent person was going to take the rap. Even more collateral damage."

She glared at him. "It's not just me, though. I have a baby to protect now. You ask any mother – you do whatever it takes. God only knows what Coop would have done when he found out, and it was only a matter of time."

Bunny could feel his anger rising. "Ara stop, would you? You could have run."

"He'd have found me," snapped Angelina. "The man's life work was chasing down people who owed him something and, make no mistake, he thought I owed him everything."

"You could have come to me. You know I'd have always helped you. I was still trying to help you throughout all this, but let's be honest, you made the classic mistake, didn't you? Thinking that because you're smart, that you're the smartest in the room. It turned out your solution to your problem became a far bigger problem than you ever could have imagined."

Bunny was standing in front of Angelina now. As he reached out a hand towards her she flinched.

"Really?"

She sniffled. "Sorry."

With his thumb, he gently wiped away the tear rolling down her face.

"I'm sorry," she whispered again. "I'm so sorry. Maybe you could—"

"Alright, enough of this," came a voice.

Bunny turned to see the bulky figure of Samoan Joe filling the doorway to the changing rooms, a gun in his hand.

"Jeez, Angelina, the whole point was to find out what he knew and who he'd talked to. You're just not a team player, are you?"

Bunny took a step away from her. "And here he is, the real brains of the outfit."

Joe started to walk towards them, a friendly smile on his face as always. He stopped to take a quick bow. "That's the thing with being the muscle, mate. Everybody assumes you're thick as pig shit. Coop thought I was a moron and the reality was I was fucking his missus behind his back. She," he said, nodding in Angelina's direction, "thought I was a dummy she could use to get rid of him and then drop me when it didn't suit. She hadn't factored in me getting myself some insurance."

"Fair play to you," said Bunny. "It was a pretty clever plan. Everybody assumed the guy in the balaclava was the murderer, but he wasn't, was he? There's no need to answer that question – he told me himself. Mr Dean is currently tied up in my next-door neighbour's kitchen."

Bunny enjoyed the moment when the smile on Joe's face faded briefly.

"I did wonder why he'd stopped answering his phone."

"Well, you just can't get the staff these days. Coop had many flaws, but firing Dean for being an incompetent idiot was a sound decision. Still, he was useful for you. I think I've got it all sussed now, but let me run you through it, see if I missed anything. One of you stabs Coop to death and then she wallops you with the fire extinguisher to throw suspicion off you."

"Bloody hurt, too."

"Ara, you're a big boy. You can take it."

Joe grinned a malevolent smile at Angelina. "I think she maybe thought she could kill two birds with one stone, hey, love? Lose a husband and a boyfriend in one night."

Angelina didn't speak, choosing instead to keep her eyes fixed on the floor in front of her.

Bunny nodded. "There's that little tunnel she can use to get in and out without showing up on the CCTV too, which is fierce handy. She nips back to Mags's apartment and firms up her alibi, so both of you look as innocent as can be. Have I got it right so far?"

Bunny looked back and forth between the two of them, but neither offered any response.

"I'll take that as a yes. Here's where Joe got a little clever, though. Like you said, got yourself some insurance ..." Bunny waggled his finger. "... just in case love's first bloom fades and herself doesn't see the two of you as lifelong soulmates. As soon as Angelina leaves, your buddy, Mr Dean, hops over the wall and grabs the knife along with a couple of tapes. The one of my meeting from the night before, giving me all the motive the Gardaí would need to pin Coop's death on me."

"Nothing personal," said Joe with a shrug. "Wrong place, wrong time."

"Sure," replied Bunny. "But then, there was the other tape ..." He looked at Angelina, who was still staring at the floor. "The one Angelina didn't know about. The one of Coop's actual murder. That one gave you all the leverage you'd ever need to ensure Angelina could never betray you."

"Not as dumb as I look, hey?"

"Indeed. I'm particularly impressed by how you got it all together so fast."

"Well," said Joe, "we had the basic plan for weeks, just waiting for the right opportunity. Then in you popped, and you and Coop started threatening each other. It was perfect. Of course, neither of you even thought about how I heard the whole thing, because I'm just the dummy standing in the corner in case somebody needs somebody hit. The whole thing went pretty well too, except Deano fucked up dumping the knife."

"Actually," said Bunny, "I feel a bit disloyal saying this, but I think the screw-up there came from the Garda Síochána end of things. They found it today, by the way. At least, that's what I'm assuming, given that the police just raided my house, where they didn't find the video tape of my little chat with Coop. That part of your plan didn't work. I'm afraid the tape in question got burned to a crisp in my neighbour Mrs Doyle's oven – not unlike one of her dreadful lasagnes."

Big Joe gave that wide grin and shrugged again. "Oh well, you can't expect everything to go to plan."

"And on the upside, Angelina here now owns the entirety of Coop's empire, and seeing as you have video evidence of her role in his killing, well, I guess that means you own her."

"Aw, you make it sound so tawdry," said Joe. "We love each other. We're having a baby together. OK, she did try to have me killed in a drive-by shooting when she realised I had a little insurance policy, but every relationship has its ups and downs."

"How do you expect to get away with all this?"

"We'll have to improvise a bit," conceded Joe, "and hope that you've not shared what you know with anybody else. I was hoping Angelina was going to get around to asking about that." He looked at her and Bunny saw something in his eyes that previously had been very well hidden. "But she clearly didn't want to. I'm guessing she was desperately trying to find a way to get you to kill me." He laughed. "She's a live wire, this one. Keeps you on your toes."

"On the other hand," said Bunny, "be fair. She did lure me here so you could kill me."

Joe nodded. "She did. And I needed to find out what you knew, so thanks for helping out with that, fella."

"Don't mention it." Bunny carried on smiling and kept his eyes fixed on the big guy.

Just a few seconds more.

Joe noticed Angelina looking over his shoulder, took a step back and spun round. Butch was still ten feet away from him. His smile disappeared for good.

"Who the hell are you?"

"Take it easy," said Butch. "I'm Garda Detective Pamela Cassidy. Put down the gun."

"No, thanks. I'm taking my shot at the big league. Ride or die. And don't bother telling me the place is surrounded, or some crap like that. You wouldn't be trying to sneak up on me if you weren't here on your own."

"Alright, Joe," said Bunny. "What's the plan now? You going to kill two police officers? Seriously, you think you can get away with that?"

Joe shrugged. "Only one way to find out."

With a scream, Angelina launched herself from the ring's canvas and on to Joe. It wasn't enough to take him down, but it was enough to divert the gun. Bunny lowered his head and charged.

Joe tossed Angelina aside with alarming ease. She landed all of six feet away and screamed a different scream, which was narrowly preceded by the sickening crack of bone.

Bunny threw his entire bodyweight behind the tackle, and yet it felt as if he was trying to take down a monolith. A nauseating jolt passed through his shoulder upon making contact. Joe sidestepped partially – not enough to prevent himself from falling, but enough to ensure he did so on top of Bunny.

The air from Bunny's lungs was expelled out of him and he felt a couple of ribs crack as the weight of all that humanity came crashing down from above. Joe rolled off him with remarkable dexterity and was back on his feet in an instant, chasing after the gun where it had fallen out of his hand in the tussle.

Before he could reach the weapon, Butch flew at him and connected with a vicious roundhouse kick to his midsection. A blow that would have felled almost any other man merely doubled him over. She then threw a couple of lightning-fast punches at his face. Her attempt to follow up with a left-footed kick was thwarted when, with another flash of unexpected speed, Joe reared back and caught her foot.

He smiled at her. But before he could do anything else, Butch managed to spin her whole body around in mid-air, using Joe's grip on her left leg as a fulcrum, and smashed the heel of her right foot into his face. It was quite possibly the coolest thing Bunny had ever seen. Unfortunately, it came at a cost. Joe still had a firm hold on her leg and used it to slam her onto the floor with a stomach-churning thump.

Despite herself, Butch screamed.

Joe stood over her, his smile replaced with a bloody sneer.

Dazed and winded as he was, Bunny tried to get back on his feet, but he was too far away. Too far to help Butch. Unless ...

Bunny drew in what breath he could and roared, "Karate Kid!"

Both Butch and Joe looked in his direction, confused.

Thankfully, Butch got it first. Summoning all of her strength, she swung her good leg around and swept at Joe's, sending all of her power through his right knee.

With a terrible howl, Joe crumpled to the ground, for the second time in his life a catastrophic injury prematurely ending a promising career.

Butch pulled herself back along the floor then, once she was out of Joe's reach, dragged herself to her feet. She needn't have worried. The big man was lost in a world of his own pain, clutching his shattered knee.

"I wasn't sure you'd get the reference," panted Bunny. "I thought that film was a bit before your time."

Butch wiped away the blood that was starting to trickle from her nose. "Are you kidding? I was a martial-arts-obsessed kid growing up in Meath. I wore that video tape out. You're just lucky I didn't crane-kick the big bastard. We should probably ..."

She trailed off as both she and Bunny noticed that Angelina had managed to limp across the hall and claim the gun. The former Mrs Hannity stood, holding the weapon in her right hand, her left arm hanging awkwardly by her side, and surveyed the room.

"What's the plan here, Angelina?"

She tried to shrug and winced. "I don't really know. Maybe you all just stay here and I make a run for it."

"You wouldn't get very far," said Bunny.

She sighed. "You're probably right."

She took a step towards Joe, who had regained enough composure to be aware of his surroundings once more. He started to clamber back to his feet.

"Think about it, baby," he said. "I'm still your only way out of this. Give me the gun."

"Baby?" said Angelina. "Baby? I'm carrying your baby and you threw me across the room, you utter bastard."

Joe lunged, but before Bunny or Butch could move, Angelina fired the gun three times.

Joe slumped to the floor.

Bunny walked slowly towards Angelina, his hand extended. "Angelina ... Love ..."

She was shaking. "I think I've made everything worse. Again."

Bunny glanced down at Joe on the floor. It didn't matter how big you were, nobody could shake off losing that much of their head.

"Just give me the gun."

Angelina took a step back and met Bunny's gaze. "There still might be ways out of this."

"Not good ones."

He could see the shock and terror in her eyes. "I've got nothing left to lose."

"Take it from me," said Bunny, "there's always more you can lose."

Her body tensed for a moment, then relaxed.

Bunny took a step forward and seized the gun from her unresisting hand.

Angelina collapsed, sobbing, into his arms.

# THE FINAL QUESTION

Bunny stepped through the doorway of O'Hagan's and patted the snowflakes off his coat. It had been the longest of long weeks and now it was snowing, which meant that the St Jude's game scheduled for tomorrow had been called off. Bloody March weather. He'd been looking forward to the match too. On one hand, it was very early to call it, but on the other, if it had gone ahead, trying to get a team together would've been like herding cats. Even allowing for the promise of McDonald's, a centimetre of snow and every pre-teen boy in Ireland lost his damn mind.

He checked his phone. He had an awful lot of missed calls. Without scrolling through them, he decided to leave everything until tomorrow. He'd spent last night in hospital, so they could check him for concussion and deal with the four cracked ribs he'd picked up, and then he'd spent today answering a lot of questions. An awful lot of questions. However, not all of the questions.

Officially, DI Marshall had been called back to Limerick on some important matter. Unofficially, the important matter was the need to be as far as possible away from Commissioner Ferguson, who apparently had quite a lot of bones to pick with him. The Minister for Agriculture's family holiday to Spain had been delayed by three hours thanks to the chaos caused by a senior officer of the Garda Síochána grossly overstepping his authority and shutting down Dublin Airport for forty-six minutes.

O'Rourke was back in charge of the investigation. For the look of the thing, he'd asked Bunny why he'd gone to see Coop Hannity. Bunny had explained that it was in relation to a third party's private matter and he was not at liberty to discuss it. That wouldn't fly in most circumstances, but in this case, nobody was questioning the nature of Bunny's involvement any longer. To use a policing euphemism, the investigation had gone in another direction entirely.

Not that there was a great deal of investigating left to do. O'Rourke's officers had found the tape of the murder of Coop Hannity in Samoan Joe's flat. It answered a great deal of questions. Bunny had been very clear with O'Rourke that he didn't want to see it – he didn't even want to know what was on it. He didn't care if it was Joe or Angelina who had held the knife in their hands. He had a strong suspicion and, given the media coverage the trial would receive, he had no doubt that he'd find out every gruesome detail in due course, whether he wanted to or not, but at that moment, he didn't want to spend one more second thinking about it.

O'Rourke was going over everything in great detail as Angelina had already hired some of the most impressive legal firepower in Ireland, and Bunny sensed they were expecting her to adopt a self-defence strategy on all counts. He didn't even know whether he agreed with that, he just knew he didn't want to think about it any more. All he wanted now was a quiet pint, and for the whole damn world to leave him alone for a while.

The first thing Bunny had done upon leaving the station was ring Diana Spain and inform her that the situation with the house had been resolved. She'd offered him a curt acknowledgement and hung up the phone. Bunny didn't know what he'd been expecting but a thank-you would have been nice. The deeds to Gringo's house were probably in a file somewhere in Hannity's house, but Bunny strongly suspected that by the time the mess of Coop's finances was sorted out, if indeed it ever was, those deeds would be lost. Legally, Angelina couldn't benefit from the murder of which she was being accused. The whole thing was going to prove a boon for the Dublin legal community. Good luck to 'em.

As soon as Bunny entered O'Hagan's a clamour of voices rushed to greet him, closely followed by Tara Flynn.

"Oh, thank Christ, Bunny. Where have you been? I've been ringing ye."

"Yeah," said Bunny, "you and the rest of Dublin." He sighed. "I'm a very popular man."

"Hamster!" shouted Tara, before realising the individual she was looking for was actually standing nervously behind her. "Oh, there you are." She pushed him forward as if presenting him to Bunny. "This is Hamster. He's studying geography up in Trinity. I hired him to set the questions and he's done a fantastic job."

"Questions?"

Tara looked exasperated. "Yes. The fecking questions. For the table quiz. The quiz that you are the quizmaster for."

Bunny sagged. "Ara Jesus, Tara. Not tonight, Josephine. It's been an absolute bastard of a week. Could somebody else not do it?"

Tara grabbed Bunny's upper arm with a strength he wouldn't have thought possible.

"Now, you listen to me, Bunny McGarry. You made me a promise. A solemn promise. Look around this room – the place is more packed out than it's been in months, and quiz nights were my big idea. Last time we had to refund everybody's money because of the ..." She paused and glanced around. "... incident. This thing needs a firm hand. You, you big lump, are that firm hand. Don't screw me over on this."

Bunny's basic survival instincts kicked in. "Only messing. Delighted to be here. Let's get quizzing."

Tara hugged him in a way that felt like a threat. "You're a good man. Like I said, Hamster has done a cracking job. He's even got musical questions in between each round based around a different song on the jukebox. It's very clever."

She pushed a roll of twenty-pence coins into his hand.

"You even get to be in control of the jukebox – for the whole night. You've been asking for that privilege since I've known you. Right, I'm going to give out the paper and pens. I'll leave you and Hamster to get acquainted."

Nicknames are funny things. Some, like Bunny's, were family traditions; others, like Butch's, were clearly ironic; and some were Hamster. Where the shaggy top of brown hair stopped and the immense beard started was anyone's guess. The only clearly visible features on the fella's face were the big, wide, scared-looking eyes, as if he were an actual hamster that had unexpectedly found itself on open ground in a hawk sanctuary. Bunny glanced around the room again. Seeing how seriously the patrons of O'Hagan's took their table quizzes, he might be right.

"So, Hamster," said Bunny. "Geography student, huh? What's your favourite type of lake?"

As soon as Bunny looked into the lad's earnest face, he could tell he was going to take the question seriously. "Oxbow."

Bunny nodded. "They are fecking great, alright. You and me are going to get on famously." He put his arm around Hamster's shoulders. "C'mon, I'll buy you a pint."

"Tara said you and I drink for free."

"I know. Figure of speech."

Bunny weaved his way through the busy pub, being careful to avoid the tables at which the teams of Terry Hodges and Mark Kind were seated. He took up his position on the far side of the bar where the microphone was and directed Hamster to the stool beside him.

"OK," said Hamster enthusiastically.

Bunny held his hand up to silence him. "First things first ..."

Hamster looked at him in confusion until, as if by magic, a pint of Guinness appeared in front of Bunny on the bar. Bunny lifted it with an air of reverence, and then, after taking the appropriate length of time to stare at it lovingly, raised it to his lips and took a long slow drink.

He placed the half-empty glass back on the counter and wiped the back of his hand across his lips. "I'll tell ye, Hamster, as you get older you'll come to realise there are very few truly perfect things in this world." He indicated the pint in front of him. "But that might be one of them."

Hamster nodded. "Tara mentioned that in previous quizzes, there had been a lot of querying of answers. I just wanted to agree a process in the eventuality of that happening."

Bunny raised an eyebrow at the young man. "The processes is, I tell anyone who is acting the gobshite to cop themselves on and remember, it's only a fecking quiz."

"But what if—"

Hamster didn't get to finish the question. Their conversation was interrupted by a heavy hand landing on Bunny's shoulder. He turned and looked up into the scowling face of one Gary Kearney.

Bunny was a big man, but even if he'd been standing up, Kearney would have towered over him. The boxer's hoodie was open over a tight T-shirt, highlighting his impressive physique.

"Here he is," said Kearney, "the man who can't keep his nose out of other people's business."

"Gary," said Bunny, shaking the hand off his shoulder. "I didn't recognise you without a referee standing over you counting to ten."

"Funny man. Let's see how funny you are after we've had a chat."

Bunny noticed that behind Kearney stood Jason Potts, the scrawny little shit who seemed to follow him everywhere, like a bad smell. Bunny kept his eyes on Kearney but was aware that the clamour of conversation in the room had died away to nothing.

He reached across and picked up his pint. "Believe me, Gary. You do not want to do this now."

"Why? Had a hard day breaking up families, have you?"

"You've got a funny idea of the definition of family."

Tara appeared behind the bar.

"We don't want any trouble here," she said in a firm voice.

"There's not gonna be any trouble," responded Kearney, "because this fucker is going to tell me where my girlfriend and her kid are."

"Over my dead body."

Kearney leered at him and cracked a knuckle. "Happy to oblige."

Tara raised her voice and pointed at Kearney. "You. Out. Now. You're barred."

Kearney looked at her. "Have women fight your battles now, Bunny, do ye?"

"Aren't they your preferred opponents?"

"We are not having this kind of shit in this pub," said Tara.

"You're right," said Bunny, standing up and making his way down the bar.

Gary laughed a sneering laugh. "Yeah, go on – run away, you cowardly Cork prick." He wafted a meaty hand in Bunny's direction and raised his voice to address the whole pub. "There he is. Your big hero. The mighty Bunny McGarry. All mouth and no trousers. Can't even—"

Gary was interrupted by Bunny kicking open the fire exit that led to the alley behind the pub. He turned and looked at him.

"Well, are you going to stand there all day flapping your gums or are ye coming?"

Two minutes later, in spite of Tara's extensive pleading, every last patron of O'Hagan's was standing in the alleyway, forming a loose circle around Bunny and Kearney. She looked from one man to the other and wondered if it was too late to call the police. Even she knew who Kearney was. Bunny might be able to handle himself, but Kearney was a professional heavyweight boxer.

He was standing with his little weaselly buddy, Jason Potts, and laughing while he engaged in stretching exercises. Bunny, for his part, merely rolled his head around his shoulders a couple of times and stared fixedly at his opponent. Tara was dimly aware that around her a great deal of wagers were being placed on the fight. Given that Kearney was a pro, with about three inches and forty pounds of muscle on Bunny, the betting was surprisingly close. Most of those backing Bunny seemed to be doing so more out of blind loyalty than any belief in his abilities.

Kearney stretched out his hamstrings, then his lower back, and then his shoulders. He threw what, to Tara's untrained eye, looked like an alarmingly fast combination of punches in the air, then turned around and started to take off his hoodie.

In that moment, Tara nearly screamed in surprise as Bunny pounced. He closed the distance quickly and, while Kearney's arms were still inside his hoodie, slammed a hard couple of rights into Kearney's kidneys. As the boxer crumbled over, Bunny launched a knee into his face, before bringing his foot down hard on Kearney's ankle. The big man howled. Even as he fell, Bunny continued to rain down blow after blow upon his form.

With Kearney on the ground, Bunny threw in a series of vicious kicks. He possibly would have kept going too, but a few members of the crowd, who had recovered from the shock, pulled him away.

The whole thing had lasted maybe forty seconds. Bunny was now being pinned up against the dumpster and Kearney was a bloody heap on the ground.

Tara and the rest of the crowd stood there in disbelief, dumbfounded by the speed and animalistic ferocity of what had unfurled in front of them.

"I'm alright," said Bunny. "Let me go. I'm grand."

The men restraining him exchanged cautious glances and then slowly stepped away.

Bunny walked forward into the centre of the circle and looked down at Kearney.

Kearney, his face a mess, pointed an accusing finger at his attacker.

"What's that, Gary?" asked Bunny, bending over. "Did you think it wasn't a fair fight? Well, maybe now you've got some idea how it'd feel for a twelve-year-old boy – fucking twelve – when a grown man comes after him. A grown man twice – three times – his size."

Bunny's voice was laced with venom now. His face was red with rage and tears ran down his cheeks. Spittle flecked his lips.

"You think you're a big man. You're not a man at all. Do ye understand me? He's a kid. A fecking little kid!"

Tara held her breath and feared for a second that the beating might resume. She doubted anyone would hold him back on this occasion.

"You can't do this," protested Jason Potts, his voice trembling with outrage. "That was assault." He indicated the surrounding crowd. "You're a guard and we've got witnesses. Dozens of them."

A moment of perfect stillness descended. Then, Tara watched as first Terry Hodges then Mark Kind turned around. Others quickly followed suit. Soon, the entire crowd except for herself and Bunny had turned their backs on Kearney and Potts.

Bunny hunkered down beside Kearney, who held up a hand in defence and winced. "You've got twenty-four hours to get out of town, and you never come back. If Janice or her son ever gets so much as a postcard from you, with God as my witness I will track you down to whatever rock you've crawled under and I. Will. End. You. Are we clear?"

Kearney nodded. Without another word Bunny walked back into the pub, rubbing a hand over his face. The rest of the crowd followed him inside.

Tara looked down at Kearney and then spoke to Potts. "Get this piece of shit out of my alleyway."

She watched as the last of the patrons trooped back indoors and then, just before she closed the fire door, Tara spat on the ground at Kearney's feet.

Bunny retook his seat at the bar and dropped on the counter the roll of coins he'd been holding in his right hand. He clutched and unclutched the fingers a few times then knocked back the rest of his pint in one go.

Hamster sat down beside him.

"Sorry," said Bunny, slapping him on the knee. "Before we were interrupted, you were asking me something?"

Hamster shook his head nervously and spoke with a trembling voice. "Don't worry about it, Mr McGarry. I ... I think you're right. I can't see anybody arguing about the questions."

Tara appeared behind the bar and spoke in a low voice. "Are you OK?"

"Sure, why wouldn't I be?"

Tara shook her head. "If you say so." She reached across and placed a full pint of Guinness in front of him with one hand. With the other she held out the microphone.

Bunny took the mic and tapped it with two fingers to confirm it was on. He cleared his throat. "Right so, folks. Sorry about the slight delay. Welcome to the O'Hagan's table quiz. I'll be quizmaster for the evening with my beautiful assistant here, Hamster. Before we start, any questions?"

There were a few seconds of silence before a female voice shouted from the back of the room, "Is Hamster single?"

Her enquiry was greeted with a cheer.

"I don't know," responded Bunny. He raised his eyebrows at the student in a questioning look. Hamster went red and nodded.

"He is indeed."

This revelation was met with more cheers and a couple of wolf whistles.

"For any interested ladies," continued Bunny, "he is currently studying geography at Trinity College. He decided not to study biology, as he has been reliably informed that he is already an expert in finding his way around the female body."

Roars and extensive banging on tables filled the room.

"OK," said Bunny. "Settle down. Settle down. Now that I'm finished playing Cupid, let's get down to some serious quizzing." He held out a hand towards Hamster. "The questions for round one, maestro, if you please."

Hamster handed Bunny a card.

"OK. Question one. What famous cricketer ..." Bunny stopped and moved the microphone away from his lips. "Hamster, can I have a quick word?"

# FREE BOOK

Hi there reader-person,

I hope you enjoyed *Dead Man's Sins*. Thanks for taking the time to read it. Bunny will be 'back to the future' in the USA in 2022. If you need a Caimh fix before then, make sure you've signed up to my monthly newsletter for free short stories, audio stories and the latest goings on in the Bunnyverse.

You'll also get a copy of my short fiction collection called ***How To Send A Message***, which features several stories featuring characters from my books. To sign up go to my website:

***www.WhiteHairedIrishman.com***

The paperback costs $10.99/£7.99/€8.99 in the shops but you can get the e-book for free just by signing up to my newsletter.

Cheers muchly and thanks for reading,

Caimh

# ALSO BY CAIMH MCDONNELL

THE DUBLIN TRILOGY

A Man With One of Those Faces (Book 1)

The Day That Never Comes (Book 2)

Angels in the Moonlight (Book 3/prequel)

Last Orders (Book 4)

Dead Man's Sins (Book 5)

MCGARRY STATESIDE (FEATURING BUNNY MCGARRY)

Disaster Inc (Book 1)

I Have Sinned (Book 2)

The Quiet Man (Book 3)

The Final Game (MCM Investigations)

Welcome to Nowhere (Smithy and Diller)

WRITING AS C.K. MCDONNELL

The Stranger Times details on the next page

Visit www.WhiteHairedIrishman.com to find out more.

## THE STRANGER TIMES – C.K. MCDONNELL

There are dark forces at work in our world so thank God *The Stranger Times* is on hand to report them. A weekly newspaper dedicated to the weird and the wonderful (but mostly the weird), it is the go-to publication for the unexplained and inexplicable . . .

At least that's their pitch. The reality is rather less auspicious. Their editor is a drunken, foul-tempered and foul-mouthed husk of a man who thinks little of the publication he edits. His staff are a ragtag group of misfits. And as for the assistant editor . . . well, that job is a revolving door – and it has just revolved to reveal Hannah Willis, who's got problems of her own.

When tragedy strikes in her first week on the job *The Stranger Times* is forced to do some serious investigating. What they discover leads to a shocking realisation: some of the stories they'd previously dismissed as nonsense are in fact terrifyingly real. Soon they come face-to-face with darker forces than they could ever have imagined.

*The Stranger Times* is the first book from C.K. McDonnell, the pen name of Caimh McDonnell. It combines his distinctive dark wit with his love of the weird and wonderful to deliver a joyous celebration of how truth really can be stranger than fiction.

Made in the USA
Las Vegas, NV
06 February 2024

85418578R00184